EVERYONE LIES

A. D. GARRETT

ISIS

LARGE PRINT

Oxford

Copyright © A. D. Garrett, 2013

First published in Great Britain 2013
by
C&R Crime, an imprint of Constable & Robinson Ltd

Published in Large Print 2013 by ISIS Publishing Ltd.,
7 Centremead, Osney Mead, Oxford OX2 0ES
by arrangement with
Constable & Robinson Ltd.

CIP data is available for this title from the British Library

ISBN 978–0–7531–9184–2 (hb)
ISBN 978–0–7531–9185–9 (pb)

Printed and bound in Great Britain by
T. J. International Ltd., Padstow, Cornwall

This book is dedicated to forensic scientists and crime analysts.

Acknowledgements

With sincere thanks to: Rachel Bowman-Sayle for advice on BCUs, FIDOs and The Dark Side; the Latvian Institute for details of Latvian traditions and rituals; Chief Inspector Dave Griffin (retd.), for the bar code quote. Finally, and very importantly, The Royal Literary Fund — a lifeline to writers since 1790.

Preface

She calls the man Vilkacis, which he likes, but only because he doesn't know what it means. Just a few stripes, he said, and she agreed, because all the girls do it, and he gave her a secret word to say if she wanted him to stop. It was nothing, the first time, and the time after that: three quick stripes, which hardly hurt at all. He was kind, and called her beautiful. He gave her twenty extra and some medication that made the little pain go away altogether.

The third time he did hurt her. And she said the secret word, but maybe she didn't say it right, or maybe he changed it, because he didn't stop; he went on and on, and even when she screamed the secret word and begged him — *begged him* — he wouldn't stop. It took a lot of medication to make the pain go away that time.

It seems foolish now, but then, she didn't know the name for this medication. Later, on the street, she learned to ask for scag, smack, candy, the goods, because on the street it's all about business. But when it's on the spoon and you're cooking it down, you can call it people's names: Henry, Helen, Brother, Boy — like family. And when you're fixed up, and everything seems washed in mellow light, she's Golden Girl. But not for long, because heroin is a Judas, a bad friend who betrays you. It is a cruel lover who goes away and makes you crazy for him. You need it more than you need oxygen, it screams in your head, *Feed me! Feed me!*

Her friends call it the monkey on your back. They're wrong. It is wild, ferocious; a beast that howls and claws and tears your flesh. The pain of the whipping and the need for the drug got tangled up together a long time ago, and now she can hardly tell them apart. Except when the need returns.

She swore he would never hurt her again, but still she lets the man Vilkacis flay her for pleasure, and all she thinks is how good it will be afterwards, when the beast is quiet.

Vilkacis has introduced a new game which he calls chequers, and now she is webbed with cuts and the pain is like fire. Heroin creates the need, but it also makes the pain go away, so when he is finished with her, she crawls off to shoot up in filthy places like this, with no sheets on the bed and stains on the mattress.

Surrounded by dirt and plaster dust and human faeces, she uses antiseptic wipes to clean her hands and the injection site and her spoons. She has two — one to crush the gear fine so it dissolves properly. She brought a bottle of water with her, and expensive citric acid she bought from the pharmacy, because the juice in the plastic lemons gets full of spores and can make you go blind. Even here, in this worst of all places, even as the beast howls and tears at her insides, she takes care. Because somewhere on the way down there's a place of perfect balance, when the pain is only a gentle warmth radiating from her skin, and the need is quiet. In these brief moments, she thinks about her family, and what she's lost, and even after the terrible things she has done it seems possible to make everything right.

She flicks her lighter flame under the spoon — not too much — she doesn't want to burn off any of the precious liquid. The drug dissolves easily; there's hardly any crap to filter, and she knows the hit will be sweet. She adds a cotton bud, then, crooning softly to steady her nerves, she takes the cap off a clean syringe and draws the liquid through the cotton wool. Injecting is the sweetest part, and even the anticipation begins to calm her. She has looked after her veins, so they look after her. She finds it easily, watching as the needle goes in, welcoming the tiny prick of pain as the sharp point pops through first the skin, and then into the blue snake of vein. She takes a slow breath, pulls back the plunger just a fraction. A tiny jet of blood spurts into the browny-yellow fluid in the barrel. Her mouth floods with saliva as she slowly depresses the plunger, watching the blood-swirl crawl back into the needle, back into her. When it is all inside her, she pulls out more blood and then eases the plunger back in a second time to wash the last traces of the drug into her bloodstream. Thoughtfully, she withdraws the needle and waits for the howling to stop.

CHAPTER
ONE

"A trivial example of observation and inference."

A. C. DOYLE, *THE BOSCOMBE VALLEY MYSTERY*

Monday morning, 9 a.m., in A12 lecture theatre, Robert Gordon University, Aberdeen. Small and slightly cramped, certainly not the best lecture theatre on the St Andrews Street campus, but Professor Nick Fennimore liked it, and always asked for it. The walls were clad in ochre-stained pine, and the seating, gently raked, ran six to a row either side of the aisle. There were several curious burn marks on the floor near the demo bench — relics of his famous "Petrol Makes a Good Fire Extinguisher" demo.

Today, fifty students were seated or slouched in the tiered seating, chatting, texting, sleeping off the weekend's hangovers. The fluorescent light reflecting off ochre walls added to the jaundiced pallor of the serious Union Street club-goers. The last few drifted in just before nine and began shedding jackets and hats and scarves. Aberdeen in winter was no place for dressing down.

Nick Fennimore was forty-two, though he could pass for thirty-five. Above average height, but not exceptionally tall, he was lean, with strong, broad hands that were more calloused than you would expect to see in a forensic scientist. He kept his dark brown hair short. Whether teaching, or visiting crime scenes — even working in ditches with the soupy remains of corpses — he wore suit and tie. Not because there was a dress code for staff — Fennimore was one of only two people in the building who regularly turned out in business wear — but after years of working with the police, that was how he felt most comfortable. He cleared his throat, the murmur of voices subsided and, after a last-minute scramble for seats, he had their attention.

"What's the most powerful tool available to a forensic scientist?"

These were first-year undergrads, several months into the course, and some of the shine had been rubbed off them. He got a muttered, slightly pained, "DNA" in response.

"Really?" he said. "The top 10 per cent of Hibernia's brightest young minds, and that's the best you can do?" This was Fennimore's preferred approach: flattery wrapped up in an insult.

Some of the more combative types sat up a bit straighter, but nobody offered an alternative.

"I know, I know . . . it's Monday . . ." He plucked a test tube from the rack in front of him. "Okay, easy question: what's this?"

"A straw-coloured liquid." This from a dark-haired lad with a short goatie.

"Interesting." Fennimore frowned at his laptop which stood open on the long demonstration bench. Still frowning, he looked at the contents of the test

2

tube. "It *looks* like wee. It's in a test tube that we use for testing wee. But you're not willing to hazard a guess that it *is* wee?"

"Not a chance."

A few people smiled.

"Why?"

"Because. It wouldn't be very scientific."

"Scientists don't guess?"

"Not unless they know all the facts."

Fennimore smiled. "Sadly, we rarely know *all* the facts. What I *think* you mean is that you believe I'm not above staging a set-up to catch out some poor alcohol-fuddled first year, and you're not falling for it."

The goatie smirked, enjoying the attention.

"Fair enough." Fennimore held the test tube up to the nasty white glare of the low-energy lights. "Okay — for the record — this is indeed urine. The problem with DNA and urine is you'd be lucky to get a few epithelial cells from the urethra. So DNA isn't likely to help you identify the urinator — even if this is an assault case and the assailant peed on the victim — and that particular perversion is not a discussion point in this lecture." It wasn't meant to shock, it was merely a statement of fact.

"So, coming back to my original question, our most powerful tool is . . ."

"Observation." Josh Brown — interesting on two counts: that he was here at all; and that Fennimore hadn't seen him. But Josh Brown had the knack of being in a room without being noticed — until he wanted to be noticed. Now, it seemed, he did.

The subject of this lecture was "Observation and Assessment". The title was listed in their course schedule and it was projected from his laptop onto the screen behind him.

"Correct," Fennimore said, "but you don't get full brownie points on account of the BIG FAT CLUE." He glanced over his shoulder at the lecture title, and a few of his audience groaned at their oversight. Fennimore slapped his head and in a fair impersonation of a generic student, said, "Mondays. Nightmare!"

They shuffled and grinned, and one or two of the girls even laughed.

He nodded to the AV tech in the glass booth at the rear of the hall. A second screen lit up on the wall to his right, projecting an image of the rack of test tubes, magnified a metre high.

"All right. Observations?"

A tawny-haired girl on the third row raised her hand. "They're different colours?" Only lately arrived from one of the smaller Hebridean Isles, she was good, but not convinced of her worth, yet.

"Colours, or shades?"

"Um . . . Both?"

"Describe them."

Embarrassed, she said, "Well, you can see."

"We can all *see*, but can you *observe*?" he said, paraphrasing Sherlock Holmes.

She blushed, frowning, but he held her gaze, and finally she accepted the inevitable, took a breath and launched in. "You've shades of lemon and honey and pale amber and caramel." Did she know that she'd described beautifully every shade of island malt from pale oak-matured Islay to sherry-casked Jura?

"And this?" He selected a test tube from the end of the rack; it shone slightly pink in the artificial light.

"That's altogether different," she said. "It looks . . . Well, it looks like somebody's been knocking back too many Sea Breezes." She got a laugh of recognition.

"Excellent." Fennimore looked around the room; now they were beginning to wake up, he could hit them with a few more facts. "Vodka, like all alcohol, dehydrates — which would concentrate the pretty pink dye from cranberry juice in a Sea Breeze. So maybe this person died of acute alcoholic poisoning. Or maybe not — but it's worth considering. Beetroot can turn urine an even more impressive shade of pink, and we might be interested in that — for instance, does this fit with accounts of what this person had for their last meal? Perhaps they're allergic to beetroot, and died of it."

Some were showing an interest, some had even picked up their pens as if they intended to use them.

"You might also note quantity, turbidity, the presence of casts. So — let's say we've observed what we can of appearance. Now what?"

"Smell," someone said.

"For example?"

"Well, diabetic urine smells weird."

"Define weird."

"I dunno, like nail polish remover."

"Which is mainly acetone, of course. In urine, it's ketones that cause the pear drops smell. It's caused by ketoacidosis — a sign that they're not taking their insulin as they should. And it's potentially fatal." Pens hovered above notepads; he almost had them. Fennimore leaned forward, conspiratorially. "When you're looking for a possible cause of death, a fatal disease could be significant."

Some of them actually did him the honour of committing ink to paper. Now they could see a point to squinting at glass tubes filled with someone else's bodily fluids.

"You also get ketonuria in anorexia — if the body is starved, for whatever reason, it starts metabolizing fatty acids — eating itself to keep the cells alive."

At the last count, 5 per cent of the UK population had diabetes — statistical probability said there would be two or three diabetics in this lecture hall alone — and he'd give good odds that every one of them knew someone who had an eating disorder.

"I was going to save this till later, but since diabetes has come up . . ." Fennimore reached below the demonstration bench and fetched out a neat rack of ten test tubes. "Diabetic urine can *smell* sweet. Have you thought how it might *taste*?"

He heard a rumble of alarm. "It's perfectly safe," he told them. "Fresh urine is sterile, and these samples have been tested bug-free — in fact all of this urine has been passed by the management." He looked brightly around the room. "So, who wants to go first?"

They weren't falling for it. Many of them sat back, folded their arms, shook their heads, the rest avoided his gaze. "You don't trust me?" he said, trying to look crestfallen.

"We'd want to see a demo first," the goatie said. A slow roll of laughter followed: they knew Fennimore couldn't resist a challenge.

He took out the first tube in the rack and stared at it for a few moments. "If I do this, you have to do exactly the same."

He waited until he nodded and muttered agreement, then shrugged, popped the lid off the tube, closed the mouth of it with his index finger, inverted it, dabbed his finger on his tongue and smacked his lips. "Sweet. So that one's diabetic." He scanned the room.

"Now it's your turn."

A few declined, but the majority were game. Test tubes were passed along the rows; he watched closely, and identified Josh Brown as the one person who had done exactly as he had. When he was sure they had all finished, he said, "Josh. What does it taste like?"

"I dunno."

"You didn't taste it?"

"No."

"Why?"

"We agreed to do the *same* as you."

"Would you demonstrate?"

Josh stood up and turned side-on, so the majority of the room could see him. He repeated the action exactly as Fennimore had performed it. A half-dozen students exclaimed in dismay, but the rest looked perplexed.

"Again, more slowly, please."

Josh closed the top of the tube with his index finger, inverted the tube, righted it, then raised his *middle* finger like he was flipping them the bird, and touched that to his tongue.

Now they understood. There were exclamations of disgust; someone even retched. "Before you all stampede for the toilets . . ." Fennimore raised his test tube and tipped the liquid down his throat to further exclamations and outraged laughter. "Lucozade," he explained.

Fennimore wrapped up a few minutes before the hour and the lecture ended with the muted applause of flip-up seats, as his students gathered their belongings and made way for the next group, already gathering outside. In the final half-hour, they had begun to look at toxicology and metabolism, and Fennimore had handed out more samples for them to identify, among other things, signs of infection (musty odour); medication for infection (the slightly sulphurous whiff of penicillin); drug habits, including ephedrine (cat pee); amphetamine (brut wine); and amyltripyline (Chanel No.5).

He turned his phone on as the last few stragglers shuffled out, and it rang immediately. He answered the call, shutting down his laptop and gathering his notes with his free hand, making way for the next lecturer.

"Yep?"

"Nick? It's Kate."

The sound of her voice blew through him like a blast of air off the North Sea. His heart thudded and he felt the tug of the past like a dangerous undercurrent.

8

"Simms," she added, as if he didn't know her voice as well as he knew his own. "Can we talk?"

You got the wrong number, he wanted to tell her. *You made a mistake*. Instead, he heard himself say, "It's been a while."

"Four years." The inevitable pause, awkward, painful to them both.

He cleared his throat. "Are you still in London?"

"Greater Manchester Police. The Met was a bit of a dead end for me, after the Crime Faculty."

"My fault," he said. "I'm sorry for that."

"I'd do it all again in a heartbeat."

He felt something shift in his chest. A burden he'd been carrying around for five years.

She started to speak, but he talked over her.

"Look, Kate, I'm in a lecture room, and I'm kind of in the way. Can I call you back?"

"No. Nick, listen to me, don't hang up."

He heard a sharp edge of desperation in her voice, and couldn't harden himself enough to close the phone. So he bundled his belongings together and stood in the corridor with his laptop at his feet among the surge of incoming students, while Kate Simms explained.

The police authority's six-monthly crime review had turned up an excess of overdoses, and she had been assigned to look into it as part of their public protection remit.

"As jobs go, it was routine, low level, something simple and undemanding for my first try-out."

First try-out? When he worked with Kate Simms at the National Crime Faculty, she was a young Detective Sergeant with a career path carved out of pure gold. Her placement there should have put her on accelerated promotion from Detective Sergeant to Detective Chief Inspector within a couple of years.

"Kate," he said, "it's been *five years* since the Crime Faculty."

"You don't need to tell me — they kept me on the naughty step for four of them."

He imagined her, a half-smile on her face, reaching for cynical from the top shelf of cop attitude. He felt a thud of guilt.

"It was a straightforward paper review," Simms said. "A box-ticking exercise. I was expected to read through the coroner's verdicts, report that it was just a bit of a spike in the numbers of deaths, nothing to worry about — it happens occasionally."

"What changed?"

"I hardly had time to divvy up the paperwork before we had another death. Except this one's got media potential and suddenly the top brass are asking for updates and demanding to be kept in the loop."

"Define 'media potential'," Fennimore said.

"You've heard of Stacey?"

"Stacey who?"

"Not Stacey — StayC, with a capital C."

"Not ringing any bells," he said.

"She reached the quarter-finals of *Stars!* Got kicked out when she was caught in one of the toilet cubicles at the venue snorting cocaine. A week later, she's found dead in her mother's back bedroom, a hypodermic stuck in her arm. Heroin. She was written up as a suspected overdose, but the pathologist wasn't convinced — she wasn't a regular user. I'd already been in touch about the excess cases so he knew I'd be interested. He expedited the toxicology, suspended the post-mortem, and called me."

"And?" The question was out before he could bite it back.

"The tox results show lowish levels of heroin, and some methylecgonine, as well."

"The methylecgonine just indicates she's a cocaine user, which you knew already — it's not necessarily suspicious."

"That's exactly what the NPIA Forensic Specialist Advisor said." When Fennimore worked with the police, the National Crime Faculty had advised police on forensic matters, but since 2007, technology and support services had come under the National Policing Improvement Agency.

"You should listen to your FSA," he said.

"I would, but the numbers are weird, Nick. We've got a sudden surge in ODs in the last six to eight months, most of them female. Why?"

Mostly female — now that is interesting. He almost allowed himself to be drawn into speculating why that might be, but he pushed away the questions that began to crowd in, the possible threads of hypotheses he could see spinning into the distance, and said, "Let it go, Kate; addicts die all the time. Follow the FSA's advice, do the review, write up your report and move on." It was brutal, but he'd made himself a promise, and he wasn't about to go back on that, even for Simms.

"I can't believe I'm hearing you say that. I don't think you even believe it yourself."

"Police business isn't my business any more, Kate. I've been there, and we both have the scars to prove it." He sounded bitter, and that made him angry. "I work defence now. That way, the only place I have anything to do with cops is in the courtroom."

The anger hardened his voice more than he'd intended, and she said quietly, "Does that include me, Nick? Is that why you changed your mobile number and moved to *Aberdeen*, for God's sake — so you didn't have to have anything to do with cops — like me?"

"Kate, you know I didn't mean —"

"Hey, you're the one who says the facts don't lie."

He said nothing.

"You work defence now? Very noble. Except it isn't, is it? It's just a way to get even with the police. I was given this case because it doesn't matter if I screw up — how about that — two hundred miles and five whole years away from the Met, and they still don't trust me. But if I screw this one up, who cares — because 'addicts die all the time'. *Right*, Nick?"

The silence that followed felt like the aftermath of a nuclear explosion.

"Sorry . . ." Her voice sounded a little shaky. "I've been bottling that up for a *long* time."

He took a breath, but she spoke before he could find the right words.

12

"I don't regret what I did. But it cost me, Nick. In ways you could never imagine."

She was right, he couldn't imagine. His career had burgeoned, while hers had withered. And how had he thanked her? By shutting her out, dropping out of her life, burying his guilt at what he'd done. But guilt had a way of sneaking around his defences, finding an unbolted door, an open window.

"Okay," he said. "Who's the NPIA Forensic Specialist? Maybe I could give them a call, talk through a few ideas."

"Just look at the reports, give me an opinion. You don't even have to come down here — I'll send them to you."

"Why so cagey?" He wished he could see her face.

"Look," she insisted, "I'm just asking you to read through the evidence, give me an opinion — that's what you do, isn't it? I mean as a forensic consultant?"

"Ye-es, but I don't usually work behind the backs of fellow professionals."

She didn't reply, and for a moment the line seemed to hum with silence. "Oh," he said. "I get it. You think my reputation will taint your investigation."

She laughed. "Why the hell d'you think I'm in Manchester? I had to distance myself from the Faculty, and Bramshill — and you."

He couldn't argue with that; it was his actions — his single-minded obsession that he *had* to be right — that had wrecked her chances. And that didn't exactly make him feel like a hero.

"Let's say I did your review," he said, still reluctant. "You know I would want all the scene details, and if these were handled as routine ODs, there wouldn't be very much. I bet nobody would have thought it worth the effort of taking scene photos — and who *knows* what tox was done —"

"Stop," she said. "I will get you everything we have. In fact, anything *anyone* has. I know what you need to work, Nick — we did the job together for long enough."

"Okay," he said. It wasn't that he underestimated her, he just needed all the details. "I'd probably make a few suggestions: tests, tox, cytology . . ." He realized with a shock that he was seriously considering this as a project.

"Uh —" She seemed to struggle for the right words. "The thing is, I'd be going against FSA's advice on this. I was hoping you could give me your assessment and even do some of the tests under the radar."

"What are you not telling me, Kate?"

"I told you, StayC's death has fired imaginations — the ACC is taking a personal interest."

"So tell him you're using your initiative — he might even be impressed."

"I doubt it." She almost spat the words.

The Kate Simms he knew never carried that kind of resentment around with her. Budgets were tight — even at his self-imposed distance from the police, he knew that — but what kind of ACC would want to stamp on thorough investigative work? His mind flew back to the Crime Faculty and, suddenly, he thought he knew.

14

"Kate, who is the ACC?"

She took a breath, let it go, took another. "Stuart Gifford."

For a moment, the steady tug of the past became a tidal wave: anger, terror, grief, so strong that he almost lost his footing.

"Nick? Are you okay?"

He couldn't answer that, so he said, "What the hell possessed you? Didn't you *know* he'd moved to Greater Manchester Police?"

"He followed *me* here — he was still climbing the greasy pole at the Met until a month ago. And, just so you know, Gifford is also the current chair of ACPO's Homicide Working Group." The Association of Chief Police Officers coordinated and developed policing strategy. "He could argue it's his *duty* to take a close look at the investigation."

He rubbed his forehead, trying to ease a throbbing pain that was building behind his eyes. "Ever feel cursed, Kate?"

"*You're* asking *me?*"

One of his students greeted him as she passed, but Fennimore barely noticed.

Simms exhaled into the phone. "I shouldn't have said that."

He cleared his throat and loosened his tie, tried hard to keep the tremor out of his voice. "If anyone's earned the right, it's you."

"I didn't call you to argue, Nick," she said. "And I swear, if I had any other option . . ." Her voice cracked, and she cleared her throat before she went on: "But my low-profile easy-start investigation is turning into something much more complicated, and Gifford is sitting on the sidelines, just *aching* for me to mess this up."

"What happened was my fault, not yours."

"I'm nobody's puppet, Nick. I made choices — of my own free will."

"But I'm not police; Gifford can't touch me, so he hounds you instead, is that it?"

"Honestly?" She sighed. "Gifford thinks I should have been kicked out for what I did."

"Jesus, Kate —"

"I told you, I don't regret it," she interrupted. "But I had to go back into *uniform* to make Inspector, Nick, and I've had my fill of neighbourhood policing: D&Ds and TWOCs and ASBOs, and endless bloody partnership meetings. I'm a detective. I want to make it as a detective. I'm asking for your help."

In five years, she hadn't asked for anything from him. He knew how hard it must be for her to ask now. He would not make her ask again.

"Okay," he said. "What've you got?"

"Names, dates, the Crime Pattern Analysis Unit's report, a few of the tox results. They're spread over several coroners, so I'm waiting on some."

"The pathologist who's dealing with StayC's death sounds friendly," he said. "See if you can get any more detail from him. He can send attachments by email, or if he only has hard copy, I can take faxes — I'll text you my office fax number."

"Okay, you'll have everything I've got within the hour. When will you —?"

"Tonight. It'll be late though."

"Fine. No problem. You can reach me on my mobile anytime. Anytime." After an awkward silence, she said, "Well, I'd better . . ."

"Kate, don't hang up." If he didn't say it now, he never would: "How's the family?" *The family*, like he couldn't remember their names. Like it had slipped his mind that Becky, Simms's daughter, and his had been inseparable. *Well done, Fennimore. No, really — nice touch.*

CHAPTER
TWO

Marta is preparing for a client. She's wearing a short red wrap-over dress, stockings, heels. She is sinuous, graceful, holds herself like a dancer. She tells her customers that she trained for the ballet, but she grew too tall; her dancing career was over by the time she reached fifteen. None of it is true, but they like the story. She has practised how to walk and turn, and tilt her head in the expressive way ballet dancers do. She wears her ice-blonde hair short, feathered lightly at the temples and cut straight along the delicate line of her jaw.

The room is clean, painted in dark red and cream, L-shaped, with a shower cubicle around the corner in the foot of the "L"; soft, fluffy towels are stacked in purpose-built shelves to the left of the shower; cream and red, to match the decor. Erotic pictures and mirrors are framed in gold; the lights can be dimmed, and usually are. A massage table stands off-centre of the room. A double bed is placed opposite a forty-inch plasma screen; access to twenty-three adult TV channels and a range of DVDs is included in the price. This is the deluxe suite: Rob is a special client.

Sol Henry escorts him in personally, slaps him on the back and says, "Marta — just like you asked. She's come in special for you."

Rob looks her over, as if he's deciding what he wants to do to her. He's a big man — broad as well as tall. Big men are often the sweetest — careful in case their clumsy hands should hurt or bruise. But Rob is not so careful. He's one of those big men who like to demonstrate their power.

Sol is shorter than his client, stocky, but he can move fast when he needs to. He shaves his head, because his hair grows in thick black curls, and he thinks that makes him look soft. He hands her a package. It's about the size of a brick, wrapped in grey plastic and sealed with parcel tape. He does it right in front of Rob. They've lost a couple of big consignments, one way or another, since she joined the firm; Rob is helping with that. She only knows this because she listens at doorways and lingers when she takes coffee in to their meetings. Now this is an official message to her: Rob is on the team. She looks at Sol, keeping her face carefully blank, and the quick sparkle of humour in his eyes says, *Yeah, life's full of surprises, isn't it?*

He places an envelope on the bed. "For you. Address is inside. By two o'clock, okay?"

She checks her watch; she has somewhere else to be at two, but if Rob is quick she can wash up, drop off the package and still make it in time. "Yes, I can do that." Her accent is Eastern European, her voice warm, well modulated.

He cocks an eyebrow. "What else you got to do, middle of the day?"

She smiles. "If I told you, you might be shocked."

Sol laughs, looks to Rob for his reaction. "She's worth her weight in gold, this one."

"You think? I reckon I could lift her with one hand." Rob looks into her eyes as he says this, sending her a message of his own.

This time Sol doesn't laugh; he looks at Marta. "All right?"

She inclines her head, and Sol turns away. His hand hovers over the doorknob, but he lets it drop and turns back.

Rob frowns. "Forget something, Sol?"

The two men lock gazes, ignoring her.

Sol touches his arm. "Be nice."

Rob's smile is a second too late to seem genuine. He looks down at Sol's hand on his arm, and up into Sol's face again, but Sol does not move, and he does not look away. Rob has been warned, and it's clear he doesn't like to be warned. But he does smile, and pats Sol's shoulder. "'Nice'? My middle name, Sol," he says with a chuckle.

Sol leaves his hand where it is for a moment longer, for just long enough, and Rob does not try to shake him off. His eyes dart left, and Sol nods, satisfied.

Rob stares at the door as if he can see Sol Henry walking slowly down the corridor. After half a minute, he turns to Marta, a thoughtful look on his face.

"What *have* you been up to?"

Marta keeps her face blank of expression. "I don't understand."

"I've never seen Sol Henry so smitten."

She hefts the package Sol handed to her. "He values reliability," she says.

"You ever curious?"

"About what?"

He jerks his chin. "About what kind of pestilence you're carrying around the city in those neat packages."

"You have saying, I think? 'Curiosity drowned the cat.'"

"*Killed* the cat."

She shrugs. "Anyway, it died." She drops the block into her shoulder bag and reaches for the envelope on the bed. "This is what I am interested in." The envelope is stuffed with twenties.

"Speaking of which . . ." He fetches out his wallet, as he has done every session, and she waves away his offer of payment, as she has done every time.

"It's taken care of," she says. "On the house."

"How about a little extra?"

She smiles a slow smile; they have danced this dance before. "Extra?"

"A speciality."

She strokes the web of flesh between his thumb and index finger. "Rob, I *am* the speciality."

"Come on . . . Just a little game."

She smiles her refusal.

"Okay, how about OWO for an extra twenty?" He means oral without protection. Most of the girls do, at no extra charge. Marta does not.

She holds up a small square condom packet between her first two fingers; the shiny bronze wrapper glints under the lights. "Your ticket for the ride, sir," she says, keeping her voice low and warm. "Real-Feel, ultralight."

He looks ready to argue and she says, "I'm afraid you must have valid ticket to enter."

A dark shadow seems to pass across his face. Rob is a man who is used to saying, "Do this," and it is done, a man who is not used to being told "no".

"You think I'm *diseased*, Marta? Worried I'll give you the clap?"

She runs her fingers lightly across his chest and feels an answering shimmer of muscle contractions up and down his torso. Heat is coming off him in waves. She moves in close, reaches up on tiptoe, her fingers resting on his shoulder, her mouth close enough to his ear to kiss. "*So*-rry, dar*link*," she whispers, amping up the accent: "No glove, no love."

She turns to leave, and he catches her by the wrist, not gently. His eyes burn with dull fury, and red-hot pain flares up her arm. Her heart skips a little; every instinct tells her to fight, but she relaxes her body, turns 180, and allows herself to be drawn into an embrace, arranging her features into an expression of wide-eyed inquisitiveness.

"Be nice," she says. It's a reminder that Sol will not take it well if he is rough with her.

The light in his eyes seems to flare, then it dies, and he flings her hand away. "All right," he says. "You win."

"No, lover," she says, patting him lightly on the cheek, "we both win."

She moves to the mirror above the dressing table, arranges her hair, checks her lipstick, using big, bold movements, so he won't see that her hands are shaking.

CHAPTER
THREE

Afterwards they shower and she sees him out, then she returns to the room and showers again, taking her time, washing all trace of Rob off her skin. She dries carefully, then sits naked at the dressing table to fix her make-up. Her wrist is bruised, but otherwise she is unmarked.

There was never any serious danger: every treatment room in the place is rigged for surveillance. Right now, she's looking into the lens of a tiny camera built into one of the screws on which the mirror hangs.

In the main office, there is a desk in front of the stockroom door; night or day, one or other of the Henry brothers will always be sitting behind the desk. If neither brother is in the office — well, you should not be, either. This means that nobody else has seen behind the magnolia white door; not the other girls — not even Rob — because Rob might be more important to the boys than she'd realized, but he is still a punter, and if he finds out what's in there, he won't like it.

Marta herself has been inside that small windowless room because Sol invited her. The other girls fantasize about a pharmacy of powders and herbs and pills stacked in boxes behind that door, but the Henrys are too careful for that. Nothing incriminating is kept close by; they have stashes all over town — she should know — she has run supplies to half of them. So that first time Sol invited her into the storeroom, she hadn't expected to see goods stacked on shelves, but she hadn't expected to see banks of screens, either. Monitors linked to DVD recorders, a column of USB drives for back-up.

She stared at the images on the screens: men in various stages of undress, fucking or being fellated by women or with their heads buried between women's thighs. "You record everything?"

Sol stood behind her and nuzzled her neck. "Mmm . . ." He slipped his hand under her blouse and cupped her breast.

"Why are you showing me this?"

He tilted her chin with his left hand, and planted kisses along the sharp line of her jaw, rotating her nipple stud between his right thumb and forefinger. "Because I trust you."

She eased away, turning her head to look up into his face. "Or because maybe this is the only place without your little spy cameras?"

He laughed. "That's what I like about you, Marta. You're smarter than the average."

"Sure, always thinking." She faced the screens again, pushing her buttocks into his erection. "Like now, I think you bring me here because you want to screw me and you don't want your brother to know."

He kneaded her breast, almost hypnotized by the girls and their punters silently humping and sucking and licking on twelve different screens. "Frank's old school," he said, his voice hoarse now. "Doesn't like mixing business and pleasure."

"So, if I fuck with you, Frank wouldn't like it."

"What Frank doesn't know can't hurt him, can it?"

She reached around to fondle his buttock with her left hand while she assessed the room. A filing cabinet; a wall safe, unlocked; stacks of CDs — recordings of men fucking and women faking. *Is it worth it? Is it worth fucking Sol for the chance of getting a good look around some other time?* Sol worked his free hand down her body to her crotch and she knew she had to make up her mind, because once he got his fingers inside her panties, there would be no stopping him. Yes, she thought. *I really want to know what's in that safe.*

This is how Marta knew Rob, standing behind her, was staring at her ass, she also knew that Sol was watching her from the monitor in the stockroom.

She looks into the small black camera lens, tricked out to look like a mirror mounting bolt, and gives a slight nod. Sol would not allow Rob to go too far. Because Rob might be a big man in the business, but Marta has her own value, and her stock rises with every new transaction: every drop-off or pick-up, every message she relays, every favoured client she entertains.

Smitten, she thinks. This so-strange word which means consumed with desire, but also *struck down, defeated.* Yes, Sol is smitten. She doesn't need Rob to tell her, she knows it — she has been working on Sol for months.

CHAPTER
FOUR

*"Not everything that can be counted counts, and
not everything that counts can be counted."*

A SIGN HANGING IN ALBERT EINSTEIN'S OFFICE
AT PRINCETON

Nick Fennimore looked up from his work. A door had
slammed further down the corridor, jarring him from
his careful check of the numbers. It was 7p.m.;
probably security, doing the rounds. He dragged his
fingers through his hair, stood up and stretched, feeling
his back creak and hearing the click and crackle of
joints realigning. The wind screaming off the North Sea
rattled the traffic lights at the corner of St Andrew
Street and Crooked Lane. He watched them change to
green as he stretched out the rucks and tangles caused
by twenty years of weekend rock climbing. Of course,
spending the rest of his days hunched over microscopes
and computer keyboards hadn't helped.

He had been working a good four hours on the data
Kate Simms had sent through. He hadn't drawn any
conclusions, yet, but he'd been reminded of one sad
truth: there is *nothing* that an addict won't do for a fix.
Post-mortem reports catalogued repeated STD infec-
tions; fallopian tubes so blocked and inflamed with

27

infection that the victims must have been in constant pain; papillomas; internal scars; old bruises overlaid with new; whip and ligature marks from S&M "games"; healed fractures. He felt sick with it.

The traffic lights changed for a second, and then a third time from green, through amber, to red, and he couldn't bring himself to go back to his reading. Time for coffee.

Fennimore had a house in the Lakes, but during term time he rented a flat near Union Terrace Gardens, which he hardly ever used; he had smuggled a day-bed into his office, and often slept over. The place was heaped with papers, books double- and triple-stacked on his shelves, and a dozen or more plastic storage boxes stuffed with case papers and journals, these crammed into corners, under his desk and behind the door.

The café had been closed for hours, but there was a small kitchen on the third floor, squeezed into a broom cupboard next to the south-east stairwell. There was no sign of Security, but he heard occasional booms as doors were opened or slammed shut. Access to the kitchen was restricted to staff, and entry controlled by a proximity card reader. He waited for the electronic lock to give the triple-tone beep which confirmed his ID, then shouldered the door open. It was a surprise to find Josh Brown at the kitchen counter, brewing coffee.

Josh seemed as startled as he was. "Professor Fennimore."

"Josh." The student had left a stack of books and papers on the coffee table; a copy of Fennimore's own book *Crapshoots and Bad Stats* among them. "Working late?" he asked.

"Case law," Josh said.

"You could read up on that at home," Fennimore observed mildly.

"Too many distractions."

Josh Brown had attended the first years' 9a.m. lecture that day, and clearly he stayed as late as he was allowed, so distractions of a romantic kind seemed unlikely. Fennimore's own flat overlooked a quiet shopping street which was usually deserted by 7p.m., but he avoided it until the necessity of sleep could not be ignored. Home — even a home away from home — was a place where thoughts you could suppress in the workplace all came crowding back. But Fennimore had lived long enough to amass a wealth of painful memories and regrets; Josh was just twenty-three.

He had been working on his thesis for five months, perfecting lab techniques he'd missed studying for his first degree. But he was a will o' the wisp — both there and not there — everybody knew him, yet nobody knew him well. He was about five-ten, his hair was gel-spiked, like most of his peers, and, like them, he wore urban fashion — hoodies, T-shirts and loose-fitting denims — but it was as though it was all an effort to fit in; his clothes, his self-effacing quietness worn like camouflage.

The coffee machine wheezed and spat, and Fennimore realized that he was staring. "Your thesis is on the influence of advances in DNA technology on cold case clear-up, isn't it?" he asked, jerking his chin towards the books and papers.

"This isn't for my thesis — it's just for interest."

His brief, uninformative answers piqued Fennimore's curiosity. "So . . .?"

"I'm looking at the Sally Clark case."

"Sally Clark. Convicted of the murder of her two infants."

"Wrongly convicted. They died of Sudden Infant Death Syndrome — cot death."

A lot of students would not have corrected him on that. Fennimore suppressed a smile. "Well . . . you know . . . a lot of people *claim* cot death . . ."

"She was cleared — the prosecution messed up the stats." Josh had a hard-to-place accent, but emotion injected a hint of Essex in the vowel sounds.

"You think?"

Josh stared at him. "The entire prosecuting argument was based on a spurious argument."

Fennimore tugged his ear. "They based their case on the assumption that if it was extremely unlikely that one child in an affluent middle class family should die of SIDS, then two dying went way beyond coincidence — isn't that reasonable?"

"*Reasonable*." Josh snatched the coffee jug from the hotplate. "They didn't even *look* at environmental factors — the house, the ambient temperatures, the . . . the fact that both babies had been vaccinated shortly before they died. They didn't consider genetics, or gender, or —"

30

"Or the possibility that Sally Clark was innocent," Fennimore interrupted.

Josh stopped. "You just said she was guilty."

"I said she was *convicted*. Of course, if they'd done a Bayesian analysis of the evidence, the case would never have come to court," Fennimore said. "Bayes would ask what is the likelihood that the deaths were caused by SIDS, *compared with* the likelihood that they were caused by murder. Statistically, it's *more* likely that two children will die of SIDS in the same family, because of predisposing factors."

Josh was quiet for a moment. "So all that was just a big wind-up?" He seemed to be deciding if he should be offended.

"A test maybe."

"How'm I doing?"

"All right, so far."

The student poured the steaming coffee into his cup and raised the jug. Fennimore picked a mug up from the drainer and Josh filled it up.

"So, you'd always use Bayes where the evidence wasn't clear cut?" Josh asked.

"Always," Fennimore said. "Wouldn't you?"

"I don't know. I never studied Bayesian stats."

"Your first degree is in psychology and law, isn't it?" Josh nodded.

Fennimore sighed. "'Combined Honours: the dilution factor' — someone should write a paper on it. You *would* have done Bayesian stats if you hadn't turned down the chance to stay in Nottingham to do your PhD in Forensic Psychology."

"How d'you know about that?" The guardedness, the willingness to take offence were back in his eyes. "I didn't tell anyone I'd had an offer from Nottingham."

"Alastair Varley telephoned." Varley was a forensic psychologist Fennimore had worked with many times over the years. "He said you're a brilliant scholar. Dedicated, curious, driven almost. He said they offered you a bursary."

Josh replaced the coffee jug, and Fennimore waited for him to explain, or at least to ask what Varley had said about him turning down a PhD opportunity with a bursary attached to it, but Josh sipped his coffee in silence.

Varley had said that Josh Brown was entirely opaque, and possibly self-destructive. Fennimore had taken the last comment as a dig at him, since Josh had ended up under his tutelage. But Varley had dropped the professional rivalry for a millisecond to make a serious point: "Josh got a double first," he said. "And nobody came to see him graduate. Nobody."

Fennimore decided that pushing Brown would achieve nothing, so he returned to the original thesis. "The second child that died had a staphylococcus infection — did you know that?"

"No," Josh said, fully engaged again, now that they were no longer talking about him.

"No reason why you should — it wasn't even disclosed to the defence. The prosecution quite perversely ignored the relevance of context, and context is always relevant."

32

Josh's eyes gleamed. "Can you recommend some texts? I want to read up on this."

Fennimore thought about it. He did need someone to talk through the drugs case. And Josh Brown wasn't afraid to argue with him. "Want a practical introduction to Bayesian analysis?" he said.

Josh gave him a long, thoughtful look, and Fennimore thought, *You might paint yourself into the background, Josh, but the camouflage will never really fool anyone — the wariness behind your eyes will always betray you.* He had only ever seen that kind of wariness in cops and criminals.

CHAPTER
FIVE

StayC's death attracted national media attention, and Greater Manchester Police forked out the cash to rent the Park Suite at the Ramada in Piccadilly Square. So what was to have been a simple statement drafted by the press office and read by DCI Simms to a few local newspaper journos became a full press conference for TV, radio and press, chaired by Assistant Chief Constable Gifford. The other members of the panel were Detective Superintendent Tanford, head of the Drugs Squad; Professor Phillip Underwood, director of South Manchester Substance Misuse Services; and Simms's own immediate boss, Detective Superintendent Spry.

The suite had been partitioned off with room dividers — one panel left open for ease of access between the two sections. Simms glanced in as she passed the press briefing room. Her heart skipped a beat — it was crammed. She counted six TV cameras, their cables snaking from various sockets around the room. Every chair was occupied, and more people milled about at the back. Simms took a few calming breaths as she walked to the GMP section next door.

Briefing notes had been set out on a desk just inside the room, and she was offered a copy by a smiling clerk.

"Thanks," she said, raising a hand in polite refusal. "I know what's in it — I wrote it."

"Take a copy."

Simms turned to face Jim Allen, head of the press office. She had worked with Jim on a couple of community initiatives when she first came to Manchester. He reminded her of a Jack Russell terrier. Small, fast, keen and constantly aquiver, as if his muscles were wired to a high voltage. Jim had come to the GMP Press Office after fifteen years as a crime reporter for the *Mirror* newspaper. He could summarize any story in fifteen words, tell you the weak spots in your briefing notes, and he had a particular knack for the visual cues that journalists used to manipulate the opinions of their readership. He took the booklet from the clerk and thrust it into Simms's hand.

"Sharks are circling, Kate. You'll look badly prepped if you walk in there empty-handed." The suggestion of poor preparation caused a few heads to turn.

Kate raised the briefing notes with a weak smile and, satisfied, they returned to their conversations. Spry and Gifford, both in uniform, stood to one side in earnest conversation. Spry was the taller of the two, grey-haired and distinguished-looking in his uniform. He spent weekends and holidays on his narrow boat on the Cheshire canals, and those who knew said he was looking to drift gently along the byways of policing into an easy retirement.

35

"The big three are here," Jim said, meaning BBC, ITV and Channel Four News. "Plus Sky, a local cable network and Music Plus — it's a Hungarian music station — apparently, StayC was very popular over there."

On the other side of the partition, the buzz of conversation from the gathered press and media sounded like a hive of bees that had been poked with a sharp stick.

"Want some help with make-up?" Jim asked, looking for someone who might give her a few tips.

Simms had already dabbed concealer under her eyes to hide the shadows caused by two days of lost sleep.

"No," she said firmly. "Thanks."

He eyed her doubtfully, but seemed to decide it wasn't worth an argument. "Keep your head up," he said. "Minimize the panda look."

"Thanks for the advice, Sir Galahad," she said, but he wasn't listening. One of the press officers had presented him with a note. "Who?" he asked.

"*Weekly News*," she said. "They say they want the human angle."

"No." He monitored the room constantly as he spoke. "No interviews. They want to ask questions, they can ask them now."

Simms listened to Jim Allen with half an ear as she watched one of his staff guide a man in a light grey suit over to the two senior officers. The psychologist, she guessed. They greeted him, speaking in low, grave tones, and the three formed a loose circle. Gifford was a square, solid man, a former rugby player, with sandy hair and small eyes that darted from face to face as he spoke.

The last of the panel of five arrived. Tanford. He was tall, well built. Solid, but not fleshy, with smoothly shaved cheeks and dark, neatly trimmed hair. Difficult to estimate his age, but he wore a long service medal ribbon, so he must have put in twenty years at least, and that would put him at over forty. Also, pinned to his tunic, a QPM — Queen's Police Medal — for distinguished service. He had the physical presence of a cop who had spent time in the field, a man who could back off a lowlife with one hard-eyed look. Spry and Gifford had made their rank through the administrative route and, as Tanford broke into the circle with the confidence of a man used to acceptance, Simms saw that they were a little in awe of him.

Jim followed her line of sight. "Hey, don't sweat it — they're here to do the heavy lifting. All you need to do is look intelligent and thoughtful."

The aftertaste of her years in the London Met wilderness soured her gullet. "What am I — window dressing?"

He seemed to consider the question seriously. "Ballast, maybe — but don't take it personally — your boss won't be saying much, either. With the ACC here, it's all about the shiny buttons and the performance targets." He looked at her. "Okay?"

She nodded. "Okay."

"You shouldn't have to take any questions, but if you're asked something direct, make eye contact, speak slowly and enunciate clearly."

Tanford had done the rounds and now it was her turn. He paused and looked down at her with a quizzical smile, but just as she put her hand out, he switched his attention to Jim Allen.

"Jim," he said, opening his arms wide as if he'd just run into an old school friend. He reached past Simms and shook hands with the press officer. "Good to know we're in safe hands. Can I have a word?" He put his free arm around Jim Allen's shoulder, edging Jim into a space a few feet from her, effectively giving her his back.

Seeing an opportunity, one of Jim Allen's assistants hurried across the room and offered her a mirror. Exasperated, Simms glanced again at Jim. His discussion with Detective Superintendent Tanford was becoming heated. Suddenly, Tanford laughed.

"Put that in a memo for me, will you, mate?" He raised his hand, fingers splayed, in a general gesture of farewell. Then he was gone.

She joined Jim Allen by the door. "Where's he going?"

"Officially? He's been called away on an urgent matter." He glared after Tanford, "Unofficially, his instincts tell him this won't go well. And Tanno's got the survival instincts of an alley cat."

Gifford called them together to establish the running order. He didn't offer Simms his hand, nor did he introduce her to the psychologist, and he never once looked her in the eye. Minutes later, they filed into the press room with Jim Allen tagged on at the end of the line to balance the numbers.

Gifford sat in the centre, Jim and the psychologist to his right, Kate Simms to his far left, on the other side of Spry.

"I would like to begin by offering my condolences to StayC's family and friends," he said. "Drugs are a blight on society, and we in Greater Manchester Police take every drug death seriously." He paused. "However, we should not lose sight of the fact that violent crime in the city and outlying areas is down, and Manchester's streets are safer and more crime-free today than they have been at any time in the last decade.

"Drugs-related crime is a priority for us," he went on, reading from a prepared statement, "and we're proud of our 'Ditch the Drugs' partnership with local communities and drugs rehabilitation services."

He handed over to the psychologist, who spoke about the nature of drug addiction, signs that parents might look out for if they suspect their children are abusing drugs, where they could go for help and advice.

A fat, grey-haired hack on the second row put his hand up. "It's all very well setting up partnerships and initiatives, but what are you doing to stop the drugs coming into the area in the first place?"

It was a hostile question, and Superintendent Tanford would have been best placed to answer it, but Gifford had been well briefed. "We have officers collecting information on drugs crime on a daily basis," he said. "We work in partnership with HM Customs and other police authorities, intercepting drugs as they come into the country, disrupting the supply chain, arresting and prosecuting dealers and suppliers and seizing their assets. Last summer, as a result of Operation Snowstorm — a joint operation between Greater Manchester Police, the Met and Customs — we took thirty kilos of heroin off Manchester's streets." He paused before adding silkily, "That's four and a half *million* pounds worth of Class A drugs out of the hands of dealers and addicts."

The journo looked put out by the good news. Simms felt his gaze settle on her, and resisted the urge to shift in her seat. "So why are drugs deaths in the region up substantially over the last six months?"

Where the hell did they get that?

Gifford began to answer, but the journalist said, "The question is for Chief Inspector Simms."

Simms remembered Jim Allen's advice and made eye contact. "The Crime Pattern Analysis Unit does a six-monthly review of crime stats across the force," she said. "They look for anomalies or unusual patterns."

"That doesn't answer my question — how many deaths are we talking about?"

"Until the review cases have been fully investigated, we won't know whether there *is* a genuine increase," she said.

"But if you're looking at 'review cases' you must have a list of names."

If she answered that she would open the floodgates — every family in the authority who had lost a child or sister or brother in a drugs-related death would want to know why their name wasn't on the list; Simms would spend more time talking to bereaved families than doing the actual review.

"The investigation is ongoing," she said, knowing she sounded evasive, feeling sweat break out on her forehead. From the corner of her eye she saw Spry lean a few inches away from her.

"'Ongoing'," the journalist said. "What does that mean?"

A woman at the far side of the room called out, "When can we expect the results of the review?"

Another shouted, "Is StayC's death linked to your investigation?"

"Can you assure the people of Manchester that StayC's death isn't part of an epidemic?"

They smelled blood. Suddenly, they were all baying at once; cameras flashed and clicked — all of them aimed at her — but neither Gifford nor Spry intervened; she was on her own. *Okay, Kate*, she thought. *You've been here before.*

She quelled a panicky flutter in her chest and took a breath, feeling the throb of her heart in her throat, and spoke over the rising clamour.

"Sometimes," she said, "tragic though it is, clusters of deaths happen simply by chance. The job of the review process is to sift through the data and establish if there's something we need to investigate, or if the increase in fatalities is just random, horrible, bad luck. That takes time, and right now, it's too early to talk about numbers or speculate about a link."

There was a mumble of discontent, but as she looked around the room, she saw a grudging acceptance, and Simms began to breathe easier.

Crisis over, Gifford stirred himself. He said that anyone with information about crime in their area could call the Crimestoppers national hotline free of charge, and completely anonymously. He gave the number as a new rumble of noise started at the back of the room. Heads turned, Gifford's words were drowned out by excited chatter, journalists got to their feet, and the crowd at the back parted to make way for a middle-aged woman.

Her hair was dyed black and cut urchin-style, with long grey strands swept right to left across her forehead. She was squeezed into an orange boiled wool skirt suit and carried an oversized Galliano tote bag in a clashing pink. It could be StayC, fifteen years on — it was Evette Lyons, StayC's mother.

"That's what they do round here," she said. "Stand back and wait for bad things to happen, then they stick it in a report so they can say they take crime serious. Well, it's all shit and shine on."

"Mrs Lyons," Gifford said. "If you would like to speak about this in private —"

"I have spoke about it, I've talked till I'm hoarse. My daughter was killed and nobody cares." Her eyes were swollen with crying and the skin of her face showed red through a heavy layer of make-up, as though her tears had scalded her skin, leaving it raw.

The TV crews were at a disadvantage: their microphones were arrayed in front of the panel; they swung their cameras around and made hasty adjustments. An Asian-looking radio reporter shoved through the crowd and thrust a microphone in front of Evette Lyons. "What do you mean, StayC was killed?"

"Don't you understand English, or are you just stupid?" Evette demanded, her face flushing a dull red under her make-up. "She was killed, murdered."

A couple of sound men snatched microphones off the table in front of Simms and directed them towards Evette and the radio reporter. Simms stole a glance at Spry, but he was staring intently at his hands, clenched on the table in front of him.

Alarmed, Gifford stood up. "Ladies and gentlemen!"

The audience wavered for a moment, unsure who to turn their cameras on, but most settled for Evette. They waited, quiet and expectant.

"Mrs Lyons," Gifford said. "I understand that you're upset, but this is neither the time nor the place —"

"Don't you talk down to me!" she yelled, her lips quivering with rage.

"I'm not — really, I'm not," he soothed, "but these allegations are —"

"'Allegations' — d'you think I'm making it up?" She took a step towards Gifford and a path opened up for her. In news terms, this was pure gold. She dug into her tote bag and came out with a fistful of papers. "Well, what d'you call this?"

She stood in front of the row of tables, and looked Gifford in the eye. "Emails. Letters. Postcards. Hate mail, every last one of them." She slapped them on the table and reached into her bag for more, then turned to face the press with a bundle of sheets in her hand. "Death threats." She swivelled on one foot, turning 180 like a pro, as the cameras flashed. "Someone wanted my StayC dead, and now she is dead, and this useless bunch of *wankers* is doing a review."

CHAPTER
SIX

Marta is lying in bed, cradled in Trevor's arms. He interlaces his fingers with hers and kisses the top of her head.

"You know everything about me, but I know almost nothing about you," he says.

It's true. In fact she knows more than she ever really wanted to know about Trevor. He is forty-nine years old, his hair is thinning and he uses Regaine because he doesn't want to lose any more. He's a teacher of English at a good independent school near the city, disappointed that he will never rise above second in department, bitter with his ex-wife, whom he calls a frigid whore — Marta doesn't point out the clash of ideas here — and angry with his daughter who dropped out of her A-level studies to work in a garden centre. "What kind of transferable skills is she going to learn from working in a fucking *garden centre?*" he wants to know. He resents his head of department, who is too pally with the kids, and an all-round, arse-licking petty politicker, who encourages extra-curricular activities — like his staff haven't enough to do — and just *loves* putting on plays and shows, *because it gives the kids what they want.* If he had half a brain, he'd know that giving kids what they *want* is not the same as giving them what they *need*. The kids, he despises, as lazy, pig-ignorant boors who have never read a book for pleasure and think that knowledge is like chicken nuggets and can be served up on a plate for them in convenient, bite-size morsels.

She also knows that he has certain sexual needs that some women would find off-putting. Because Trevor likes the girlfriend experience, but only if the girlfriend he pays for is really, really clean.

She has to brush her teeth with Trevor's toothpaste and gargle with Trevor's mouthwash before Trevor will kiss her — a feature of the girlfriend experience which Trevor likes very much. Trevor insists on bathing her before he fucks her. Not a sensual, sexy shower, with lots of lather and gentle friction, but a businesslike and uncompromising scrub down, paying special attention to her hands and belly button and arse. Then he'll hand her the sponge with an apologetic smile and say, "My turn."

What Trevor knows about Marta is her name — Marta McKinley; her nationality — Russian; her favourite colour — red. She has a liking for cats, her promising ballet career was ended when she grew too tall. She has a mother and two sisters — identical twins; she let this slip after she heard that Trevor used to visit a set of twins who worked for the Henrys in the year before Marta came to England.

"Is any of what you told me even near the truth, Marta?" he asks.

She smiles. "You know I'm good in bed." She avoids the word "fuck" — Trevor doesn't like her to use what he calls "obscenities". "You know I'm a good listener." She gently disengages her hand and strokes his chest. "Don't I make you feel nice?"

He traps her hand before she can work lower. "No," he says. "You make me feel cheap."

She chuckles softly. "Shouldn't that be my line?"

"It's not funny, Marta. I'm serious."

"Me too." She struggles onto one elbow and he reluctantly lets go of her hand. "Look, Trevor. You get what you pay for and a little extra — otherwise, why would you come back?"

"You really don't know?"

She sees hurt in his eyes, and decides she doesn't want to know. "You're confused," she says. "This is a trade: you want something, I give it, for a price."

"Jesus, you sound like my wife."

She widens her eyes, smiling a little. "You *paid* her?"

His eyes darken. "She got the house, the kid, half my earnings, and the damn car — what d'*you* think?"

She thinks it is strange that he put his daughter in his list of belongings, but she smiles, says, "Love is like war: easy to begin, hard to end."

He huffs a laugh. "You got that right."

"Sex is easier." She leans forward and kisses his chest, his stomach, his abdomen; he smells of sex and desire. She reaches across to the dish on the bedside table for a new condom. "Sex is not so complicated." She tears open the packet, eases the rubber from it. "More fun?"

47

He sit up, twists to grip her elbows and searches her face, his eyes filled with a frantic urgency, as if he is convinced she's hiding something deeper, something more meaningful than the exchange of sex for cash. Finally, he shoves her away, plucks the condom from her fingers and throws it across the room. "I don't want that," he says, as though the thought of having sex with her disgusts him.

She remains calm, warm, sweet. "What can I do for you?"

"Tell me about yourself."

"What do you want to know?"

"Anything. Tell me about when you were a kid."

"I wanted to be a ballet dancer —"

He frowns, petulant. "You already told me that. Tell me something new, something interesting."

"I had boring childhood in boring town. This is why I came to England."

His eyes fill with tears. "Am I asking so much?" he pleads.

Marta suppresses a sigh and strokes his arm. Most men leave after they've fucked her, but there is still ten minutes on the clock, and Trevor will take every minute owed. "Okay. I've never told anybody this . . ." She settles in his arms and makes up some new stories — the small dusty town she came from; her family's vegetable patch and the chickens she would feed as a child and which terrified her because they pecked her legs — and it makes her tired, because now she'll have to remember all this stuff.

When the half-hour is finally over, she watches him tuck these intimate details of her life near his heart, like a lock of her hair, and hates him for it.

He's dressed and, eager for him to go, she swings her legs over the side of the bed and reaches for her silk night robe. He catches her hand and entwines his fingers in hers, turns her hand over and begins kissing her palm. She thinks it's an overture to more sex, but he holds her arm straight and examines the crook of her elbow.

"What are you doing?" She snatches her hand away. "You think I am junkie, Trevor?"

"I'm sorry," he says, immediately. "I'm just concerned. It was on the evening news, didn't you see it? Girls are dying — bad drugs, they think."

She throws on her robe and fastens the silk cord tight. "I work nights, Trevor. I don't watch news." She moves to the door. "And I don't do drugs."

"Marta, please, it's only because I care about you. *Please*," he says again, and she softens her eyes, even though what she wants to do is slap his face.

"Of course," she says. "Come, I'll see you downstairs."

He is reassured, and flattered, too, because he doesn't know what all the girls know — that she is walking him down to reception to make sure he leaves.

After he has gone, she can't recall her mother's face. Georgs, Veronika, little Toms; they've all vanished. She locked them in a dark room with the rest of her past when she came here, and now she can't find the key. For a second she can't breathe, starts to panic.

"You all right?" Amy is working reception tonight because Sharon, the old pro who usually does it, has called in sick. Amy is brunette, tanned and slim, though the tan is sprayed on. She has brown, heavily lashed eyes, and there is not one atom of human compassion in them. "You shouldn't let them get to you, Marta."

To hell with it. Marta turns on her heel and heads back through the archway. It's only half an hour until her shift ends, and anyway, there is no one waiting in the lounge. She turns left, into the kitchen. She opens her locker and takes out her purse, slides the fee from Trevor into the wallet section. She keeps a photograph of herself with Veronika in the ID section. It reminds her why she's here, and she touches it, for good luck.

Candice is sitting at the table, fully dressed, drinking coffee.

Marta's phone is in her locker. She checks her text messages: one from her mother. Tweets from two friends who know nothing about what she does for money, sent at one in the morning from a club in the city. She follows a link to "yfrog" and finds a picture of them dancing, laughing. They look very drunk, and very happy.

Candice sniffs every few seconds, like she has a cold, and sits hunched over, both hands wrapped around her cup, although the place is always overheated. As she bends to take a sip of her drink, she shows a half-inch of dark brown grow-back at the roots. Her make-up is three shades too dark for her complexion, and completely fails to hide the heroin sickness underneath.

Marta's phone jingles — another text. She feels a shiver of excitement — it's from Gary. "Ready for a F2F?" — a face to face — for the first time.

Candice finally realizes there's someone else in the room. "Oh," she says. "Hiya." Her eyes go to Marta's phone. "Boyfriend?"

Marta shakes her head, smiling.

"Oh," Candice says again. "Business."

"I suppose," Marta agrees, although it's a very different kind from the usual. It's a professional relationship, sure, but one which does not make her feel ashamed, one that she is proud of. *A face-to-face meeting?* Yes, she thinks she is ready. She smiles to herself, texts back. "Will call U."

Candice sets her cup down and twirls a lock of hair between her fingers, squinting at the ends. Her hair has been bleached so many times that it has started to break around the hairline.

"Marta, love." She talks in the singsong voice which means she's about to ask for something. "Couldn't borrow us a tenner, could you — for the kids — buy them breakfast?"

For the kids — it's always for the kids. Candice has three and, if you believe her, the whole Chinese economy couldn't generate enough money to keep them fed and clothed and happy.

"What about what you just earned?" It's a rude question, and Marta already knows the answer, but she doesn't want to be seen as a pushover.

Candice shrugs, embarrassed. "Still paying Frank back on last week's advance. You know how it is with kids." Under the table, her foot starts a rhythmic tapping. "Don't get me wrong, I love them, and all that, but I swear, if it isn't food, it's coats, or uniforms or school trips, or shoes."

Unthinking, she pulls at the brittle hairs at the rim of her hairline, plucks out a tuft. She stares at the stubs of broken hair for a moment, then rubs her fingers together, watching them fall to the table. "See that? Know what does that to you? Having *kids* does that to you."

Marta shakes her head. It is heroin, and working double shifts, and alcohol substitutes when she couldn't get a proper fix that did this to her, but Candice is strung out, her brain screaming for a fix, and she can't admit the truth. She wipes her nose with the heel of her hand, turns her pink-eyed gaze on Marta. "Don't ever have kids, love. First they ruin your figure. Then they ruin your life. It's not like them babies in the Cow & Gate ad, laughing their little socks off."

Marta thinks again of her nephew, and how he seems to carry the sun in his smile, and the way his laugh can make her heart swell with so much joy that she has to put her hand to her chest to stop it from bursting.

Candice's foot-tapping becomes a frantic, angry rattle, like a resentful child intent on annoying. She flicks her thumbnail against the mug handle, setting up a constant *pingpingping* in time with the nervous tapping of her foot. "Take, take, take — that's all it is with kids. Always wanting *something*. I swear, I stick

52

my nose round the front door, the first words out their mouths: 'I want'."

"Candice."

"I mean — what about what *I* want?"

"*Candice.*"

"What?"

"It won't help," Marta says.

"What? A tenner to buy my kids breakfast *won't help?* If it shuts them up for five minutes, believe me, kiddo, it'll help."

A shadow falls across the doorway, and Marta sees it's Amy; she looks from Marta to Candice, a sardonic smile on her face.

"Forget it, Candice. She thinks you'll spend her tenner on smack."

Candice looks at Marta like she had snatched her cup and poured her coffee over her head.

Marta says, "I didn't say that —"

"We all know she's been working double shifts, moonlighting at the new place," Amy says, talking over Candice's head.

Candice slides lower in her chair and Amy bends to catch her eye, talking loudly, as if she is deaf. "You should be rolling in cash, sweetheart. But you're not, because it's all going in your saggy veins. And if working double shifts isn't enough to keep the monkey off your back, an extra tenner isn't going to help. Now, is it?"

Candice blinks back tears, wipes her nose with the heel of her hand again.

"Leave her alone." Marta takes a card from her purse and places it in front of Candice.

"What's this?" Amy says, picking it up to read it. "A drop-in centre?"

"It is for Candice," Marta says, plucking it from her fingers and placing it in the other girl's hands.

Candice stares from the card to Marta as though she has suggested taking up embroidery to curb her cravings.

"I'll pay for cab, go with you, if you like?" Marta says.

Candice licks her lips, shoots a look at Amy, her eyes pleading for a way out.

Amy laughs. "Go on. Ask nice, she might stop off at your dealer's on the way."

Frank and Sol don't allow drug deals on the premises.

"And when you're all smoothed out, you can go and get a sausage and egg McMuffin 'for the kids'."

Candice stares down at her hands and a tear falls into her coffee cup.

Marta looks into Amy's face, trying to understand why she would want to make someone as pathetic as Candice cry. Suddenly, she sees it. Amy's eyes are bloodshot, pupils way too big. "*Hypocrite.*"

"Wh —?" Amy knows what she means before the question is fully formed. She's been sussed. "Oh, right," she says, folding her arms. "I forgot. You're Saint Marta of *Just Say No*. You don't need nothing to see you through, do you, Marta?"

Grateful that she's no longer the butt of Amy's sarcasm, Candice joins in. "Yeah. Why don't you fuck off, Miss I'm-too-good-to-get-high? You think I should try rehab? Been there, done that, got the fucking cavities to prove it. I mean, do you know what methadone does to your teeth?"

Marta closes her eyes, trying not to remember. "Yes, Candice, I know."

"Well, don't talk to me about rehab then. And anyway, you *need* something to get you through double shifts sucking men's knobs sixteen hours a day. Right, Amy?"

Amy is offended. "What you asking me for? I'm not the smackhead skank, working double shifts to feed a habit."

Candice wraps her arms tight around her middle like she's just been punched. "Fuck off," she whispers. "Just fuck off, Amy."

Marta turns to Amy. "Shouldn't you be in reception?"

"I came on a message," she says. "Frank wants you."

Amy must see her hesitation because she says, "Go on, she'll be all right with me."

"No, I won't. Make her go away," Candice sobs.

"You heard her."

But Amy stays where she is. "You got it wrong. We're best mates, me and her."

"I fucking *hate* you." Candice is red with humiliation and rage. "You're a fucking *bitch*, Amy."

Amy smirks. "Watch this." She takes two ten-pound notes from the tiny handbag she carries to stash her tips, places them on the table. "There you are, Candy — for the kids," she says imitating her high-pitched singsong voice.

Candice wipes her hands over her face, dries them on her jeans, stares at the money as if she's afraid this is part of Amy's cruel game.

"Go on then, if you want it."

Candice's hand is shaking as she reaches for the cash. "Cheers, Amy," she says, her voice bright, but she can't disguise the crack in it. "I'll pay you back. Next week."

"Sure you will." Amy keeps her eyes on Marta. "See? Best mates." She waits a moment, relishing Candice's humiliation.

Then, satisfied, Amy turns her back on them and saunters out, heading back to reception.

A second later, she's stumbling backwards through the door, wild alarm in her eyes.

Frank comes in after her. She's brought up short against the kitchen table and her ankle gives way. She lurches sideways, grabs the table edge to steady herself, and he moves in close, bends her backwards over the table, plants his hands either side of her. They are strongly muscled and the index and middle knuckles enlarged from heavy punch bag training.

"I told you to fetch Marta."

"I did, Frank." Her voice is a breathless squeak. "I told her she was wanted."

"Yeah? 'Cos I heard a lot of screeching and name-calling, but I didn't hear my name." Frank is taller than his brother and, unlike Sol, he's proud of his hair, which he wears long and curling, tied loosely in a ponytail. He's suited and newly shaved, but he looks like a roadie from a rock band — which apparently he was, back in the nineties. His eyes are so near black you can't tell the iris from the pupil.

Amy tries to avoid Frank's eye, but his face is inches from hers and he keeps moving, so that unless she shuts her eyes, she can't escape him.

Marta quietly slips her phone back into her bag and replaces it in her locker. The discreet click of the lock distracts him for a second, and the danger passes.

"Get out front and earn your keep," he says. He keeps his hands on the tabletop so Amy has to squirm and duck beneath his arms to get past him. Now there is nothing between him and Candice. She flinches under his gaze, clasping the money between her two hands, hiding it like a guilty secret.

"You — go home — and get yourself straight before you come back for tonight's shift." Candice jerks to her feet.

"Marta — if you wouldn't mind?"

Marta sees a flash of surprise and envy in Candice's eyes: she'd heard the respect in his tone. Marta straightens her shoulders and smiles. "Of course."

The corridor to the office is narrow, and he walks slightly behind her. She can feel the pulse in her throat; there is no way out except back the way they came, and she doesn't think Frank is in the mood to give way.

"Just curious," he says. "Most of the girls dabble a bit. But you never touch the stuff — why is that?"

"I have . . . reaction," she says.

"What — like an allergy?"

"Sort of . . ." She smiles crookedly. "Kind of a lockjaw? Makes me want to bite down." She snaps her teeth to demonstrate, and he chuckles.

They're outside the office, and he grips the doorknob, but holds the door closed and looks down at her. "You got your reasons, and you don't want to say. That's okay, I respect that. But don't be causing me grief with the other girls. We clear?"

She holds his gaze, but only for a second. "Clear, Frank."

Sol and Rob are in the office. Rob turns as Marta comes in, gives her the once-over. The dressing gown she threw on so that she could see Trevor out is very short and cut very low, yet it's only Rob's gaze that makes her feel dirty.

Sol eyes her appreciatively and Frank gives him a sharp look. Then he closes the door, and for a moment all of the men regard her.

"Can I do anything for you, gentlemen?" The innuendo is intentional, automatic, and — importantly — it's what they expect.

"Maybe."

Frank sits behind the desk, and Rob positions himself by the filing cabinet to her left, props one elbow on it and rests his chin on his fist. Sol remains standing. The brothers have an instinct, like wolves: they know at any moment in a situation which of them should take the lead. This time, it's Sol's turn.

"There's a new parlour down the road. Some of the girls have been moonlighting."

Marta looks from Sol to Frank. "Not me."

"*Woof!*" Rob laughs. "Defensive."

"We've heard the girls like it there," Frank says. "Giselle has missed her Wednesday session here . . ." He checks the rota in front of him. "Three weeks in a row, and the other girls . . . well, they seem restless."

This is what they do, she thinks: they call you in and make observations, instead of asking a direct question or making an accusation you can easily deny. So you end up guessing what they know, sweating over the lies you've already told, in case they've found you out, and of course you say the wrong thing, prove yourself a liar. She keeps her head up, but avoids his gaze.

Sol sits on the edge of the desk, his legs stretched out in front of him. "I'll be straight with you, Marta — we're losing custom. Now, normally Rob would take care of that. Rob's got contacts, connections. He knows people who can make problems go away."

Rob-the-fixer smiles to himself, looks into her face to see if she's impressed, but his eyes keep drifting to her breasts. She wants to know more about Rob's contacts, and what he's going to fix for the boys, but Sol and Frank are suspicious of people who ask questions. That's all right — she's patient; she can wait — it's not by accident that they have given her this new information; it's a sign that they trust her.

"The owner, George Howard, is an accountant," Sol goes on, as if he's addressing a seminar. "In the National Audit Office, or was, before he got restructured in the bonfire of the quangos, and you know what that means."

Marta is not even sure what a quango is, but thankfully, he doesn't wait for an answer.

"He's a bean-counter. Worse, he's a *government* bean-counter. He just doesn't have the kind of history that Rob can use. He's getting annoying," Sol says. "And he won't agree to a private sit-down to sort it. So we've negotiated a compromise: we meet in public, at a bar of his choosing in the city centre. We talk, you join us, you leave with him, work your Mata Hari magic." He grins, spreading his hands, as if to say, *What could be simpler?*

She feels a stab of alarm, seeing where this is going. "But I like it *here*," she says.

"Very heart-warming," Frank says. "But he didn't say you'd have to work for Howard exclusive, did he?" It's a reprimand. Not a warning, so far, but a reminder that Frank hates interruptions.

She arches an eyebrow and folds her arms, because he also despises weakness, and a fearful woman is weak. "Okay . . ."

"It'll take a while," Sol says. "Don't worry about that. Take your time, get it right. We just want some inside info so we can persuade him not to expand into other areas of supply. You can carry on working here, see him on your evenings off." They can't know that her evenings off are fully occupied.

"You think of everything," she says. "Except how I can get paid — I mean, if I'm working in his parlour, I

60

can't ask this George Howard to pay me for . . . um . . . entertaining him. And this *is* business."

Sol laughs softly, and he and Frank exchange a look; she knows they will already have considered this. "How does standard hourly rate sound?" Sol asks.

She purses her lips. "This is not standard work."

Rob works his tongue around his front teeth, but he doesn't speak.

Sol cocks an eyebrow at her. "You're a cheeky mare." He looks at his brother like he's asking for confirmation. She doesn't see a nod or even a flicker of the eyelids — maybe it's the wolf-pack telepathy — but something passes between them, and Sol says, "Fifteen per cent over the odds."

"And a bonus for any useful information of course," Frank adds smoothly.

"Let me think about it," she says, although she is already rearranging her schedule in her head.

Frank's eyes begin to harden, but he seems to decide to give her some leeway. "Well, don't take too long over it, eh? We're losing money."

CHAPTER
SEVEN

"It is the nature of an hypothesis, when once a man has conceived it, that it assimilates every thing to itself, as proper nourishment; and, from the first moment of your begetting it, it generally grows the stronger by every thing you see, hear, read, or understand."

LAURENCE STERNE, *TRISTRAM SHANDY*

Fennimore set up a link in the video-conferencing centre in the computer suite. The facility was housed in a windowless room which had Skype access via a webcam: a smooth black egg-shaped device above the digital projector screen with a lens wide enough to accommodate up to ten around the conference table which ran the length of the room. Fennimore sat at the head with Josh Brown seated to his right. The room smelled of new wood and warm electronics.

Fennimore clicked the Skype link and seconds later Kate Simms's face appeared on the screen.

Four years ago, Simms's brown hair was straight and glossy and hung to her shoulders. Now, it was almost as short as Josh's — though she was anything but androgynous. Her eyes were light brown and long-lashed, and she had a face that most women would remortgage the house for. Fennimore shifted his gaze from her face to the webcam. "Kate — you cut your hair."

"Hello, Nick," she said, her voice warm, amused, gently chiding. "Who's your friend?"

He had forgotten Josh in his shock at seeing her. "Josh, this is Detective Chief Inspector Simms. Kate, this is Josh Brown. He's not a friend — he's a PhD student. I've enlisted his help."

"You'll learn to forgive his rudeness," she said, smiling in the general direction of the student, not quite finding the line of sight. "The professor's social graces got stunted by his passion for scientific accuracy."

Josh sat side-on to the webcam, frowning at the blank screen of his laptop, which stood open on the table in front of him. "Not a problem," he said.

She maintained her focus on the student. Fennimore had spent an hour going over the stats with Josh again; the student had argued, challenged, disputed and recalculated every step. Now, watching him shift uncomfortably, avoiding the blind gaze of a woman 350 miles away, Fennimore was reminded again of the student's almost pathological reserve.

"Before we begin, let's get this straight, Josh," Simms said. "None of this is for general discussion, understood?"

"Understood."

"Look at me, Josh."

He did, but his gaze slid quickly back to his computer.

"Nothing — I mean not so much as a *gnat's fart* of this — gets out to your friends, your drinking buddies, e-buddies or girlfriends. If I see one word of this on the Web —"

"Woah." The student's awkwardness vanished; he sat up and stared into the webcam. "You've got an investigation to protect — fine, I get that — so yeah, let's be straight. I don't text, I don't tweet, I'm not on Facebook — or any other social network for that matter — and I don't have a girlfriend. I study. I eat. I sleep. But mostly I study."

Fennimore heard the slight harshness in the vowel sounds again, like a whiff of salt air and sea asters from the Essex marshes. He sat back and watched his friend assess this young stranger through the distorting lens of digitization and distance. After a few moments she said, "So, what's the verdict?"

"The first thing we had to establish was whether the data's solid, or an artefact."

"Which is it?"

"I've analyzed data for the past five years of quarterlies and compared them with the figures you gave me from the Crime Pattern Analysis Unit — straight stats, based on actual numbers of overdoses — and aside from a small blip four years ago caused by a batch of particularly strong heroin, the figures are remarkably consistent, until the last three quarters, that is, when the rate goes up, and stays up.

"Now, as you get more deaths over the norm, it's less and less likely that your excess deaths are just a wee blip and you have *thirteen* deaths over the expected norm —"

"I know this, Nick," she broke in. "I *gave* you the numbers — just tell me, are they real?"

He folded his arms. "Any plod with a GCSE in maths could tell you the numbers seem a bit high. But you want something you can quote with confidence, and I can't give you that without the stats."

She took a breath and exhaled slowly. "You're right, I'm sorry, I need the stats." Before he could accept her apology she added smoothly, "Just skip the lecture, okay?"

He smiled. "Okay. In simple statistical terms, I am 95 per cent certain these deaths are significantly above what you would expect."

"So the CPA Unit was right," she said. "They're real."

"Really real," Fennimore said.

She didn't speak.

"You don't seem overjoyed."

"Did you watch the news?"

He nodded. "I thought you put your case very well. All that stuff about clusters happening by chance, the function of the review process, the futility of speculation — really, it was bang on the money."

"Thank you."

It was also, almost word for word, a little lecture he'd given her when they worked together at the National Crime Faculty, but now didn't seem a good time to mention it, and Simms went on:

"Funnily enough, nobody quoted me on that. They did quote Evette Lyons extensively, though: 'Police incompetence,' she said. We ignored the real threats against her daughter 'while we dicked about with our computer spreadsheets'."

"Does she think you should ignore the other victims just because her daughter happens to be in the news?" Fennimore said. "Come on, Kate, she's bound to blame the police — she can't very well blame herself, can she? She's talking crap."

"And as a smart-arsed scientist you probably know the adhesion co-efficient. Me, I'm just a thick-headed cop, but I do know shit sticks, and Stuart G —" She checked herself, glanced at Josh Brown. "*My bosses* won't want to blame themselves, either."

"Stuart Gifford is a bureaucrat —"

Another quick glance towards Josh. "For *God's sake*, Nick."

"What? You think names should be changed to protect the stupid? Gifford might be a pillock who was born with a pencil up his arse, but even he wouldn't be so vindictive."

She pinched the bridge of her nose and took a moment, then spoke slowly and clearly. "Gifford is interested in two things: The Rules, and Gifford. He's been in post for a month — not even long enough to tack his family photos up on his office wall. He will not take the fall for this and, conveniently, his least favourite police officer happens to be standing on a narrow ledge hanging on by her toenails." She pushed her fingers through her hair, laced them on top of her head and left them there like she was trying to keep her brains from bursting right through her skull.

Watching her, frowning hard, looking inward, fighting to keep it together, Fennimore felt a tidal wave of shame. "Kate —"

She raised a finger. "No. Do not do that. Don't you *dare* feel sorry for me."

Josh busied himself with his laptop, pretending he couldn't hear them.

"I don't," Fennimore said, keeping his gaze on her. "But I do want to help."

"I got a call from the *Mirror* twenty minutes ago," Simms said. "Tomorrow, they're running the front-page headline 'STAYC MURDERED?'. They wanted a reaction quote. Now, I could remind them that StayC died in her own bed in her mother's house, while her mother was downstairs watching *Hollyoaks* on TV. But they'd only say that where she died is irrelevant, because someone might have put something in her heroin before she bought it. I'm in a real bind here, Nick."

"Well . . . StayC's death does look like it's part of a pattern, rather than a one-off, and as one of thirteen drugs deaths above the norm, it's far less likely she was murdered."

"*Less likely*, but you can't rule it out. Look at it from the other end of the telescope — it's probable her death is linked to *twelve* others." She peered at him. "And that makes a much more interesting article."

He shrugged. "I'm sorry, Kate, I can't do any better than that until we've re-examined the evidence, and that means going back to the beginning, looking at it all over again. I can do that with you if it helps?"

She hesitated, but he could see her thinking it through, and after a few seconds she gave a nod of acceptance.

"Who've you got working with you?" he asked.

She gave him a cynical smile. "According to the press release, 'a dedicated team of officers'. In reality, there's me, two Crime Pattern Analysts and a Scientific Advisor — and it's just me working on it full time."

"We'd better get started then, hadn't we?" He turned to Josh. "For context, the import of illicit drugs to the UK is estimated at between four and six billion pounds per annum." The student's fingers rustled over the keyboard, typing as Fennimore spoke. "Factor in the fifteen billion spent on crime and health costs every year, and you have an industry worth twenty-one billion — which is 25 per cent more than legitimate pharmaceutical companies made in exports last year."

Nick Fennimore knew all of this because it was his job to know, and because some numbers just stuck. There were some he couldn't budge, like how many children are abducted every year — between six hundred and a thousand; like the average age of an abducted child — ten; like the number still missing and unaccounted for — around two hundred. His daughter was ten at the time she disappeared, and, five years on, she remained one of the two hundred who stayed missing. It made him weak to think of Suzie among those two hundred children, frightened and alone — or worse — in the hands of monsters. Nick Fennimore, scientist, logician, did believe in monsters. Not the fairy-tale kind that were easy to spot, so you could point them out and keep your children from harm — the monsters of his nightmares walked on two legs, and spoke like you and me, and called themselves men.

He drove those thoughts from his mind, or at least squeezed them into a corner where they would stay quiet for a while. After years of trying, he had learned that he could keep them at bay working fourteen-hour days dealing with statistics of a more endurable nature.

He reached into his laptop bag and fished out a sheet of A4 paper and some whiteboard markers; Fennimore disliked linear note-taking, preferring instead to work through complex ideas using mindmaps, a visual tool that used a tree branch format combining key words, symbols and colour. He wrote "EXCESS DRUGS DEATHS" in block capitals in black ink at the centre of the sheet, and with an artistic flourish he drew a rough gravestone around it. Swapping from black to orange, he added a side branch to the right of the gravestone and wrote "CHARACTERISTICS" along the line.

"We have twenty ODs in all," he said. "Thirteen extra deaths above what you would expect in the last eight months. If something in the deals is killing them, it's likely to be in *all* the deals." Josh furrowed his brow ready to ask why, and Fennimore added, "It's more efficient to make up the deals in bulk — think industry, production lines."

"If it's in all of the deals, it can't be very toxic, or we'd have more deaths," Simms said.

He wrote "LOW TOXICITY" on a side branch.

"Unless it's only poisonous to some people," Josh said.

Simms said, "We've got fifteen female victims out of twenty."

"Interesting." Fennimore wrote "SELECTIVE?" on the diagram, then added a sub-branch and wrote "GENDER BIAS?"

"It's not something we'd see on routine toxicology, or it would have turned up on normal post-mortem," Simms said.

Fennimore nodded. "It's also fast acting, because a lot of these deaths happened within an hour of injection."

"How could they tell that?" Josh asked.

"The body treats heroin like any other toxin," Fennimore said. "As soon as it's injected, the liver gets to work on breaking it down into something safer. At the post-mortem the pathologist will prepare tissue and fluid samples from different parts of the body. Urine is taken direct from the bladder, blood is usually syringed out of the femoral artery. You can estimate how long the heroin was in the body by comparing the drugs found in wraps or syringes recovered at the scene with the concentration of metabolites in the decedent's blood and urine."

"Plus, there were witnesses to some of the deaths," Kate added, "and they all say the victims died fast."

"We need to re-interview those witnesses," Fennimore said.

"I'm in the process of tracking them down," Simms said. "But addicts aren't the easiest people to keep tabs on."

Josh was frowning at his laptop screen. "Heroin's usually cut with all kinds of crap to bulk it up, isn't it?"

Fennimore nodded. "More heroin, bigger profits."

"So, if they injected purer stuff than they were used to, they'd overdose and die before the heroin is metabolized, so you'd get low metabolites — like we've got here."

"Good reasoning," Fennimore said. "But we would also expect to see high morphine levels in the blood, and that's not showing in the lab results we have so far." He looked pointedly at Kate. "On the other hand, we haven't seen all of the reports yet."

She rolled her eyes. "These weren't suspicious deaths, Nick — they were routine drugs overdoses, done as standard hospital post-mortems by hospital pathologists. It's not like a nice tidy Forensic Post Mortem — I can't just go to one Home Office pathologist and come back with a bundle of files under my arm. I'm dealing with four pathologists on different shifts in two different hospitals."

"I understand that," he said, "but I do hate to theorize with so little data."

"You'll have the rest by tomorrow," she said. "But if we can narrow the field today, I can direct my efforts, waste less energy and stay within budget."

He nodded. Since the government squeeze on public finances, budgets had been slashed. Politicians called it "making difficult choices" and urged "prioritization" —

an ugly word for abandoning the disenfranchised. Simms was telling him that she had to justify and cost every investigative decision she made, because management priorities said these were only addicts and not regular human beings. It was number two on his list of reasons for quitting police work.

"So far, we know that they didn't die of a genuine overdose," Simms said. "What else could have killed them?"

"What about the death threats against StayC?" Josh said. "You said whatever killed them must be in all the deals — maybe it was poison."

Fennimore thought about it. "Strychnine is out — that would show up on a regular PM tox screen. Arsenic and antimony would be the obvious choice. But they're too slow-acting — you're talking hours, weeks, even months, depending on the quantities in the deals. Cyanide must be a possibility," he said, half to himself, adding it to the list.

"Come on," Kate said, breaking into his reverie. "Addicts are desperate, not suicidal — cyanide smells of bitter almonds, and one of the top ten rules of safe injection is if it smells funny, don't inject it."

"You're right," he agreed. "And although most men can't smell it, all women can — so you would expect more men than women among your victims." He placed a cross next to cyanide.

"What about an interaction?" Josh asked, pausing briefly from his typing. "You know — there's not enough morphine in the deals to kill them, but something they used to cut the deals increases the effect?"

Fennimore added "CUTTING AGENTS" to the diagram.

"Other opiates like papaverine and codeine would be the usual suspects," Fennimore said, "but they're both on the regular PM tox screen, and they don't show up in our deaths." He tapped the pen on the tabletop, feeling mildly intoxicated by the whiff of solvent from the tip. "It *might* be a side effect, of course . . ."

"Well, whatever it is, it must be cheap," Simms said.

Fennimore looked at her in question.

"Like you said, it's all about profit margins."

"Everything's cheap if you nick it," Josh said without looking up.

Fennimore stopped writing, and Kate peered at the student through the webcam. He continued scrolling through his notes, but sensing the scrutiny, he looked up. "What?" he said. "I'm just saying maybe whatever it was could've come from a pharmacy break-in or a factory or something."

Fennimore shrugged, added "CHEAP/STOLEN?" on a new branch, and leaned back from his creation.

"So, some form of contaminant." Kate looked into the distance. "Wasn't there an anthrax scare up in Scotland a few years back?"

"Yes," Fennimore said. "But anthrax victims get very sick — At post-mortem, you would see swelling of the lymph glands, abscesses, ulcers at the site of injection — I can't see all of that being missed, even on a regular PM, even across two hospitals and four pathologists.

These victims looked like drugs overdoses, Kate. They injected, blissed out, didn't wake up."

Kate pushed her fingers through her hair again. In their Crime Faculty days, when she wore her hair long, Kate would lift it from the nape of her neck to cool it, and more than once, as they worked through evidence, it had taken heroic self-control not to lean across and kiss the vulnerable curve of her neck.

"The fact is, until we know what really killed them, we won't even be able to separate the normal deaths from the excess ones," Fennimore said.

Kate stood abruptly. "Keep thinking," she said. "I'm going to make myself a coffee that would blow the lid off a pressure cooker." She walked away, leaving a blurry image of a kitchen table, cupboards beyond. A few moments later, they heard the rumble of a kettle boiling, like a distant rock fall. Fennimore rubbed the centre of his forehead, trying to massage his frontal cortex into action. The sound of Josh's typing continued, like the soft patter of rain against a window.

"We know the deaths are real." Fennimore raised his voice to carry over the sound of coffee-making, wishing he'd thought to make up a flask. "I mean, that they're not a random blip in the stats — so there must be a common thread."

"No shit, Sherlock." Simms reappeared, a steaming mug in her hand.

Fennimore ignored the jibe. "If the deaths *are* caused by a contaminant," he said, thinking aloud, not sure where this stream-of-consciousness was taking him, "it was probably added locally, because if it got into the

74

drugs earlier in the supply chain we'd be seeing a lot more deaths across a much wider area — maybe even nationally —"

Kate stopped, the coffee mug halfway to her lips. "Say that first bit again."

"I said whatever-it-was, it was probably added locally."

She set her cup down and glanced at the notes beside her. "I'm looking at a list of names and locations." She pulled out a map and snatched up a pen. "If I mark where the victims were found . . ." Her eyes darted left and right as she studied the list, found the locations on the map and marked each one off. After a few minutes, she held up the map.

"Most of them are in Cheetham Hill, pushing out as far as Waterloo Road to the west, and Queens Park to the east — it's a *tiny* area, Nick." Her gaze shifted from the map to the list. "Only one vic was found out of area — in Piccadilly Gardens, right in the city centre, two miles away. That's practically the far side of the moon for some of these girls, but I happen to know there's a drop-in centre for addicts in Piccadilly, so maybe it's not so strange . . ." She set down the list and studied the city-centre map again. "Okay . . ."

"Talk to me, Kate."

"What if a new drugs refuge or rehab unit opened in Cheetham Hill," she said. "That would screw the numbers, wouldn't it? I mean, more druggies in the area, a greater probability of drug-related deaths?"

"Yes." Fennimore's head began to buzz with excitement. "Yes, it would. But you would expect a corresponding decrease elsewhere."

"I'll talk to the inspector at Cheetham Hill," she said. "He would know if there's a new drop-in centre or refuge in the area. And I'll ask the Crime Pattern Analysts to look for any unexpected drop-off of deaths anywhere else in Manchester." Her eyes were bright and eager, and she fidgeted on her chair as if tiny sparks jolted through her muscles.

He felt charged with her energy. "Okay," he said. "While you're doing that, Josh and I can look at the paperwork. But Kate —"

"I know, I know," she said. "You need the rest of the coroners' reports."

"That's only the start of it. I'll also need the toxicology results on all the cases, so we can assess the methods used, to see what may have fallen through the cracks. If you can find any remaining drug deals taken from the victims' possessions, get them analyzed. If you're lucky, the blood and urine samples will have been stored at the mortuary or hospital path lab; ask for a wider tox screen on those — that's if the coroner will pay for it."

"I think I've got enough here to convince him," she said.

"Excellent."

"But, Nick — it'd take three or four months for a regional toxicology unit to get around to it . . ."

Fennimore felt the dangerous tug of the undertow again. She hadn't asked him outright, and she could send the samples elsewhere, but if he wanted to help Kate — and he did — he would have to get involved in a way he swore he never would do again.

"All right," he said. "If you can get permission, I'll screen them in the labs here." He glanced at Josh, but the student was focused on summarizing his notes on his laptop. "You don't need to mention my name."

"Okay."

"And you'll need to talk to the pathologists about other possibilities."

"Like what, for instance?" Kate asked.

"Inflammation of the brain, cardiac myopathy in case it's bacterial, signs of anaphylaxis in case they've all been stung by a curiously persistent bee — ask them to be creative."

"Anything else?"

"Any further details about the sequence of events: who was with them, anything out of the ordinary in the social set-up."

"I'll talk to the witnesses, see if I can get help to canvass the families, too." She came to a halt, her face troubled.

"What?" he asked.

"I'm thinking about that *Mirror* headline tomorrow. They want to know what Greater Manchester Police is doing to show we care. 'More tests' is going to sound a bit lame."

"All right," he said. "Josh, could you send a copy of your notes through to Kate?"

Josh nodded. "It should be in your inbox —" he hit "send" "— now."

Fennimore scanned the bullet-pointed outcomes of their discussion and nodded his approval.

13 EXCESS DRUGS DEATHS

CHARACTERISTICS
- Low toxicity
- But fast!
- Negative on tox screen

  - Wider screening needed?
    - Need blood/urine samples
    - Original tox screens
- Localized: Cheetham Hill
  - New clinic?
    - Check with C. Hill DI/CPA unit
- Selective: More females??
- Cheap: Stolen?

POSSIBLE CAUSES
- Contamination
  - Poison (unlikely)
  - Anthrax X
- Cutting agent
  - Side effect?
- Strong heroin? X
- Other?
  - Need ALL coroners' reports
  - Talk to pathologists
  - Brain inflammation?

- Cardiac myopathy — bacterial?
- Anaphylaxis?
- Social set-up/events leading to death

Simms laughed suddenly. "It's the locality again," she said.

Fennimore adjusted the document so he could view the bullet points side by side with Simms's image on Skype.

"A clinic *could* be acting like a honey pot to addicts, but it still might be something in the deals that's killing them — we just haven't worked out what, yet. This really is a *very* small area, which probably means one particular dealer."

"A manhunt." Fennimore grinned. "The press will love that."

Josh had begun packing away, and Simms reached for the keyboard mouse to end the session, but Fennimore raised a hand to stop her. "Kate."

Her hand hovered over the mouse button.

Fennimore turned to Josh. "Go ahead."

He waited for the door to close behind the student then leaned in close to the table mic and lowered his voice. "My name stays out of this."

She frowned. "We already agreed that."

"We did. But that was you wanting to keep on the right side of Gifford. This is me, Kate. At some point, somebody will ask who's been advising you. I don't do well in the media spotlight." He heard a tremor in these last few words, and a shadow of pain and compassion passed fleetingly behind his friend's eyes.

He felt an unexpected flood of emotion, a tightening of the muscles around his heart. "I —" His throat closed and he couldn't say any more.

"Hey," she said, "you already screwed up my career once, Fennimore. Anyone asks who's been advising me, I'd sooner say it was aliens sending messages through my iPod." She reached forward and her image vanished from the screen.

Fennimore smiled. It was exactly the right thing to say, and said with exactly the right amount of conviction. That one brief glimpse of compassion in her eyes had almost finished him — he couldn't have borne her sympathy.

CHAPTER
EIGHT

Dip is secured to a chair with duct tape. He is naked. Tufts of hair gather like plucked feathers at his feet — they have shaved his head. His hands are bound behind his back and tape has been wrapped around his upper torso; his legs are taped to the front legs of the chair, so he can't close them. He knows this is a deliberate choice, and he has a good idea — no, not good, nothing about this could ever be good — but he does know what they are going to do to him, because laid out on a box two feet away are a soldering iron, a hammer, two sets of pliers and a Slendertone kit — the old kind, but with the electrodes stripped back and crocodile clips attached in place of the pads.

The chair is placed dead centre of an empty retail unit in Salford. It's already dark, and lighting is provided by the headlamps of his boss's Merc. The temperature has dropped to two degrees above freezing, but he's sweating.

"Boss, whatever you think I did, I didn't do it." He tries to sound calm, reasonable, but he's speaking too fast and he can't get any strength behind the words.

His boss looks at the two men who brought Dip in. His face is a study in concentration. "Ready?" he says.

Dip knows Beefy, but the other one is new to him. Beefy is six four and weighs as much as a small horse. He moves behind Dip's chair. The other one stands to the side, his hands crossed in front of him. He is short and lean, like he didn't get fed right when he was a kid, and his skin has the grey smudged look of a night worker or a convict. His neck is tattooed from his collar to his jawline. His eyes are small and dark and he has sharp features, like a jackal.

Behind him, the big man shifts his weight, his shoes whispering on the concrete floor. Dip cranes his neck, anxious to see what he's doing.

"I swear, Boss. I —" Pain explodes in his nose. Jackal is fast as a whip — he didn't even see it coming.

"Hey! Wait till you're told."

Jackal takes a step back, but looks pissed off about it.

The boss leans closer. Dip's eyes and nose are streaming and his heart feels like it's trying to crawl out of his throat.

"You're all right," his boss says. "It's not broken. Not even bleeding — but when I want you to speak, I'll ask you a question. Are we clear?"

Dip nods, and his boss's eyebrows twitch. "Yes, Boss."

The boss straightens up, satisfied. His eyes flick to Beefy. Dip sees a flash of something then he's suffocating. He opens his mouth, sucks hard, tastes plastic. He struggles, sees his boss watching him thoughtfully, as if he's trying to understand what Dip wants. His mind is filled with *Can't breathe*. He fights the bindings; they're too strong. Beefy twists the bag tighter. *No air.* His boss's face fades from the edges, Dip's heart slows, falters.

He hears voices, first, in the dark. He knows he's not dead, or if he's dead, he's in hell, because it's his boss's voice he can hear, and Beefy's. He tries to be still. They are discussing which to use next: Slendertone or pliers. Beefy is standing at the box, helping him choose. Jackal is standing where he was before, so Dip thinks he can't have been out for long.

"Let's ask him. Which d'you want, Dip?"

The boss's back is turned to him, but he must have X-ray eyes or something, because when Dip shakes his head, he says, "Mate, you got to choose. Slendertone or pliers?"

"I never messed you about, Boss. I always played it straight."

"I know it's a big decision. I'll give you a minute." He reaches inside a padded shoulder bag, takes out a laptop computer, turns it so that Dip can see the screen.

Oh, shit, they're going to record it. They're gonna put me on fucking YouTube. His wife would see this. His fourteen-year-old son.

His boss makes a final adjustment, standing on the far side of the box and crouching to eye level with Dip, checking the height.

"Made up your mind?" he asks.

"I won't choose. Please don't make me choose. I didn't do nothing."

"D'you think we should go with the pliers?" the boss asks Beefy. "I think we should go with the pliers."

"Boss, please, Boss. What the fuck —"

The boss laughs. "What the fuck? What the fuck? You can see it going round and round inside his head, can't you? *What the fuck did I do?*"

The boss balls his hand into a fist and raps once, hard on Dip's skull. "Think. You know what you did. Now make up your mind."

Beefy hefts the pliers, a question on his face. The yellow plastic of the handles is stained a brownish red.

"I can't. I can't."

His boss says, "The pliers."

"No."

"I think that was a decision, Beefy."

Beefy frowns, but he sets the pliers down.

The boss picks up the grey pebble-shaped controller for the toning machine, and offers the Jackal two metal rings. "Put these on him."

"Cock rings? You want me to touch his cock?" Jackal shoves his hands in his pockets.

"You're just out from four years in the nick — don't tell me you're squeamish."

Jackal ducks his head so low between his shoulders his neck disappears.

"Oh, for fuck's sake." The boss ditches the cock rings, flings the wires at him instead. "Here, use the clamps."

Dip feels the bite of metal in his scrotum, and he howls.

84

His boss slaps him, open-handed, across the face. "Don't be such a baby."

Jackal attaches the second clamp and Dip screams again.

"I mean it," the boss says. "You're getting on my nerves — shut the fuck up."

Dip presses his lips together, but can't quite stifle the sound.

The wire jacks are connected to the controller and the boss squints at it. "Okay, so . . ." He presses a button and Dip jerks, but feels only the tearing pain from the metal clamps. Even that begins to fade, receding to a dull throb.

"You have to press that one, Boss," Beefy says, pointing.

"Pleaseboss, pleaseboss. Pleeeease."

"Oh, this one?"

Dip shrieks. Molten steel pours down his cock, his balls are aflame. He fights his restraints. He screams, pleading for it to stop, but the words don't come out right.

"What? I don't know what you're saying, mate. You're not making sense. You've changed your mind? You want the pliers, is that it?"

He's crying, he doesn't want the pliers, he doesn't want anything, except to make it stop.

His boss presses a button, and the pain subsides, but he can still feel the aftershock as tremors rippling across his lower abdomen. His thighs are shaking, rattling the legs of the chair, sending it jittering a few inches across the floor.

"Please stop," he whispers.

"I know what you're thinking," the boss says. "Should've gone with the pliers. Don't feel bad, Dip. Everyone makes the same mistake. Pliers are messy, so they go for the electrics. I mean, it's not even plugged into the mains — it's not like it can kill you, is it? Thing is, these things are designed to spread the shock over five-inch-wide stick-on pads, so they really pack a punch. The crock clips are what — a quarter of an inch? You're getting a concentrated jolt of electricity. And with electrics, you're wired direct to the nerves. Nothing's more painful than that — passing a *kidney stone* isn't more painful than that."

The shaking gets worse; Dip's whole body is so racked with the aftershocks he can hardly speak. "J-just t-t-tell me w-w-what you want to knnnnnow. I'll t-tell you a-anything."

"W-w-w-what I w-w-want to kn-n-n-ow?" the boss mocks. "Okay. I want the truth."

Dip shakes his head, crying, blubbing and gulping helplessly, tears and snot streaming down his face. "But I don't know what I did."

"If that's the way you want it," his boss says, "I can go all night with this. 'Cos it's really no effort, see?" He lifts the pebble-shaped control. "How do we crank this up?"

"No-no. Wait, wait, wait. I'll take the pliers. Please, Boss, don't —"

His boss looks at Beefy. "He wants the pliers."

Beefy shrugs and his boss turns to Dip, a chiding look on his face. "Sorry, Dip, lad. You made your choice." He adjusts the control. "Let's see if we can speed things up a bit."

The hurt is so intense, so beyond anything he has ever experienced, he feels he must die. But it goes on and on. Something seems to snap inside him like a rubber band and he looks down, horrified. His flesh steams, he can smell burning.

"I'm on fire. Oh, no, oh Jesus, I'm on fire — *oh Jesus God* I'm burning!

For one sweet, blessed, holy second, the pain stops.

Jackal says, "He isn't burning. He's just pissed himself."

"Oh, that's all right, then," the boss says. "Good conductor, piss." He looks down at the control in his hand and Dip says: "The consignment. It's got to be the consignment." He wants to tell them what they want to hear, but the one bad thing he did is the one thing he knows they can't know about.

The boss's hand drops. "Now we're getting somewhere. The van. Three weeks ago."

"I did everything to the letter. I parked it in the Tesco 24/7 in Didsbury, locked it, walked away." His boss strokes the pebble that works the electric like it's some kind of Zen relaxation. "I posted the keys at the agreed drop, just like it said in the docket."

His boss doesn't speak.

"Look — did it get nicked, 'cos if it got nicked, it's nothing to do with me. I swear —"

"Did I say you nicked it?"

"No, Boss."

"No, Boss. That van stayed on the car park for ten days. It got ticketed seven times, but it never got towed. Know why, Dip?"

Dip shakes his head fearfully.

"'Cos the police were watching it, and they weren't gonna let some car park Nazi tow it, because they wanted to catch the boys who were about to pick up 30 K's worth of high-grade heroin. They were tipped off."

"No." Dip swings his head left and right in wide, sweeping movements. "No, Boss — I'm no grass."

The boss nods to the Jackal and Dip flinches, but the Jackal walks to the computer. A Lucozade-orange view of the entrance to Tesco's car park lights up the screen.

"This is the twenty-first century, Dip," the boss says. "Surveillance society. Big Brother. Security footage." The recording switches to an image of one of the bays. "Oh, look, that's you, driving in. Just like you said."

Dip sees himself get out of the van. He looks over his shoulder, checks all around, making a big thing of it, and now he's embarrassed because he looks like some guilty amateur. Embarrassed when he's tied to a chair naked with electrodes attached to his balls — it'd be funny if he wasn't so shit-scared.

"Hang on," the boss says. "Wind back a bit." Jackal obliges. "Isn't that you getting into the back of the van? Now, what would you do that for, when you were told to lock up and get the *fuck* out?"

"I wanted to make sure nothing showed through the windows." *It's all right. Just keep your mouth shut. He can't know.* "I'm not lying. I seen some lads hanging around and I thought they looked a bit dodgy, so I "got in the back to check everything was out of sight."

"Very conscientious. Highly commendable." He waits a moment. "And that took you ten minutes?"

Dip swallows, hears a dry click. *He can't know. Just stay calm and stick to your story.*

"'Cos if you look at the little clock, here, you'll see that the security camera times you getting into the back of the van at 6.05 and getting out again at 6.15."

"I dunno why," Dip says. "Must be something wrong with their clock."

"No, Dip. There's something wrong with your head." He pokes Dip in the centre of his forehead. "You're insulting my intelligence with that shit. You got in the back of the van with the . . . what did he call it?"

"Consignment," Beefy says.

"Consignment, that's it." His face is so close Dip can smell his breath — it smells like vodka and raw meat. "And you ripped me OFF."

"No. No. No-no-no-no." His heart is going so fast it's a miracle it doesn't burst. "No. Boss, I wouldn't do that."

The boss looks at Beefy. "He says he wouldn't do that."

Beefy's eyes track over Dip's face. He's seen that flat look on Beefy's face once before. Just before he glassed a bloke in a pub.

"Show him." The boss stands aside so Dip has a good view of the computer.

The screen changes. The orange tint of the car park footage is replaced by a greenish glow which Dip recognizes as an infrared image. They're inside the van.

But that's impossible. Dip's brain tells him it's impossible, it can't be real, even though he knows he did all of the things he can see himself doing on the screen.

"Trust is all very well, but safeguards are better," the boss says. "We put some surveillance of our own in place, see. Police found it, of course. Took a while to get a copy from their evidence store — annoying I had to pay for it twice, but worth the cover price."

Oh, shit. He knows. Oh, Jesus, he knows.

His boss looks from the screen to Dip. He bursts out laughing, claps his hands. "Your face — I swear, I want a picture of that."

"Here's the bit you wanted, Boss," Beefy says.

The boss turns again to the computer, folds his arms.

On the screen, Dip takes out a knife and cuts a small slit in the duct tape seal on one of the bags, catches the powder in a baccy tin.

"Oh," the boss says, like he's never seen it before. "OH. Look at that — that isn't just a little taster, a finger-dab of sherbet. That's gotta be ten grams. What's that worth, Beefy?"

Beefy says, "Seven, eight hundred?"

"Seven or eight hundred." He looks at Dip. "How d'you explain this one? Don't tell me — it was a quality assurance check, wasn't it, Dip?" He rams his face to within a hair of Dip's. "Is that why you were pilfering nearly a grand's worth of my property?"

"Boss, I —"

"Shut up." He moves back to the monitor. "We're just coming to the best bit."

On the monitor, Dip takes a roll of silver duct tape out of his jacket pocket, cuts off a strip and reseals the bag. The boss turns 180 degrees and wags a finger at Dip. "You went tooled up, Dip — that's premeditated, that is. That's going equipped."

"I'm sorry, Boss. I'm really, really sorry. I never did nothing like that before."

"I know. 'Cos we've been watching every vanload for the past eight months. Just after we lost 30 kilos of the stuff last summer — three mill of drugs. Of course the cops inflated that to four and a half, but that's cops for you. Anyway, that's beside the point — the point is, this one time, *you* decide to steal from me."

"No, no, honest to God, I'm telling the truth."

"The problem is, Dip, I can't believe a word you say. You've lied and lied and lied."

Dip shakes his head, tears coursing down his face again. Because now he knows he's going to die.

"Now, I'd be willing to believe this was a one-off, except you didn't get arrested. Now why is that?"

"I don't know. I swear I don't know."

"I'll tell you why: because you were useful to them. You'd just done them a big fat favour — helped them out with their performance targets. You sold us out."

"No, Boss, no." He's so sick with fright he can't even say it like he means it.

"Except we know they're watching. So we watch them watch the van for ten days, and then we watch them drive it away and impound it — 'cos even GMP Drugs Squad've got the brains to know when they've been sussed. You, however, are a different story. You carry on like nothing's happened. Did you think I wouldn't find out who grassed me up? Find them and their families and punish them till nothing's left but bones and scraps of meat for the rats to gnaw on?"

Dip's eyes widen. No, not his family — they didn't deserve this. Not Julie, not Daniel. "Boss, I swear I never —" The world is white fire. His skin is melting. It stops for a second, and he slumps forward, gasping. His nose, his mouth, his eyes should be gouting blood. He doesn't know why he isn't dead. He wishes he was.

"Thirty K."

Electricity rips through him, tearing a scream out of him.

"What percentage is that of three million?"

Dip gulps air.

The boss lifts his chin. "Dip, I asked you a question: what percentage of three million is thirty thousand?"

Why is he asking this? Dip tries to think past the fire in his groin, the torn muscles in his abdomen. Tears squeeze out from under his closed lids. He can't control the muscles of his face.

He feels a slap and he screams.

"Open your eyes."

He does.

"Now answer me."

"I dunno, Boss! I swear."

He turns to the other two, grinning. "He swears — like he needs to convince me he's a dumb fuck." He looks at Dip. "Thirty thousand is one per cent of three million. Chickenfeed, compared with what we lost last summer. But worth it to catch the bastard who grassed us up for that one."

Dip's eyes open wide. "Nooo-oooo!"

"You know what we do to grasses, Dip?"

"But *I'm not I'm not I'm not.*" They'll rape his wife in front of his son and they'll force his boy to watch while they cut pieces off her.

"I'll bring them here," the boss says. "I'll kill Julie and Daniel, and then I'll gouge your fucking eyes out so it's the last thing you see on this earth."

He shocks him again. And again. And again.

Dip swears on his mother's life. On his wife's, on his son's. He stole, but he's no grass. He begs them not to touch his wife, his son. They shock him until he feels like his lower half has turned to liquid and he begs to be allowed to die. He passes out a dozen times, but they revive him and shock him again. He swears he *is* a grass, that he told the police everything he knows. He gives them names, and he is so fevered with shock and pain he doesn't even know if they're real or made up. He tells them where to find the spare key to his house, hidden under a rock in his front garden, gives them the code for the alarm, so they can take his wife, his son, if only they will make the pain stop.

"I think we're finished here."

The boss's voice comes from far away. It's getting light, and they've turned off the car headlights to conserve the battery.

"So, is he a grass?" Beefy asks.

"Nah. He didn't sell us out, did you, Dip?"

Dip is past speaking, but he groans because a failure to respond will be punished.

The boss slaps his cheek affectionately. "He's a thief, but he's not a grass."

"All that screaming, there's not a mark on him." Beefy seems to find it a marvel.

"Well, that's no frigging *good*."

Dip responds to the anger, tries to lift his head, but it's too heavy. He wonders how he will ever be able to hold his head up and look a man in the eye again.

"I mean," the boss says. "How'm I supposed to make an example of him if you can't see nothing wrong with him?"

Beefy shuffles a bit, and Jackal says, "Dunno, Boss."

For half a minute all Dip can hear is his own breath stuttering and catching in his throat.

The boss clicks his fingers and Dip jerks so violently that Beefy has to steady the chair so it doesn't topple. "Look at me, Dip."

Dip tries, fails.

"Lift his head. I want him to see this."

Beefy moves behind him, grabs him by the ears and pulls his head up.

94

The boss picks up the soldering iron. "Cordless," he says.

Dip forces himself back into the chair, as if he could merge with the plastic, come out the other side. In his mind he's already running, five miles down the road.

"Four double-A batteries, over a thousand degrees of heat. Bloody miracle of science."

"No. No, no — you stay the fuck AWAY from me." In his head, his voice is a roar of rage, but his voice is ruined by screaming; he can hardly even hear himself.

"Hold him steady," the boss says. "I'm about to get creative."

CHAPTER
NINE

Kate Simms stared at the tall man in the Gieves and Hawkes suit reading her whiteboard notes. Something in the set of his broad shoulders was definitely familiar.

"Can I help you?" she asked.

He swung to face her, and she recognized him instantly: Detective Superintendent Tanford. For a lot of men she knew on the force, good posture was a function of the combined restraint and buttressing effects of uniform. Put them in a suit and they slumped. But not Tanford: he held himself well.

"Ah." Tanford spread his arms wide. "DCI Simms!"

He offered her his hand and she took it. His grip was firm, his hand warm; she sensed strength in it, though he didn't seem to feel the need to prove that to her.

"Did you want something in particular, sir?"

"Let's call it professional interest." He nodded to a map on the wall; coloured pins marked the location of every drug death on her list. "I heard you've been digging up bodies all over Cheetham Hill."

She frowned slightly. "I don't recall asking for an exhumation, sir."

"Sense of humour." He chuckled softly. "I like that. But I was speaking metaphorically, of course."

"Of course."

"You've got the pathologists jumping, with your requests for tox screens and full PM reports and samples . . ." He looked at her, his head cocked on one side, waiting for an explanation.

She gave none.

"You did a stint at the National Crime Faculty — when it was still called that. Five years ago — that'd make you Nick Fennimore's protégée, wouldn't it?"

She tensed. Every new post she had taken up since the Crime Faculty she'd had at least one visit like this from the higher ranks. She knew the routine by heart: they told Simms her own history, as if she didn't know it well enough, implied that it was her own flagrant disregard for the rules that had made her fit only for the shit jobs nobody else wanted, and finished with a warning that she had better do as she was told.

"Fennimore's wife and child went missing," Tanford said, bang on cue. "Rachel and . . ." He tapped his hand against his thigh, trying to force the name. "Nicky . . . Becky . . ."

"Suzie," she said, her throat tightening.

"Suzie, that's it! Wife turned up dead five or six months later, as I recall. Was he ever in the frame for that?"

"No, sir." It felt like a betrayal even saying that much.

"No, course not." He shook his head. "Sorry — crass of me — some other case . . . Did they ever find the daughter?"

She shook her head, not trusting her voice.

"Still, they say Fennimore was the best — some of it must've rubbed off. So I'd love to know what you're thinking."

She controlled her breathing, thinking, *No, you fucking don't.* "I'm just here to review the evidence, sir," she said, saving him the trouble of saying it.

"Well, your review is playing havoc with my performance stats," he said.

No department head liked anyone messing with their stats. Especially not a disgraced cop who had compromised a major investigation. Simms and Fennimore had burned through tens of thousands worth of NCF resources in the ten days after they found his wife's body. Rachel's car was found in a National Trust car park in Cumbria, a hundred miles from where her body was discovered. Simms had allowed Fennimore access to the car and forensic evidence recovered from the deposition site, compromising both as potential crime scenes. She had let him near aspects of the investigation he had no business being near — because like it or not, as the husband, Fennimore was a suspect. And because of Simms, he was all over the evidence; Gifford had never forgiven her for that.

Tanford frowned down at her.

Here it comes, she thought, steadying herself for the onslaught.

But he broke into a grin. "I've got to hand it to you," he said, "the street's buzzing with it."

Simms stared at him in wonder; she didn't know how to respond. This was the point in the conversation where he was supposed to remind her that she was only here under sufferance, and he was *praising* her?

"I suppose StayC's mum going off on one like that has made things even worse for you?" he said, apparently oblivious to her confusion.

She gathered her wits enough to say, "Hasn't made it any easier, sir."

He took a step closer. He smelled of expensive cologne and peppermint breath fresheners. "It's a knockabout game this," he said. "And sometimes the wrong person gets elected as punch bag."

"Sir," she said neutrally.

They stood apart for a moment, each reappraising the other.

He gave her a searching look, suddenly earnest, serious. "Have you got what you need, Chief Inspector?"

"Sir?"

"The Assistant Chief Constable has a reputation for . . . um . . . *efficiency*." He said the word like it had inverted commas around it for ironic emphasis, wrapped it up in a sneer for good measure. "Likes to squeeze every last penny from his budgetary pound, our Stuart." He looked around at the CID office, busy with detectives working other cases. "I'm guessing the best he could rustle up for you is a corner of this CID office, a whiteboard and a couple of clerks."

She avoided his eye; he wasn't far wrong.

He puffed air between his lips. "That's Stu for you," he said, taking her silence for acknowledgement.

"Thinks he's done a good job if he hands money *back* to Whitehall at the end of the financial year."

She didn't contradict him, but she had the sense not to be heard agreeing with him in front of an office full of cops. A Detective Superintendent with an impressive conviction rate and twenty years on the force might get away with implying that the Assistant Chief Constable was an arsehole; a recently promoted DCI with a dodgy history would not.

"Take my word for it — the tabloids will soon get bored with StayC and the ODs." Another dry chuckle. "Now wouldn't that make a great concept album?"

She offered him the ghost of a smile and he seemed to regret his levity.

"Look," he said. "Why don't I loan you a couple of my lads — they know the Manchester drugs scene, and they've got the muscle to deal with the local scumbags."

"That's a generous offer, sir," she said, the ambitious, selfish part of her thinking that the presence of two of his hand-picked "lads" would make it easier for Tanford to take the credit if she solved the case.

"So what d'you say? I can have them here in an hour," he said.

Was she just being stubborn? She could certainly use the manpower; but she smiled and said, "We're doing okay, thanks."

She braced herself: if he took offence, she could chalk up another powerful enemy on a growing list. But the superintendent didn't seem to take it at all amiss. He peered at her with a quizzical smile on his face.

100

"Triumph and disaster," he said at last. "Imposters, both. And I should think whichever it is at the end of this, you'd rather meet either one on your own terms." He regarded her seriously. "I respect that. Here." He handed her his card, then held out his hand again and it swallowed hers. He stopped mid-shake and looked into her face, his dark eyes locked with hers. "Anything you need, Kate. Anything at all."

"Thank you, sir," she said, hearing the wariness in her own voice.

"You can call me Tanno. Will you take a bit of advice from an old soldier, Kate?"

He still had her hand and she was half convinced he wouldn't give it up until she agreed to hear him. "Always glad to learn from others' experience, sir."

"*Tanno*," he said. "C'mon, Kate, you can call me Tanno, can't you?"

"Yes, Tanno," she said.

He nodded, satisfied, but still didn't release her hand. "It's true what they say about life on the high crags of management," he said. "It's lonely and bloody cold. Policing at this level, nine-tenths of the game is about being able to manage the politics."

She raised her chin, ready to nod, but not sure where he was taking this.

"I've got a nose for these things," he said. "The high-ups on the job are taking flak from all the press interest, getting a bit twitchy, which — don't get me wrong — is not a bad thing *per se*. But you might be on the point of kicking up a real shit-storm with those dainty size sevens of yours."

He released her hand and took a step back. "Kick up a shit-storm, you're bound to get some on your shoes. So — mind you don't tread it into the carpet."

Kate thought she caught a sharp glimmer in his eyes, then it softened to something like concern, and she wondered again if she should accept his offer. But half a decade of senior-level disapproval had made for uneasy professional relationships, and a habit of isolation and distrust in Kate Simms. So she let him go and hoped she wouldn't regret it.

CHAPTER
TEN

The corridor is full of people in no particular hurry. Marta pushes through to her locker. She has a change of clothes in a Next bag, but she's running very late, so she stashes her rucksack, padlocks the door and shoulders her handbag, then she's off at a run, dodging and squeezing through the press of bodies. She feels a guilty thrill that she has sat with these good, honest people all morning with a brick of heroin hidden in her bag.

A minute later, she's out on wide, windswept Oxford Road. A friend sees her and waves. Marta points to her watch, shrugs, mimes "call me", then heads for the city centre at a trot. Sol is waiting in his bronze Lexus near the corner of Whitworth and Princess Street.

She slides in beside him and he turns to tell her she's late. The surprise on his face almost makes her laugh.

"When did you start dressing like a student?"

She's wearing denim jeans, trainers, a grey funnel-neck jacket done up to the neck and a coral pink scarf knotted at the throat.

"Is disguise," she says. "You don't like?"

He grins. "You kill me, Marta, I swear."

Sol turns the wheel one-handed, accelerating effortlessly into the traffic and, in minutes, they are on Cheetham Hill Road. He's taking Marta to drop off an urgent delivery of goods; Frank didn't want him to go, but Sol said he needed to see for himself how bad things were.

The Lexus is warm and quiet and smells of new leather. She settles in and lets Sol's lecture wash over her. He's telling her that of all consumer goods, drugs are damn near recession-proof.

"Recreational, mood-altering, mind-altering; uppers, downers, rev-up, wind-down or knock-you-out-cold — narcotics buck the trend," he says. "But it's not worth a candle if you can't get the goods out to your customer base."

To hear Sol speak, you would think trading in drugs is like any other regular business. He talks about sourcing issues, cash flow and distribution problems. He calculates profit margins and balances them against customer satisfaction, just like a regular businessman — except Sol carries a gun and his competitors have more to worry about than aggressive price-cutting.

"Sol." She has seen a queue of stationary traffic ahead.

He sees it too and pulls in to the kerb because, for once, Sol does not want to draw attention to himself. He turns off the engine and stares in horrified silence through the windscreen. Twenty police officers and Police Community Service officers are working slowly up the street towards them.

"Jesus," Sol murmurs. "No wonder Bug's been screaming."

He grips the steering wheel and eyes the mass of uniforms like he's just uncovered a nest of rats in a dung heap. "How'm I supposed to get product out to my retailers with this lot sniffing around?" *Retailers* — this is what he calls dealers. "This is severely fucking up my distribution channels, Marta."

They are fifty yards down the street from Bug Nelson's flat. Bug is one of their mixers — he cuts the imported heroin according to the brothers' instructions, then his team packages it into small bindles for street sales. Sol and Frank don't allow trading close to the mixer's house, but the heroin still has to go in and deals have to come out. Marta can see one or two addicts threading their way through the shoppers; Cheetham Hill Road is on their way to where they want to be — to the street corners and alleys half a mile away, where they know they can buy a fix.

The police are stopping people passing by, handing out leaflets, ducking into shops. "The *Stars!* girl made them take notice," Marta says.

He shakes his head. "This isn't taking notice, Marta. This is going through the motions. D'you really think these arseholes actually give a shit?"

She raises her shoulders. "I think, maybe, some."

He snorts. "Yeah, and you hire your body out by the half-hour because you want to bring comfort to lonely men. *Grow up*, girl. This just happens to be what they have to do to pick up their monthly pay packet. Give them a better financial incentive, they'd snatch your hand off."

She looks at a young PCSO on the other side of the street. The cold has chafed his cheeks apple-red and he smiles at an addict whose skin is so grey it looks like he has been shaped from the dirt in the gutter. "You think so?"

"I know so."

Ahead, a girl turns the corner onto the main road, sees the mass of uniforms and ducks back the way she came.

Sol groans. "This is *killing* our trade."

"You should maybe talk to Rob," Marta says.

He whips round so fast she flinches. "The *fuck* d'you mean by that?"

A jolt of adrenaline shoots through her veins. She pouts a little. "I make silly joke." Normally, Sol responds well to her pouts. Not this time.

"That wasn't a joke. I know a fucking *joke* when I hear one — I got a sense of fucking humour — and Marta? I'm not laughing."

"I'm sor —"

He cuts off her apology.

"What the *fuck* do you know about Rob?" The tendons in his neck stand out like ropes.

"He is customer," she says in a small voice. "I know only what he tells me."

"Oh yeah? And what *exactly* has he been telling you?"

The situation is spinning out of control. She didn't mean that Rob told her something, but if she says that now, it will look like she's denying the truth. It will look like she's lying. She faces Sol. "I only mean that if you have trouble with police, always Rob is the one you go to."

He glares at her, one hand on the steering wheel, the other gripping the leather of her seat back. He could snap her neck one-handed.

"Sol, I am the one who carries your —" she glances out of the window at the police and lowers her voice "— your goods. Just the other day, you hand me valuable —" again, she darts a look at the police "— *package* when Rob is standing right next to me. I need to know I can trust him."

"*You need to know?* It's my product, *my* fucking money — you just need to do what you're told."

She could leave it there, but his eyes are dark with suspicion, so she goes on: "I think —" She puts her hand on her chest to stop her heart beating so fast. "Maybe, one afternoon, I make delivery and police are waiting."

Sol laughs. She hides her confusion and relief with annoyance. "What's so funny?" She backhands his arm. "English prison is not funny."

He laughs harder.

"What?" she demands, allowing a little petulance to creep into her voice, knowing that the danger has passed. "I'm scared and you laugh at me."

He plants a kiss on her mouth, but has to break off because he's still laughing. "Let me worry about Rob," he says. "You just stick to what you're good at."

She takes a breath, blows it out between her lips. "Men are crazy."

He takes her hand and kisses the palm, puts her hand to his face and moves in again to kiss her on the mouth, slides his tongue between her teeth and shifts his hand to her thigh, works his thumb into her crotch.

A sharp hammering on the window and they almost leap apart.

It's the police.

Sol curses softly, winds the window down and cranes his neck to look up at the policeman. "Everything all right, officer?"

A bitter northerly wind screams down Cheetham Hill Road, bringing with it the smell of rain. It whips up grit and rubbish and flaps the lapels of the policeman's jacket. This is a man who looks like he has been rained on one too many times.

"Take it off the streets," he says.

"What, exactly?" Sol is smiling, but there are chips of flint in his voice, and such sudden violence in his eyes that Marta can almost smell the blood already. She thinks about the brick of drugs in her handbag at her feet and prays. "Just saying goodbye to my girlfriend, mate."

The policeman looks at Marta in her jeans and sensible coat. She smiles her brightest smile, knowing that her skin glows with good health and her eyes are clear and sparkling, and waits for him to realize he's made a mistake.

"Sorry, miss," he says and she lifts her shoulder, glances away to show she's embarrassed to have been mistaken for a hooker. She doesn't speak, because to a policeman canvassing addicts an Eastern European accent will always create suspicion.

"You lot are out in force today," Sol says.

The policeman sniffs, jerks his chin at the young officer who is trying to press a flyer into the grey addict's hand. "That Stuart Cordwell's got a lot to answer for."

Sol laughs; Cordwell is the producer of *Stars!* He pats Marta on the knee. "Off you go then, sweetheart. Give your mum my love. I'll pick you up later — just give me a buzz on my mobile."

She swivels in her seat, turning away from the policeman to look at Sol, her eyes wide. Can he really mean her to walk past twenty cops with 6,000 pounds' worth of heroin in her handbag?

Sol grins, leans past her to make eye contact with the policeman. "D'you mind, officer?" he says pleasantly.

The policeman steps away from the car to give her room to open the door, and Sol reaches into the well and lifts her handbag onto her lap. He slips his left arm around her and pulls her close as if to peck her on the cheek, but his fingers dig into her shoulder, working her collarbone into the socket until she can almost feel it give.

"I'm a bit soft on you," he whispers, "so I let you take a few liberties." His lips are so close to her ear that she can feel the heat of his breath. "But Frank hears you spouting off about Rob, he'll cut your fucking *tongue* out, nail it to his bedroom wall." He takes the soft lobe of her ear between his teeth and gives it a painful nip before he lets her go.

Her knees are trembling so hard that the fifty-yard walk to Bug's place seems like a mile. Bug lives on the third floor above a row of shops. Access is at the back of the shops, through a gate into a back yard, and up the fire escape. This is the only way in or out. The door is plated with steel on both sides. It has a spyhole, and a slide hatch, big enough to admit the kind of delivery Marta is paid to make, one briquette at a time. There is no bell or knocker on the door, because Bug does not admit casual callers, and since an incident involving a fake postman with a special delivery, his post is held at the sorting office, three miles away. There is a rumour that the "postman" was returned to sender by special delivery the day after in twelve separate parcels.

She stands at the top of the steps and looks into the small black eye of a camera above the door. After a few seconds, she hears the rasp of metal on metal and waits for the hatch to open. But the entire door opens outwards, forcing her to take a step back. A hand snakes out and seizes her wrist, and she is dragged inside.

She gives a small yelp of protest and Bug slams her against the wall.

"Shut up!" He holds her still while he slides four bolts across, one after another with his free hand.

Steve Nelson was called "Bug" as a kid, Sol had told her, because he was small and the bigger kids bullied him and stamped on him so many times, they used to say he looked like a squashed bug. "He was my mate. I protected him, when I was around, but I wasn't always around, and Bug was a daydreamy sort of kid — he just didn't have the instincts that keep you safe on the street. D'you get me?"

Marta had told him she did, and meant it.

"Those lads got too cocky. Maybe they didn't notice him getting bigger, or maybe they didn't think it was important, because they got bigger an' all," he'd said. "Bug was just shy of his thirteenth birthday when five of them started in on him — shoving, punching, kicking — you know, Bug-baiting. Out of nowhere, he starts swinging at them with two copper pipes. Now, he'd filled those pipes with ball-bearings and they were *heavy*. The boys who survived said his eyes bugged out like they were on *stalks*. So now he doesn't mind being called Bug."

Bug pins Marta against the wall and shoves his face into hers.

Her muscles jump and twitch; she has no control over them. Sol must have called him from the car. Her ear throbs from the bite, and darkness pulses behind her eyes, threatening to overwhelm her.

"Where's the gear?"

His eyes remind her of the brown clay in her mother's garden, but the colour shifts constantly and she sees flashes of something dangerous, like lightning in a dust cloud. She can't hold his gaze. "It's in m-my . . ."

"Speak the fuck up!" He slams the wall with the palm of his hand and she feels the vibrations through her body.

"My bag. It's . . . it's in my bag."

He lets go of her and snatches the bag from her hand. He is wearing a T-shirt with the sleeves rolled up. His arms are lean, the muscles under the skin twisted together like steel cables. His upper arms are a mess of blurred prison tattoos — crosses and spiderwebs — but on his right forearm he has a crisply rendered image in black and red — an executioner with an axe slung over one shoulder. The blade drips blood at the executioner's feet and a grotesque bug feeds on the blood.

She presses herself against the wall, and he unzips the centre compartment and thrusts the handbag back into her hands.

"Come on then."

"I . . . I don't understand."

"Well, I'm not gonna root round in a tart's handbag, am I? What the fuck you take me for?"

Marta forces down a wild urge to laugh. *Men really are crazy.* She fumbles in her handbag, spilling tissues, lipstick, keys onto the grey floorboards, and finally brings out the briquette.

He takes it from her. "About fucking time. Been waiting for this since yesterday."

"Police are everywhere," she says.

"Don't need to tell me. Fucking dibbles." But he's almost forgotten her. He carries the block of powder

112

away, holding it in both hands, as if he's afraid to drop it.

Marta realizes for the first time that they are not alone. Three women — two young, one middle-aged — are seated around a long glass table; all wear dust masks. Next to the middle-aged woman is an electronic kitchen scale. None of them look at her, and their silence feels like an interrupted argument.

One of the women is tearing strips of paper and cutting them into squares, ready to make the bindles, another is breaking open capsules — some orange and white, some brown and grey — and pouring the white powder from them into a growing pile. The empty shells lie scattered around her chair, like the empty cockroach egg-cases. There are two windows, both closed. The room is overheated and the air smells sharp — slightly acrid — like burnt matches.

Bug jerks his chin and the middle-aged woman stands and takes the block from him. "Stick to the recipe, yeah?" he says.

She nods, shifting her gaze from the drugs in her hands to Marta for the briefest instant. Then she returns to the table, places the briquette down carefully, and picks up a craft knife.

Bug paces to the window and stands watch there.

The women hunch over their work, avoiding eye contact; to Marta it seems that the walls echo with this man's rage, and she feels their lack of spirit beginning to infect her.

She speaks loudly, deliberately, into the silence: "I go now."

The one who is shelling the capsules convulses with shock, drops a pill into the mound of powder and shoots a look at Bug to see if he has noticed.

Bug remains at the window, arms folded, looking down into the street. He doesn't reply and Marta draws back the first door bolt.

"Touch the next one, I'll break your arm." He doesn't move, doesn't even look at her, but Marta lets her hand fall.

"You might as well make yourself comfortable." He tilts his head to indicate a sagging blue sofa at the far end of the room. "Bathroom's through the door to your right."

Marta doesn't move.

He shrugs. "Please yourself. But you'll never get all three of them bolts open before I get to you."

Three more bolts. Even if she did get them open and out of the door, she would have to make it down the fire escape, out through the back gate, down the alley, forty yards or more to the street; she wouldn't stand a chance. But Sol wouldn't kill her for saying one stupid thing, would he? No — even Frank wouldn't do that. Her scalp prickles, thinking of other things — unsaid things, secret things — that would get her killed for sure, if they knew. But she has been so careful — how could they know? She checks the bathroom and discovers it has no window, drifts past the bedroom door and sees bars bolted to the inside of the window frame.

Sol's words come back to her; he said he could buy anyone's loyalty, it was only a matter of finding the right price. Bug Nelson continues staring down at the street, the women go about cutting and mixing and bagging the deals, and a black, terrifying thought lodges itself in Marta's mind. That if she disappears, she has told so many lies no one will know where to look for her. She is invisible. Already gone.

CHAPTER
ELEVEN

"We want to make sure the thing you're looking for is on Google 100 per cent of the time."

ERIC SCHMIDT

The girl in the picture has dark brown hair, grey eyes, like her mother's. Her face has lost its childish roundness, the dimple in the left cheek; her nose is longer and narrower than in the earlier versions, her hair a shade or two darker. The mouth is fuller, but it still has a slight upturn, a readiness to smile.

The door flew open and the papers stacked on Fennimore's desk lifted and settled again like birds rudely flustered.

"Nick, I think I've found something." It was Josh Brown.

Fennimore's desk was placed at ninety degrees to the window so that he could look out at the crossroads and gain the widest view of sky. It was 2p.m., and the sun was already low, bathing his office in pink light. He turned to give the student his attention but Josh looked past him, staring at his laptop monitor.

"Are you on Photoshop?" Josh asked.

Fennimore swivelled to face the screen again and reached for the mouse.

"Wait a minute," Josh said, coming further into the room and leaning over him to get a better look. "Are you using age-progression software?" He snapped upright. "Oh, shit, sorry — is that your daughter?"

Fennimore closed the screen carefully and swung round in his chair to face the student. "What the hell do you know about my daughter?"

"Nothing. I don't know anything."

Fennimore stared into Josh Brown's face, and felt adrenaline rip through him so fast his fingertips burned.

The student held up his hands. In his left, he carried a bundle of papers, in his right a laptop. "I swear, I wasn't snooping. I was trawling for your research publications."

"What's wrong with using Athens, like everybody else?"

"I did." His eyes kept darting away. "But there was a two-year gap, and I wondered why. Look, what can I say? It's all over the web. Google Professor Nick Fennimore, you get a hell of a lot more than an academic CV."

Fennimore was sharply aware of what Josh Brown had been too diplomatic to say: Google Nick Fennimore, you get "disappearance" and "kidnap" and "murder".

"So, Google Josh Brown, what do you get?"

Josh shrugged. "A couple of actors, a kicker with the St Louis Rams, a born-again rock star. I'm not there, Professor. Like I told the Chief Inspector — I haven't got a web profile, and I don't want one." The hot, itchy embarrassment was gone from his eyes, replaced by something unfamiliar. Anxiety, perhaps.

"Yes, I remember you said that, and you do seem to go out of your way not to be noticed — yet you work like a man out to make a name for himself." Fennimore stared hard at the student. "You're just a bundle of contradictions wrapped in a conundrum, aren't you, Josh?"

"Look," Josh said. "I'm sorry I barged in like that. I'm sorry if you think I've been digging around in stuff that's none of my business. I didn't mean to invade your privacy, and I didn't mean to offend you."

Seeing the student's pained expression, Fennimore realized he was being overbearing. What if Josh *had* done a little internet research — wouldn't it be hypocritical to condemn exactly the kind of curiosity he encouraged in his students? Especially when half the undergraduates did exactly the same. Some of the brighter girls even asked shyly if there was any news, delicately avoiding any specifics of the news they were enquiring about. He shrugged, irritated with himself.

"All right," he said. "What've you found?"

The relief on the younger man's face was palpable. "A pattern in the post-mortem results." He stopped. "I mean a possible pattern." Then, frowning, he said, "No, I mean an actual pattern, but with a possible explanation."

"Let's see it."

While Josh was occupied laying out the folders, Fennimore reopened his laptop. The digital image he had been working from occupied the bottom right quarter of the screen — a face that was recognized across Europe — Fennimore's daughter at the age of ten. He had taken it himself, five years earlier, just four days before Suzie vanished. His little girl would be almost a woman now. He saved the image and minimized the screen.

CHAPTER
TWELVE

Kate Simms was about to start re-interviewing witnesses to the drugs deaths. In response to her request for more officers, her superintendent had allocated a detective sergeant and one newly promoted detective constable. DC Moran had six years of street policing experience, most recently in Cheetham Hill, and had already tracked down two more witnesses through her contacts in the area.

Moran had sad, gentle eyes and a round face, framed by fine brown hair. The lads called her Mouse, but Kate Simms had seen her file, and she knew that DC Moran's appearance had nothing to do with the person within. They agreed that Moran would take the lead in the first interview, with an addict who had witnessed the death of her sister.

Jordan Fitch was shivering, and her nose dripped like a broken tap. DC Moran handed her a tissue and a cup of hot sweet tea.

"I'm really sorry what happened to your Jade," she said, unwrapping a chocolate bar and placing it between them, as if they were a couple of mates out for a cuppa and a bit of a consoling chat.

Jordan warmed her hands around the paper cup. "Jade wasn't even into it that much." Her body twitched as if some invisible tormentor prodded and pinched her ribs, her back, her face. "She was more into coke, a bit of weed. She had a good job, you know, in this nice restaurant in the city centre, so she didn't have *time* to get high, you know, regular."

"So what happened, you know, when it happened?" Moran asked, falling easily into Jordan's rhythm of speech.

Jordan shivered so violently the tea in her cup slopped over the sides. "Oh, shit, I'm rattling," she said. "I'm just rattling, you know?" Kate Simms stirred, but didn't interfere: DC Moran was the expert in this situation.

"I know," Moran said, touching the woman's hand lightly. "We'll get you sorted as quick as possible, after we're finished here, yeah?"

Jordan took a fresh tissue, wiped her nose, balled it up and clamped her hands around the cup again. "Losing her like that was horrible." Her body twitched. "I seen people die before — my feller died of an overdose, but he kind of drifted off, you know?" She looked into DC Moran's face. "He were *peaceful*. But Jade . . . It was horrible. No, it was . . ." She groped for the right word. "It was *ugly*. And my little sister wasn't ugly." She stared fiercely into Moran's face. "She *wasn't*."

"*Course* she wasn't," Moran said gently. She waited a few seconds, and when Jordan was calmer, she said,

"Jordan, I know it's awful talking about it, but we really do need to know."

They had her witness statement but it was brief and unhelpful.

"I'm not *well*," Jordan appealed to Simms. "I'm really sick."

"I know you want to help your sister," Moran persisted in that same quiet, coaxing manner.

"I do. I *do*, I want to help, but . . ." Jordan wrapped her arms around her stomach and began to rock. After a time she wiped her face and nose on the sleeve of her jacket, clenched her hands into fists and forced them onto the table.

"All right," she said. "For Jade . . . I'd bought a few wraps off —" She checked herself. "Off a street corner. We shared a flat, see, and I was in the bedroom getting . . . you know . . . fixed up, and she bounced in all happy 'cos she'd got the evening off. She wanted me to sell her a wrap, and I had a few spare, so I said okay."

"Was there anything odd about the deal when you were cooking it up?" Moran said.

Jordan shook her head. "It were a normal — if there was owt wrong with it, I swear I would of stopped her. Anyway, I'm quicker than her, 'cos she's not really used to it, so by the time she's injected, I'm already high. Suddenly, she starts gasping like she can't catch her breath. And she looks at me. Like she wants me to help. But I can't — it's like a dream and I can't do nothing, you know? Like one of them dreams where you're trying to run and you can't?"

122

DC Moran nodded, sympathizing.

"No!" Jordan banged so hard on the table that the tea cup skittered sideways. "Stop it. Stop *doing* that. Stop being so fucking *nice* to me." She began to cry, and two red spots bloomed on her cheekbones, as if her tears burned her skin. "You know I'm fucking lying." She gave a hiccuping sob and covered her mouth.

Simms glanced across, and Moran lifted one finger, a signal that she should wait. Jordan tore a bundle of fresh tissues from the box, blew her nose and sat up straight.

"I was mellow, you know?" She avoided their gaze as she spoke, frowning instead at the tissues balled in her fists. "*I* was fine, so in my head I knew nothing was really wrong. Truth is, I was feeling too fucking *good* to be bothered." Her mouth twisted into a sneer of self-hatred. "I couldn't be *arsed* to help my little sister when she was choking to death 'cos *I* was feeling fine."

Kate Simms spoke up, following Moran's example, speaking softly, keeping any moral judgement a country mile away from her tone. "None of this is in your witness statement, Jordan."

"No?" Jordan frowned in the effort of concentration. "I told them." She knuckled the centre of her forehead. "I *think* I did."

Kate Simms glanced down at the signature on Jordan's witness statement. DS Renwick, ex-Drugs Squad. He was on her team now.

Jordan was looking from Simms to DC Moran; suddenly her shoulders slumped. "What the fuck's it matter — who's gonna listen to a smackhead, hey?" Her eyes were full of bleak acceptance and despair.

"Me," Simms said. "I'm going to listen, Jordan."

CHAPTER
THIRTEEN

Over the Skype connection, Simms could see Fennimore and an untidy and overstuffed bookcase a few feet behind him; the building's video conferencing facility was unavailable and they were Skyping laptop to laptop.

Fennimore wasn't classically handsome, but his intelligence and confidence made up for any slight imperfections. He had an interesting face: straight, dark eyebrows and a narrow nose, grey-blue eyes that readily lit up with delight, or more commonly mischief. But she'd noticed in their Skype conversations that his features were less mobile than when she had known him well, and that when he wasn't smiling — or teasing — a quiet seriousness settled in the lines around his eyes.

He was in his shirtsleeves, tie loosened, short hair ruffled; he always did run hot when he was doing fuzzy stats.

"Josh is here," he said.

A blur, then the student appeared on her monitor, behind the professor. He jerked his chin as a form of greeting then disappeared off the screen.

"I was about to call you when I got your text," Fennimore said.

"What have you got?"

"Show me yours and I'll show you mine," he teased.

"The local DI confirms there are no new clinics in the area, so that theory's out," she said, humouring him — this wasn't a power play, just Fennimore's need to base his thinking on as much evidence as he could gather. "We're still working on the dealer angle, but nothing so far.

"I've re-interviewed several of witnesses to the drugs deaths. One of them gave a very clear account of her sister's death." She summarized Jordan's description of her sister's breathing problems in the minutes before she died. "And Jade wasn't the only one. I've got three more who say their friends were 'breathing funny' when they died, another says the victim was snoring for a bit, then just stopped breathing."

"That is interesting."

"I thought so. I had a word with the Home Office Pathologist who did the post-mortem on StayC. He said he'd found a slight swelling in her larynx. I asked the hospital pathologists who performed post-mortems on the other victims to review their findings in the light of this — three have got back to me."

Kate had started work at six that morning. It was now 4.30p.m. Breakfast had been coffee and a banana. She'd skipped lunch entirely, but she felt turbo-charged with adrenaline as she continued:

"Two victims showed signs of inflammation in the laryngeal passages. One had mucus secretions in his

126

lungs, but he'd had a chest infection for a couple of weeks, so it wasn't noted as unusual. In every case, the symptoms were minor."

"We need to look at the histology," Fennimore said. Tissue samples would have been taken at every post-mortem.

"Already done that," Simms said. "StayC's slides were held up in the system, but the Home Office Pathologist got them fast-tracked; he said the histology suggested a possible adverse drug reaction, so I asked the hospital pathologists to check their tissue samples —"

"How come they hadn't already checked?" That was Josh.

"Apart from anything else, it costs money," Fennimore said. "They had a cause of death — drugs overdose — so there wouldn't be any reason to make any further investigations."

"And the more subtle symptoms were dismissed as insignificant," Simms added.

"Tell me about the histological sections," Fennimore said, bringing them back to the evidence.

"They showed signs of cell maceration," Simms said.

"Uh . . . maceration?" Josh again, sounding apologetic, but determined to understand everything.

"It is what it sounds like," Fennimore said. "On microscopic examination, the cells look mashed up. They rupture and die. It can happen when the body becomes flooded with histamines."

"Histamines — so it's an allergic reaction?" Josh sounded excited now.

"It *could* be." Fennimore looked at Simms. "Josh has been comparing post-mortem reports. A lot of the victims had penicillin in their urine at the time of death."

A sharp spike of excitement shot from the base of Simms's spine to the crown of her head. "You're kidding me! StayC was warned to stay away from penicillin two months ago — she was on a course of antibiotics and it brought her out in a rash. Also, the Home Office Pathologist noted a penicillin smell in her urine at post-mortem." She fixed on Fennimore's blue-grey eyes. "This could be our cause of death, Nick."

He winced slightly, and she could see that she'd offended his scientific sensibilities.

"We're talking about drug addicts and prostitutes here, Kate — they're not exactly choosy about what they stick in their bodies. These people are seething with nasties at one time or another — of *course* some of them will be taking penicillin."

Kate wasn't discouraged. She had expected a cautious response from Fennimore — he never let enthusiasm spoil his objectivity.

"We've been doing a Bayesian analysis," he said. "Looking at two propositions: either the penicillin in the victims was from the drugs deals or it was legally prescribed by a doctor. Our results say there's a strong likelihood that the penicillin in your addicts' urine was from contaminated drugs deals."

A strong likelihood. The term was designed to help non-mathematicians understand the relevance of the

128

numbers — and though it might sound unscientific, Simms knew that it was founded on careful calculations.

"Okay," she said, "the penicillin was in the drugs deals. But what's the likelihood that it actually killed them?"

He smiled. "You haven't forgotten *everything* I taught you at the Crime Faculty, then?"

"Only a few minor details, but, hey, they're just facts — I can always look them up. Pity you seem to've forgotten all the subtle social skills I taught you."

He dipped his head in mock apology. "It is an excellent question, though, because despite its bad press, penicillin isn't all that deadly. Allergic reactions happen, but they're relatively rare, and usually mild. Depending on which study you read, you'll get full-blown anaphylaxis in fewer than one in a hundred people. And only one in eight *million* will actually die of it."

She sighed impatiently. "You seem to be arguing against your own case, Nick."

"I'm not *making a case*, I'm looking at the evidence, Kate, and that means looking at it from every possible angle."

"All right." She understood his irritation, but her superintendent was screaming for answers and so far all Simms had was a fist full of maybes. "But if this is going to end with you saying we need to look elsewhere for what killed these people, can we get to the bad news — soon?"

"The fact is," Fennimore said, "that despite all the arguments *against* penicillin being the culprit, the numbers say that your victims are *one thousand* times *more* likely to have died from penicillin than from anything else. Context is everything, Kate — you know that — so when we add in the new factors you've just given us: cell maceration, swelling of the victims' airways, hyper-secretion of the bronchial mucosa —"

"Penicillin is our cause of death."

He looked into her face. "Almost certainly."

She clenched her hand into a fist, her blood positively fizzing with a new flood of adrenaline. She had a case. Not just the sad what-a-waste deaths of a few hopeless addicts who didn't know how to measure their dosage — a *real case*, with criminals to track down and bring to justice. She nodded, considering, thinking how she would present it to her boss, and her brief sense of triumph was rudely elbowed to one side by a whole new set of questions.

"Problem?" Fennimore said.

"I'm wondering why so many deaths if penicillin isn't particularly deadly," she said. "And why so many women?"

"Hm . . . that is a facer, isn't it?" Fennimore rested his chin on his fist and stared at a point to the left of the screen. "Most cases of penicillin anaphylaxis happen with a sick person being cared for in a family situation," he said. "An anxious parent or spouse notices the signs and calls for an ambulance." He continued to look off to the left, and she could almost see him picturing the tableau: a mother wringing her hands as paramedics leaned over her stricken child. "But addicts shoot up with other addicts. If they're high, they're not watching out for anyone else — you only have to listen to Jordan's story to know that."

"So they send for help too late, or not at all." Simms nodded. "Okay, that makes sense. But it still doesn't account for the number of female victims."

"Ah, yes, the gender bias . . ." He picked up a pen. Although she couldn't see it, she knew he would be doodling, mapping, writing down random words. "Women are more prone to allergy than men," he said, and then fell silent. For a full minute, he said nothing. It would have been easy to do a web search, but Fennimore had a phenomenal ability to dredge up obscure facts from his memory and, though he would never admit it, he did like to show off.

"Allergies happen when a sensitive person is exposed to an allergen — obviously. Sometimes just once will do it, but often it's after multiple exposures. Studies show that if people are given penicillin on many occasions and on an irregular basis, it increases the chances of developing an allergy even where none existed before. Those are exactly the circumstances these women would find themselves in — antibiotic treatment for chlamydia one month, gonorrhoea the next, maybe a course of antibiotics for a bronchial infection," he said, thinking it through as he spoke. "Add to that bad hygiene, dirty needles, dirty punters — their immune systems were severely challenged, which heightens the risk of sensitization and an allergic response further down the line."

131

"A perfect storm," Simms murmured, leaning back in her chair. But just as her mind turned to the machinery she would employ to accelerate into the next stage of the investigation, she had a realization that jammed a great iron spike into the works. "One problem with your logic, though — none of our victims showed obvious signs."

Fennimore didn't even break stride. "They wouldn't have to go into full-blown anaphylactic shock for it to kill them," he said. "You know addicts sometimes die of positional asphyxia?"

Simms nodded. "Of course. The head slumps forward onto the chest, obstructs the airways."

"And since breathing is already suppressed by the heroin, they die," he said. "Add into the mix even a *mild* reaction to penicillin — like StayC's — and you'd greatly increase the risk of death."

Her mood lifted. "And the death could easily be mistaken for an overdose."

Fennimore nodded, his eyes gleaming with satisfaction. "Josh has discovered something else that might be relevant." He looked over to his right. "Tell the Chief Inspector about the clusters." He turned the laptop and the screen seemed to pitch. Kate Simms experienced a moment of unexpected vertigo, then the student appeared on the monitor.

Josh seemed unnerved, almost literally blinking in the spotlight, but after taking a second to steady himself, he said, "Seven of the penicillin deaths happened in the last five months — that's statistically significant — and I was thinking maybe the suppliers

132

are cutting the deals with more of the stuff than they did when this all kicked off eight months ago."

"Why cut it with penicillin at all?" Simms said. "I mean, I know it's about maximizing profit, but why not use bicarbonate or benzodiazepines or whatever else they generally use?"

Fennimore appeared, shoulder to shoulder with the student. "Penicillin is relatively easy to come by, it's dispensed as a nice white powder, making it a good lookalike if you want to bulk up a heroin consignment; it's water soluble, so it wouldn't do anything in the cooking to put an addict off using it. It's a bit smelly, maybe, but in a medicinal sort of way, and maybe Josh's theory was right — it cost them nothing because they nicked it."

Simms tapped her desk, thinking. "So either they got greedy, decided to bulk the deals up just to make more money, or they lost a delivery."

"It'd have to be a big one to disrupt their supply for over half a year," Fennimore said, off camera.

"Operation Snowstorm." The room seemed suddenly brighter, her brain cells zinging from a fresh flood of adrenaline. "Gifford mentioned it at the press conference — 4.5 million pounds' worth of heroin was seized. That was eight months ago — exactly the time when the first death happened." She grinned. "Cause of death *and* the trigger for the whole mess in one night — good work, guys." She flicked her laptop mousepad with her fingertip, eager to get her team working on the new information.

"Whoa, wait." Fennimore's hand blurred as he raised it to stop her. "We do still have to confirm by analysis that it *is* actually penicillin in the urine."

"Yes, right, sorry," she said. "I've had the okay to use your university for the analysis. If I sent you some samples from the OD victims, how quickly could you turn them around?"

"Are these urine samples, or did you find some nice easy-to-process deals?" Fennimore asked.

"Actual deals found with the bodies. Eight from Evidence, so far. Some of the wraps got flushed or nicked by other users before Emergency Services arrived on the scene, but I do have three untouched wraps from StayC's bedroom."

"We could do those in twenty-four hours," Fennimore said.

"Thanks, Nick. I'll courier them to you and send on the rest as they turn up."

She ended the call and walked two doors down from her own office to the CID room. It was empty, except for Detective Sergeant Renwick who was sipping coffee, and Ella Moran, typing up her notes from the interview with Jordan.

Renwick was forty-two; recently divorced, he was a member of the GMP cycling club, he used the gym at headquarters regularly and kept himself in trim. He dressed like a business rep, favouring bold striped shirts and ties.

"Looking for anyone in particular, boss?" Renwick swung his office chair to face her.

"You were in drugs, weren't you?" she said, remembering his signature on Jordan's witness statement, the hopelessness in Jordan's face when she said, "Who's gonna listen to a smackhead?"

He looked momentarily flustered and she said, "Come on, Renwick, it's not a trick question."

"Four years," he said. "Why?"

"Were you involved in Snowstorm?"

His eyes searched her face. "You think Snowstorm is linked to our OD vics?"

Moran looked up from her computer screen, but Simms kept her eyes on Renwick and raised an eyebrow, waiting for an answer to her question.

"Yes, I was in on Snowstorm," he said. "Four and a half million —"

"Thanks," she interrupted, "I've heard the press release. Did you shut down the local operators?"

In the silence that followed, she heard the soft click of Moran's typing, but she seemed to have lost her rhythm.

"We got the transporter — a local haulage firm that was going under when the recession hit, then miraculously started turning a profit."

"You didn't get the wholesalers, the suppliers?"

He seemed embarrassed. "It was all a bit last minute. Customs got a tip-off something was coming through. Just the name of the haulier and the number of vehicles — Day's Haulage, based in Salford, which is why we got drafted in to handle this end. We let the trucks through in the hope the suppliers would show up at the warehouse."

"But they didn't."

"No. Steve Day said he ran the whole thing. His drivers backed him up."

"But you didn't believe him."

He stuck his chin out and grazed the back of his hand along the edge of his jaw, thinking, his gaze locked on something halfway across the office. A second or two later he shrugged as if to say, *What the hell.*

"If you want my opinion, Steve Day hasn't got the nous. I think he's so shit scared he'd rather do a life sentence than give up his bosses' names."

One more piece in the puzzle, she thought.

"You don't mind me asking, why the interest?" Renwick said. "Snowstorm is someone else's problem."

"Not any more."

"How d'you mean?"

She looked at them both; DC Moran had stopped working on her report altogether, and was waiting for her answer with just as much curiosity as Renwick. "Because when Snowstorm took thirty kilograms of their goods at a stroke, I think Day's bosses started bulking their reserves with penicillin."

CHAPTER
FOURTEEN

"Gambling is a principle inherent in nature."

EDMUND BURKE

"Diane B., aged sixty-nine, found in the back garden of her home in West Yorkshire. Cause of death: exsanguination."

Nick Fennimore pulled up the next slide on his PowerPoint presentation. It showed a plump woman lying on her back on a lawn; she was fully clothed, her head turned slightly to the right, the collar of her blouse stained red. She had been partly covered with a housecoat, and three pink spots had seeped through from beneath it. A red-brown streak, like a question mark, stained the patch of grass above her right shoulder.

"Diane was a chronic alcoholic. She was on prescribed diazepam, and she had a volatile relationship with her husband — also alcoholic. Their arguments were frequent and violent."

The greenhouse itself was wood-framed and rank with weeds and clumps of grass. A green plastic patio chair stood at the far end, next to a bundle of clear plastic and a few discarded plant pots.

He clicked to a post-mortem close-up. "You can see the stab marks in her neck, here. The distance between

137

the two puncture marks was five centimetres. A pair of scissors found near the body matched the wounds."

Fennimore was talking to forty-plus MSc and PhD Forensic Psychology students at Manchester Metropolitan University. A smattering of academics had turned out alongside the mixture of new graduates and older students, some of whom were serving police officers or data analysts retraining for a career step-up. This was an introduction to working with professionals in related disciplines. He had shown them two other case studies, demonstrating how Bayesian analysis helped in making investigative decisions. He had given them a brief history of his own unusual career path: failed genetics student; successful gambler; betting agent, Scene of Crime Officer; chemistry graduate, toxicology specialist, three years as scientific advisor to the National Crime Faculty. Now a scientific consultant, reviewing cold cases, with a particular interest in miscarriages of justice. They already knew his academic credentials.

"The investigative team had formed two hypotheses — murder, or accident. They arrested the husband. But surely there was a third explanation." He gave them a moment to form their own hypotheses before naming his: "Suicide.

"I worked with a clinical psychologist on this one — we performed a joint physical evidence and behavioural review. He said there was little to suggest she'd been suicidal. Before you ask, no, I didn't forget to mention she was an alcoholic taking prescribed anxiolytics. But she'd made none of the preliminary arrangements you would expect of a suicide; there was no recent history of self-harm — in fact no recent change in behaviour at all — no tentative wounds. And no note. Plus, women in her age group are more likely to choose self-poisoning, rather than violent means."

The next image was just outside the greenhouse. The victim's slippers sat neatly on the grass; the insoles and fur trim were spotted with blood. "The drip pattern suggests she was standing — those nice round splodges indicate that the blood dropped vertically, and not as a result of impact or cast-off from a weapon."

He used a laser pointer to circle the top left corner of the photograph, where one of the slippers was partially hidden by a clump of weeds. "For the botanists among you, that blood-spattered clump of vegetation is hedge mustard. You'll see that it's also flattened. She — or her assailant — pulled the scissors out. She clamped her hand to her neck, staggered about a bit, stepped out of the slippers at some point, fell backwards." He clicked to the next slide, showing Diane B.'s body a short distance from her slippers. "In this instance, blood distribution would be the same for accidental self-injury or attack, and the pathologist suggested an accidental cause was 'most unlikely' — hence the husband's arrest for murder.

"All of this was pre-Bayes." He smiled. "But you know I like my stats." They did for sure — about fifty copies of *Crapshoots and Bad Stats* were stacked on a table just outside the lecture theatre, with a keen bookseller ready to take their money.

"I wondered what the odds were on accident versus murder. I went to SCAS — that's the Serious Crime

Analysis Section. It had three hundred and thirty-two murders on file. In six, the murder weapon was a pair of scissors. All involved multiple stab wounds."

He caught a couple of frowns of disapproval among the academics. "I know, small sample size — I accept your silent disapproval — so I asked International ViCLAS for some data." This was the Violent Crime Linkage Analysis System, a computerized tool used by police forces across Europe and in Canada. "Of about nine thousand homicides, three thousand were stabbings — but just ten of those were with scissors — it's just not a popular weapon. Of those ten, all the victims were stabbed multiple times. All of them."

He paused. "But Diane B. had been struck just once — no sign of struggle, no defensive wounds, abrasions or other injuries."

He saw a few accepting nods in the audience.

He clicked to the post-mortem slide again. "Mrs B. has two puncture marks — both blades penetrated her neck equally, so the fatal injury was caused by one blow, with the scissors held only *partly* open. The wounds are at right angles on the left side of the neck. The pathologist said it would be impossible to produce those wounds accidentally, because Mrs B. was right-handed. Try it for yourselves." They did, and there was a satisfied murmur of agreement.

He frowned at his audience. "Looks bad for Mr B., doesn't it?"

He circled the puncture marks on the post-mortem photograph with the laser pointer. "And those wounds are unusual, aren't they? Hard to imagine how she

140

could have done that to herself. Diane and Mr B. had been arguing shortly before she died. Objects were thrown. Even worse for Mr B., the pathologist said that adaptive functionality ruled out an accidental stumble. You know — the drunk who places his feet very carefully, talks a tad slower, but without a hint of slur, and drives very, *very* precisely."

He got a few smiles of recognition. Those who'd taken the academic route would be recalling sources, articles, psychosocial theories — or their own undergraduate binges. The police in the audience would know it from experience — policing city centres on Saturday nights, or battling their own demons — or perhaps a bit of both.

"At that time, I was a Forensic Science Service toxicologist. I completely disagreed with the pathologist's evaluation. Mrs B.'s blood contained three times the legal limit of alcohol for driving — as well as diazepam in the moderate therapeutic range. She was drunk and drugged.

"Now, a habitual drunk might be able to walk a line, speak clearly, drive apparently well. But challenge that careful, conscious control with a change in conversation, a slight jostling of an elbow, someone braking suddenly and all equilibrium is lost — disaster quickly follows." He could see them anticipating his report conclusions, but still not quite able to reconcile the facts with an accident.

"Mrs B. had been taking cuttings from her geraniums, so she was holding scissors." He picked up a pair of kitchen scissors he'd laid out ready on the bench, holding them in his right hand as if he was about to use them to cut paper. "She's on her way out of the greenhouse."

He clicked to a photograph of the greenhouse interior, looking towards the door. A few sorry-looking geraniums cluttered a wooden bench along one side; beyond that, the doorframe cast a faint shadow over two loops of blood on the packed earth floor.

"Notice the uneven surface." He circled the lumps and bumps with his laser light. "Add into the equation alcohol, diazepam, the well-worn slippers, a slight lip at the base of the frame; she catches her toe, puts her hand against the frame to save herself." He mimed the action. "It's a natural reflex to spread the palm and fingers to try to regain balance." The scissors in his hands were now partly open. "This wedges the handles against the frame at shoulder height, with the points of the blades turned straight towards the holder." He continued the mimed fall, only turning his head away as the points approached his face. Now the tips of the blades pricked the left side of his neck, and they could see that the momentum of the fall would drive the blades deep into the flesh.

"Accidental death suddenly looks a far more likely explanation."

There was a murmur of approval in the room. Fennimore closed the blades and placed the scissors thoughtfully on the bench.

"So —"

The lecture theatre door opened and Kate Simms stepped through. Fennimore took a breath and

142

experienced a momentary dizziness. He hadn't told Kate of his visit to the city — pure cowardice — he was scared of the emotions that seeing her face to face would stir up.

A slight rumble from the audience made him realize he'd made a misstep of his own, and he dragged his eyes from Kate to the expectant faces in the auditorium.

"It's still speculation." Judging by the dead-eyed look, this was from an ex-cop; the type that had barnacles encrusted around the heart. "Opinion."

"Backed by statistics," Fennimore said, mildly. "Accidental injury can happen to anyone — which in the UK gives you a pool of around sixty-one million possible candidates. The murder pool, by comparison, is fewer than a thousand a year, so even if Mrs B.'s injuries are a hundred times more likely to be malicious than accidental, it's still *six hundred* times more likely that this was an accident."

"You're saying it must be an accident because murders are rare? But people *are* murdered, Professor."

"And the statistical rarity of murder is not accepted as a defence argument. Fair point," Fennimore said. "So, we go back to the evidence."

He pulled up the slide he'd been saving till last. "Re-examination of the scene photographs of the greenhouse revealed apparent shallow indentations on the left-hand doorframe, five feet from the ground." He highlighted the marks with the pointer. "These were a physical match to the scissor handles."

He'd been relishing this moment, yet he delivered the coup de grâce with his eyes on Kate Simms: "The coroner's verdict was accidental death."

He left them to study the slide while he studied Kate. Now that he'd got over the shock of seeing her, he found himself unexpectedly cheered by her presence and he had to curb a foolish impulse to grin. It was as if a tight cord had unravelled from around his chest; and he felt unreasonably happy.

She wore a trouser suit — she'd probably come straight from work — and it fitted her perfectly. Kate used exercise for stress relief, and she had the lean physique of a distance runner. He could see from the way she held herself that she was pissed off. *Possibly with me*, he thought. *Ah, well.*

"I'm often consulted in cases that have already been investigated by scientists, police, pathologists, psychologists. I'm no cleverer than they are, but perhaps I think differently." He shrugged his shoulders in a practised gesture of self-deprecation. "I have been called weird."

He got a laugh — not a kindly one from the crusty ex-cop.

"I don't mind that — weird is useful in what I do, because most scientists, psychologists and police officers are *not* weird, with the odd notable exception." He couldn't resist adding: "Meet Detective Chief Inspector Kate Simms." He raised his hand in introduction.

Kate's eyes widened, and for a moment he thought she would bolt for the door, but by the time they turned to look, she was composed, even smiling. "Well, I can vouch for the fact he's weird."

CHAPTER
FIFTEEN

"For every observation, every result, we need to think, how does this help in this particular case?"

NICK FENNIMORE

They headed north-west in Kate Simms's car, along the redbrick canyon of Oxford Street, towards the Midland Hotel, where Fennimore was booked in for the night. Greater Manchester was the most complex and densely populated urban area of the UK outside of London. The county covered 492 square miles and ten metropolitan districts, but these warehouses and office blocks, built for the cotton and coal merchants of the nineteenth century, marked the outer boundaries of the old city. These same towering buildings now housed the global headquarters of international corporations and banks.

Two miles out of the city centre, they hit traffic and Simms slowed the car to a crawl, muttering a curse under her breath.

"What's got you rattled?" Fennimore said.

"Who said I was rattled?"

"Come on, Kate. You go to the trouble of tracking me down, you gatecrash my lecture —"

"I mean why would I be rattled?" she interrupted. "The case is solved; we got our man."

Josh Brown had emailed the results from Aberdeen: StayC's drugs and the other deals all contained penicillin. The hospital pathologists had confirmed anaphylaxis in case after case — the supposed overdose victims had been killed by penicillin in the heroin they injected. But that only gave them a cause of death — it didn't solve the case.

Fennimore stared at Simms, wanting an explanation.

"Yeah," she said. "How about that? A street-level dealer coughed to the lot."

"He just gave himself up?"

She barked a laugh. "He didn't actually grow a conscience. It was a Drugs Squad arrest. Anthony Newton — that's the dealer — ran a red light right in front of a patrol car. They pulled him over. He had fifteen wraps of heroin on him. Drugs Squad got a search warrant and found another twenty in his flat." She turned to look at him full on. "Newton caved in straight away — said he was just trying to make some easy money on the side, slipped a few milligrams of penicillin into the mix. He said he feels terrible, he didn't know it'd do any harm. He thought it might even do some good."

"Touching," Fennimore said. "Drugs dealers aren't usually so public-spirited."

"No," she said. "They're not." She shifted gear, accelerating past a slow-moving line of cars into a gap in the traffic.

Fennimore couldn't understand why she was so angry. He swivelled in his seat to get a better look and she glanced at him sharply.

"What?"

"Your case is solved, Kate," he said. "What's the problem?"

She faced the front again. "Back at the Faculty, you always said that for every observation, every result, we need to think, how does this help in this particular case?"

"That still holds true — so?"

"We know how the victims died, we've got the culprit, the press are happy, the CPS is happy, the review criteria are satisfied, the families have justice. But it doesn't *help* the case, Nick. It stops it dead."

"Because?"

"The anaphylaxis victims go back months, yet the constituents are exactly the same."

"O-kaay?" He had no idea where she was going with this.

"You're always saying context is everything."

"I am. And it is."

"So a street-level bozo, maybe with a habit of his own, gets hold of some stolen penicillin. Which he carefully rations, cutting his deals with it for over *eight months*?" She shook her head. "No, it doesn't make sense, Nick. Street-level dealers aren't that organized. They don't hold on to drugs for months — they blow the lot within days, hours even."

"Hm."

She glanced at him. "Is that 'Hm, you're right' or 'Hm, that's pure speculation'?"

"It's 'Hm, you *could* be right.' You need to talk to the dealer."

She sighed. "Yes, I do. But Newton is already banged up in Strangeways on remand."

"That was quick."

"Well, they did have a confession. But Newton was in police custody for *two days* and nobody told me. Tanford called after they'd charged him and taken him to prison."

"Now, why would he do that?"

"I don't know. Maybe he's pissed off with me because I turned down his offer of help. Maybe he's teaching me a lesson." She turned to him and her eyes sparked like static in amber. "You're missing the *point*, Nick."

"No," he said, "I'm not. I know that now he's been charged, Newton doesn't have to talk to anyone he doesn't want to. My guess is he isn't talking to you."

"He isn't even talking to his own legal counsel."

He shrugged. "Maybe he did grow a conscience after all."

"Come *on* — the moment I started re-interviewing witnesses, local intel reported a drop-off of arrests for heroin possession and an increase in addicts signing up for methadone treatment. We release info that the excess deaths were caused by penicillin and there's *another* drop in drugs arrests — bad merchandise is bad for business. Then Newton shows up, just *dying* to confess."

"Put it that way, it does sound convenient," Fennimore agreed.

She told him about Operation Snowstorm, and the haulier who claimed responsibility for the entire drugs shipment. "The suppliers are still out there, Nick. I think the penicillin went into the deals higher up the supply chain. The suppliers can't afford to take more losses, so they hand me a rogue dealer to save me the trouble of actually investigating the case."

Fennimore nodded. "And at the same time reassure their customers that their heroin is safe."

"Got it in one," she said. "Anthony Newton is just some lowlife they paid or intimidated into taking the fall."

"What does your boss say?"

"That a major drugs inquiry is way out of my league, and well beyond my brief. He warned me not to mess up the chance to start rebuilding my career."

"Ah."

"What *is* it with the monosyllabic answers?" Simms demanded.

"I don't want to distract you from your driving."

"There's nothing wrong with my driving."

He nodded towards the queue of stationary traffic straight ahead.

Her head snapped front. She braked inches from a rear-end smash. "*Shit*, Fennimore, why didn't you warn me?"

"I did."

"I meant *sooner*."

He didn't answer. He didn't know why he took risks, and he didn't care to speculate.

The traffic was backed up by two coaches dropping passengers outside the Palace Theatre for the evening performance of *Mamma Mia!*

Simms kneaded the wheel, breathing hard through her nose as they waited for the pensioners and families to disembark. For a while neither said a word, but when the last coach in the queue started to edge out in the traffic, Fennimore nudged Simms's elbow. With one last resentful scowl, she turned her attention to the road, squeezing past the second coach.

When they were back in the stream of traffic, Fennimore asked, "Has the preliminary tox screen been done on the wraps they found on Newton?"

She nodded. "Tanford sent me a copy. They're waiting on the quantitative analysis, but the basic constituents are a good match to the drugs found in our penicillin vics." Her phone rang. "Oh, hell," she said. "What time is it?"

"Seven-thirty."

She groaned, slipped her mobile phone from her coat pocket. "Kieran, I'm sorry, I —" She broke off.

Kieran. Her husband. Fennimore looked out of the passenger window, trying not to listen. A second later, the phone was thrust into his hand. "What are you —?"

"Put it on speaker," she said softly. She jerked her head right, as a police car cruised slowly past. The driver wagged his finger at her and she mouthed "Sorry."

"You promised, Kate," Kieran said.

"Look, love, this is a big inquiry."

"What inquiry? *North West Tonight* says it's solved — a man has been charged."

"It's not that simple."

"Tell that to your son."

Son? Fennimore glanced at her, but she kept her eyes on the road, her hands gripping the wheel so tight he could see the rim distort.

"Mummy?" A small, tearful voice.

Simms took a breath, pressed her thumb to her top lip. Then she cleared her throat and said brightly: "Hi, Tim!"

"Are you coming home?"

"Not yet, sweetie. Mummy has to work."

"But you *promised*." Echoing his daddy's words.

Oh, boy . . .

"I know." She bit her lip, frowning, and Fennimore turned his head, wishing he was a thousand miles away.

"I'm really, really sorry. But you go to sleep like a good boy and I'll come and kiss you goodnight just as soon as I come in."

"I don't *want* to go to bed. You promised you'd read me a story."

"Oh, God . . . Kieran, are you there?"

"Yes. I'm here, Kate. Just remember while you're working on your 'big case' that you have a son who needs to see his mother from time to time, and a daughter who's trying to adapt to a change of school as well as a move — because of *your* job, mark you — which has dragged her two hundred miles away from home and friends and everything she knows."

"Has Becky said something? Is she all right?"

"If you were here occasionally, you'd know."

"Kier —"

"Don't worry," he said. "I'll deal with it. Like I always do."

152

A few tumbling notes told them the line had been disconnected. "Shit." She slammed the wheel with the heel of her hand. "I'm sorry you had to listen to that, Nick."

Fennimore stared stupidly at the phone in his hand. "How old is he?"

"Kieran? Thirty-five, going on fifteen."

They had arrived at the baroque frontage of the Midland Hotel, a Victorian mansion of red brick and brown-glazed terracotta. Opposite, the circular dome of Manchester Central Library glowed greenish-white under spotlights.

Kate pulled in to the kerb and closed her eyes briefly, pinching the bridge of her nose. "Tim is four."

For a moment he was stunned. "When were you going to tell me?"

"You haven't exactly been around *to* tell. Please, Nick, don't *you* start."

He was ready to argue, but seeing the weariness, the misery in her face, he realized that he had no claim to righteous indignation.

She put the car in gear. "Look, I'd better go."

"Come and have dinner with me — we'll talk."

She took the phone off him. "I need to try and sort this out with Kieran."

"Go home the way you're feeling right now, you'll only argue." She hesitated and he said, "Come on, it'll do you good to talk."

She gave him a hard stare.

"About the case," he said. "Just about the case, all right?"

"One drink," she said, suspicion written all over her face. "Then I've really got to go."

She stayed for dinner. They agreed that she would forward full analyses of the seized wraps as soon as she had them from the drugs squad. Fennimore would make a comparison with her excess overdose cases. It was the best they could do, since Newton was refusing to speak to her — or anyone else.

She stood, clipping her phone onto her belt, and reached for her purse.

"On me," he said. "I insist."

She seemed to struggle with herself for a moment, then smiled her thanks. "I probably couldn't afford it, anyway." She dropped her purse into her handbag.

"Kate, sit down a minute?"

A frown crossed her face. "Nick, I don't want to talk about Tim."

"I know," he said. "This isn't about your son — I want to explain why I left without telling you."

"Not necessary," she said.

"I know," he said again. "But it's long overdue, and I need to say this. Please?"

She sat down again and worried the corner of her napkin.

"After they found Rachel, I was a wreck."

She nodded, not making eye contact.

"When Rachel and Suzie —" His throat closed up and he had to stop for a moment. "When they first disappeared, I tried to convince myself she'd found someone else, that she was punishing me — I don't

154

need to tell you how things were between us, back then. But no matter how mad she was at me, Rachel wouldn't prevent Suzie getting in touch, so I knew — after twenty-four hours — I *knew* something terrible really had happened."

His wife had been found, strangled, five months after she and Suzie had vanished. The pathologist estimated that Rachel had been alive until a few days before her body was discovered.

"When they found Rachel . . ." He took the napkin from Kate's hands and folded it in half with meticulous care. "I kept thinking if I'd known for sure from the start that someone had them, maybe I would have worked harder — we both know the first twenty-four hours are crucial —"

"You did everything you could, before *and* after they found Rachel," Kate broke in.

He shook his head. "Thinking about Suzie — still out there, all alone — it felt like I'd abandoned her. I felt so guilty that I went way beyond my powers. I misused police resources." He made a second fold. "I interfered in a police investigation." He folded the napkin corner to corner, making a triangle. "I involved you."

"Jeez, Nick, how many times do I have to tell you?"

Right through the internal investigation and disciplinary hearing Kate had bitterly resented any suggestion of victim-hood, any hint that she had been manipulated.

"I know," he said. "You made a choice, and you don't regret it. And I want you to know that I appreciated that — I never said it, and I should have. But I was a scientist — independent of police regulations — I knew they couldn't touch me. And I knew what the consequences might be for you. I was nine-tenths out of my mind just then." In truth, he was so mad with grief that there were whole chunks of time he couldn't remember.

"Knowing that I might have saved them, if I'd been faster or smarter or tried that little bit harder, was more punishing than all those months of not knowing if they were alive or dead. I begrudged every coffee break I'd taken, every meal, every hour of sleep —" He took a breath and it stuck in his throat. "But no matter how crazy I was, no matter how driven and obsessed, I knew that I had no right to involve you, and I didn't give a damn. I didn't think about how it would affect you, and I didn't care." He placed his hand on the folded napkin, unable to look her in the eye.

"You've got it all wrong, Nick." She dipped her head to look into his eyes. "You told me a thousand times to walk away. When Gifford found out what we'd been doing, you put yourself between me and him like some old-time warrior." Her mouth twitched a little at the corners. "Which I did not need. Because, Nick, I'm a big girl. I make my own decisions, and I fight my own battles."

"You can't fight the system, Kate."

"Screw the system," she said. "I made Chief Inspector. I moved on." She peered into his face. "Did you?"

156

"Rachel is dead, Kate. Suzie is gone." He exhaled, realizing only then that he had been holding his breath. "I've accepted that."

"And yet you run your age-progressions and carry a picture of Suzie as she might look at fifteen, and you search every face of every teenage girl you see in the street."

He stared into her eyes. "How did you know that?"

She smiled softly. "I know *you*. Does even a day go by when you don't wonder where she is?"

"Not a minute," he said. "Not a second."

In truth, it took an act of will not to break those five years down and count every tick of the clock since he last saw his little girl; it took a conscious effort not to calculate all the instances of fear and pain and hopelessness she had experienced.

"I've seen things," he said, starting cautiously, testing his voice. When he was sure it would hold out, he said: "I *know* things — terrible things — that make me wish . . ." It was too awful to say, but he said it anyway: ". . . that Suzie *is* dead."

She rested her hand on his and the warmth of her skin on his made him weak.

CHAPTER
SIXTEEN

"Most so-called anomalies don't seem anomalous to me at all. They seem like nuggets from a gold mine."

FISCHER BLACK

Fennimore stood beneath the giant screen on the concourse of Piccadilly railway station, his laptop and tote bags at his feet, watching StayC singing her heart out in mime on-screen. The news ticker below trailed her post-mortem findings:

"Penicillin allergy killed StayC . . . Drugs peddler, Anthony Newton, confesses he 'cut' heroin with antibiotic . . ." The video cut to StayC's weeping mother, hugging a framed photograph of her daughter. The tickertape read: ". . . Police not looking for anyone else in connection with the inquiry."

He waited, but the text-stream rolled round to the beginning again; there was no mention of the other twelve dead addicts. Fennimore gave a mental shrug. *That's showbiz.*

His mobile rang and he fished it out of his overcoat pocket.

"Nick, are you still in Manchester?" Kate Simms. Her voice was tight with contained excitement.

"Just barely."

The Tannoy bing-bonged and platform ten was announced for his train. He glanced up at the departure board. "I can give you five minutes."

"This will take much longer. D'you have to leave today?"

Today was Saturday, and in the three days since Kate had gate-crashed his lecture, Fennimore had addressed a seminar for senior officers and presented a paper at a Forensic Science conference in Manchester. "Depends on what you've got. I was planning to take the rest of the weekend off, head up to my place in the Lakes."

"Stay right where you are — I'll pick you up."

"Uh, d'you want to tell me why?"

"Look, I can be there in ten minutes."

"Kate, my train *leaves* in ten minutes." He watched passengers stream past him, heading for his train. "You might at least give me a good reason why I should miss it."

She took a breath and he heard it catch. "We've got another body."

He scratched his forehead and looked up into the arched glass roof of the building. "It's tragic, and I'm sorry for the victim and their family, but Kate, you're bound to have a few more while the tainted deals work their way out of the supply chain."

"This isn't a drug death, Nick. This one is murder."

Forensic Pathologist Dr David Cooper, already in theatre blues, met them at the door of the mortuary, trim and bearded, standing five foot four in his three-inch Cuban heels.

"I should've known it was you when Kate told me you'd worked out the penicillin connection from the stats." Dr Cooper had lived the past fifteen years in the more refined air of Knutsford, twenty miles south of Manchester, but his vowels still carried the smoky tones of the city.

Fennimore grinned and offered his hand. "Kate's tame pathologist."

Dr Cooper squinted up at him. "Wild and free, mate — always will be."

Kate Simms looked from Fennimore to Cooper. "You two know each other?"

"We worked on a miscarriage of justice case, two years back," Cooper said.

"Three."

"Still going all *Rainman* about the numbers, Fenn?"

"Still wearing the lifts, Coop?"

"I hope this isn't going to turn nasty," Kate said, but lazily, like she might enjoy a scrap between two geeks.

Cooper angled his foot and gazed appreciatively at his boot. "These beauties've saved my deltoids from untold agonies. Adjustable tables are fine and good, but if it wasn't for these heels, I'd be walking around looking like the Honey Monster's short-arsed uncle."

Kate stifled a laugh, which Fennimore guessed was what Cooper had been aiming for all along. "DCI Simms said you have a body we should see?"

"Get yourselves booted and suited. I'll walk you through my findings."

He plucked a pair of elasticated booties from the shelves to the left of the post-mortem room and slipped them over his heels while they struggled into gowns, caps and booties of their own.

"What makes you think this is linked to Kate's deaths?" Fennimore asked.

"The victim's urine smelled of penicillin," Cooper said. "CSIs found a cling film wrap near her body. Preliminary analysis of the contents suggested the same composition as StayC's drugs stash — two key components being diamorphine and, yup, you guessed it, penicillin."

"So it *is* another anaphylaxis victim?" Simms threw Fennimore an apologetic glance. "You said it was murder."

Cooper smiled. "You missed the PM, but I thought you'd want to take a look anyhow." He pushed through the door and held it, releasing the unmistakable whiff of sanitized decay.

The body on the table was bleached white by the surgical lamps. There were bands of paler, shiny flesh on her fingers and toes. Reddish bruising showed on her ribs and abdomen. The T-incision — which Cooper preferred to the Y-incision popularized by TV pathologists — had been stitched closed with thick green thread, strong enough to bind the seams of a canvas duffle bag. Fennimore knew that the internal organs were packed in leak-proof bags under the stitching.

The face was almost gone.

Simms stepped around him to get a full view of the body. "My God," she whispered.

Impossible to guess what this woman looked like in life; her nose was mashed flat, bent to one side, her jaw, her cheekbones, the right orbit, all crushed. Whoever had done this had beaten her flesh to the consistency of ground meat.

For half a minute, they stood there like mourners around a coffin, breathing the cool air of the mortuary. The ventilation system's downdraught dragged most of the smells away, but no ventilation system could ever completely eradicate the perfume of disinfectant and slowly putrefying flesh.

Cooper was first to break the silence. "Fingerprints came back negative — she's not on the system and there's no missing person report. Early- to mid-twenties, dumped in an alley at the back of a city-centre hotel, sometime Thursday night or early Friday morning. She was naked. The only item still on the body was a tongue stud — her mouth was so full of blood the killer must have missed it when he took the rest. As you can see, someone gave her a thorough going-over."

Simms pulled her gaze from the woman's ruined face. "Cause of death?"

"Well, it wasn't an overdose," Cooper said. "Among other injuries, she had a ruptured spleen, fragments of the orbital socket embedded in the brain, and her liver, kidneys and lungs had all haemorrhaged." He leaned back against the bench that ran along one wall; behind him, a whiteboard. "But my report will say she drowned." Simms crinkled her brow in question and he said, "In her own blood. It was in her stomach, trachea and lungs. I found clots of the stuff in her larynx."

"Pure rage," Simms breathed.

Fennimore doubted that rage could ever be pure. But he had seen enough of death to recognize the attack on this young woman as distilled, uncontrolled hatred — whether that hatred was for this one woman, or all of womankind, time would tell.

Cooper strode to the door, his boot heels clumping on the tiles despite the muffling effect of his booties. He bumped the door open with his backside and roared, "ALI!"

A few moments later, a middle-aged woman appeared, still fastening the back of her gown. "Will you stop bloody doing that?" she said.

Cooper pointed left and right. "DCI Simms, Professor Fennimore." He turned to the mortuary technician. "Ali."

She scowled, ignoring their guests. "Near gave me a heart attack."

"Can you give me a hand with this?" Cooper said, returning to the far side of the table.

"I'm only in the next room. I mean would it be too bloody much to just bloody knock?" She continued muttering as they turned the body face down.

The buttocks were criss-crossed with fine wheals, white in the centre, with reddish lines either side, like a railway track. Where the tracks crossed, there were pinpricks of blood.

Fennimore winced.

"A riding crop," Cooper said. "Or something similar, but I'd go with riding crop. It's the instrument of choice in S&M interplay." He shot a look across the table at Kate Simms. "So I'm told."

Kate fixed him with a stony stare. "I understand the bruising, but what caused the white lines?"

"The blood gets forced to the sides by the impact of the rod — or whatever — so bruising occurs either side of the line of contact. The cross-hatching is particularly painful. The stripes are precise. The darker lines indicate slightly older bruising." He followed the line of one of the darker tracks with his pinkie finger.

"How much older?" Something about those marks niggled Fennimore.

"Maybe an hour or two. She was also raped, choked with a wide strap and resuscitated several times," Cooper said. "Analysis indicates that the morphine was administered quite late on — whoever did this wanted her to feel every blow. Oh, and speaking of blow . . ." He lifted the body's right arm, turning it so that they could see a puncture mark on the inside crease of the elbow. "I found only one site of injection — and I was very thorough — nothing in the armpits or groin, in the finger knuckles, ankles or between the toes. I'd be willing to bet that hair analysis will confirm this young lady was not a regular user."

"A prostitute without a drug habit. I suppose it's possible," Fennimore said, doubtfully.

Cooper set the arm down with surprising gentleness. "What makes you think she's a prostitute?"

164

"Small holes in both nipples, probably from rings or studs," Fennimore explained. "Slight chafe marks or indents on the third and fourth toes, indicating toe rings. And of the thirteen penicillin victims, all the women except StayC funded their habits with sex work — statistically, it's likely she did, too."

"Except this one didn't have a habit — at least not a drug habit," Cooper said. He bent closer to the corpse. "Here's another interesting thing." He circled a small patch of skin an inch below the victim's left shoulder blade, a faint red mark, slightly curved.

"Bruising?" Simms said. "A fingernail, maybe?"

Cooper picked up a small black box from the bench behind him. He pressed a button and it flickered for a second, then flooded the area immediately in front of it with bright light. "Ali, could you get the overheads?"

The technician moved to the light switches and, a second later, the room was in darkness, except for the violet-tinged light from the box.

Cooper played the light over the mark and the faint red blemish became a jagged circular outline in purple, as though the skin had been imprinted with dye. "Forensic light sources — you've got to love 'em," Cooper said, grinning like a schoolboy with a new Xbox. The saliva on his teeth luminesced yellowish-green.

"The edges look crimped," Simms said.

"A beer bottle top?" Fennimore suggested.

"Precisely. Funny thing is, the CSIs didn't find anything like it at the scene." Cooper shone the light on the purple coronet of bruising again. "There was nothing under the body or within thirty feet of it that could have left that mark."

"So she was killed somewhere else," Fennimore said.

"The investigating officer disagrees," Cooper said. "He thinks she's just another druggie prostitute who went for a twenty-quid jump behind the wheelie bins with the wrong punter."

"One injection site, and we're supposed to think she's a hard-core addict?"

"I didn't say *I* believed it. If she *was* a prostitute, she was high class, so she wouldn't need to sell it cheap in a filthy back alley. She was tortured and this is supposed to've happened behind a hotel on a Thursday night? Do me a favour — you'd've heard the screams from Piccadilly to Deansgate. Added to that, there was no blood spatter — in fact, there was hardly *any* blood at the scene. The hotel was the dump site."

Simms stared hard at the pathologist. "The SIO *does* know all this?"

"I told him what I've just told you, and he had the additional benefit of being at the post-mortem." Cooper watched Simms, testing her reaction. "But his head was jammed so far up his arse he didn't seem to hear a word I said."

"You're pissed off," Simms said, folding her arms. "I can see why you would be, but I don't know what you expect me to do. All we've got so far is a tenuous link to my penicillin deaths."

Fennimore looked again at the body. There was something else — something he'd missed, something about the injuries. He glanced at the whiteboard on the wall behind the bench, his fingers itching to pick up a pen and start doodling.

"D'you mind?" he said.

Cooper shrugged. "Go for it." He nodded to the tech and the spotlights flickered on.

Fennimore took a red marker pen from the trough at the base of the board and sketched a body outline at the centre. He marked it "VICTIM", in block capitals. From that, he drew a main branch and labelled it "KNOWNS".

"You're not about to do a Donald Rumsfeld, are you, mate?"

Fennimore gave Cooper a dusty look. "We know that she was early- to mid-twenties, natural blonde. Height?"

"Five seven," Cooper said.

"Last meal?"

"She'd had a surf 'n' turf meal four hours before she died," Cooper told him.

Fennimore added that to the diagram. "Possibly a sex worker." He added sub-branches to the diagram as he spoke. "COD — drowned in her own blood."

A ripple of emotion passed across Simms's face — revulsion, or something more complex — then she seemed to brace up. "She was raped, flogged and beaten."

"Ligature marks on the wrists and ankles," Cooper added, nodding, now, seeing the point of the exercise. "And she was healthy — no signs of addiction."

"Okay." Fennimore capped the pen and replaced it with green. "I'm calling that an anomaly." He drew a new main branch on the left of the diagram, and labelled it.

As he wrote, Simms said, "Addict or not, she *had* been injected with the same drug mix that killed our penicillin vies."

He noted that and added a circle to the top of the board. Inside it, he wrote "PENICILLIN DEATHS" and connected it to the body outline with a wavy line. It floated like a thought balloon over the rest and he stared at it, until Simms said, "Earth to Fennimore."

"I was just thinking, this case is rife with anomalies, isn't it? Her good health and lack of addiction suggest she would have people who cared about her, but there's no MisPer report, and then there's the location. All due respect to the investigating officer, it doesn't fit a stranger murder, does it?"

"Girls do get dragged off the street," Cooper said, playing devil's advocate.

"Yes, but an opportunistic attack is what it says," Fennimore countered. "It's unplanned, disorganized. You would expect the assailant to attack, then flee. There were four hours between her last meal and the moment this girl died. Like you said, her killer took his time: he tortured her; raped her; he moved the body; he removed things *from* the body. All of that takes planning, organization."

He swiftly sketched a new sub-branch and labelled it "ORGANIZED ELEMENTS". "The flogging would have to've taken place elsewhere. It would involve physical restraint, which is controlled, organized. He

168

cleaned up afterwards — no blood, no spatter, no jewellery."

"Except for the tongue stud," Cooper said.

"But he missed that because he'd smashed her face to a pulp," Kate added. "That's not controlled, Nick."

"Another anomaly," he agreed.

Cooper raised a finger. "Should have said — the nipple studs were unscrewed or unclipped. Deaths like this, they're usually torn out."

"He breaks her jaw and crushes her orbital socket into her brain, but he carefully unscrews her nipple studs." Fennimore added it to "ORGANIZED ELEMENTS", and immediately an alternative came to him: "Unless she only wore them for work, and this was a nice quiet meal with a friend . . . Any more new and interesting gems you'd like to contribute, Coop?"

"Oh, I'm a superhighway of info, Nick, mate. Ali . . ." He picked up the box again and the mortuary technician lifted her chin in acknowledgement. But she kept her eyes on the diagram, watching Fennimore add new lines, new key words, as she moved to the light console.

"If we're looking at anomalies . . ." Cooper nodded to Ali and the room went dark again. He directed the eerie glow of the lamp over the victim's shoulders.

Fennimore moved closer. In the penetrating light of the UV source, he saw other faint areas of bruising. "Bites?" he said.

Simms frowned. "That's hardly unusual in a sex attack."

"No, but these don't look right to me — they're faint. Almost tentative." Cooper tracked down the body, and purple bruising, invisible in normal wavelengths, appeared and faded, appeared and faded, like objects in a car's headlamps. He stopped at the striations on the victim's buttocks, and the cuts of the riding crop showed in cruel detail. "And tentative doesn't seem to fit with this guy, does it?" he said.

"Are you thinking there were two assailants?" Fennimore said. "One more confident — and more sadistic — than the other?"

"Don't ask me about psychology," Cooper said. "I'm an evidence man. You asked for anomalies, I'm giving you an anomaly."

"I've thought of something else," Simms said. "None of the penicillin victims died violently, but this —" She looked at the body on the table as if she was seeing it for the first time. "This is ultra-violent."

Fennimore followed her line of sight; the hairs at the base of his scalp prickled and again he experienced that niggling sensation that he'd missed something. Suddenly, he had it. The waffle effect of the whipping — he'd seen it before. He fished out his mobile phone and speed dialled the RGU faculty office manager. She gave her name and title in slow, precise Aberdonian.

"Joan. Can you do me a favour?"

"Would that be *another* one?" she said. "Because you *do know* I'm already typing up the report you left with me when you swanned off on your little field trip?"

"Joan, you know I couldn't function without your organizational brilliance."

170

She sniffed, always suspicious of a compliment.

"DCI Simms sent me a bundle of coroners' reports —"

"Is that the lassie from Manchester police? Such nice manners."

He'd wondered how Kate had got his mobile phone number — and the details of his lecture at Manchester Met — now he knew.

"I'm with her now," he said. Kate raised her eyebrows and he added, "She sends her regards. Those reports," he went on, before Joan could engage him in a swapping of pleasantries. "They're in my office. You couldn't just . . ."

She complained, but that was Joan — never truly happy unless she had something to complain about. Within minutes, she was in his office and had dragged the relevant box from under his desk.

"You're looking for Rika — that's R-I-K-A — no surname."

"I have it," she said.

"Excellent. Can you look at the pathologist's report — about halfway down the second page. I think it's para five." He could visualize the layout and paragraphing of the report almost as clearly as if it was in front of him.

"You know I don't like looking at these things," she said.

"It's all right, Joan, there are no photographs. Only a description."

"As if *that* makes it any better," she grumbled. "Here it is —"

"Wait a minute — I'm putting you on speaker."

"'There are recent whip marks on both buttocks,'" she read, in her high flutey voice. "'Thin white "rail-track" wheals, with purple bruising either side. Bruising shows characteristic waffle effect, probably caused by subsequent application of —'" She broke off. "For heaven's *sake*."

"I'm sorry, Joan," Fennimore said, "but it's important."

She drew breath and began again mid-sentence: "'. . . probably caused by subsequent application of riding crop at right angles to the first wounds. Older bruises are present under the rest.'"

They all looked at each other.

"Well, thank you so very much for spoiling my morning," Joan said. When nobody sympathized or apologized, she said, "Is that it? Because I do have a mountain of work waiting to be dealt with."

"That's it. Thanks, Joan. And Joan . . ."

"Yes?"

"You are a pearl among women. And nobody appreciates you as much as I do."

"Get on with you," she said, but she sounded less huffy.

Fennimore hung up and pocketed his phone.

"There's no Rika on my list of penicillin deaths," Simms said.

"She died of a genuine overdose," Fennimore said. "I remembered the whip marks from the post-mortem report — the method is very unusual."

Simms looked to the pathologist for confirmation. "First I've seen at PM," he said. "I'll leave it to *Rainman* Fennimore to work up the numbers, but I'd say it's pretty much unique." He looked from Simms to Fennimore and back again. "I mean what's the chances of two bodies with the same dodgy drugs in them showing up with the same injuries?"

"I'd have to check the Injuries Database to answer that," Fennimore said coolly. He glanced at Simms in warning; Cooper wanted the current SIO off the case, blown out of the water, and he wasn't above using Simms as his Exocet missile. But she raised her eyebrows and Fennimore caught a glint of humour in her eyes. She knew exactly what Cooper was up to.

"Best get cracking then," she said. "I'm going to need those numbers to have any hope of convincing my boss."

Fennimore couldn't help smiling; she really intended to prise the case from the current SIO's fingers. He turned to the board and added the new link, then stood back and folded his arms, studying what they had:

KNOWNS
- Female — early-mid twenties/5′ 7″/blonde
- Assault — beating/flogging, multiple rapes/ choking/ligatures
- Whip marks unusual — v. painful — riding crop
- Cause of death — drowned/own blood
- Last meal — surf/turf
- Piercings/toe rings — sex worker?

ANOMALIES

- Fingerprints not on NAFIS/ no MisPer report
- Body location (hotel)
  - Dump site, not torture site
  - Risk of potential witnesses
- doesn't fit stranger murder
  - body moved
- Victim healthy
- Victim not addict, but drug wrap near body, heroin in body
- Organized elements
  - clean-up
  - restraints
  - flogging
  - no spatter/no blood
  - studs unscrewed, removed
- Disorganized elements
  - blitz attack (face)
  - tongue stud still in mouth (missed by killer)
- Bites tentative

LINKS TO PENICILLIN DEATHS

- Same drug composition as penicillin victims
- Similar whip marks on genuine OD victim — "Rika"

A second later, the overhead lights came on, and they all clustered around the diagram; Simms and the mortuary tech on one side of the table, Fennimore and Cooper on the other.

"Now what?" Cooper said.

"I'll research the injuries." Fennimore looked at Kate. "And I think we need expert advice on the psychopathy."

She nodded. "D'you have anyone in mind?"

"Alastair Varley. He's based in Nottingham — I'll give him a call — and in the meantime . . ."

"We investigate," Kate said. "If she was a sex worker, she probably worked out of a sauna or massage parlour." She was already racing ahead, working out where the evidence was taking them, where they might find the data they needed. "We'll do a canvass of the local knocking shops, see if any of the punters have a reputation for that kind of thing."

"Have you got the manpower?" Fennimore knew that most of her team had been reassigned after the dealer gave himself up, and until Simms was officially tasked with the murder investigation, she would be working with very few resources.

She shrugged. "I've got a reliable DC, and I can do some of the legwork myself."

"I can call Josh," Fennimore said, "ask him to do a virtual check of restaurants in the area — see who was serving meat and seafood combos on the night in question — most of them have their menus online, these days."

She nodded. "Great."

"Which leaves me with what?" Cooper said.

"The one witness we already have," Fennimore said, looking at the body.

Cooper tilted his head. "The SIO did pull his head out of his arse long enough to ask for a DNA profile so we can run her through the database, but if she's not on NAFIS, let's face it, she's not likely to be on the DNA database." NAFIS was the National Automated Fingerprint Identification System. "There was no usable DNA on the tongue stud — too much of her blood. But we got dermal tissue from the fingernail scrapings, and we swabbed the bites and took vaginal and anal swabs. They might yield something. What else do you want?"

Fennimore stared at the board. "Okay," he said, working through the evidence, selecting the best options given what they had and what they needed to find out. "She's healthy, she's well cared for. You'd expect her family to be missing her, worrying about her, but there's no MisPer report. So maybe she's not from here. Stable Isotope Analysis of the teeth — that'll give us where she grew up."

The pathologist nodded, a slight frown creasing his brow. "And if she's been in the UK for less than a year, it'll show in her hair and nails — we should be able to identify country of recent origin."

Fennimore shot Simms a quick grin. "We should have her postcode and social security number by Thursday next."

Cooper shook his head. "SIA is a specialist lab job. There's only one decent lab in the UK I know of — it'll take weeks."

"The lab is in Dundee," Fennimore said. "I happen to know the head honcho. I'll have a chat with him, see if we can do better than that."

Cooper looked from Simms to Fennimore and back again. "And who did you say is going to pay for all this — not that I'm bothered, so long as the bill doesn't land on my desk, and I get my Home Office Post-mortem fee."

"You make a start," Simms said. "I'll work out the logistics."

CHAPTER
SEVENTEEN

"I suspect the secret of personal attraction is locked up in our unique imperfections, flaws and frailties."

HUGH MACKAY

"What do you make of Cooper?" Simms said.

Fennimore and Simms were at the back of the hotel where the body had been found. All that remained to mark it as the final resting place of their anonymous victim was a tangle of blue-and-white crime scene tape, fluttering from a wheelie bin. Cobbles showed through the tarmac like blisters on a burns victim. A sheer, windowless wall formed one side of the alley, the rear wall of the hotel the other. Four giant wheelie bins were lined up against the hotel wall, two either side of a steel door. The alley stank of bins and urine and — incongruously, wafting from the hotel kitchens — fresh bread.

"He's all right."

"Spoken like a man."

"All right, he's an oddball, but he does cut up dead bodies for a living," Fennimore said. "Why d'you ask?"

"Just wondering why he was so keen for me to take the case."

Fennimore smiled. "Your paranoia is showing. Have you got those photos?" Cooper had printed off the crime scene photos before they left the mortuary. They stood shoulder to shoulder, studying them.

"Here." Simms pointed to a patch of scabby tarmac a few feet from the rear wall of the building.

Fennimore oriented the printout so that they could both picture how the body had lain in relation to the hotel. He took a step back and looked up. "I count ten windows," he said. "All with frosted glass, all of which are probably sealed shut, anyway."

"I'll find out," she said.

They walked on, past the stream of crime scene tape fluttering like a banner from the dumpster, the stink of rotting fish and decaying cabbage sharp in their nostrils. Fennimore crouched, peering closely at the pits and potholes, noting a splash of white paint on the cobbles about ten yards from where they were standing.

Simms turned three hundred and sixty degrees. "It's a good place to dump a body: access both ends, no observation points from above, wide enough for a bin lorry to fit through, but not so wide you'd park your car and leave it while you shopped in the town centre. Enough cover from the bins, so anyone passing the end of the alley wouldn't see her. Bastard had local knowledge."

"And you wonder why Cooper wanted you on the case."

"Make sense, Fennimore," she said.

"I thought I was the one who's supposed to be clueless about these things," he said, a small smile on his face.

A van turned in from the main road and stopped short behind Simms's Mondeo. The driver leant on the horn. Simms flashed her badge and ID, still waiting for an explanation.

Fennimore stood up, brushing street grime from his hands. "Okay. You're thorough. You're not satisfied with the obvious explanation. You cared enough to treat a routine review with the seriousness it deserves — you thought about it, and you asked questions and you found out the truth."

She puffed air between her lips. "You seem to be implying that he actually cares."

"Of course he cares. Who spotted the link between your drugs deaths and StayC? Who smoothed the way for you when you had to go back to the hospital pathologists and tell them they'd missed the actual cause of death on close to a dozen cases? They could easily have closed ranks on you, but Coop massaged egos and persuaded them to go back and check their findings — he made it possible for you to establish penicillin as the common cause. And today, he could have sent in his report and shrugged his shoulders at the laziness and incompetence of the senior investigating officer, but he didn't. He called you in — again. Why? Because he knew you'd do the job right."

"Hm." It didn't seem to register. She stared past Fennimore to the steady flow of traffic on the main road forty or fifty feet away.

"And of course he fancies you something rotten."

She nodded and turned one hundred and eighty. Now he knew she wasn't listening — a comment like that would usually warrant a sharp rebuke and possibly a dead arm.

She was looking towards the far end of the alley, another thirty feet distant, where her car was parked. "This is what — eighteen feet wide? Our killer could just roll in here, dump her, and roll out —" She stopped. "What are you staring at?"

You, Kate. You. He said quietly, "I've missed you, Kate."

"Nick, stop it. I'm married, and I want to stay that way."

He should have grasped the chance to clear the air; they needed to talk about the real reason he had left without a word four years ago, and she needed to explain why she hadn't told him about her four-year-old son. But Fennimore did what most men would do in his position — he changed the subject.

"How are you going to square this with your boss?" he asked.

"I've got half a dozen reasons why this isn't a stranger rape, Nick. Added to which, I've got a direct link to the tainted deals in my case, and the similarity between the whipping injuries. I'll square it."

"Look, Kate," he said, "If I'm brutally honest, I can't lose. Even if this goes no further, I'll have a new case study for my lectures, some good stats, a few photographs. But you —" He wasn't sure how to say it

181

without sounding patronizing. "You have to be sure you want this, because —"

"I know." Her eyes sparked, but he could see the uncertainty behind them. "If I mess this up, there's no coming back." She stubbed her toe against a loose cobblestone. After a few moments, she looked into his eyes again; this time he saw defiance and determination. "But I want this, Nick. I feel like I'm being played for a mug. All of this is connected — I know it is. I want to find out how, and I want to catch whoever did those things to the girl in the mortuary."

The ripple of emotion he'd seen in the Post-mortem Room again disturbed the stillness of her brown eyes. "He didn't just kill her, Nick — he annihilated her."

CHAPTER
EIGHTEEN

Detective Superintendent Spry was not easily convinced. He just wasn't sure he wanted the added complication of supervising Kate Simms in her first Category B murder investigation, especially coming straight after the short-lived glory of solving the penicillin deaths. His instinct, he said, was to quit while they were ahead. Someone else had already been tasked with the murder; he could arrange for them to talk, Kate could pass on her thoughts. It wasn't that he believed she couldn't do it, he told her, but she still had a lot on, what with the paperwork and this being her first major investigation flying solo.

Simms reminded him that she had spent three years at the National Crime Faculty, and *he* reminded *her* that her stint with the boffins hadn't exactly ended in bouquets and accolades. He added with a pitying smile that things had moved on in the four years she had spent cooling her heels on community partnership committees.

Simms argued that it was because of her that the excess overdoses in the review had been reclassified as manslaughter; that she had made the link between the drug deaths and the faceless corpse.

"In fairness," Spry said fastidiously, "it was the pathologist who made that connection."

"The pathologist called me because the DCI tasked with the investigation wasn't listening and he knew I would," she said, echoing Fennimore's words. "It was obvious the body was dumped, and the level of violence goes way beyond an opportunistic attack."

Spry gazed at her with weary patience. "Yes, well, now the investigating officer is aware, and if you leave it with him I'm sure he will —"

"Sir," she interrupted. This was her work — she wasn't going to just leave it with a stupid lazy dope who couldn't find his own arse with both hands. "How's it going to look," she said, "when it comes out that Greater Manchester Police failed to investigate the fact that the murder victim had the same drugs inside her as StayC and the rest?"

Spry bristled — ever since the embarrassing confrontation, news programmes had played clips of StayC's mother at the press conference, shouting, pointing her finger at Gifford, Spry beside him, alarmed, a cartoonish grimace on his face, fingers gripping the edge of the table. The same footage was shown when StayC's cause of death was given as penicillin allergy, and again after the arrest of Newton, the dealer.

"Your tone is offensive, Chief Inspector," he said, flushing angrily. "Moderate it."

"I'm sorry, sir," she said, "but the conspiracy theorists are still muttering about the death threats

184

against StayC. Ignore the drugs link to a violent murder and they'll start screaming 'cover-up'."

The colour seeped from his face as he thought about it. He agreed to talk to the investigating officer. He wasn't keen to share — even less keen to give the investigation away — but after two days of wrangling, a box file of case notes appeared on her desk and Kate Simms got the call to say that she had been allocated a Major Incident Room. An hour later, Dr Cooper emailed her his full post-mortem report with his good wishes.

Details of the investigation would be logged onto the Home Office Large and Major Enquiry System — HOLMES2. Every ambitious young detective relished their first HOLMES investigation — that word "Major" stood out as a career landmark — it was their opportunity to be noticed.

HOLMES had been in use across the UK for over twenty-five years, evolving to make best use of twenty-first-century computer technology. It was designed to organize, cross-reference, index and interrogate the many thousands of lines of inquiry that major investigations and disasters could generate.

"But the system is only as good as the information you put into it," Simms said, for the benefit of the newbies who didn't know better and the old hands who thought they did. "Garbage in, garbage out." She got nods of approval from the techs; her team of twenty included a HOLMES2 receiver, document manager and four indexers. "With good information, HOLMES2 can do a lot of things — it can narrow down a list of suspects, establish links between events and individuals, suggest new lines of inquiry." She spread her hands. "It can practically make you a nice brew after a hard day's canvassing, but *only* if you feed it clear, accurate, detailed information."

"Bear that in mind when you're knocking on a stranger's front door at the end of a long day, with your shoes soaked through and freezing cold rain dripping down the neck of your overcoat."

She waited a few more moments, allowed herself the first smile of the briefing. "Lecture over — let's get to work, shall we?"

She called up her first PowerPoint slide and projected it onto the screen behind her. In five minutes, she took them through the penicillin deaths and the arrest and confession of Anthony Newton, the dealer.

"Is it right he sold StayC the heroin that killed her?" someone asked.

"That's what it says in his confession."

She went on to summarize what they knew about the body found behind the city-centre hotel. Josh Brown had narrowed down the number of restaurants in the area serving seafood and meat combos to four. She wanted CCTV from the streets around all of them, and at both ends of the alley where the body was found. She set out a timetable for morning and evening briefings, and outlined the processes for reporting and task allocation, establishing Detective Sergeant Mark Renwick as their first point of contact. Renwick was trained in the use of the HOLMES system and had fifteen years' experience — the last seven on the drugs squad. He would double up as her HOLMES Room Action Manager and Office Manager. It would be his job to allocate tasks and make sure they were entered into the system promptly — which meant DS Renwick would have the overview of everything going on in the Incident Room.

"Stable Isotope Analysis gives the victim's country of origin as the Baltic States," Simms said. "Toenail and hair grow-out suggests she'd been in the UK eight to twelve months. She had DNA under her fingernails, but it doesn't match anything on the DNA database — so whoever it belongs to, they're either new to the UK or they have no criminal record."

This information had come minutes earlier from Nick Fennimore; he was back in Aberdeen, but ready to take her calls, anytime, he said. Reading his notes again, she remembered something.

"Ella, wasn't Rika from the Baltic States?"

Ella Moran checked the paperwork on her desk. "Yes, Boss." Ella sat side-on to her desk, plump in a plain white blouse and a dark grey trouser suit: the trousers wide to give her thighs room if she needed to run; the jacket boxy. Her hair, mousy brown and too fine to hold a barrette, was combed behind her ears.

Simms clicked to a post-mortem photograph of Rika's face. "Rika — we don't have a surname — died of a genuine overdose, so she's not on our list of penicillin deaths. She's linked to the murder because she'd submitted to some nasty S&M in the months before she died." The next slide showed the whip marks on Rika's buttocks, and there was a collective hiss from the team.

"I know," Simms said. "It's not pretty." She clicked to the next slide, a photograph of the murder victim, showing the same angry, painful-looking web of stripes. "This criss-cross pattern of injuries is highly unusual." She flicked back and forth between the images of Rika and the murder victim. "So unusual, in fact, that they were probably inflicted by the same person. Now, the whip marks on our murder victim were perimortem — she was flogged during the assault that killed her — which means whoever inflicted the injuries on Rika is probably our killer.

"Our murder victim had drugs in her even though she wasn't an addict. She may, however, have been a sex worker, like Rika. The composition of heroin in the murder victim was the same as we found in the penicillin deaths, which were all around Cheetham Hill — so she probably lived in the area. Maybe she knew Rika, maybe they worked together, or at least for the same massage parlour. Our killer could be a regular at one of the salons — maybe Rika even introduced our vic to the killer."

There was a murmur of excitement — this was a good, solid lead.

"We need to canvas massage parlours and saunas," she said. "Talk to the girls. Do they know anyone with a rep for this kind of thing? Has one of the girls gone missing in the last few days?"

Renwick shifted in his seat and cleared his throat diffidently.

"Sergeant?" she said.

"These girls move about a lot, and the physical description won't make it any easier." He dipped his head apologetically. "I mean, we've got a slim girl, mid-twenties, five seven tall, blonde hair, blue eyes." A slight grimace. "You could be describing about 90 per cent of the girls."

"So," she said, "we take it slowly and carefully, and we follow up every possible lead."

"Yes, ma'am, but —"

"They won't be keen to talk, and they might be wary about talking in front of their bosses or their peers," she said, cutting him short before his helplessness infected the rest of the team. "So hand out business cards, tell them they can call Crimestoppers, remain anonymous. Exercise tact." She looked at Renwick. "Do you think that will be a problem, Sergeant?"

"No," he said. "No, ma'am."

"Guv," she said. "You can call me Guv, or Boss, or Chief Inspector." She looked around at the shiny eager faces of her team. "I don't like to be called 'ma'am'. Clear?" She got an uneven chorus of, "Yes, Boss" and "Yes, Guv".

Simms wrapped up the meeting a few minutes later. On her way out, she glanced at Renwick. "My office, Sergeant," she said.

She sat behind her desk and left him standing.

"Look, Boss, I didn't mean to piss on your parade back there, I was just —"

"You're an experienced officer, Sergeant Renwick," she interrupted. "You must know how important morale is in any investigation, especially one with as much stacked against it as this one."

She riffled through a stack of papers in her in-tray and placed in front of him the sloppy, incomplete statement he had taken from Jordan Fitch.

"Jordan Fitch is an addict," Simms said. "Her sister — who, by the way, was not a serious user — was one of the penicillin victims. Jordan watched her little sister asphyxiate. She remembered every detail. Said she'd told the same story to the officer who took her witness statement."

"Sorry, Boss," he said, "I don't . . .?"

He didn't even recognize the name.

"Read it," she said. "Tell me what's missing."

She watched and waited for him to make the connection. At first she saw bewilderment, then concern. A fraction of a second later, he saw his name as co-signatory, and he blurted out, "Oh, sh—"

"It's like I said — garbage in, garbage out," she said. "If you'd bothered to listen to Jordan, the tainted drugs could've been off the street months ago. Lives could have been saved."

He closed his eyes briefly and hung his head. When he opened them again, the whites showed a panicked urgency. "Boss, I —"

She raised a finger. "Stop. I don't want excuses or self-justification. I expect you to do your job, because that's what you're paid to do. Okay?"

"Yes, ma'am — uh, I mean yes, Boss," he stammered.

"I expect you to be thorough, efficient and precise. I expect you to be an example to every individual out there. Are we clear?"

"Yes, Boss."

"All right," she said, "you can go."

He turned to leave, but at the door he hesitated, spun on his heel and stood to attention. "Boss, I messed up — big time," he said. "I'm sorry. It won't happen again."

Taken aback, for a few seconds she eyed him suspiciously. He flushed under her stare, but held her gaze.

"The younger members of the team will look to you for guidance," she said. "Don't let them down."

He braced up. For a second she thought he might salute, then her mobile phone rang and she glanced away to take it out of her desk drawer. When she looked again, he was gone.

CHAPTER
NINETEEN

"Action is the antidote to despair."

JOAN BAEZ

It was 11p.m. Nick Fennimore sat at his office desk, waiting for Kate Simms to Skype. He drummed his fingers on the mouse pad, checked that the volume on his laptop was turned up, took a sip of coffee, discovered a crusting of mould on its surface. He set it to one side, picked up the hot coffee he'd just prepared and sipped that.

Still no call. He tapped the mouse pad, just to be sure, paced to the window and watched the sleety rain hiss against his office window for a few minutes. He stopped himself in the act of checking the volume setting on his computer again, realizing his impatience wasn't about the case, it was about Kate Simms's call.

He shook his head and returned to the window to watch the slushy mix of ice and water melt. Rivulets formed and merged and changed direction, and he tried to predict patterns in the seemingly random tracks on the windowpane.

At 11.23, the two-note alert tone sounded and he sat at his computer.

"Sorry about the delay," she said. "The debrief went on for a bit, and I wanted to check a few details before I spoke to you." She was seated at a desk, the window behind her a square of black, the wash of cold fluorescent light from above casting shadows under her eyes. "Have I kept you from anything important?"

Since his return, Fennimore had spent his days lecturing, his evenings brooding. Thinking about Kate's four-year-old son, working for a few hours on the aged-up image of his daughter. He was on the point of launching the picture onto the web a dozen times, but every time he had aborted at the last second. He knew about the con artists who trawled for people like him, hoping to turn a profit from others' misery. Sometimes it seemed that his notoriety made him a prime target for every new-age crystal fumbler, seer and pendulum dowser on the planet. They would turn up at his book signings with a dream, or a map already felt-tipped with a search grid that was sure to lead him to his daughter. Sometimes shy, tremulous, hypersensitive, sometimes steady-eyed and solemn, they fell into two broad categories: well-intentioned but deluded, and the worst kind of manipulative.

So, he filed the new version of fifteen-year-old Suzie safely on his laptop and trawled the net himself, looking at missing persons sites and forums, getting nowhere, the trail being too old, far too cold.

But Simms didn't need to know any of that, so he told her he'd been marking students' scripts and working on a book outline — which was true, at least in part — you could get a lot done if you only slept four hours a night.

"What've you got?" Fennimore asked. She had left a message on his voicemail that afternoon, requesting the Skype conversation. "It sounded urgent."

"We've been hammering the local saunas and massage parlours for the past three days," she said. "Nothing. Then we get a tip-off via Crimestoppers — a local sauna owner — seen with blood on him the night of the murder, scratches on his face and hands.

"Claims he'd had a skinful — can't even remember getting home. I've fast-tracked his DNA profile. And we've already got a match from his dentition to the bite marks on the victim."

Fennimore recalled the purplish marks on the victim's body, blooming under the pathologist's forensic light, like invisible ink on a page.

"We also found a smashed phone in a sewer directly outside his place."

"The victim's?"

"We don't know; it's been raining here since you left on Sunday night, so it's been under water and gunk since then. The SIM card is gone."

"What about the IMEI?" The IMEI number would enable them to trace the phone back to the factory that produced it and — with luck — from there to the service provider.

"If I had that," she said, "I'd be listening to the answerphone messages right now, mapping out a timeline and list of suspects from the phone log and contacts."

194

"Tetchy," he said.

"Tired," she countered. "Sorry." She swept a hand over her face. "The IMEI has been scratched out."

"That doesn't mean it's irretrievable."

"Nick, there's nothing *to* retrieve."

"It might appear that way, but, hear me out. In most new mobile phones, the number is on what looks like a piece of paper, stuck to the main housing, behind the battery."

"I *know* that." Irritation was etched between her brows. "But as I said, the paper —"

"But it's not just paper," he interrupted. "It's a laminate. The paper is sealed behind a bonded plastic sheet. Scratch it, it can look like you've destroyed the number, but it's only the plastic you've destroyed."

She nodded, looking brighter. "I'll send it to the lab tonight."

"They might look for DNA, too. I know, it's been under water," he added hastily, "I was listening — but skin cells can get trapped in seams in the casing and saliva spray carries buccal cells which can lodge in the mic hole. It's an outside chance, but it would give you a definite match to your victim."

"Okay," she said. "I'll give it a try."

"What d'you know about sauna guy?"

"George Howard," she said. "There isn't much *to* know. He's been in the business for six months, maybe a bit longer. No arrests, no convictions."

"So, not on the DNA database. Unusual, in his line of work."

"Until recently, he was an accountant with the National Audit Office. When the NAO got canned, he decided to invest his redundancy payout in a business venture."

"Well, that's the British entrepreneurial spirit for you."

"The local Field Information Development Officers have been monitoring him, on and off, since last autumn. He's not doing badly for a start-up business in the current economic climate; covert surveillance shows a steady flow of punters, and he's hiring new girls all the time."

"But he hasn't fallen foul of the law, till now?"

She shook her head. "His website is carefully worded: customer pays for the room and companionship — anything else is the choice of consenting adults. He's operating out of a large detached Edwardian house in Cheetham Hill. Discreet signage, parking around the back. There's a veterinary practice on one side and a solicitor's office on the other — so no neighbours to upset. His private accommodation is on the ground floor, the girls' rooms on the upper floors. He also has the basement rigged out as a dungeon. Scientific Support have already taken away a variety of whips and riding crops."

"Any link to the tainted heroin?" he asked.

"They've turned up a small quantity of drugs in the rooms: speed, Viagra, cocaine, a few tabs of E. No heroin — and not enough of the rest to charge him with supplying."

"Careful man."

"Accountant," she said, as if that explained everything. "And National Audit Office, too. Which makes me wonder why he'd dump a body halfway across town —"

"And ditch the phone a few short steps from where he lives. It does seem odd, doesn't it? You'd think a man like that would be a meticulous planner."

"You would," she said. "I could really do with some psychological insights from your Professor Varley, but he's in back-to-back meetings in London till Thursday and my boss tells me that ACC Gifford wants 'A swift resolution and efficient use of resources' — and you know what Gifford thinks about my use of resources."

He knew all right: "Wasteful, irresponsible, a wanton misuse of taxpayers' money," Gifford had said of their unofficial investigation into Rachel's death.

Simms nodded, seeing the unspoken words in his face. "We'll know if it's sauna guy under the victim's fingernails by tomorrow morning. And if it is, I'll be under pressure to charge him. You know how this works, Nick — if I charge him, I won't be able to question him. I already lost the dealer that way, I don't want to lose this guy."

"But you've got ninety-six hours to question him without charge."

"Not without a Magistrate's Extension," she said. "Which my superintendent would have to request, and since he thinks the dental match to the bites is proof of guilt, that's just not going to happen." She sat back in her chair and for a moment her face blurred.

"This whole thing smacks of nomination," Fennimore said, bitterly. "Find your suspect, build a case, send him down."

She puffed air between her lips. "What can I tell you? It's hard to argue with six and a half billion in spending cuts. They're a gift to men like Gifford. They prove he was right all these years — it really *is* all about the bottom-line."

Fennimore was silent for a while. "What d'you need from me, Kate?"

She took a breath. "I've sent Professor Varley the files; he's agreed to look them over and we'll meet here in Manchester, Thursday afternoon. I need to buy more time to question Howard and gather evidence, which means convincing my superintendent that Howard might be a sleaze, but that doesn't necessarily make him a killer. It'll take more than slight inconsistencies in the PM findings to persuade him that there could be another assailant. And if there are other suspects, I need to identify them fast." She stopped and stared straight out of the monitor at him. "Nick, I need you here."

He hesitated, but he was already wondering who he needed to speak to, to enable Josh to coordinate the forwarding of lab analyses to him, simultaneously working out the earliest scheduled flight to Manchester in the morning.

CHAPTER
TWENTY

"Every contact leaves a trace . . ."

EDMUND LOCARD

". . . But the tricky bit is finding the contact points and recovering the trace."

PROFESSOR NICK FENNIMORE

Fennimore's plane touched down in Manchester at eight twenty. Kate Simms was waiting for him, looking trim in a skirt suit, the jacket nipped in at the waist.

"Thanks for coming," she said, talking fast, already heading for the exit. "We're in the short stay. You're at the Midland again, yes? We'll talk as I drive. I'll have to drop you at the hotel and run — I've delayed the briefing till 9.30, but I can't keep them waiting any longer than that."

"Hey, slow down, take a breath," he said.

She smiled, slowing her pace a little. "Sorry, I've been running on caffeine since this kicked off."

"That's okay. Just don't have an aneurism — I'm rusty on my first-aid skills."

They crossed to the short-stay car park with jets screaming overhead, the sun bright and the air crisp and cold under a clearing sky.

On the first floor of the multi-storey, she pointed her remote key at her Mondeo. "I've put together a file for you. I'll update you as we drive." She opened the car boot and Fennimore dumped his tote bag, keeping hold of the laptop in case he needed it during their impromptu meeting.

She reached to slam the boot lid and he caught a flash of red on the collar of her blouse.

"Cut yourself shaving?" he asked.

"What?"

He indicated on his own shirt and she pinched her collar between finger and thumb, tugging the fabric and squinting down at the damage. "Jam. Oh, Tim . . ." she groaned. "I *really* haven't got time for this."

She ducked into the boot and dragged a small vanity case to the front. "You go ahead — file's on the dashboard." A second later, the rear passenger door opened and she slid into the seat behind him.

He turned just as she finished stripping off her blouse. "See anything of interest?" She twitched her eyebrows. "In the file, I mean."

He swivelled to the front, chastised, and picked up the buff folder. The file contained a bundle of documents and photos. The first photograph showed Howard's hands, palms down on a table, fingers splayed, scratches visible on both, bruises on the knuckles of the right.

"We've had the results," she said, pausing to curse her cuff buttons. "It's his DNA from the swabs of the bites, his DNA under her fingernails."

The next image was a close-up of Howard's left hand. The scratches ran parallel from wrist to knuckles, ending in half-moon indents where the nails had found purchase and dug right in. The close-up of his right hand showed abrasions and bruises on the knuckles.

"We have CCTV footage — possibly the victim — climbing into an unidentified car near Livebait restaurant on Lloyd Street in the city centre at 10 p.m. last Thursday." By now, Simms was behind the wheel. "Male driving — photo's in the file." She had the key in the ignition and pulled out of the bay before he found the picture.

It was raining heavily. A woman sheltering under an umbrella was leaning to open the passenger door of a sleek BMW. Someone had tried to sharpen the image, but rain and reflections from the road made it impossible to see anything more clearly defined than a hulking shape at the steering wheel.

"Partial index," he said, tilting the picture to get a better look. A taxi parked at the kerb had cut off the last three letters of the number plate.

"Yep." She spun the steering wheel, turning onto the down ramp like a rally driver, and he slapped his hand onto the stack of pictures as they shifted on his lap. "MA12 — which covers cars registered for the first time in Manchester and Merseyside between March and August 2012. The DVLA sent a list. D'you know how many hits we got?"

"A lot?"

"A lot." She shoved her credit card into the slot at the barrier and rested her arm on the window frame, her fingers twitching, practically beckoning the machine to return the card.

"I don't suppose the partial matches Sauna Guy's car?"

"Cars," she said. "Plural. A Mercedes, a Mini Countryman as a runabout, a twelve-year-old Volvo estate — and, yes, a Beamer. No match to the index." She lifted one shoulder as if to say, *But number plates can be faked.*

"The Volvo is interesting," Fennimore said. "The other cars scream conspicuous consumption, but a turn-of-the-century Volvo?"

"Apparently he keeps that as a reminder of what he could afford to drive as a more 'respectable' member of society."

"Hm . . ." he said. "A Volvo estate's also a more practical choice for body disposal."

"Well, if he did use it to dump the body, he hasn't left a single trace — in that, or any of the cars."

"Disappointing, or possibly telling."

"Meaning that he didn't do it?"

"I wouldn't go that far — he could've used an accomplice's car."

"*If* he had an accomplice. Again, there's no physical evidence pointing to that."

Fennimore looked again at the picture. "This could be our victim," he said. She was long-legged, and showed them off in a thigh-length skirt. The shadow of the woman's umbrella sliced diagonally across her face, catching only a tantalizing glimpse of short blonde hair and an eye.

"What about the restaurant staff?" Fennimore asked.

"One of the waiters remembers her. Slim, early twenties, pale blonde, blue eyes — *gorgeous* blue eyes, he said — elegant, foreign-sounding."

"And her companion?"

"Big bloke, older than her," she said.

"That's it?"

"I think his attention was elsewhere. He did say her companion was a lousy tipper."

"Very useful." A thought flashed into his head, but Simms anticipated the question.

"Before you ask — he paid cash."

"Big Bloke likes his anonymity." He stared at the dark blur in the car.

"Mr Howard — Sauna Guy, if you like — is small and rather slight. And he was drinking in the Derby Brewery Arms, a mile up the road, from nine till midnight. Landlord confirms."

By now, they were on the M56 motorway, barrelling towards the city.

"She died about four hours after the meal," Fennimore said. "She could easily have met Sauna Guy between midnight and 2a.m. Or she could have gone with this man —" he tapped the photo "— and Sauna Guy joined them later. Or she could have been murdered by somebody else entirely."

"Yup," she said. "That's a bloody great hole we've got in our timeline."

Fennimore read in silence for a few minutes, checking the lab reports on the swabs, trying to think of a way to fill that hole. As he sifted through the photographs a second time, he realized there was something missing.

"I can't see any CCTV images for the hotel."

"We didn't get any," she said. "There's a blind spot on the street cams both ends of the alley."

"That's a happy coincidence for the killer."

"Local knowledge again," she said.

"What about the phone? Anything back from that yet?"

"The lab's working on the DNA from the phone mic, and I'm still waiting on the IMEI number."

"We need those phone records, Kate. They could tell us who she is, who she knows, even where she was on the night she died."

She speeded past a slow-moving lorry and jinked left onto the off-ramp. From here it was a straight run all the way down to the Mancunian Way.

"I know that," she said. "I've got Sergeant Renwick chasing it. But we can't rely on the phone, Nick. We have a suspect who can't account for his actions or whereabouts — the DNA tells us he was with her — but did he kill her?"

Fennimore cocked his head. "If I approached this using Bayes, I'd be looking at the likelihood he *didn't* do it."

"That's a given," she said dryly. "What I need to know is what we should be looking at, evidentially."

"Contact points."

She shook her head. "We already looked at contact points — the lab results were inconclusive. We got a mixed profile from anal swab — not good enough for a match — and semen in stomach, but the DNA was destroyed by stomach acid."

He looked out of the window. They passed winter woods and retail parks which quickly gave way to a mix of Victorian red-brick houses, tight against the street, and jaundice-yellow new-build maisonettes, their backs set to the roadway.

"Okay. The digested semen in her stomach tells us that she must have had oral sex, perhaps before dinner or just after," he began slowly, working it out as he spoke. "Something might have lodged behind her teeth — you should ask for dry swabs of the back of her incisors."

She shook her head. "Cooper was right — there was too much blood in the mouth — it destroyed the semen evidence."

"Semen is mostly liquid — easy to dilute, easy to wash away," Fennimore countered. "With a dry swab, you're looking for epithelial cells."

"From the penis," she said.

"They stick well to the teeth, and the backs of teeth best of all."

She nodded.

"It might be worth taking an external swab of the perineum, too. Same reason: during sex — consensual or otherwise — the perineum is the most likely place for skin-to-skin contact."

"Even if the assailant wore a condom?"

"Even if."

"Okay."

He knew they were approaching the hotel as the density of sandstone railway bridges and warehouses increased. He leafed through the paperwork, studying the reports more closely. "The lab found nothing of interest on his clothing, but they did find her blood on his shoes?"

She shrugged. "They always keep the shoes."

He nodded. "I'd like to know exactly where the blood was found," he said. "Is it in the seams, on the laces, on the toe-caps? Was it dripped? Is it transfer, or is it spatter? We need to know exactly how it got there."

"Okay, you'll have it."

He reached the end of the reports and then turned back the pages, thinking he must have missed something.

"What?" she said.

"Odd, there's no trace at his massage parlour."

"Oh, there's plenty of *trace*," she said, with a grimace. "Just nothing from her." She took a sharp left after the GMex centre and skimmed neatly onto the cobbled paving of the hotel's drop-off point.

"He might have taken her elsewhere, I suppose," Fennimore mused. "But it is odd . . ."

Simms checked her watch and her fingers began tapping nervously on the steering wheel. The car was still in gear and she hadn't even engaged the handbrake. "I'll talk to Cooper about those additional swabs," she said and, when he still didn't move: "I'll email you as soon as I have anything."

He wasn't listening. "I mean, why would he take her somewhere else, when he has a torture room in-house?

And if he *did* use his own torture room, how is it he managed a forensically thorough clean-up, yet carelessly dropped her phone down a drain outside his own house?"

Simms's fingers stilled and she turned to him. "You think he was deliberately set up?"

He gave her a pained look.

She rolled her eyes. "Let me guess: you're not ready to make that assessment until you have more evidence."

He grinned. "You read me like a book."

"Yeah," she said. "A textbook. With complicated maths and tables, and smart-arsed questions at the end of every chapter."

She waited for him to get his tote bag from the boot, then zipped off before he had a chance to say goodbye, leaving him at the drop-off point with his tote bag at his feet and the file and his laptop tucked under one arm. He smiled to himself, watching her tail lights flash once, before she scooted right into Mount Street.

As he shouldered his bag, a car swerved out from behind a delivery van and followed her, accelerating fast.

CHAPTER
TWENTY-ONE

Detective Superintendent Tanford was standing in front of the whiteboards as Kate Simms entered the Major Incident Room. Post-mortem photos of their unidentified victim had been Blu-tacked to the board and he was studying them intently. Around him, the office was a scene of quiet activity. The HOLMES2 operatives were corralled off in one corner of the room, behind office dividing screens, where they could get on undisturbed with the exacting task of accurately logging the hundreds of items of data that came in every day.

It was after 9 a.m., and the majority of Simms's team had already put in an hour and a half of work. Those who had been out canvassing had begun drifting back in, ready for the briefing. They carried machine-dispensed coffee cups and plastic-wrapped sandwiches, or pastries in lieu of breakfast.

She nodded in greeting to a few as she walked to the far side of the room.

Tanford continued his scrutiny of the board, feet planted squarely a foot apart, hands on his hips, but as she reached his side, he said, "Funny how things can change overnight, isn't it? I mean last week you were Cinderella, sweeping up the fag ends of other people's parties, and now . . . I heard you'd bagged this one off DCI Anders." He laughed softly. "Must've had to arm-wrestle him for it — all that extra overtime his lot will have to forgo."

She didn't comment.

He let his hands drop and turned to face her. "Well, the important thing is, you got your man — again."

"You got the dealer, sir."

He slid her a sidelong glance. "Not still sore about that, are you, Kate?"

"I'm sorry, sir, I don't think I know what you —"

He waved away her awkward protestations. "Come on, Kate. You wanted to solve StayC and the ODs all by yourself — of course you're pissed off." He chuckled. "I know I would be."

"Well, we're all on the same side," she offered, thinking she'd need to work on her poker face.

"That's the spirit," he said, still smiling. "Anyway, you can claim this one all for yourself." He jerked his head towards the board, and the photographs of their murder victim.

She grimaced. "Not really."

"No?"

"A tip-off from Crimestoppers," she said. "You might say it fell right into my lap."

"We all need the odd bit of good luck to get the job done, Kate. But as Louis Pasteur said, 'Chance favours the prepared mind'. You're having an impact — getting yourself noticed by people who matter. Some think you've been badly treated since Crime Faculty; the way you handled the review — and now this nasty murder — shows what you're really capable of."

Her pulse quickened. Did she dare hope, after five years, that she was shaking off the "untrustworthy" tag?

"Gifford's not quite sure how he feels about it, of course — but you know what? Fuck him, and his brand of policing by tick-box." He stopped, looked down at her. "I've shocked you."

"No, sir, I —"

"No," he said. "I've put you on the spot — I should be ashamed of myself. Wasn't I the one who told you half of this job is handling the politics?"

She shot him a sly look. "I believe you said nine-tenths."

A smiled twitched the corner of his mouth. "Well, 70 per cent of all quoted statistics are made up on the spot."

"Is that right?"

"No idea — I just made it up." He frowned in mock exasperation. "And what exactly do I have to do to get you to call me Tanno?"

"Nothing — Tanno." She smiled. "It's just going to take some getting used to."

He gave her a comical look. "Fair enough." He stared at her for a few seconds longer, as if he found her a puzzle. "So, what gave you the connection between your murder and StayC and the ODs?"

"Composition of the heroin," she said.

"Our paths do seem destined to cross, don't they?" He chuckled, turning to scrutinize the board again. A post-mortem photograph of "Rika" was tacked next to the murder victim, below it, another, showing the bruises and the waffle effect of the riding crop on her buttocks. Tanford planted the broad pad of his index finger dead centre of the picture. "Who's this?"

"Overdose," she said.

He glanced down at her. "So?"

The noise of conversation behind them told her the team was almost ready for the briefing, but Tanford had offered her his support and friendship and she didn't want to rebuff him by letting him know he was in the way. So she delayed checking her watch, and answered his unspoken question.

"They're up there for comparison, sir."

He tilted his head in question.

"The whip marks — they're similar to the murder victim's."

She saw him work it through in his mind, and finally, he shook his head and turned back to the pictures. "If you're hoping to link back to earlier assaults, you'd have to prove the whipping was non-consensual. Prostitutes will do just about anything to feed a drug habit. Anyway, most of these girls are so off their faces I doubt they'd reliably identify Howard."

She wondered if she should confide in him — tell him her doubts about the tip-off.

He seemed to sense her hesitation and studied her closely. "Unless you're thinking this Rika will lead you to someone else. You don't believe Howard is the killer, is that it?"

"I don't know, sir. But I'd feel happier if I knew where Howard went after the pub on the night of the murder."

"You've got his DNA under her fingernails. His teeth marks on her body. How do you explain that if he *didn't* do it?"

"I haven't made my mind up either way, sir," she said, adding reluctantly, "But there are anomalies — a gap in the timeline; no trace of the victim at his premises; none of his girls knows her." She'd already been through this with Superintendent Spry, but she sensed that Tanford would give her a more sympathetic hearing, and although he had no say in how the investigation was run, he had already proved a good ally.

He nodded, encouraging her to go on.

"The pathologist is sure this woman *wasn't* an addict; and why the hell would the killer strip the body, yet leave a wrap of drugs right next to it?"

"Why indeed." He gazed up at the ceiling and smiled. "I must admit, that one's got me completely foxed. I suppose DCI Anders would have labelled it 'murder of a hooker with a habit', and let it be. She's lucky she got you."

He glanced at the room; a few were observing them surreptitiously. Tanford took her elbow and turned her in towards the notice board, away from the curious eyes of her team. "But your resources are limited, Kate. You need to build the best case you can with the evidence you've got."

212

"I agree, sir. But only after we've gathered all the evidence available."

"Kate, you're looking for a connection between this Rika and your murder vic because they were both flogged — that's not evidence, it's wild supposition."

"No, sir — I'm looking for a connection because their injuries are *distinctive*."

"Well, I don't know who you're getting your info from, but I'd be careful of getting too hung up on this." He flicked one of the photographs with a fingernail, suddenly exasperated. He seemed to collect himself, and went on more calmly, "You'll always have men who like to inflict pain on women, Kate. And you'll always have women who are willing to let them. There's nothing 'distinctive' about that."

Without solid stats on the injuries from the National Injuries Database, Simms wasn't willing to tell him he was wrong, but she did feel the need to defend herself, so she said, "The forensic pathologist said it's the criss-cross pattern that makes it unusual."

He moved in closer to the board so that he could get a better look. "Is that so . . ." He traced the lines on the photograph. "This pathologist wouldn't happen to be David Cooper, would it?"

"Yes," she said, on her guard now.

"Little man. Cuban heels?" He smiled to himself. "You know his motto — 'If you can't autopsy it — screw it.'" He laughed. "Well, you know little men."

She faced him, feeling suddenly — and completely irrationally — defensive on the pathologist's behalf. "I don't believe I do."

He scratched his forehead and looked contrite. "Sorry — really — that was uncalled for. It's just — I'm having a hard time following your logic."

Simms wasn't about to explain herself again. This time she did check her watch, and made sure he saw it.

"I'm holding you up," he said. "I barge in here and mess up your schedule — questioning your decisions — and I know you're not answerable to me. I'll understand if you bar me out of here from now on. But I just want to say one more thing and then I'm out of your hair. Okay?"

She thought about it. "If it takes thirty seconds or less."

He nodded, and now he seemed completely serious. "People are expecting good things of you, Kate, but it's easy to get hooked up on the seedier details of a case like this. That's not intended as any kind of criticism of you and, for all I know, you're the exception that tells the rule to go diddle itself. But, Kate, I've worked this kind of case more times than I'd care to admit, and I'm just warning you — it can happen."

Simms eyed him coolly. He seemed sincere, his concern genuine, and she felt she owed him an explanation for that, if nothing else.

"I've got someone checking the numbers on the cross-hatch wounds," she said. "And I've arranged a consultation with a forensic psychologist."

Simms half-expected him to tell her she was wasting her time and a slice of her budget, but he gave her an opaque look and said, "I've held you up. Apologies."

214

He strode from one end of the room to the other and people gave way to him. Simms called her crew to order and, while she waited for the noise to die down, she spread her notes out on a table next to the whiteboards. When she had silence she looked up. Tanford was standing in the doorway watching her. If she was pushed to it, she would have said that he looked disappointed.

He gave one sad shake of his head before he turned and left.

Simms listened to reports from the HOLMES manager, DS Renwick, the detective coordinating the trawl of massage parlours, and the two constables working through CCTV footage outside Livebait restaurant. CCTV had yielded nothing useful, there was no further information about Howard's whereabouts on the night of the murder, and none of his girls would admit to knowing the victim.

"The DNA says he was with her," Simms said. "Maybe his girls are too scared to speak out against Howard, or maybe they didn't know her because our victim was from another salon and she was seeing him on a try-out. Which would explain why they're being cagey, but not why we're drawing a blank at the other massage parlours."

Renwick seemed reluctant to speak, but when nobody else did, he cleared his throat. "Um, we're the cops, Boss," he said, a half-smile of apology on his face. "That's how it goes."

He was doing it again — telling them it was all too difficult, that they might as well give up. "Go back to the massage parlours," she said, trying to curb her irritation. "Make them understand that if they want us to go away, someone has to speak up. *That's* how it goes, Sergeant."

"Yep," he said, sitting up like she'd jabbed a sharp finger in his ribs. "Yes. Sure — yes, Boss."

She looked around at her team. "A case can turn on a single question — so you've got to keep asking. The more you ask, the better your chances of coming up with that big breakthrough. For instance, the pub landlord is sure Howard knew the men he was drinking with, so why does Howard swear otherwise?"

Renwick glanced uneasily at the constable next to him. "He's a liar?"

"Everyone lies, Sergeant. But why would Howard lie about the two people who might be able to alibi him?"

Renwick shrugged, at a loss.

"Maybe it's because they *can't* alibi him," she said. "Or maybe Howard is protecting his drinking buddies. And who was our victim's dinner partner; why hasn't he come forward?"

"Sorry, Boss." Renwick again, avoiding her gaze, but determined to speak. "We don't know if the girl in the picture *is* our victim and, if she is, this guy paid for her company by the hour — there's any number of reasons why he wouldn't want to hold his hand up to that."

"Good — fair comment on both points." Now he was thinking. "But we still need to eliminate him from the inquiry, and if he won't come to us, we need to find him."

"How're we supposed to —?"

"The mobile phone — if it's hers. Do we know that yet?"

He frowned at the paperwork on his desk. "Not yet, Boss. The lab's working on the DNA. We'll have the results by the end of the day. They say the identity number's a bit trickier."

She stared at him until he met her gaze, gave him a look that said, *Do you really think I care what they say?*

"I'll get on to them," he said. "Right away."

Fifteen minutes later, the briefing over, tasks allocated, Simms called Howard's solicitor to let her know that she would be interviewing her client. Thirty minutes after, having caught up on a wodge of paperwork, she headed down to the interview suite.

Renwick appeared, breathless, outside the interview room, a panicked look on his face. The custody sergeant must have warned him.

"Boss," he said. "I know I got off to a bad start, but I swear, when I interviewed Howard, I was thorough."

"I read your interview notes, Sergeant — the interview was fine."

A custody officer approached from the opposite direction, walking slightly behind Howard.

"So why —?" Renwick nodded towards the prisoner. Howard's solicitor arrived — a woman — attractive, perhaps mid-twenties, from one of the more expensive law firms in the city. They shook hands, the custody officer standing by Howard's elbow.

"It's like I said, you've got to keep asking questions."

"I can do that," Renwick said. "You've got enough on, and anyway, best to have continuity in the interview process, eh?" He smiled, but couldn't keep the note of pleading out of his voice.

He was right, on all counts — Simms's job as senior investigation officer was to administer, direct, guide and manage her team. Interviews were not typically conducted by officers of her rank — taking over from Renwick could reflect badly on him.

Howard was deep in conversation with his solicitor. "Take a look," she said. "Tell me what you see."

He was standing too close to his lawyer, touching her arm, her shoulder, to emphasize his point. And when the solicitor stepped away, polite but strained, he closed the gap again.

"He's a bit touchy-feely," Renwick said.

"I bet he requested a female solicitor," she said. "Trying to make us believe his regard for women isn't all about what goes on between the sheets."

"Oh," Renwick said, "you think he'll let his guard down with a female interviewer?"

"I think he'll judge me by my looks, Sergeant."

Renwick's quick appraising glance was unintentional, purely reflex. Simms arched an eyebrow, and he flushed and apologized.

She smiled. "It's all right. But you see what I mean?"

She was about to move on, but he spoke again: "Uh, Boss — what you said about the girls being scared . . ."

She nodded, encouraging him to go on.

"Made me think. I asked around and —" He passed a sheaf of papers to her. "Well, you might want to have a look at this before you go in."

Simms skimmed the text. "This is good work, Sergeant," she said, and Renwick fought to keep the smile off his face. "This could give me exactly the leverage I need."

CHAPTER
TWENTY-TWO

George Howard wore Italian wool trousers, slip-on shoes of polished leather and a casual maroon shirt under a matching cashmere sweater — bought new by his solicitor, under his instruction, after his clothing was seized by Scientific Support.

DCI Simms stared at him. All that red, and yet he was still grey. Grey hair, dull grey eyes, an ash-grey shadow of growth on his chin.

"Before we begin," his solicitor said, "my client would like to make a statement."

Simms felt a slight tingle of excitement in her chest. Had he remembered something from the night of the murder? She couldn't read anything in his face, and he avoided her eye, spreading his fingers on the table and staring instead at the healing scars on the backs of his hands.

"All right," she said. "I'm listening."

He cleared his throat and began, raising his voice slightly, as if he was addressing a seminar. "I run a successful business," he said. "Current footfall stands at around six visitors per hour. I charge twenty-five for the room per half-hour. Factoring in parties and seasonal specials like the Santa's Helpers extravaganza last

220

Christmas, and the Chocolate Indulgence weekend I'm planning for Easter —"

"Spare me the infomercial," she cut in.

"Very well." His tone became brisk. "I'm currently averaging a turnover of fifteen thousand a week. In my first year of trading, including the parties, I estimate pre-tax results of around 850 K." He leaned forward, linking his scarred hands on the tabletop. "Think about it, Chief Inspector. Why would I jeopardize that?"

Why indeed, she thought. "And yet you were seen with blood on your clothing the night of the murder."

"An anonymous tip-off," the solicitor's tone said, *anyone can accuse . . .*

"You have scratches on your left hand that look like defensive wounds and abrasions on your right that look like you punched someone or something — hard," Simms went on.

He curled his fingers and drew them back towards his body.

"How does that square with your daily footfall and your average weekly turnover and your pre-tax results?" She replayed in her head what she'd just said, and did a double take. "Wait a minute — you're planning to pay tax?"

"Of course I'll pay tax," he said, shocked. "It's the law."

She almost laughed. "Is that what they teach you at accountancy school? You don't need to complicate your life with inconvenient concepts like morality, just so long as you obey the letter of the law?"

His flat grey eyes held hers for the first time. "I was like you once," he said. "When I was young enough to still feel self-righteous about such things. As an auditor, I played by the rules and worked for the common good. I uncovered misspending and poor accounting and even a few high-profile frauds, and I saved millions of pounds of taxpayers' money. Millions. Shall I tell you my reward, after twenty-six years of playing by the rules, Chief Inspector?" His mouth twisted, as though he'd felt a sharp pain. "A redundancy notice. Three days before my fifty-second birthday." He shook his head, the memory obviously still raw.

"So to hell with the common good," she said. "But hey, you pay your taxes, which makes you a model citizen, right?"

He shrugged. "It makes me someone who plays the rules to his advantage." He looked at her. "Tell me you've never done that."

She hesitated and as he eyed her, curious, she tried not to think about the lies and the half-truths she had told her superintendent only that morning.

"I thought so," he said with a satisfied nod. "I provide a service. Comfortable, clean surroundings, fair treatment. My ladies don't get ripped off — by me or their . . ." His eyes drifted away for a moment, as he searched for the right word.

"Punters," she said.

"Companions," he countered, his eyes fixed on her again.

"Let's talk about the eight hours between midnight last Thursday, and the following morning, Mr Howard."

His eyelids flickered and he looked quickly away. "I told your sergeant everything I know."

"I doubt it."

"I am not a violent man, Chief Inspector," he told the tabletop.

"Really?" she said. "You're sticking by that story?"

"It isn't a story."

"Think hard, Mr Howard." His head was still down, so she fixed her gaze on his crown, wishing she could shine a light inside his skull, see what he was hiding, because he was hiding something. She was sure of it.

He stared at the backs of his hands, a frown of concentration on his face, and she could almost see him riffling through the efficient storage and retrieval systems of his memory.

"You maintain that you have never violently assaulted a woman?"

His eyes flicked up to hers, alarmed, and she placed an arrest sheet in front of him — the paperwork Renwick had given to her outside the interview room.

He glanced at the name on the sheet. "Chloe?"

His solicitor frowned: the name was obviously new to her. "George, perhaps we should —"

"She was bruised black from the chest down," Simms said.

He shook his head.

His solicitor sat forward, placing a hand on her client's arm. "George, I think we should speak in private."

Howard brushed her off. "I was never even charged."

Of course Simms knew that. If he had been charged, his DNA would already be on record.

"You're a practical man, Mr Howard. So maybe you paid her off, wrote it down as an operational expense."

His hands closed into fists. "That's *outrageous*." He'd missed the sarcasm entirely — more appalled by the suggestion that he would fiddle his expenses sheet than by the notion that he would beat a woman until her flesh was the colour of a ripe aubergine.

"George."

Howard finally turned to his solicitor. "Chloe was out of control. I struck her off my list after I found her passed out in one of the rooms, a hypodermic still in her hand. Some weeks later, her pimp boyfriend beat her up for withholding money from him."

Which is exactly what the file said. But Simms hadn't been looking for a confession — only to rattle him. She smiled and a muscle began to jump in his eyelid.

He pressed his fingers into his eye sockets to quell the tremor in his eyelid. "Look, I conduct three . . . interviews a week."

"Oh," she said. "Nice euphemism. Do you 'sample the goods' during these 'interviews'?"

He shot her a brief, disapproving look.

"Both the interviewees *and* the ladies already using my facilities are happy to allow the management to . . .

224

how shall I term it?" He gazed at a point a few inches above Kate Simms's left shoulder.

"Dip his wick?" she offered.

His eyes snapped to hers. "There's no need to be coarse."

"Hey, I've seen what's on offer on your website — don't lecture *me* about coarse."

He sucked in his cheeks and looked away again.

"For clarification," his solicitor said, "Mr Howard does not 'offer' anything on his website. The ladies state their preferences and specialities, which are on the website for illustration purposes only. What goes on behind closed doors is a private matter between consenting adults."

"Mr Howard just rents out the rooms by the half-hour. Yes, that's very helpful. Thank you," Simms said. "*For clarification*, perhaps Mr Howard can tell me who provides the condoms and the role-play costumes and the sex toys and triple-X-rated films? Oh, and let's not forget the Viagra — compliments of the house."

The solicitor began to speak, but Howard held up his hand. "Since you've seen the list of services, you will know that the range of experiences available is imaginative and comprehensive. And the young ladies —"

She huffed air through her nose at "ladies", interrupting his flow, but he persevered anyway: "The *ladies* in question are far from inhibited." He looked directly at her, defiant and unashamed. "I have a constantly changing roll call of twenty attractive girls willing to indulge my every whim, to cater to my wildest fantasy. Why would I need to use force?"

"For some men, use of force *is* the fantasy," she said.

He looked at her blankly.

"Oh, come on, Mr Howard — I've seen your Dungeon Room."

"That's for the clients. My predilections run in a different direction."

"So, tell me, Mr Howard — I'm interested — which way do your 'predilections' run?"

She had thought to rattle him a bit more, but he gave her a long, speculative look.

"I prefer blondes," he said, his eyes skimming her own brown hair.

"Blonde," she said. "Like the victim."

"Blondes with nice curves and large breasts. I like them chatty, bubbly, but not too assertive."

Another jibe at her. Time to nudge him off balance again.

"Tell me about the men you were drinking with at the pub." She saw something like panic behind his eyes, gone before she was sure it was there.

He rallied. "Now *your sergeant* likes brunettes. He —"

"We're talking about you, Mr Howard," she interrupted.

"I couldn't help noticing how he looked at you." There was a sharpness in Howard's eyes she hadn't seen before, like light reflecting off a knife blade.

"The landlord thought you knew the men."

"Your sergeant looks at you the way my clients look at the girls."

The solicitor leaned across her client, a look of alarm on her face. "George."

George Howard's eyes didn't flicker. "Detective Sergeant Renwick likes the athletic type. I can tell."

"The pub landlord says you arrived at the same time."

"They happened to arrive at the same time," the solicitor said. "That does not mean they were together."

Howard leaned back to get a better view of Simms. "You're quite athletic, yourself, Chief Inspector."

The solicitor tapped Howard's hand and muttered under her breath, "*George.*"

Howard twitched her hand away. "Would you like to know what he was thinking, while you were having your serious, professional conversation?"

"Why won't you tell us who you were drinking with on the night of the murder?"

He leaned forward across the table, a wicked grin on his face. "The one thing — the *only* thing — in Sergeant Renwick's mind was how you would look naked."

"That's *enough.*" Simms slammed the table with her hand and Howard flinched as though she'd slapped him.

Simms breathed hard through her nose, and the silence in the room felt loaded with meaning.

Finally, the solicitor said, "Mr Howard has made his statement: he fell into conversation with the two men. He doesn't know them. He doesn't know their names."

"I don't believe that," Simms said.

"I've told you everything I know," Howard said, avoiding her eye again.

"Not everything. You didn't drive that night. Why?"

"I went out for a drink. I didn't want to lose my licence. As I told you, I play by the rules."

"You went drinking on your own, with all those lovely women to choose from?"

He said nothing.

"Were you planning to meet someone?"

"I don't remember."

"The victim perhaps?"

"No."

"But you just said you don't remember, Mr Howard. How can you be so certain you weren't planning to meet the victim?"

He shook his head.

"Perhaps you met her later."

"No."

"Mr Howard," she said. "If you didn't know the victim, and you didn't meet her in the hours before her death, why is your DNA under her fingernails?"

"I don't know."

"Look at your hands, Mr Howard. Your skin is under her nails."

His face paled to the colour of salt.

"Why are the bites on the murdered woman's body a match to you?"

"I told you I —"

"You sank your teeth into her flesh, and you expect me to believe you don't remember?"

He flinched and screwed up his eyes as if against a sudden phosphor-flash. "Stop," he said.

"The place must have reeked of blood, and *you don't remember?*"

His eyes widened, and he stared past her with a look that almost made her turn to discover the horror that had melted through the walls to hover over her shoulder.

"Mr Howard?"

He shuddered and blinked down at the scrapes and scratches on the backs of his hands.

"Are you all right?"

Sweat beaded on his forehead like condensation on a glass, and he covered one hand with the other, thrusting them into his lap where they could not be seen.

"Is there something you want to say?" She looked at him, willing him to speak. "Something you want to tell me?"

He shook his head.

Simms kept her voice low and even. "Take your time." She waited and he looked like he wanted to spit in order to get a bad taste out of his mouth.

"I'd like some water," he said.

"In a moment."

"My client is requesting a break," the solicitor said.

Simms kept her eyes on Howard. "Did you remember something? Is that it?"

He shook his head.

"Mr Howard, look at me."

But he just shook his head again and swallowed, his Adam's apple bobbing convulsively. He stared at his hands in his lap and, in the silence, she heard a constant *tick, tick, tick,* as he picked at the scabs.

CHAPTER
TWENTY-THREE

The debrief was set for 8p.m., and many had arrived half an hour early to type up reports and complete task sheets. Those who had been canvassing saunas came in from the dark smelling of cold city air, and dripping with sleety rain, the ice still melting from the shoulder pads of their winter coats. Sergeant Renwick was the last to arrive, clipboard in hand.

"Okay, the sooner we get cracking, the sooner we can all go home," Simms said.

Renwick nodded to her and hurried to his desk.

"Who did the check on Rika?"

"Me, Boss." She located the detective who had spoken. He was slouched in his chair, a paunchy, grey-haired officer in his mid-fifties; the type who should have retired on an ordinary pension after twenty-five years' service, but was holding out for the better deal guaranteed by doing the full thirty.

"Do you have an actual name, or d'you just go by 'Me'?"

He sat up. "Beasley, Boss."

"Well, Detective Constable Beasley?"

He raised his shoulders. "Nothing to report, Boss," he said.

"Really?" She stared at him. "Nothing? So, what, you wandered the streets calling her name, and nobody answered, is that it?"

He shuffled in his seat. "I spoke to people — nobody'd heard of her."

She nodded. "People. Is that what you're going to write in your report?" He gave her the truculent look of a teen, unfairly picked on, but didn't answer. "*Who* did you speak to? *Names*, Constable. *Where* did you speak to them? *When?*"

One of the younger officers opened his notebook and began surreptitiously reading over his notes, which was exactly what Simms intended.

"Details, Constable," she said.

Beasley suddenly realized that she wasn't going to let him off the hook, and began thumbing through his notebook.

"Um . . . I haven't had a chance to type it up yet, but . . ." He found the relevant pages and gave her a list of locations and names.

Most were street names of working girls — a lot of them would be false, but that wasn't the point — she was sending a message that she would not accept sloppy work.

"Times?" she said.

"Between about two and five, Boss," he said.

"Hm." She looked at him. "So, if one of the girls works a particular street corner at a particular time, and we need to speak to her again, you expect one of your colleagues to hang around for *three hours* because

232

you couldn't be bothered to write down the exact time?"

"No, Boss." He frowned at his notebook as if furious with it for letting him down.

Simms didn't want to crush him — or make the rest of the team afraid to speak up — so she said, "Okay. So, no word on the street. Who else did you speak to?"

His eyebrows twitched, like he didn't understand the question. "There is no one else — we haven't even got a full name for her, Boss."

A fresh wave of frustration shimmered through her, but she curbed the impulse for sarcasm and said, "Did you speak to the coroner? Did you call the SIO who dealt with her case? Has anyone been asking after her? Has her family been in touch?"

"Uh . . ."

"Burial records," she said. "Where's she buried? Who paid burial expenses — a friend, a relative, or the state?"

Sweating, he flipped back through the pages as if the facts he hadn't bothered to establish might magically appear.

"Details," she said again. She looked around the room. "I expect every one of you to use your initiative. I expect clear, precise summaries of the work you've done, and I do not expect you to prejudge a task too dull to do it well." She paused, nodded to let them know that the lecture was over. "Okay, who's dealing with the CCTV?"

Three younger officers raised their hands. Simms had widened the search area, calling in camera records from the streets further from the restaurant and the dump site; these three had spent the day running backwards and forwards through hours of video recordings. They were red-eyed and queasy-looking, as if they'd just stepped off a rollercoaster. One look at their hunched shoulders told Simms they had nothing.

"You're doing a good job," she said. "Important work, so keep at it — we need to trace her dinner partner, and if we can get a better image of the BMW approaching Livebait, or anything near the dump site, it could give us the break we need."

They nodded, tired, but their heads came up and they looked less defeated.

"How're we doing on the mobile phone?"

Renwick scrabbled for a flimsy in the mess of papers on his desk. "DNA's a match to the vic."

"The DNA," she said, unable to quell her impatience. "Is that it? They *still* haven't come up with the IMEI number?"

"They say they'd rushed the DNA through, like they'd done us a big favour — you know how it is since forensics went commercial."

Since the Forensic Science Service went bust, lab work had become a free-for-all, with firms undercutting each other, vying for nice, cost-effective automated jobs where they could press a button and let a machine do the rest. Recovering a number off a scratched and water-damaged scrap of laminate was manual, labour-intensive, skilled work — which made it a less attractive commercial prospect.

234

"The IMEI gives us access to her service provider," she said. "If the victim called the BMW driver — and she probably did — we'd have him, and a hell of a lot more besides."

"I told them all that," Renwick said. "I said they'd better pull their finger out — we're not paying them to do half the job. I *told* them — we need that number, and I'll stay on their case till we've got it."

It sounded like bluster, and Simms wondered if he'd taken the same feeble tone with the lab, but humiliating her office manager in front of the team wouldn't help, so she said, "First thing tomorrow, call them and put a rocket under them."

He nodded, eager to please.

"What about Howard's drinking buddies — has anything turned up there?"

"Mouse." Renwick glanced over his shoulder to Ella Moran, evidently relieved to be able to direct attention away from him. "D'you want to tell the boss what you got?"

All eyes turned to Detective Constable Moran. Two experienced male officers had already been taken to task, and as one of only three women in the room — including Simms — Moran must be acutely aware that she had to make this good.

"I talked to the landlord at half ten this a.m.," she said, her voice firm and clear. "He said he had nothing more to add. So I went in again at 1p.m., spoke to some of the lunchtime regulars, but nobody recognized Howard's picture or the descriptions of the men he was with. I tried again, five until seven — no joy. I'll drop in

235

on my way home, see if I have any luck with the night-time drinkers."

Simms looked around the room. "Detail," she said. "Initiative." Having made the point, she said, "Okay, my turn. Preliminary forensic reports from Howard's premises haven't shown up any trace of the victim, so far."

Renwick shrugged. "All that means is he took her elsewhere."

"Possibly," Simms said, pleased he wasn't afraid to challenge her, despite the verbal pummelling he'd just had. "But Land Registry only has him listed for the one property. So we need to know if he registered anything under a business or trust name — maybe even in the name of a friend or relative. We're looking for a house, a flat, a storage facility. He's a man who likes his cars — does he work on them himself? Maybe he has a garage or lock-up — if he has, he's hiding it. Could be he's renting. So we look closely at phone records, bank and credit card statements — if he took her somewhere else, I want to know where."

Sergeant Renwick looked over at the HOLMES2 manager. He pointed to his own chest, then to the manager — they would work on task allocation together.

Good. "Anything from the massage parlours?" Simms asked.

Kilfoyle, the constable leading the canvassing team, was young and soft-featured. He dipped his head apologetically. "No, Boss. The description we've got's a bit generic — there's just so many twenty-something

236

blondes out there, and a lot of them are Eastern European."

Renwick scratched the stubble under his chin, embarrassed. "It's like I said, Boss."

Simms knew it — when she worked in the Met, only about a quarter of sex workers were actually from the UK.

"Any owners whose feathers seem particularly ruffled?" Simms asked. "Any of the girls who seemed more nervous than you'd expect?"

"Um . . ." Kilfoyle looked uneasily to his team; she could see he was expecting a bollocking.

"Okay," she said. "Keep handing out those business cards. Make sure they have the Crimestoppers number. Keep pushing. I'll see if I can squeeze some extra money from the budget to get you out there during the night — catch the late shift."

That perked them up. Overtime was a word everybody liked to hear.

She looked around the room. "But for every good thing, there is a price to pay," she said, allowing herself a smile. "Who has outstanding reports still to be logged on the system?" In the exchange of glances she could almost hear them say, *Uh-oh* . . . She waited for a show of hands. "I want them written up and handed in *before* you head for home — clear?"

Detective Superindent Spry had asked for an update before she went home for the night, and Kate Simms headed southeast from Collyhurst Station to the shiny glass and stone offices of the new Greater Manchester

Police Headquarters. A trip out to the old HQ, a short step from Man United football stadium, would have meant a slog to the other side of the city, but the new offices were only a short hop from where she was stationed and she made the journey in under five minutes. It glowed blue, standing out against the more modest business offices around it, an entire block of glass and steel.

Spry had a double-size room on the edge of an open-plan office on the third floor. She knocked at his door and heard him clear his throat noisily before calling her in. He didn't look up from the pile of papers on his desk.

"I understand you missed this morning's briefing," he said. "Being late for morning prayers sets a bad example, Kate."

Great, she thought. *There's a snitch on my crew.* When she didn't answer, he raised his eyes to meet hers. They were heavy with sleep, and she wondered if she had interrupted a little snooze.

"I put the time back a little, sir, that's all," she explained.

"Kate." Spry's broad face was concerned, avuncular. "A good start is essential for the team. You can't keep changing times of briefings, disrupting the day's tasks."

She stopped him before he made a prat of himself by getting onto the touchy subject of childcare. "I was consulting on the evidence."

"Oh," he said. "NPIA advisor being helpful, is he?"

The local National Police Improvement Agency advisor would be the person to go to for advice on

238

forensic matters — if she didn't have Fennimore to turn to. But she did, and since she hadn't spoken to the NPIA advisor since he'd advised her to shelve the drugs deaths as sad-but-inevitable, Simms diverted Spry's attention away from the actual question by telling him how far they'd got with the collection of forensic evidence and performance of tests, stopping short of admitting that she had her own private consultant advising her, and one which the ACC would certainly not approve of.

Detective Superintendent Spry listened to the list of tests completed and requests made, the canvassing of saunas and checks on CCTV footage. "Isn't this overkill? You have your suspect."

"I have a suspect, but I'm not convinced he's our man."

Spry looked mildly horrified. "Howard's DNA is on her, her DNA is on him. Stop faffing about and charge him."

"His DNA is *on* her, but not *in* her, sir."

"So, he wore a condom."

"Maybe. If he did, the perineal swabs will still find evidence of him."

"And if the evidence is there, will that convince you of his guilt?" he asked.

She hesitated.

"For God's sake, Kate."

"There's no evidence of her on his premises, and nothing in his cars, sir," she said.

"He was careful, cleaned up afterwards."

"Nobody cleans up that well. Howard is still refusing to name the men he was drinking with, we still haven't found the man the victim was with at the restaurant. If the killer intended to make it look like she was an addict, he botched it — and George Howard is too careful for that."

"Who knows how a man will act in that situation — he'd just killed a woman!"

"The lab says the victim's blood on his shoes wasn't caused by spatter, it was smeared."

"So he rubbed his shoes over. You said yourself, Kate — nobody can clean up every spot of forensic evidence."

"If the smearing was caused by an attempt to clean up, you would still expect to see some spatter, but there was none *at all*, sir. This was all transfer — it could be someone used a bloody item of clothing to put it there."

"All I've heard so far is 'could be', and 'maybe'," Spry said.

"There are too many things that don't add up."

He stared at her as though she was completely incomprehensible to him. "You're running a criminal investigation, not completing *The Times* crossword, Kate. There are bound to be unanswered questions."

She opened her mouth to answer, but he raised a finger in warning.

"I pulled strings to get you this investigation. I put the district SIO's nose out of joint, prising the case out of his grabby little hands to give it to you. If you make a mess of it . . ."

It was a threat and a warning, and an expression of anxiety — if she messed up, it would reflect badly on him. She looked into his broad red face, frustrated. The risk of personal embarrassment overrode any concerns he had about justice. Well, Simms wasn't above playing on his professional vanity.

"I appreciate your support, sir," she said, trying to sound sincere. "I know how much is riding on this. And I really don't want to foul up. Which is why I'm being ultra-careful. George Howard is seriously wealthy — he can afford the best defence — and we've got gaps in our evidence, a whacking great hole in the timeline. We don't even know who the victim is, yet — his lawyers will tear us *apart*."

"And the press would love a chance to give us a kicking," Spry added, pressing her argument home for her.

She smiled. "Well, we don't have to help them lace up their boots, do we, sir?"

CHAPTER
TWENTY-FOUR

Simms's meeting with Nick Fennimore meant another trip back into the city. Parking for the Midland Hotel was in the NCP car park at the rear of the building, below what used to be Manchester Central railway station and was now an exhibition centre. The car park sprawled over an acre underground. At this late hour the parking bays lay mostly empty, and Simms found a free spot a hundred yards in, on the main level.

There were steps to ground level on Albion Street, where she wanted to be, but the car park was laid out in a grid, and underground, in the dark, it was hard to get her bearings. She stood by her car and turned three-sixty. A car pulled into a bay thirty feet from her own; its brake lights flashed once, then the engine fell silent. The late-night hum of traffic washed around her like fog, and she started off down the main inlet, hoping to pick up a sign so that she could get her bearings. Halfway down the row, she saw it: Peter Street and the Midland Hotel. The arrow pointed back the way she'd come — she was heading the wrong way.

Cursing softly, she turned — saw a movement off to her left. The driver of the car that had followed her in, maybe. But she couldn't see him. She stood still and listened, heard the gritty slither of shoe leather on cobbles. She peered into the shadows. Saw the movement again; closer this time — a hooded figure. He ducked back behind one of the archway pillars. She looked in the opposite direction, back along the bays. A second figure seemed to be lurking near the stairs to the street.

The hooded figure had disappeared. Go forward, or back? Every archway was a hiding place. A place for someone to lurk and pounce. Going back the way she'd come would take her to the quieter end of the street — further from help, if she needed it, and towards the waiting figure and the foot of the steps. Forward would take her nearer the Midland, and safety. Forward, then. She took a few steps, saw a movement deeper into the shadows.

Her heart thudding, keeping her eyes fixed on the spot where she'd seen the movement, her ears straining for the slightest sound, she reached for the Casco baton in her shoulder bag. The weapon weighed just a pound, but it was made from hardened aircraft alloy steel; used deftly, a seven-stone woman could bring down a rugby prop forward with a couple of well-aimed strikes. She headed north, towards Peter Street, keeping to the centre of the bay, hearing sly footsteps in the echoes of her own. A car revved somewhere behind her and she heard a distant squeal of tyres. Ahead she saw a sign for the stairs and she cut right fast, taking the steps two at a time, waiting at street level for whoever was following.

Nobody came.

At the head of the steps, fifty yards down the road, she thought she saw someone, but he ducked down when he saw her. She waited. Still nothing. A young couple strolled past her, arms entwined. The girl turned in her boyfriend's arms to get a look at her and whispered something. They laughed and they walked on, the girl snuggling closer. Simms crouched at the steps. Nobody. She deployed her baton, flicking the steel shaft to its full twenty-one inches, and inched carefully down the stairs.

Fifteen feet from her, a figure in dark clothing, moving fast. He was on her in a second.

"Police," she yelled. "Stay back!" She took a step back, raised her baton over her right shoulder, her elbow tucked neatly to her side, her left arm forward to maintain distance between them.

His face white with shock, he raised both hands, as if she'd pointed a gun at him. He was no more than a kid. Nineteen, twenty years old, maybe, dressed in black, his sweater badged with the Midland Hotel's logo.

"Shit," she muttered. *Shit, shit, shit*.

CHAPTER
TWENTY-FIVE

"Rule no.1 — they always keep the shoes."

PROFESSOR NICK FENNIMORE

They settled for sandwiches and a beer in the Octagon Lounge.

"You look pale," Fennimore said. "Are you all right?"

"Fine," Simms said, scanning the foyer.

"Kate?"

She looked at him, and for a second he thought she looked spooked. "I'm *fine*, Fennimore. Long shifts, and Tim's been cranky at night, me not being there."

They found a table and ordered beer, and Simms ran through the latest findings, including the lack of evidence on the sauna owner's premises and the fact that the blood had been smeared onto George Howard's shoes from a piece of fabric.

"Hmm," Fennimore said. "Planted?"

"Is there any way of knowing that?" Simms asked. "I mean for certain?"

"Unlikely," he said. "The lab will have retained any fibres but even if the evidence *was* planted, you would have to find the original piece of fabric they used, and my guess is that it will have been burned or dumped."

"Sounds about right," she said. "Howard's story is he noticed blood on his clothing and shoes when he woke up and assumed he'd been in a fight, so he got rid of his clothes, but not the shoes." She shook her head, puzzled. "Why *do* they always keep the shoes?"

"Easy to replace a pair of trousers," Fennimore said. "But breaking in a new pair of shoes — bloody nightmare."

She half smiled.

"You haven't identified the victim yet?"

"No. And Howard still maintains he has no recollection of her."

Their food arrived. The waiter lit the candle on their table and Simms began to object, but then she shrugged as though to say it wasn't worth the fuss, and focused on her sandwich.

"D'you think you've convinced your boss to give you more time?" Fennimore asked.

She raised her right hand, wobbled it, her left hand still holding her sandwich. "His instinct for self-preservation might keep him onside for a bit longer." She sank her teeth into her salmon on wholemeal and rolled her eyes back in her head, groaning with pleasure.

He watched her, admiring the creamy-white skin of her neck, the artless way she tore into her food.

She chewed and swallowed. "First bite I've had since breakfast."

It was close to 10p.m., and she had picked him up from the airport just after eight that morning. He wanted to tell her she should take care of her health, but thought better of it and turned to his own plate, deciding how best to attack the burger he'd ordered.

"So, shall we brainstorm?"

She'd taken another bite of her sandwich and she rotated her finger, inviting him to go ahead.

"Okay," he said. "We have more hints of another presence, but we're still hobbled by that four-hour gap in the timeline."

"I've got people working on that," she said, wiping her mouth with her napkin. "But don't hold your breath."

"And we have behavioural and physical anomalies."

"Are you talking about blood on the shoes?" She eyed him shrewdly, the sandwich halfway to her lips. "Or are you holding out on me?"

He smiled. Nothing much got past Kate Simms. "I've been looking at the DNA results."

"What DNA results?" She put down her sandwich. "Are you telling me you got the DNA results from the teeth and perineum in less than twelve hours?"

"No, I'm telling you I got them in less than *seven* hours." He shrugged modestly, like it was no big deal, though he had schmoozed and promised help with review papers and called in favours to move Kate's samples up the waiting list.

"There's not much to do here except wallow in hedonism," he said, gazing up at the high vaulted ceiling, gold-edged mosaics, and swatches of bronze chiffon draped across the arches. "Boredom sets in fast."

She read him in a second. "You pulled in a few favours. That was a nice thing to do."

"Like I said, I was bored."

"Keep working on those social skills, Nick." She smiled and picked up her sandwich happily. "So what did you get?"

"I'm afraid they weren't good enough to load onto the database as a scene sample."

"You couldn't search the database?"

She was so crestfallen he felt bad for stringing her along. "But that doesn't matter at this stage — we wanted to compare the profile from the victim's swabs with George Howard."

"You've lost me," she said. "If we can't check the scene profile against the database . . ."

"A direct comparison of profiles is nothing to do with the database — it's a job done in the lab by your friendly local scientist." He gave her a slow smile. "Or in this case, by *my* friendly local scientist."

She sat forward, eagerly.

"The DNA from the back of her teeth did *not* come from Howard."

"Proof there was more than one attacker," she said.

She looked so pleased that it pained him to have to say, "Proof *she had oral sex* with someone other than Howard shortly before she died. It doesn't prove that person was her attacker, Kate. And it could be a mixed profile — some of the DNA *could* have come from Howard."

She waved away his objections. "You're not going to spoil it for me — this is the best news I've had all day."

248

She took a swallow of beer. "You said the results told you two things."

"The perineal swab yielded a partial profile which contains some of the same DNA as the swab from the teeth."

"Same person."

"Maybe," he said. "Or maybe not. With what we've got at the moment, we can't exclude two donors. Now, that might be Howard and A. N. Other, or it might be just an unknown male — no Howard there at all."

She sighed. "Look, Nick, I've been sitting on committees and organizing community partnership meetings for the past four-and-a-half years, so I'm a bit rusty on the DNA stuff. Plus, I'm really, *really* tired. Can you break it down for me?"

"Okay. In crime scene stain analysis we don't try to type the entire DNA molecule — that's actually the Human Genome Project, and thousands of scientists are working on that full time. Instead, we look at a more manageable ten loci on the DNA and see what version — or allele — of the DNA is present. Sure, there are some alleles on the swabs that match Howard's profile, but *all* of us share four or five alleles."

"You're saying it could just be a coincidence that Howard and the attacker share some common alleles?"

He nodded.

"So, what d'you need to rule him in or out?"

"A full profile from the partials would be nice," he said.

"You're thinking LCN?"

She was talking about Low Copy Number; the LCN process could be used to produce a DNA profile from just a single cell isolated at a crime scene.

"We call it LTDNA these days — Low Template DNA."

"You say tom-*ayto*, I say tom-*ahto* — it won't tell us anything we don't already know — that there's someone on her that isn't Howard."

"Actually, it might — you haven't forgotten how we actually create a DNA profile?"

She gave him a look that said, *I might be rusty, but I'm not brain dead.* "We take a tiny sample of DNA from a swab or whatever, then multiply it lots of times to provide us with enough DNA to analyze by SGM whatsit." This was Second Generation Multiplex Plus — the current set of probes used in the UK to analyze the ten loci used on the database.

"Correct," he said. "Now, most of our DNA is the same — mine, yours, the waiter who served our meals — and that's not much good for identification purposes."

Simms rolled her eyes at the mini-lecture, but used it as an opportunity to finish her sandwich.

"Fortunately, we also have bits of junk DNA which don't code for anything, and are highly variable from person to person, making it easier for us scientists to differentiate one person's bits of junk from another's. These unique sequences of base pairs are called short tandem repeats because they're short — just two to five base pairs long — and they repeat many times in tandem."

She mumbled something that sounded like, "It does what it says on the tin."

"So we take the fragments of DNA and multiply them — typically twenty-eight times for SGM Plus, but with LTDNA, that's increased to thirty-four times. Which might not sound like a lot more, but each iteration *doubles* the amount of DNA. With SGM Plus, you're well into the hundreds of millions, but LTDNA multiplies the original fragments by *billions*."

Simms dabbed the last few crumbs from her plate. "So we'd see stuff that was previously invisible?"

"Or we might see 'stuff' that isn't actually there."

She sighed. "Because?"

"Because every time you double your DNA fragments, you also double any degraded material, so you can get mini-peaks on your graphs — alleles which drop in and out, appearing and disappearing at random, like background noise."

"If it's unreliable, why do it at all?"

"Because the real peaks will still be there, and in the same proportions — you just have to apply stronger protocols for collection and interpretation, so you don't botch the results."

She nodded thoughtfully, wiping her mouth with her napkin. "Call it what you like, it sounds expensive and time-consuming."

"It is."

"And not something I could ask you to do in your university lab."

"No," he confirmed. "There are only two or three labs in the country equipped for LTDNA."

"And I'm thinking this process can't be rushed."

"Your thinking is, as always, impeccable. So, the question is, are you willing to bet a few thousand of your budget on a test that might tell you nothing?"

She shrugged. "My only other option is to charge Howard with murder and hope nothing turns up in the future to make his lawyers scream miscarriage of justice."

She sat back, pensive, an anxious frown creasing her brow. Requesting the LTDNA tests would also be tantamount to telling her boss, "You're a fool. You're wrong, I'm right, and I'll prove it if it kills me." Which was not the best way to make friends — especially when you already had a reputation for bloody-mindedness. Fennimore didn't envy her position, and he certainly wouldn't try to influence her one way or the other. But maybe he could give her something else to think about, something that might even help the case.

"Want to hear my other news?" he said.

She took another thoughtful sip of beer. "Sure."

"I also checked the National Injuries Database for the cross-hatch whip marks."

She looked at him over the rim of her glass. "You *have* been busy."

"It was that or bet my entire consultation fee on an outsider in the three o'clock at Chester."

"What consulation fee?"

"The one you're going to pay me retrospectively."

Her eyebrows twitched. "So, what did you get?"

252

"Three examples showing exactly the same injuries: same weave, same thickness, same sort of force, by which I mean just drawing blood. And *exactly* the same criss-cross pattern of strokes. Which I'm reliably informed is very unusual in consensual S&M, and could only have been done if the victim was fully restrained."

"Only three on the database? I wish Tanford was around to hear that," she said.

He raised his eyebrows in question.

"He said there's nothing unique about men hurting women."

"That's true, but it's the *means* that sets this sadistic misogynist apart from the common herd. The database turned up something else — all three victims were addicts and prostitutes, and all three reported kidnap-assault."

She set her drink down and stared at him. "Kidnap-assault?"

"Sounds a bit like our victim, doesn't it?" he said.

"I don't suppose we have a name for the abductor?"

"We've got E-FITs." He reached into the breast pocket of his suit jacket and handed her a sheet of paper.

She scrutinized the three computerized images. "These are different men," she said.

"I don't think so."

She pointed to each image in turn. "Middle-aged, with collar-length hair. Young, with buzz-cut. Youngish, close-cropped hair."

"One of the victims was eighteen, the other two were in their thirties — to a teenager, twenty-five is middle-aged," he said. "Plus, the attacks happened six months apart, and hair length is . . . adjustable — as you would know." He eyed her tragically short hair and she rolled her eyes.

"Look at the shape of the jaw," he said. "The same. The nose is . . . similar."

She snorted, and he turned the paper to get a better look. "Okay similar*ish* — and they all said he had big hands."

"Not much of a description, is it? A dark-haired, square-jawed man with a nondescript nose and big hands."

"Addicts," he said. "Minds on the fix beforehand; out of their minds on the fix after."

"If the injuries are so distinctive, why weren't the crimes flagged as a possible serial offender?"

"A database is just a sophisticated list," he said. "You have to ask it questions if you want it to tell you what it knows. As you said, from the descriptions, they might have been three different men. He shrugged. "Prostitutes. Addicts. Easy to dismiss. The investigators probably didn't even consult the database."

A shadow crossed her face, but she nodded, accepting the reality. "All right. The victimology's the same: all three victims addicts, all of them prostitutes — like Rika — and maybe our murder victim, too."

"Yes — interesting factoids for Professor Varley to consider when he works up a profile for you."

"Was this in the Manchester area?"

He shook his head. "That's where the similarities end. Two incidents were in Newcastle, one in Hull."

"We should speak to them," she said.

"Sorry, Kate," he said. "One OD'd, one committed suicide."

"That's a high mortality rate," she said. "This was when?"

"The first attacks happened four years ago, the last, eighteen months later."

"We both know that serial offenders like this never stop," she said.

Fennimore nodded. "Which means he moved away, or something stopped him — like a prison sentence, an accident, illness."

"Or he got better at covering up," she said. "What about the third victim?"

"Tanya Repton — the girl from Hull." He took out an image he'd printed off from Tanya's police file that afternoon.

Tanya Repton was the eighteen-year-old. She looked ten years older. She had arrests for possession of heroin and cocaine, shoplifting, and soliciting — these last two she claimed were to support her habit. Her skin was the pale sick colour of dead fish. She had a small pointed face with thin, greasy blonde hair — brown at the roots — and a cold sore on her lower lip. But the most striking thing about her was her eyes: they were flat and grey, and would have been unremarkable, except the iris of her right eye had what looked like a jagged brown tear from the pupil to the outer rim. She stared into the camera lens with a look that said she knew what life held in store for her and it was completely without hope.

"We'll speak to Tanya then," Simms said.

He shook his head. "She dropped off the radar. Humberside police don't have a current address for her."

Simms took out her phone and scrolled through the contacts.

"Who are you calling?"

"Liz Dromer," she said. "She set up a drugs rehab programme in Hull after her son died of an overdose."

She pressed the call button, and a second later someone picked up. "Hi, Liz," she said. "Kate Simms."

A pause.

"No, I'm in Manchester, now. All those stories you kept telling me about the friendliness of the northerners? I thought I'd come and see for myself." She listened a moment. "Ah, you know, work in progress. Listen, Liz — you with someone?"

It seemed she wasn't, because seconds later, Kate was telling Liz Dromer about the three attacks in her area, and the possible link to a case she was working on. When she'd given the outline, she listened again, said, "No — I understand," gave Liz the girl's name and disconnected.

"She said she can't promise anything, but she'll ask around."

"So the Community Partnership work was good for something then?"

She took the jibe in good part. "I did get to know some good people," she conceded. "Liz being one of them."

He nodded. "And what's your work in progress?"

"That was the private part of the conversation." It was a slap-down, but amber flashes of humour in the dark brown of her irises took some of the sting out of it.

She checked her watch and her shoulders sagged. "Half past ten — Kieran'll be furious." She opened her bag to drop her phone into it, and it buzzed. She checked the caller ID. "Superintendent Tanford," she said.

CHAPTER
TWENTY-SIX

Kate Simms braced herself, pressed "answer", and with more enthusiasm than she felt, said, "Tanno, what can I do for you?"

"You've got me on your caller ID," Superintendent Tanford said. "I'm flattered." She didn't know what to say to that, and he went on, "Actually, Kate, I think maybe *I* can help *you*." He lowered his voice. "Are you free to speak?"

She looked around the restaurant. It was beginning to empty, most people moving over to the sofas and banquettes in the lounge area to take their coffee.

"Go ahead," she said.

"Your murder suspect."

"George Howard. What about him?"

"We've had intel he's supplying drugs."

She frowned. "If he is, he's not doing it from his business premises or his flat."

Across the table from her, Fennimore raised his eyebrows. "Drugs?" he mouthed. She nodded.

Tanford exhaled into the phone. "The search turned up nothing? You're sure?"

"All we found were some Viagra pills, a few tabs of E, a taster of cocaine — just enough for a few lines, not enough to charge him with supplying. No heroin."

"None at all, eh?" Tanford made a sharp *tsk* sound. "This one is a cautious bastard, isn't he?"

"We are looking into the possibility he owns other properties in the area."

"Our intel was very specific about the address — his sauna. You're telling me the sniffer dogs picked up no trace?"

Kate felt a pang of uncertainty. "POLSA advised against use of dogs." This was the Police Search Advisor, a trained specialist who advised on searches of crime scenes. "He said there was a risk of DNA transfer and hairs fouling up the trace evidence."

"There was nothing to stop you sending them in *after* the scientists finished up."

"We had no reason to suspect him of dealing," she said.

"Your murder vic was shot full of smack — where'd you suppose that came from?"

She didn't answer — she didn't know where it had come from — but she'd discounted Howard because if he *had* been set up, it couldn't have come from him. She'd been guilty of stupid, circular thinking every bit as sloppy as Superintendent Spry's.

"Look, Kate," Tanford said, "I don't want to scare you, but ACC Gifford talks about your fuck-up at the National Crime Faculty like it happened last week. He's just gagging for a chance to relegate you right back to your touchy-feely committee work in community partnerships."

Fuck-up. So that's how he saw it. And now she'd fucked up again.

Fennimore was trying to catch her eye, but she stared at the tabletop, face burning.

At the other end of the line, Tanford gave an irritated sigh. "It's such a bloody shame — you'd make a good SIO, given half a chance." He paused, and she waited for the axe to fall on their mentor-mentee relationship. Eventually, he said, "Fuck it — why not? Listen, I want to help you out here, so why don't you make the request?"

For a second, she was speechless — he was giving her the chance to call in the search team. Tanford was covering her back. "Well, that — uh . . ." For the briefest moment she wondered what was in it for him, but she slapped that suspicious little gremlin down. "I . . . I don't know what to say."

"Say you weren't satisfied with some of the answers Howard was giving in interviews, you got suspicious. I don't need to tell you how to bullshit, do I?"

"Got an 'A' for it on Board exam, sir," she said, deadpan, and heard an appreciative chuckle. "But what I meant was I don't know how to thank you."

"Don't." She could hear the wince in his voice. "It's not like this is entirely of your own making. You're bound to make a couple of mistakes on your first solo major investigation. Learn from them — move on." He disconnected before she could embarrass them both by thanking him again.

Fennimore raised his eyebrows. "Good news, or bad?"

"Bit of both, I think," she said, feeling slightly dazed.

Detective Superintendent Spry dropped by Kate Simms's office at 6.15 a.m. The dogs turned up a cache of drugs hidden in a false joist under floorboards at George Howard's flat. With it, a purse containing a photograph of a woman, a nipple stud and its stay, and a key ring with Yale door key, locker and two Chubb padlock keys. All of them had been wiped clean of fingerprints, but the CSIs caught a couple of partials off the key ring, sufficient for a match to the murder victim. There was no ID in the purse. The woman in the photograph was Slavic-featured, and had long, wavy brown hair and dark eyes — so, not their victim.

"Couldn't have worked out better for you, Kate." Spry rubbed his hands, smiling.

"You think so, sir?" The quantity of drugs was relatively small.

"I know so." He looked sharp and rested, snappily dressed in a charcoal-grey suit and white shirt, fragrant with expensive aftershave.

Simms straightened her jacket, acutely aware that she was wearing the same suit and blouse that she'd worn the previous day, and was smelling more vagrant than fragrant.

"A hundred grams of heroin," Spry said. "More than enough to charge Howard with possession with intent to supply." He cocked his head and looked at her through half-closed eyes. "What made you decide to go back with the sniffer dogs?"

"Howard knows the two men he was drinking with the night of the murder — I'm sure of it," she said. "I wondered if he was protecting a business connection he'd rather keep from the police — massage parlour, a constant stream of Eastern European girls — drugs seemed a good bet."

He stared at her for a long time; Spry might be lazy, he might be coasting in his mind's eye towards a gentle retirement on the slow waterways of the Cheshire plain, but he still had a cop's instinct for bullshit.

"Tanford seems to've taken a shine to you," he said, watching for her reaction.

Simms kept her expression carefully blank.

"Play it clever," he said, "Tanford could do you some good with the likes of the ACC." He held her gaze a moment longer, letting her know that he knew she'd sold him a line, and that Superintendent Tanford was tugging one end of it. He went to the door, but turned back, looking positively cheery.

"You won't be needing the incident room any more; that should free up at least a dozen staff." He raised his hand and was on his way down the corridor before she could reply. But Detective Superintendent Spry was not built for speed and she caught him easily.

"Sir," she said, "I need my team at full strength — I have several lines of inquiry still running."

He stopped and looked at her like she was a wilful but charming child. "I do hate to repeat myself, Kate," he said. "But you have enough on George Howard to charge him on *several* counts — his dental match to the bites, his DNA from the bites *and* under the victim's fingernails. And now the drugs connection." He gave her an exasperated look. "What else could you possibly be looking for?"

"I'm still waiting on evidence from the victim's mobile phone number," she answered. "I've got people checking CCTV footage over a wider area of the city centre — searching for the BMW our victim was seen getting into on the night she died. And I'm waiting on forensic tests — I've asked for LTDNA on the perineal and teeth swabs. The evidence points to a second person being with her around the time she died."

"Another punter," he said firmly. "You know these girls have a high client turnover."

"It might be — but if it *was* her mysterious dinner partner . . ."

"Why this constant need to complicate everything?" Spry flushed, impatient. "The honest, straightforward, simple fact is — you already *Have. Your. Man.*" He finished at shouting pitch, and Renwick, walking passed them in the corridor, shot her a sympathetic glance. Spry broke off, and stood for a few seconds, breathing through his nose, clearly trying to regain his composure.

"The National Injuries Database came up with three other attacks," Simms said. "Women abducted and tortured in the same way as our murder victim. I want to establish if George Howard can be linked to them." It was partly true at least.

"Look, Kate," he said. "You're not the only game in town. I cannot justify a team of twenty staff — plus overtime payments — so you can tinker about, tying everything up in a nice silk bow."

"Sir, I —"

"No, Kate," he said. "No. Do you know how many staff we've lost since 2010? A quarter of Manchester's entire police force — half of those were frontline officers. The few we have left should be out doing police work, not faffing about with paperwork."

Which was rich, coming from a man who spent entire weeks of time faffing about with paperwork.

"I'd like my first major investigation to go the distance, sir," she said. "It's no good me charging Howard if I can't make it stick." It was an appeal to his professional vanity; it would not look good for Spry if she fouled up after such a promising start — he would be tainted by association.

Spry eyed her suspiciously. "All right, I'm listening." She took a breath, but he raised a finger in warning. "Just listening," he repeated. "I'm not saying I've changed my mind."

She nodded. "If we knew who she had dinner with, it might help us to identify the victim and establish the course of events. Less wriggle room for Howard. If we can discover her name it might give us a direct link to Howard's massage parlour." It might, but she wouldn't bet on it. "At least let me get the IMEI number off the phone, see if we can recover her voicemail."

He thought about it, standing in the corridor with her staff passing by either side of them. He was looking

264

at her, but she could almost see the back-of-an-envelope calculation he was doing in his head.

"All right, here's what you do. Follow up on the phone. Call in the lab results, assess the evidence so far. Keep the HOLMES team while they get the database up to date. But chasing this phantom BMW is a waste of time, and why you're still canvassing the saunas is beyond me. Anyone involved in either of those tasks can go back onto regular duties."

"Sir — I'd still be losing half my team."

He waved away her objection. "Reality of post-recession policing, Simms — a lesson you had best learn sooner rather than later. Identify the victim," he went on. "Consolidate the case — but don't spend money you don't have on tests you don't need, and do *not* go inventing non-existent leads."

Simms watched him make his flat-footed way to the stairwell. As soon as he was out of sight she went to her office, closed the door and picked up the phone.

Fennimore was already up.

"Well, don't you sound annoyingly fresh and bright," she said.

"Amazing the effect of a good night's sleep," he said. "How did the search go?"

He listened without interrupting while she summarized the main points, including her conversation with Spry.

"All of which sounds like good news," Fennimore said. "So why am I sensing doom?"

She raised her shoulders and let them fall. "I dunno, Nick — every time I find another kink in the course of the investigation, something pops up to whack it back into shape for me again. I hassle the dealers on the street and someone steps up and admits to tainting the deals. I rattle the sauna operators and suddenly Howard drops into my lap — courtesy of Crimestoppers, mind you, so I can't check the source. I ask for additional tests on the swabs, and *hey presto* the victim's belongings turn up in Howard's flat, along with a nice little stash of heroin."

"Everyone makes mistakes, and criminals do sometimes get cocky," Fennimore said.

"But it doesn't make sense!"

"Hey, I'm on your side," he said. "I'm just doing that thing I do."

"What," she said, "stating the bloody obvious?"

"It's sometimes the best way to reveal the obscure."

"Very gnomic," she said, knowing she sounded childish and sulky. He was playing devil's advocate, she knew that. But she was hot and prickly and in need of a shower and breakfast and a few hours' sleep. She closed her eyes, trying to find a point of equilibrium, but the room began to spin and she saw a vivid image of the murder victim, her face pulped to blood and raw flesh. Her eyes flew open again and she took a few breaths.

"Okay." She tried to put her thoughts in order. "I checked with the FIDO for Cheetham Hill." Field intelligence development officers, or FIDOs, gathered basic intelligence on criminal activities in their local neighbourhood.

"There hasn't been so much as a *whisper* of George Howard being involved in drugs. Yet Howard —

266

ex-government auditor, a man who pays his taxes *because it's the law* — is now in the frame for possession with intent to supply a class A drug."

"He also runs a massage parlour, Kate — that's not what you'd call a legitimate business." She heard the quizzical humour in his voice.

"Sure," she admitted. "But Howard is too careful to make a basic error like this. He stays just within the boundaries that would make prosecution economically unviable for the CPS and he runs the business like it's a bloody insurance office. He's got his events schedule planned for the year, his pre-tax results all worked out — he's even set up an online savings account labelled 'tax fund'. Keeping a hundred grams of heroin on the premises isn't cocky or careless, it's stupid and lax, and in Howard's book that would be *really* criminal."

Fennimore was silent for a few moments. "Well, if *he* didn't put it there . . . then someone else did."

"Well, duh!" It was one of her teenage daughter's phrases of the moment, and Simms instantly regretted it, but Fennimore went on as if he hadn't heard:

"They're Howard's drugs, or they aren't his drugs — it's as simple as that. The question is how to establish which is the correct proposition." He sounded intrigued, relishing the challenge.

"How do we do that?" she said.

"We'll need a detailed analysis of the heroin, obviously. DNA trace on the threads of the nipple stud bar. Since he unscrewed it, rather than ripping it out, we won't have blood all over the stud, so there might

267

well be some good clean epithelia from his tongue or buccal cells from his lips in the screw threads."

She took notes, grimacing slightly at the grosser details, but inwardly smiling. One of Fennimore's best qualities was that he took every hypothesis seriously. He might tear it to shreds in the discussion that followed, but only in the interests of good forensic science.

"The photo you found in the victim's purse — is it professional, or a photo booth?"

The question stumped her for a moment. "I don't know, let me think." She knew there had to be a good reason why he was asking, and she rubbed her forehead, trying to stimulate the brain cells into some kind of activity. It came to her slowly, out of a fog of tiredness. "Photo booth," she said. "Why?"

"Photo booth pics are still tacky when they come out of the machine. If we're lucky, the brown-haired beauty in the picture touched the edge of the print before it was dry, and you'll get a nice partial at the very least."

Simms emailed the lab to make the additional request, still cradling the phone between her shoulder and her ear.

"Anything else I can help with?" Fennimore asked.

"You couldn't rustle up a few students to augment my team, could you?"

"If you're serious, Josh Brown has been agitating for more to do. I keep telling him he has a PhD thesis to work on, but I think he's been bitten by the investigative bug."

"I'll keep him in mind," she said. It wasn't that she distrusted the student exactly, but he made her uneasy.

268

He was hiding something, and until she knew what that was, she would never feel entirely comfortable with him.

She looked at her notes, and couldn't bring herself to make the next call.

"Problem?" Fennimore said.

"I'm a bit nervous about requesting the DNA trace on the nipple stud," she said. "Spry was very specific about not spending more money on lab analysis, so . . ." She stuttered to a halt and hoped he would jump in and rescue her.

He exhaled into the mouthpiece. "All right . . . I do happen to know someone at the DNA lab at Wetherby. I can get it done fast, under the radar. If or when you get something useful, you can enter it in the books."

CHAPTER
TWENTY-SEVEN

"If you must play, decide upon three things at the start: the rules of the game, the stakes, and the quitting time."

CHINESE PROVERB

Fennimore was watching the TV in his room with Joe — José González — the hotel concierge. Joe was off duty until the evening shift; Fennimore had struck up a conversation with Joe on his first visit to Manchester, when he'd asked if there was a betting shop nearby. They had discussed their mutual interest in turf accountancy and Fennimore discovered that González studied form, betting on the outsiders with a sporting chance. Fennimore, on the other hand, studied the odds and bet on the best statistical chances. Complementary skills, so far as he was concerned. Today, they were up eight-hundred-and-twenty on an initial stake of fifty pounds each. Taking the advice of the Chinese proverb, they had agreed the stakes and the quitting time, which guaranteed neither one of them would walk away out of pocket, and engendered a warm glow that Fennimore refused to acknowledge as smugness.

He and Joe had a hundred riding on a four-to-one shot in the three o'clock chase at Sedgefield. His mobile rang as the horses rounded the bend and entered the back straight for the last time. He checked the caller ID and answered.

"Kate," he said, one eye on the screen. "How're you holding up?"

"Right now, I'd give a week's salary for a good night's sleep," she said.

The horses were out in the country on the far side of the course, beginning to spread out as the leaders pushed on for home.

"Got a minute?" She did sound tired, but he heard a tremor of excitement in her voice.

Soon the riders would be rounding the final bend, disappearing from view in the dip as they turned into the straight until the leaders reappeared, jumping over the last fence. Fennimore always thought that sudden reappearance was the most exciting sight on any racecourse in the UK, but the slight quaver of eagerness in Simms's tone had him hooked, and he motioned Joe to turn the sound down.

"A minute, an hour, a lifetime for you, Kate."

"Bollocks," she said, then, "Sorry — tiredness brings out the Tourette's in me. Nick, we got two partial fingerprints from the edge of the photograph."

"And . . ." He kept his eye on the screen as the horses took the last few fences, their horse still on the bridle in fourth place, Joe urging it on, but Fennimore was listening, knowing there was more — she wouldn't have phoned him unless there was more.

"We got a link to a tenprint from one of the excess ODs — a genuine overdose that is — not one of the penicillin victims."

He felt a happy surge of adrenaline. "Let me guess," he said. "Rika."

"The very same. I asked a forensic anthropologist to do a comparison of the photo booth image with Rika's PM photo — it's her, Nick. Our murder victim was carrying Rika's photo around in her purse."

Fennimore turned away from the TV. "Even your superintendent couldn't dismiss that as a coincidence."

She gave a short, coughing laugh. "He pointed out that since we don't know who Rika is, it hasn't 'progressed the investigation in any measurable way'."

"He really is a pillock, isn't he?" Fennimore said.

"Well he's right, I suppose — it doesn't give us her real identity," Simms said. "We know from the coroner's inquest that she had no ID on her at all, not even a bus pass."

"Trafficked?" Fennimore asked.

"Maybe, but I'm going to play that possibility down for a bit, until I've got something more definite."

She was hedging. He didn't blame her — any hint of gangland connections or an international dimension would almost certainly lose her the case — the Intelligence and Security Bureau would swoop in and snatch the investigation from under her nose. Fennimore knew Simms well enough to be sure she would *not* want that. He was surprised to realize that neither would he.

"Anything new on Rika?" he asked.

272

He heard her puff air into the receiver. "Only that the state paid for her burial." Renwick had turned that one up.

Behind him Joe roared in Spanish at the TV, leaping to his feet in an unconscious effort to be the first over the last fence.

Fennimore stuck a finger in one ear and pressed the phone to the other, raising his voice over Joe's yelling. "So, what will you do?"

"Work the case until they shut it down around me." He could practically see the stubborn jut of her chin.

"I've had a team out for two hours, doing the rounds of the massage parlours with Rika's photo booth picture," she went on. "Either they're stonewalling us, or they really don't know her."

"Rika did die almost a year ago," Fennimore said. "And massage parlours have a rapid turnover — nobody stays long. Some of the girls give up, quit the life."

"Not Rika," Simms said. "She had a serious drugs habit — she couldn't afford to quit. And if her habit got to be a nuisance to the management, they'd've kicked her out onto the street without a second thought —" She stopped suddenly.

"What?" he asked.

She laughed. "You've just given me the angle I need. Fennimore," she said, "I think I love you." A silence followed, heavy with meaning. She hung up before he could think of something to say.

Fennimore turned to face the room again. The TV was still on, though the volume was off. Their horse was

273

making a steaming circuit of the winners' enclosure, and Joe had left a note on the coffee table: "I'll pick up the winnings and drop your share in this evening, *Brujo*."

Another win. He should be pleased. He *was* pleased. But a share of easy money suddenly seemed dull set against the possibility of closing the case. With Kate.

Simms walked fast to the Major Incident Room, trying not to think about what she'd just said to Fennimore.

Some of the team were out canvassing. Of the ten remaining, three were HOLMES operatives. She had already delivered the bad news about staffing cuts at the morning briefing; there was a reek of defeat in the place. She had a quiet word with Ella Moran, asked her to run off a bundle of colour copies of Rika's post-mortem photo on the office printer, and called the rest to order.

Simms held up a spare copy of Rika's smiling image from the photo booth, and looked around the room. "Rika didn't look anything like this when she died," she said. "She was a drugs-wasted mess." She held a copy of the post-mortem photograph next to it. "*This* is what she looked like when she died."

Moran started handing out the PM photographs and they began to sit up and pay attention. "We're moving the search to the streets. Go to the corners; talk to the sex workers and addicts who might have known her. Show them the PM photo side by side with the photo booth image. Ask if they knew her. If they did, we need to know where she came from, if she ever told anyone her family name, or the name of a friend from home who was here in the city. A good-looking girl like Rika probably started out working in the saunas. Find out which.

"Our murder victim was carrying Rika's picture around in her purse. We don't have a clear picture of what *she* looked like — she was too badly beaten. We *do* know she was probably working as a prostitute. She wasn't a regular drug user, so she was healthy. And she'd never been subjected to whipping before the night she died. She was a natural blonde. Ask them to look at Rika and try to picture her with a slim blonde woman: long legs, short, straight hair, early twenties." They were making notes, eager, heads up, ready to get to work.

"Now, I know a lot of you will be back on normal duties tomorrow. You'll want to clear your desks, get reports written up." She gave them a deadpan look. "Fill in your expense sheets."

She got a ripple of laughter.

"So. I'm not going to force anyone — I'm asking for volunteers."

Four or five hands went up immediately; Ella Moran's was one of them, standing at the printer with a handful of postmortem pictures in her hand. "I worked that beat in uniform, Boss," she said. "I know some of the girls. If you want, I could —"

"Go ahead, Ella. Call me direct if you find anything — anything at all."

DC Moran dumped the rest of the photos onto one of her colleagues, then she was out the door.

In Renwick's absence, Simms worked on task allocation with the HOLMES2 manager, devising a schedule with the volunteer canvassers. In twenty minutes they were on their way, stuffing photographs into their pockets and hooking jackets and overcoats from the back of chairs. Simms posted a spare on the whiteboard next to her post-mortem photo and alongside the list of penicillin-related deaths.

As she turned she saw Detective Superintendent Tanford at the door, standing back to let the team out. He nodded to the last officer and stepped inside.

"I was passing," he said. "I heard you'd been told to scale down — thought I'd come in and commiserate. I know you feel there's a lot more to do." He jerked his head in the direction of the door. "And judging by what I've just seen, you intend to get it done. I've got to hand it to you, Kate, I expected to find a demoralized rabble, but I'm almost knocked down in the rush of folk aiming to make the best use of the few hours they've got left. I knew you were good — I never guessed you were inspirational."

Simms bit her cheek to suppress a smile; she had the feeling that Tanford would consider that too girly.

"The photo in our murder victim's purse belonged to Rika," she said. "They were close."

He stared at her. After a few moments he tapped his fingers to his upper lip and a smile ghosted at the corners of his mouth. "Well, well, well. That . . ." He shook his head, picked up a spare photo and studied it. "That's just . . . fantastic. Shows what you can do if you just keep turning over stones, eh, Kate?"

276

Her mobile rang and she dipped her head in apology. "Go ahead," he said.

"Boss, it's Mouse." Apparently Ella Moran had embraced her nickname. "I've spoken to a few of the girls. No one recognized the photo, but someone said I should talk to a girl called Candy — she had a mate called 'Rita'. A foreigner, she said."

"Good. Where can we find this 'Candy'?"

"This time of day," Moran said, "she's usually round the back of Piccadilly Gardens, trying to score."

Simms guessed that if she was going to get anything useful out of their witness, she would need Moran's sensitive touch. "Where are you now?" she asked. "I'll pick you up." Moran gave her a location and she disconnected.

Tanford was still there, watching her, that half-smile playing on his lips. "Still turning over stones, Kate?" He stepped aside with a mock chivalric bow, and waved her on.

Her office phone was ringing as she stopped in to grab her coat and car keys. It was reception. "There's a Doctor Fenn at the desk," the receptionist said.

Simms's mouth dried and her heart began to pound thick and hard.

"He's asking to speak to you, ma'am."

CHAPTER
TWENTY-EIGHT

"Heroin is a Judas, a bad friend who betrays you. It is a cruel lover who goes away and makes you crazy for him."

RIKA

Fennimore saw Kate Simms steaming like a freight train through the glass doors at reception. She wore a woollen coat buttoned to the throat; it was minus five outside and a thick bank of dirty white cloud was creeping towards the city from the Pennine moors. She buzzed herself through, pulling a leather glove onto her left hand like she meant to do battle. Fennimore stood to greet her.

Eyes glittering, jaw set hard, she extended her ungloved hand. "Doctor," she said, "This is . . . unexpected." Her formal courtesy sounded like a poorly veiled threat. She gripped his elbow and steered him to the door. "I'm afraid I can only spare a few seconds — if you wouldn't mind walking with me?"

Outside, she said, "What the *hell* are you doing here — has something happened?"

"Nothing happened," he said. "That was the problem — I was bored."

"You ran out of money."

278

He considered telling her that he was another two hundred to the good, but couldn't think of a way to say it without bragging, so instead he shrugged, said, "Where are we going?"

Kate gave a frustrated groan, turned on her heel and started walking. "'We'," she said, "are going nowhere. *I* am going to the car park; *you* are going back to your hotel."

He loped alongside her. "Wouldn't it be quicker to cut through the building?" The car park was around the back.

"And what if someone recognizes 'Doctor Fenn'?" She carried on at a pace — three sides of the building to gain access to the car park — and he matched her stride easily, which only seemed to infuriate her more. "You're not supposed to *be* here, Nick. I'm not supposed to even be *talking* to you."

"Okay," he said, stalling for time. "But you'll have to drop me — I let my cab go."

She stared at him. "You really think I'm that naive? Hire another one."

"Here?" He turned full circle. This stretch of Rochdale Road was home to the police station, a self-storage unit and a low-cost car park. It was a long, cold walk back to the city. "You see a taxi rank? Black cabs don't hang around police stations, Kate. And a minicab will take thirty minutes to haul out here — I'll freeze to death."

"You could walk it in twenty-five."

"Wrong shoes," he said, looking down at the polished toes of his black Derby lace-ups.

"You should have thought about that before you came out here to ambush me."

She pretended to hunt for her car along the rows of vehicles, and there was something in her agitation, the way she avoided his gaze — he was certain that she was thinking about what she'd said to him over the phone.

"Leave, Nick," she said. "Now."

He couldn't go back to the hotel — he would drive himself mad thinking about what she'd said, and the mistakes he had made five years ago.

"Tell you what — I'll call for a cab, go and wait in reception."

Her eyes widened. "You wouldn't dare."

He began to think he might just get that ride in her car. "I'll just . . ." He jerked his thumb over his shoulder and began to retrace his steps.

"Nick, I'm warning you . . ."

"Don't worry about it," he said, still moving. "I've been out of police work for an age. Who's going to know me?"

She swore softly, and he knew she was about to cave in, but he waited to hear the chirp of her alarm as she clicked the remote key before he turned, careful to keep the smile off his face.

She gave him a look that would melt steel.

"Hey, come on," he said. "You wouldn't even have known that was Rika's photo if it weren't for me."

She couldn't deny it. But it didn't take a lesson in Kate's famous social skills to tell him she didn't like it either.

"You will stay in the car," she said, jabbing the ignition key at him over the roof of the car. "You will *not* speak to anyone."

They stopped to pick up someone at Cheetham Hill. A plump young woman with fine brown hair and a pleasant face. Fennimore vacated the front seat, held the door for her and offered her a beaming smile.

"Hello," she said. It sounded like a question.

"Nick," he said, opening the rear door.

"Detective Constable Moran." She slid into the front seat. "Mouse, if you like."

"Mouse?"

"New nickname," she said. "I'm trying it on for size."

He took the back seat. "Nice to meet you, Mouse. I'm —"

"Walking if you say another word," Simms interrupted.

The young constable threw a puzzled look at her boss.

"Don't worry about him," Simms said. "He's not even here."

There was a time when Piccadilly Gardens was a no-go area, but regeneration since the IRA bomb in the nineties, and a zero-tolerance approach from Greater Manchester Police had effectively reclaimed the gardens from the pushers and addicts who had plagued the area up to the end of the noughties. During the day, at least, the gardens and fountains had once more become a place for families and office workers to relax,

281

take the sun, enjoy the green oasis in the heart of the city.

But the need for heroin is a tyrant — the addicts simply adapted, hovering at the margins, ghosting at the edge of visibility. Goods were bought and sold instead in the narrow streets and dark alleyways that served as service access for the office blocks and shops that fronted the square.

It was here they found Candy. She looked one step away from collapse — two stones underweight, pale and half frozen in a denim jacket and cut-off jeans in the sub-zero temperatures. She shifted from one foot to the other, the cuffs of her jeans loose on her thighs, her legs mottled purple with the cold.

She saw them pull up at the kerb ten feet down the narrow roadway and started walking. She moved slowly, as if her bones ached, as if even the brush of her clothing against her skin caused her pain.

Kate Simms slid the car into first and trundled alongside her.

"You talk to her," Kate said quietly.

The young officer wound down her window. When she'd first spoken, Fennimore recognized her accent as generic Northern — flat vowels and elongated "o"s, but as she spoke to the young hooker, it metamorphosed to the nasal sounds of broad Mancunian.

"Hiya, Candy," she said. "Don't worry, love, we're not here to hassle you."

"That's nice, *Officer Dibble*." Candy jammed her hands into the pockets of her denim jacket and kept walking. "In that case, you can fuck off."

Simms kept pace, while Moran tried again: "I were just talking to Tami-Marie — she said you might be able to help."

The use of a name was as good as an introduction. Candy stopped and bent at the waist to look inside the car. She was so emaciated that the muscles and tendons running down her jaw were visible working under her skin. Her eyes looked huge in her wasted face; her eyebrows were plucked bare — or they'd fallen out — and she'd redrawn them high on her forehead, which, together with her sunken cheeks and sallow skin, gave the impression of a startled wraith. She eyeballed Simms, then leaned in at the window to get a look at Fennimore.

"Who's he?"

"Oh, don't worry about me," he said. "I'm not even here."

She pouted and he saw that she had inexpertly covered a large sore on her upper lip with Vaseline and foundation.

She ignored him, addressing the two women instead: "Looks like a fucking punter in that get-up."

She opened the passenger door, letting in a blast of cold air. "Well, shove up," she said, practically sitting on Fennimore's lap. "I'm freezing my arse off out here."

Shifting to the offside passenger seat, Fennimore glanced out of the rear window and caught a glimpse of a car crawling past the end of the road. A punter: where addicts were drawn, so was their source of income. She perched next to him with one buttock on the seat, but a moment later shifted her weight onto the other buttock.

"First off, it's Candice," she said. "Not Candy."

Moran swivelled in her seat. "Sorry," she said, her tone solemn and respectful. "Candice."

"I don't know who Tami-Marie thinks she is, calling me Candy. I mean what if I started calling her Tami, or Tam —"

"Candice." The officer who called herself "Mouse" was firm, but not sharp.

Candice fiddled with the broken and bleach-damaged hair that formed a fringe on her forehead, raking and primping it. She couldn't sit still. "Well, I'm just saying," she muttered.

"We thought you might know this girl," Moran said, gently but firmly bringing her back to the subject. She took a colour copy of Rika's photo booth picture from an A4-sized leather portfolio and passed it through the gap between the driver's and front passenger's seat.

Candice stared at the picture. She raised her eyes to the young constable and reached out tentatively, as if asking permission. Moran gave her an encouraging smile and she took the photograph in her trembling fingers.

"Rika," Candice said. "She were lovely."

"Tami-Marie thought her name might be Rita," Moran said.

"Rika," Candice said, all offended sensibilities again. "She was from Latvia, for fuck's sake. Who heard of a girl called *Rita* from Latvia?"

Simms whipped round. "What part of Latvia?" If they could pinpoint the place, they could have her full name in days, rather than weeks.

284

"What're you on about?"

"Which city — did she say?"

"Duh!" Candice said, bugging her eyes at the stupidity of the police. "Latvia *is* the city."

Moran took over. "Latvia's a country, hon," she said.

"Well, how'm I supposed to know?" Candice squirmed constantly, taking some of the weight off her bony behind by hanging on to the grip over the door. "She said Latvia. Just Latvia. I'm not bloody Google Earth, am I?"

"We didn't even know that she was from there till just now," Moran said, placating. "Tami-Marie said you and Rika were mates."

Candice nodded. "We worked out the same sauna. But Rika got fucked up on the drugs and doing . . . stuff she should have stayed well clear of." She began tugging at the scrunchy, pulled it out and retied it so that her thin, scraggy ponytail sat on the crown of her head. "She died."

"I know," Moran said. "I'm really sorry, Candice."

Candice's eyes sparkled with tears for a second, but she blinked them away, wiped her nose with the heel of her hand. "Yeah, well, like I said, she got fucked up."

"But we're looking for another girl; someone who was close to Rika."

She eyed first Moran, then Fennimore. "Maybe she doesn't want to be found."

"We've already found her," Simms said, watching for Candice's reaction in the rear-view mirror. "She's dead, too."

285

Candice's eyes narrowed. "It's that girl they found at the back of the hotel, isn't it?"

"We're trying to identify her," Moran said. "She was blonde, blue-eyed. We were thinking maybe she worked with Rika — she had Rika's picture in her purse."

"No." Candice shook her head. "I worked with Rika, I never saw her with no blonde. She was *my* mate. Rika always said I was the only friend she had over here." The possessiveness of her tone was unmistakable.

"Maybe she knew her from Latvia then?" Moran said.

She shrugged, still resentful. It seemed strange that she could feel jealous of a dead girl.

"Short blonde hair," Simms added.

Fennimore remembered the glimpse of a young woman getting into a BMW outside the restaurant and gave her the waiter's description. "Long legged," he said. "Elegant — gorgeous blue eyes."

Candice gave him a sharp look. "He *sounds* like a punter an' all."

"This girl wasn't a user," Moran said. "I mean, most girls need *something* to get them through, but not this girl."

This seemed to chime a chord with Candice. "*Ohmigod*," she said. "Saint Marta of the Just Say No." She smiled like it was a horrible joke. "So she's dead?" The look of spiteful glee on her face a reminder that unkindness passed down the chain from the powerful to the ultimately powerless gets smaller and meaner with every step.

"Why d'you call her Saint Marta?" Simms asked.

"Because. She called Amy a hypocrite just 'cos she likes a little pick-me-up on the late shift, and there's *her* —" She broke off, as though a sudden jolt of electric current had shot through her.

"What, Candice? What did she do?"

"Nothing," she said.

"Why do you call her a hypocrite? Was she carrying drugs for someone maybe?"

Candice's eyes flared wide, then dulled, as though she had deliberately shut down something inside of her. "She didn't do nothing. Just she was full of shit."

"Did she have a surname?" Kate asked.

"McInley. Silly mare thought it sounded English. I told her it was Scotch, but she said she didn't care, and I said she should care. I mean since when did the punters want *English*?" She would have gone on, but Moran intervened.

"Who did she work for, Candice?"

"One of the saunas," Candice said evasively.

"Wouldn't people have missed her?" Fennimore said.

"Oh, yeah, she were very *popular* — had her own set of regulars and everything."

"But it came as a surprise to you that she was dead," Simms said.

Candice eyed her in the mirror. "I don't work there no more — it's a bloody rip-off what they charge for rooms — I decided to go freelance."

Nobody contradicted her.

"So," Moran said, "this Marta — what can you tell us about her?"

Candice folded Rika's picture in half and tucked it inside her jacket. "Depends on what you got to offer me."

Simms said, "What d'you need, Candice?"

"Not what you think." She looked offended. "I'm not just some tart looking for a bit of easy cash, you know."

"Look," Simms said, "we haven't got time to mess about."

"You think I have?" She winced and shifted her weight again. "Time's money, and you've already had ten minutes worth of mine."

"We really need to know who this girl was, Candice," Moran said. "So whatever you can do to help . . ."

She chewed her inner cheek. "They took my kids."

"They?" Simms said.

"Well, it wasn't Daddy Warbucks, was it?" she snapped. "Fucking Social, who else? I want them back."

"You know how it works, Candice, love," Moran said. "You'd have to get yourself straight, first."

"How'm I gonna do that?" she demanded.

"I could maybe get you bumped up the list for rehab," Simms said.

She snorted. "Rehab. Fucking joke. They're *my kids* —" She broke off, and reached for the door handle. "Forget it," she said. "Thanks for the warm." A second later, she was out of the car and two steps down the road.

Fennimore got out the other side and Kate was quick to follow. Moran was slower, watching Kate for her lead. She had good instincts, Fennimore thought. Knew when to take point position and when to hang back.

"Candice."

She flipped him two fingers and carried on walking.

"This bad shit Rika got into . . ." Fennimore saw Kate's warning look, but he went on: "Was it S&M?"

She wheeled to face him, her eyes wide with shock, but she recovered quickly. "Why?" she asked, her face twisted in contempt. "Get off on it, do you, love?"

"Was it caning? Maybe whipping? A hit of some good stuff to ease the pain after — is that the kind of bad shit you mean? Are you into the same shit now, Candice, because I noticed you seem to be in some discomfort."

The thin mask of contempt dropped away completely and she stared at him, horrified.

"Fuck off," she said. A gob of spittle gathered at the corner of her mouth. She was shaking — he didn't feel proud of that, but she wasn't leaving, either.

Simms put herself between the two of them, taking the chance of another shot at persuading her. "We can protect you, Candice," she said. "But only if you tell us what you know."

Candice looked over her shoulder, her eyes glittering with hate and shame. "He can fuck right off out of here, or I will."

Fennimore turned his back and started walking, his head down, though he felt a rising excitement. The discrete packets of information were starting to interconnect: Rika and the murder victim were both tortured, almost certainly by the same man. They injected heroin from the same source. They knew each other, and well enough for the murder victim to carry Rika's picture around in her purse. They both knew Candice, both worked at the same sauna. He suspected that Candice had been subjected to the same torture as Rika and their unidentified murder victim. Sets, subsets, overlapping data — the Venn diagrams of scientific investigation. Soon they would find more intersections — names, places, times, events — and they would begin to understand their significance. Finally, the picture would come into sharp focus. Then everything would make sense. And at the back of it, like a tune that kept repeating over and over in his head: *Fennimore, I love you.*

He glanced up and saw that the kerb crawler had returned. His car was idling at the junction, twenty-five yards down the road. He caught a dull glint of something; the driver had wound down the window. Cocky sod: two women and a man talking to one of the girls in the same car screamed police, and most of the kerb-crawling types would have run a mile. He stared at the car, parked side on at the junction; as the distance closed, he saw that the driver wore sunglasses and a beanie hat. He had one arm stretched out across the doorframe; the angle seemed odd — like he was shielding something.

Fennimore increased his pace, and his heart began to thud. *What the hell?* He shielded his eyes and the punter jerked back inside the car. As the punter lifted his arm off the window frame, Fennimore saw a telephoto lens.

"Hey!"

Simms turned and he pointed to the car, already running. "Camera!" he shouted.

The driver shoved the camera away from him, but he was slow to shift the engine into gear.

Fennimore put on a spurt, yelled again, "HEY!"

Ten yards. Eight. He was going to make it. The engine whined, then caught; the car fishtailed down the narrow roadway. He made the last few yards, rounded the corner at speed, ran a few more yards, then stood still, trying to read the number plate. The car was forty yards down the road. Too late. Too *fucking* late.

It slewed around the corner into the traffic. Horns blared. Tyres screamed, he heard the roar of the engine, then it was gone.

Kate skidded around the corner a second after him. She looked at him and he shook his head, gasping for breath, his hands on his knees. She wasn't even breathing hard. She kicked a can and it ricocheted off one of the buildings.

"Who?" she yelled, fury crackling in her eyes. "Who the hell *was* that?"

He shook his head again and she turned and walked back towards the car. He was still catching his breath when she got to the corner. He heard her curse, then she was running again.

"Ella!" she shouted.

When he got to the corner the young constable was lying on the ground, her hands covering her face.

CHAPTER
TWENTY-NINE

*"A lie with a purpose is one of the worst kind,
and the most profitable."*

FINLEY PETER DUNNE

Ella Moran was coughing and choking, her hands tight
to her face.

"Ella, what happened?" Kate shouted.

The young constable gritted her teeth. "Pepper
spray."

Fennimore was already calling emergency services.

Moran whooped and spluttered.

"Help is coming." Kate Simms knelt beside her.
"Ella. *Ella*, take your hands away from your face."

She roared into her hands. "Bugger, bugger, *bugger*
— it hurts."

Fennimore gave their location to the operator while
Kate prised Moran's hands away from her face. Her
eyes were clamped tight shut.

"You need to try and open your eyes, increase your
blink rate."

She turned her head and tried to rub her face against
her jacket sleeve, but Simms stopped her. "Ella, listen
to me — remember your training — the more you do
that the worse it'll be. You *can't touch your face*."

She coughed and retched. "I know but it bloody *hurts*." The upper half of her face was one livid red welt.

Fennimore pocketed his phone. "What can I do?"

"Help me get her up." Simms gripped the young officer's wrists as she writhed and groaned battling with her instinct to rub the irritant off her skin.

Simms nodded to Fennimore and he put his arm around the young constable's shoulders. "Come on," Simms said. "Try to sit up."

They got her to a sitting position and long threads of mucus trailed from her nose and mouth, but neither of them tried to wipe them away — it would only prolong the pain.

Sirens approached through the traffic. "I'm okay," Moran said. "Get after her." Simms hesitated, and she yelled, "For God's sake, Boss, go!"

Fennimore said, "Go ahead, I'll look after her."

She ran, only returning as the crew was lifting Ella Moran into the ambulance. She was alone. Ella Moran's eyes were open — just. She was blinking furiously, trying to wash the capsicum out of her eyes; her eyelids looked swollen and red, and her skin was puffy and inflamed, but she was breathing more easily.

"How is she?" Simms asked.

"We'll irrigate her eyes before we set off to the hospital," the paramedic said. "It'll make her a bit more comfortable."

"Boss, did you find her?" Moran asked.

"No, but don't worry about it, Ella — she gave us the lead we needed." The driver got back into the van and his partner climbed inside.

"Ella," Kate called, as he shut the doors, "take it easy. I'll check on you later."

They sat in the car for a few minutes, Simms staring through the windscreen at the patched tarmac on the narrow back street. She gripped the wheel as if she was already driving on treacherous roads through dangerous territory.

At last, Fennimore said, "Was he watching Candice, or you?"

"I don't know." There was something in her tone that told him there was a "but" at the end of that sentence.

"Kate, what are you not telling me?"

She sighed and shook her head as if she was regretting what she was about to say before she even said it. "Yesterday evening, parking up at your hotel, I got the feeling I was being followed."

Dread settled under his ribcage like a solid lump. "Why didn't you say?"

"Because I thought I was mistaken. I mean, why would anyone be following me?"

"You have pissed off some bad people just recently."

"I'm a cop. I wouldn't be doing my job if I didn't piss off bad people."

"Well, that's all very fine and macho, but they won't feel bound by your rules of engagement."

For a second her game face slipped and a sliver of fear shone in her eyes; he saw that she was trying to tough it out and he was being an arsehole.

"Kate," he said, "I —"

"Forget it." She started the car. "You've always been crap at apologies. "Candice gave me the name of the salon she worked out of — want to come?"

Frank and Sol Henry's massage parlour was located on an industrial estate in a low-rise, low-rental retail unit. The spiked aluminium fencing around the yard and shabby blue paintwork suggested a car repair shop rather than a knocking shop, and the next-door unit was occupied by a plumbing trade warehouse. The sign — "Francine's" — was painted in an ornate script: the only hint of the kind of trade that went on inside.

Five cars were parked on the patched concrete in front of the building: a Lexus, a Merc, two Ford Fiestas and a Ka. No BMW. Kate opened the door and they were greeted by a blast of heat that nearly knocked them back into the car park. The reception area was furnished with a couple of leather sofas; a tanned brunette wearing way too much make-up and very little else sat at the desk on a high stool, leafing through a copy of *Hello!* magazine.

She looked Kate Simms up and down and said, "Sorry, love, this is a gentlemen only service."

"Haven't you heard of equal opportunities?" Simms said. She produced her warrant card. "Boss's office through here, is it?" She was through the archway and into the narrow corridor towards the back of the building before the brunette had the chance to uncross her legs.

Fennimore heard a buzzer in the distance; the office door opened before they reached it and a man barred their path.

"Police," Kate warned.

He looked past her, locking gazes with Fennimore. "Yeah, and what's he?"

"He's a police consultant, and he's with me." Fennimore was relieved to be under her guardianship, and more than happy to let her do the talking on this occasion.

She held up her warrant card. "Detective Chief Inspector Simms." His gaze shifted momentarily to her card, then back to her and Simms said, "Your name, please, sir."

"Frank Henry," he said, but he didn't budge.

"We can have this conversation in your office, Mr Henry, or we can talk about your murdered employee in your reception lounge," Kate said, her voice hard. "Your choice."

"We don't employ anyone here — except a cleaner." This from a stocky man with a shaved head who had appeared from the reception lounge. "All masseuses are what you call free agents — we just manage the facilities." He pronounced it "massooses", American style. He edged past Fennimore and offered Kate his hand. She didn't take it.

"Fair enough," he said. "Sol, Frank's brother. Let's take this inside, eh, Frank?"

Frank barred the way for a second longer, then turned his back and went into the office. He seated

296

himself behind the desk, while his brother perched on the edge of it.

They couldn't have been more different, these two men. Frank was tall and wiry, his hair worn long and loosely tied back, hippy-style, but there was nothing New Age or hippy-style about the flint in his eye. Sol was bald and built like a nightclub bouncer, yet he seemed to have inherited all the family's affability genes.

"Off to a bit of a bad start, there, Chief Inspector," Sol said, with the superficial bonhomie of a businessman. "When reception presses the red button, it usually means trouble — so the adrenaline starts pumping, you get me?" He didn't seem to expect an answer, because he went on, "So, who's been murdered?"

She didn't answer that one immediately. Instead she took out the photograph of Rika. "D'you know this girl?"

"Rika," Sol said.

Frank's left hand, nearest to Sol, twitched, but he didn't speak.

"She worked here for a bit last year — she was heavily into smack and we . . . uh . . ." He seemed to be searching for a suitable euphemism.

"We parted company," Frank supplied helpfully.

"Rika wasn't murdered," Sol added. "It was her habit killed her."

"But Rika knew your murdered employee."

Sol gazed at her with innocent expectation.

It was a punt — they didn't have a positive identification, only a suggestion that their murder victim worked for the Henrys and this from a street prostitute whose brain was addled with drugs and sickness.

Sol began to shake his head, but the stillness in the room, the brothers' careful avoidance of each other's gaze, told her she was right.

"Marta McKinley," Simms said. "Blonde, five seven, mid-twenties, Slavic features, blue eyes?"

The brothers looked at each other, and Frank nodded. "Marta."

"Would this be the body behind the hotel?" Sol asked, his expression solemn, concerned.

"You know about 'the body behind the hotel'. You've had at least two visits from police canvassers in the last week," Simms said. "And you didn't make the connection?"

"We thought she'd defected to a rival sauna owner," Frank said. "We've had a problem with that recently."

"But you would recognize the description, wouldn't you?"

"I might've — if I'd heard it," Frank said. "Sol?"

Sol shook his head. "I must've been off the premises when they came."

"Convenient."

Frank glared back at her, his eyes black and hard as polished stone.

Simms didn't waver.

"We liked Marta." Sol again, brokering the peace. "The client-base liked her — she brought in return

298

customers and referrals. And the other girls benefitted from the old recommendation gambit, as well. You know the kind of thing: 'If you liked that, you'll love this.'" He looked at Simms as though anticipating a nod of understanding and approval. All he got was a blank stare.

"Who's been poaching the girls?" she asked.

"George Howard," Sol said, as easily as he'd told them Marta was one of their girls.

If she was surprised, she did a good job of hiding it. "What made you think Marta had gone to this George Howard?"

Frank leaned across his desk and buzzed through to reception. "Amy, can you come through to the office, love?"

Amy appeared a moment later — it turned out to be the brunette with the spray-on tan. Since their arrival she'd put on a pink silk dressing gown with feathers at the cuffs and collar.

"When Marta didn't show up for work last week you told me she'd said something to you — what was it?"

"You mean about the try-out?"

"Yeah," Frank said. "Where was that?"

She shrugged and her upper half jiggled outrageously, but the gown covered enough to enable Fennimore to focus on what she was saying, rather than on her moving parts.

"I dunno," she said. "Up the road at that new place — Georgina's."

"Georgina's is what George Howard calls his parlour," Sol added.

"What day was this?" Simms asked.

"D'you mean what day did she tell me, or what day she was going for the try-out?" Amy said.

"The try-out," Simms said slowly and clearly — a definite clue to Fennimore that she was only just keeping her patience.

Amy answered lazily: "Dunno, love. You'd have to ask her PA."

Sol said, "Hey, you — manners."

She put a finger to her lips and worried at one long nail. "Dunno," she said again. "I wasn't really listening."

He jerked his chin and Amy slouched out of the room.

Sol smiled apologetically. "Like I said, the girls are free agents, but Marta was on a good screw here — 'scuse the pun — we knew she'd be back. Even kept her locker for her."

"I'd like our CSIs to take a look at that."

Sol beamed like a salesman who'd just closed a deal. "No problem. Anything we can do to help, eh, Frank?"

Frank kept his eyes hard and stony on Simms.

"You should have a word with George Howard though," Sol said.

Frank folded his arms and leaned forward a bit, staring into Kate's eyes like he was trying to see what was behind them. "Oh, she already has, Sol."

She didn't confirm or deny, but he went on: "Howard's place has been closed ever since police arrested a fifty-three-year-old man — stands to reason."

"You *do* keep a close eye on the competition," Fennimore said, and Frank's eyes fixed on him for a few uncomfortable seconds.

Sol laughed. "Nah, a few of the prodigals came back, looking to be reinstated onto the rota after your lot strung police tape across his driveway, that's all."

"Ironically, we'd had a sit-down with Howard the night Marta buggered off," Frank said.

"The night we *thought* she buggered off," Sol corrected him.

"When was this?" Simms asked.

"Last Thursday."

"You seem very sure."

Frank tapped the year planner on the wall behind him. "Rotas," he said. "Marta was supposed to do Wednesday, Thursday, Friday last week. She didn't show up for her Friday session."

Marta McKinley's body had been found in the early hours of Friday morning.

"Where did this sit-down take place?"

"The Derby Brewery Arms on Cheetham Hill."

"So you can alibi him," Simms said.

Sol raised his eyebrows. "He does *need* an alibi then?"

"Oh, he needs it all right — he just doesn't seem keen to involve you gents."

"Well, that's a bit weird, isn't it?"

She smiled, unconvinced. "Not if you threatened him."

Frank's head jutted forward. "Does he say we did?"

301

Fennimore could see the cords standing out in his neck — this was a man who took his weight training seriously, the kind that ran on adrenaline and testosterone. Big muscles, small nuts and simmering anger and resentment made for a volatile mix, but Simms eyed him coolly.

"Mr Howard won't say anything about his drinking buddies," she said. "He won't even say he *was* drinking with anyone."

"Look, chief." This from Sol again. "It was a friendly drink. We advised him it wasn't good form to poach the talent."

"Very civilized."

"He's new to the game," Sol said, spreading his arms wide to demonstrate his generous spirit. "You've got to allow a bit of leeway."

"So why is he refusing to name the two men who could vouch for his whereabouts on the night Marta died?"

The two men in question looked at each other. "Guilty conscience maybe," Sol said.

"Meaning?"

"You never said *when* Marta died. We met him about nine, poured him into a taxi just after midnight." It all tallied with what the landlord had told them. "So, us-as-alibi only works if Marta died between nine and midnight, am I right? And if you was to ask, we'd have to say Georgie-Porgie was very well oiled and a little bit argumentative when we waved bye-bye to him." Sol's eyes darted from Simms to Fennimore. His weren't as dark as his brother's, and Fennimore could see the sparkle of mischief in them. "So, are we his alibi? Or not?"

She countered with a question. "Where did *you* go when you left the pub?"

"Party," Frank said.

"Where?"

"My place," Sol said. "A few of the girls, nice bit of sushi, a few bottles of Cristal on ice. Was a good night. Come to think of it, Marta was supposed to join us, but she never showed up."

"And this party went on till what time?"

He stroked the rim of his earlobe with one finger. "Oh, I'd say, six-ish?"

Frank nodded in agreement. "Funny Howard wouldn't give you our names."

"Yeah," Sol said. "You should look into that."

"Oh, I will," Simms said. "And we'll want to speak to all the girls again."

Frank looked like he might balk at that, but Sol said, "You can take the canteen and one of the upstairs suites. I'll call the off-duty girls in as well if you like."

"That's very cooperative of you, Mr Henry," Simms said.

Sol grinned. "Better get it over in one go than have a marked car sitting outside the shop for a week, waiting to scoop them up, eh, chief?"

Outside, Simms said, "It just keeps looking worse for George Howard."

"It does, doesn't it?" Fennimore agreed. "Of course, Howard is competition — the Henry brothers have a vested interest in getting him off the scene, by whatever means."

A silver Mondeo turned in from the main road and slowed, indicating a right turn into Francine's.

"So what's the plan?" Fennimore asked.

"The first thing is to check their story," she said. "I'll get someone over to the pub with a mugshot — ask the landlord to confirm it was the Henrys he saw with Howard."

"A mugshot? Really, Chief Inspector — that's blatant stereotyping."

She said, "If you'd care to put a tenner on it?" She didn't actually smile, but her eyes crinkled a bit.

"You can keep your cash, and I'll keep mine," he said.

The owner of the Mondeo locked up and sauntered into the massage parlour.

Simms dialled the incident room on her mobile. "Renwick, can you do a VIN check for me?" She gave him the registration number of the Mondeo. Seconds later, she said, "Great — keep a note of the name and address, I might need it later." She asked for information to be gathered on the Henrys and for him to send someone back to the pub to verify the brothers' account of their meeting with George Howard. "And can you find out who sent in task reports for the two visits to their massage parlour?" She paused. "Francine's, that's right." She listened for a moment. "Not logged, yet . . . Can you chase that? . . . Thanks. I want to interview one of the girls myself, then I'll head back. Can you send out a few from the canvassing team to talk to the girls here? Hang on a second."

She covered the mouthpiece and spoke softly. "You need to disappear, Nick."

He was reluctant. The snap-happy man who was following her was still out there. But he knew that if he said a word she would laugh him down the street as a patronizing chauvinist. As he hesitated, the owner of the Mondeo hurried out of the salon as if he'd just been told his house was on fire.

"Sir," Simms said. "You need to go back inside."

The man avoided looking at her, fiddling with his remote key. He fumbled the switch, and when he opened the door the alarm went off.

Simms flashed Fennimore a smile. "Who says policing can't be fun?"

She walked towards the Mondeo and Fennimore watched her present her warrant card and take the keys from the driver's trembling fingers to shut off the alarm. Then she ushered him politely, but without a scintilla of doubt that he would do as he was told, inside the building.

CHAPTER
THIRTY

Amy was slumped in her seat, hands between her knees, frowning at the tabletop. It was Ikea utility, stained with coffee rings and gritty with spilt sugar. Methadone gave them a sweet tooth, and the stats said that most sex workers were on heroin or methadone — or both.

"I told you everything I know," the girl said, a petulant frown creasing her brow.

"Amy, I'm not trying to get you into trouble," Simms said. "I just want to find out who did this to Marta."

"What d'you want me to say — I hardly knew her."

"Did she talk about family, or friends? Where she was from? Where she lived in Manchester?"

"Oh, no, Marta was too cool for that. Mysterious Marta never told you nothing about herself. Maybe if she'd shared a bit, not been so stuck up —"

"D'you think you could've stopped what happened to her, Amy?" Simms asked, holding back from adding, *Would you have stopped it if you could?*

She shrugged.

"Can you help me see to it that it doesn't happen to any other girl?"

Amy pondered on the question, a look on her face like she was deciding on pink or red lipstick. "All right," she said. "I'll tell you what I know, but like I said, she wasn't the chatty type. All's I know is what she told the punters. They were all full of it: their exotic Russian doll."

She lapsed into a pouting silence.

"And what did they say?"

"Doesn't matter," Amy said, irritated. "It was a pack of lies anyway — different story every day of the week. Don't know how she kept track."

Simms wondered if Marta *hadn't* been able to keep track, and one of the men had taken offence. But she quickly dismissed the idea. Wasn't sex work all a lie — pretty young women faking orgasms with fat middle-aged men? Marta's punters paid for her time, her body and her cooperation, and as long as she maintained the pretence, why would they care?

A boyfriend, on the other hand, might take strong exception to being lied to . . .

"Was she seeing anybody?" Simms asked.

The frown stayed on Amy's face, but for a second, Simms thought she saw a flicker of the eyelids, a flare of recognition, then Amy began to shake her head. "A regular maybe? Someone who took a particular interest in her."

The frown deepened for a moment, but Amy sat slowly upright. "Yeah. As a matter of fact, yeah, there was someone." She met Kate Simms's eye boldly, gave a little flick of the head. "Clever Trevor."

"Clever?"

"Thinks he is, anyway. Schoolteacher — told me he worked at the local comp." She snorted. "Yeah, and I'm Katie Price." She gave Simms a scornful look. "I went to that school — they'd have ate him alive. *And* he's weird."

"There are all kinds of weird, Amy . . ." Simms said, thinking, *S&M weird?*

"Clean freak." Amy wrinkled her nose. "Made us scrub down before he'd touch us."

"So, he does see the other girls?"

"Not after Marta. Once she was on the rota, he only had eyes for her. Always mooning after her, he was. 'Marta, don't you know I care for you?', 'Marta, let me take you away from all this.'"

"She told you this?"

"Didn't need to. Always making a show of himself, he was. Hanging around, just hoping to catch a glimpse of her, even if he was too skint to pay. Clingy bastard." She shuddered. "Marta started bringing him downstairs after the sessions, just to make sure he went. Then last week, he books a half-hour, she comes down, as per usual and — as per — he's on at her. Same old *blah-de-blah* about her being better than this. He wants to save her, give her a decent life. Well, she turns on him. 'I don't need saving, Trevor, and even if I did, you are the last man in the world I would turn to.' I've never seen her so angry. She even swears at him, calls him a fucking pervert — and that's not Saint Marta at all."

"*Saint* Marta?" she said, thinking about Candice.

308

Amy's eyes widened. "Don't tell Sol I said that. He'd kill me if he heard me bad-mouthing her."

"Sol have a soft spot for her, did he?"

Amy rolled her eyes. "He's a man, isn't he? And I wouldn't call it *soft*, exactly."

"Good that you can see the funny side."

The girl checked her out, seeing if she was messing with her, but Simms kept her gaze level, her face open and sympathetic.

"Well, you got to find some way through, right?" Amy said.

"Right," Simms agreed, solemnly.

"See, Marta always thought she had to 'save' people." Simms tut-tutted sympathetically.

The girl's mouth twisted into a cruel little smirk. "Joke is, the only difference between her and Trevor was *she* didn't have a hard-on for the girls she tried to save."

"Was there any girl in particular Marta tried to save?"

"Candice." She didn't even have to think about it.

Candice, whose special friend was Rika, who in turn was a special friend of Marta's. All three of them linked like daisies on a chain.

Simms wrote the name down as if it meant nothing to her, kept her eyes on the page and her voice casual, interested, but not overly so, while the pulse jittered in her throat. "Is Candice around today?"

"Long gone. Hopeless bloody addict, always on the lam for a few quid. Not for herself — never for herself — it was always 'for the kids'."

"Any idea where she went?"

"Like *I* care?" The emotion riding in Amy's eyes was hard and unforgiving and mean.

Candice was the common link. If Fennimore was right — if she had submitted to a whipping — she might even know Marta's killer. They *had* to find her.

"I suppose if an addict gets desperate, she'll do just about anything to itch that scratch," Simms said, keeping her tone conversational.

"Wouldn't know."

Too close to home, Simms thought. *Better change tack*. "Did you know Rika?"

Amy's gaze shifted to the left, as if someone had come into the room, but the only two things behind Simms were the kitchen sink and a fly-spotted mirror.

"Amy?" she said.

"Haven't been here that long," the girl said, licking her lips.

"Rika had whip marks on her buttocks. D'you know who might have done that to her?"

"A lot of the punters are into bondage games."

"These were more than 'games'."

She fiddled with the sugar bowl. "I'm not into that shit."

"No," Simms soothed. "But girls talk."

"Not me."

"What, never?"

"D'you think it's all tarts with a heart, looking out for each other like on the telly?" she sneered. "I got my own problems. I don't wanna hear that stuff." The door opened and her eyes grew big in her head.

"Everything all right in here, ladies?"

Simms turned angrily to face Sol Henry. "I'm conducting an interview in here, Mr Henry," she said.

"Heard voices raised," he said, a soppy grin on his face. "Our Amy can be a bit of a cat." He hissed and mimed a paw-swipe, claws out.

Amy was already up. "I gotto go home," she said. "Things to do." She swept past Sol, but he caught her by the arm.

"If the Chief Inspector is finished with you," he said. There was no threat in his words or his tone, but the girl stopped dead and looked anxiously at Simms.

She stood, offering the girl a business card. "You can let go of her now, Mr Henry."

Sol Henry looked down at his meaty fingers, pressed into Amy's flesh, then up to the girl's face before releasing her.

"You see Trevor, give me a call," Simms said.

As the young masseuse fled, Simms was in no doubt that the call would come only with Sol Henry's permission.

Renwick met her at the door of the incident room with a sheaf of notes in his hand. "Pub landlord has positively ID'd Sol and Frank Henry as the men he saw drinking with George Howard. And I asked someone to look up the Henrys' arrest record." He handed her a sheet, and held up a second flimsy between finger and thumb. "Carol Watson — aka Candice, aka 'Candy'. Addict and prostitute. Three children — all taken into care ten days ago, prosecution pending."

311

There was no denying Renwick had made a bad start, but he had worked damned hard since. She smiled. "Good work, Sergeant."

He didn't return her smile, but he looked pleased. She scanned the notes.

"No address?"

He shook his head. "Landlord kicked her out with six months' rent owing."

So, Candice was in the wind; in a city as big as Manchester there were a million places to hide.

"Okay," she said. Maybe Ella would know who to ask, then she remembered with a thud that DC Moran was still in the hospital and made a mental note to swing by. She began to move on, thinking Renwick had finished, but he shuffled a bit to his right, blocking her way, eyes down.

"Boss." He lowered his voice. "The Super's in your office. He doesn't look a happy bunny."

She nodded, made another move, but he stopped her again.

"The other thing you asked for — the canvass on Francine's."

"Got a name?" she asked.

"Beasley."

Beasley — again. If he'd done his job right, they could've had the victim's name two days ago. Simms stared at him, her blood fizzing and popping under her skin. "Talk to him," she said.

"Will do."

"And when you're done with him, send him to me."

She watched Renwick make his way to the water cooler where Beasley was chatting up one of the HOLMES operatives. *Later*, she thought. Right now she needed to find out why Spry had hiked over from headquarters for the second time in a day.

Detective Superintendent Spry was wearing a heavy overcoat; he carried good-quality leather gloves in his right hand. The cold came off him like November mist; he must have come straight up from the car park. His high colour was more muted than normal, but it was as if someone had adjusted the saturation values on a digital image — he just seemed greyer — and by the look on his face, he hadn't made this special trip to the hinterland to congratulate her on the breakthrough in the case.

He declined a seat, and they stood at arm's length in her small office.

"When did you last speak to your NPIA advisor?" he asked.

"I don't know . . . it's been frantic. I think I rang him a few days ago."

He nodded, watching her closely. "A few days. You're sure of that?"

She began to speak, but he interrupted.

"It's actually been a full week, Kate." He waited for that information to sink in. "Which means you haven't consulted your forensic specialist advisor once on the *entire* murder investigation."

Stupid, she thought. *Bloody careless — you could have at least thrown him a bone.*

"Do you know where I found all this out?" Spry demanded. "At an ACPO Homicide meeting — I've come straight from there to share this news with you.

"You've been on committees, Kate — you know how these meetings are. Sometimes the only highlight is coffee and a McVitie's digestive halfway through. So," he said, "let me paint you a picture: I'm supping my coffee, engaged in chit-chat, and your NPIA advisor starts having a good old bitch about how this new DCI in Manchester blew him off when he offered his expertise in a murder investigation. You do know who chairs ACPO Homicide, don't you, Kate?"

Now she knew where this was going. She felt sick. She avoided his gaze, but Spry jutted his head forward, into her line of vision, unhealthy colour creeping into his face. He was not going to let this go until he had an answer.

"ACC Gifford, sir," she said.

"Full marks, well done. Now, Assistant Chief Constable Gifford happens to be standing next to me at this moment, so hears this, and he is not pleased. It's almost comical, the look of horror on the advisor's face. He was just having a bit of a moan, filling in the silence with idle gossip, and suddenly the ACC's involved. Of course he wants to know the details — which is embarrassing," he went on, talking through gritted teeth. "Because I. Couldn't. Tell him." By now, he was puce from the neck up.

Grovel, or attack? She thought about Tanford's advice about political savvy; decided grovelling would leave her self-respect in shreds and gain her nothing.

So, with a mental shrug, she said, "You might recall that the NPIA advisor told me there was nothing to investigate in the overdoses. I requested the tests, which proved otherwise. *I* proved that StayC's death was caused by a severe allergic reaction. And it turns out our murder victim has a direct link to Rika — one of the heroin deaths — and Rika has a direct link to Francine's — a massage parlour that has only just appeared on our radar."

Superintendent Spry opened his mouth, then shut it again, a frown of complete consternation on his face, and she forged ahead.

"We now have a name for the murder victim — Marta McKinley — not her real name, admittedly, but we're almost there. Marta worked for the same massage parlour as Rika — circles within circles, sir."

"If these two girls are connected," Spry said, sniffing an opportunity to criticize her methods. "Why was this massage parlour missed out on the canvass?"

"It wasn't." She thought about Beasley, but managing a lazy team member was her job, not her superintendent's, so she said, "But until my visit today *nobody* recognized the victim's description."

"What do we have on the owners?"

Simms raised an eyebrow — he was actually showing an interest. She sorted through the handful of pink slips Renwick had handed her and read from the sheet:

"The older brother, Frank, has a couple of arrests for assault and a conviction for GBH going back to the nineties — apparently he was a roadie for a rock band. Also a caution for possession of marijuana and a six-month spell inside for cocaine — possession with intent to supply — see above. The younger brother, Sol . . ." She skimmed the sheet. "Assault . . . assault . . . burglary. All teenage stuff — nothing from the age of twenty."

"Fairly clean, given the business they're in," he said.

"And now we know Marta worked for them, they've decided to cooperate. One of the girls has said Marta had a blazing row with an obsessive client only last week. He hasn't been seen since."

Spry frowned. His brow cleared for an instant, then he was frowning all over again. He slapped his gloves into his hand. He started to speak. He stopped. She saw him setting the advantages of a quick completion of the investigation against a humiliating turnaround and release of his favourite suspect if it turned out that Marta's obsessive client was the killer. Only recently the landlord of murdered landscape architect Joanna Yeates had won his libel claim against eight tabloid newspapers, and he was planning to sue Avon and Somerset police for wrongful arrest. The fallout from a mess like that would certainly cast a pall over a Detective Superintendent's dull but spotless career.

Spry thrust his gloves into his pockets and his hands came out white and empty. When he clasped them as if in prayer, she knew she'd won the battle.

She waited for his introductory gambit — his statement of the non-negotiable in his climb-down. "You can't sideline your specialist advisor," he said.

"No, sir." No harm in being magnanimous in victory.

"You *do* have a good suspect."

316

"Plausible, anyway," she agreed, not willing to give that much ground on Howard. "But Marta's obsessive client — we need to trace him."

Spry sucked his teeth. "All right. I can give you a bit more time, but I'm standing firm on budgetary considerations — I will *not* go back to Gifford and tell him you need more staff."

She saw a flash of white in his muddy eyes and thought, *Oh, dear Lord, he's scared of Gifford.*

Back in the incident room, she gave officers who were running interviews at the sauna a brief update. She wanted anything they could get on "Trevor".

"We need more to go on than he's 'weird'." As she spoke, she scanned the room. Ella Moran was standing near the back, a band of redness across her eyes and upper face. "As of now, I want the girls interviewed here, rather than at the salon." She was thinking about Sol Henry, his chunky fingers bruising Amy's arm. "Trevor's taste for prostitutes is obsessive, and probably long-standing. He told Amy he was a teacher — he said local comp, but she says not — so maybe one of the easier schools, further out. You all know the area better than me — I'm just an ignorant Southerner."

A few of them smiled; all of them looked eager to make a start.

"Ask the girls if he ever let slip what subject he taught — we could cross-check it against school staff lists. Or did he drop a name — maybe a pupil, or a member of staff who was giving him a hard time. If he complained about traffic on the way over to the salon, did he name a particular road? Anything that could help us narrow the field."

She sought out one of the admin staff. "Contact the CRB, see if there's a Trevor on their list." Since 2002, anyone who applied for a job in schools had to go through a Criminal Records Bureau check; the rules applied only to new applications — so if Trevor had been in post for a while, he wouldn't be listed, but it was still worth a look. The meeting broke up a few minutes later. On her way to talk to George Howard, she paused to speak to DC Moran who by now was inching towards her desk with one hand shielding her eyes.

"Ella, what on earth are you doing here? You should be at home."

"I'm fine, Boss."

"You look terrible." She resisted an impulse to seize the constable's arm and lead her to a chair.

"It's just the after-effects. They washed all the nasty stuff out with baby shampoo at the hospital — said I'd be right as rain in a few hours."

"Okay. Take a few hours off, come back when you're fit."

Her chin came up, but when she tried to look Simms in the eye, she squinted and blinked as if she was looking straight into the sun. She lowered her voice. "Boss, it was me found the lead that took us to Francine's."

"Yes," Simms said. "It was. And we wouldn't have Marta's name now if it weren't for you. I won't forget that, Ella."

The young constable hesitated, and Simms understood — it was still hard for a female officer to get noticed for the right reasons in policing. "I won't let anyone else forget it either," Simms added.

George Howard was wearing a pale-blue shirt with a blue-and-mauve paisley pattern tie. His house was still locked down, and the shirt still held its creases from the shop wrapping. This was the third day since his arrest, and Howard didn't seem quite so sure of himself.

"Why didn't you say you were drinking with Frank and Sol Henry on the evening of the murder?" Simms asked.

His eyes widened — only a fraction — but she caught it.

He said, "Are those the men you keep trying to place me with?"

She smiled. "You, with your spreadsheets and profit predictions and pre-tax results, expect me to believe you didn't know about your nearest rivals?"

He shrugged and Simms said, "Could you respond for the tape, please, Mr Howard?"

"I went for a drink at my local," he said. "If, as you say, they also run a business in the area, it's not so strange that we would bump into each other from time to time."

"That doesn't answer my question," she said. He shrugged again. "They say that they had arranged a meeting with you."

He shook his head, then leaned forward to speak into the recorder. "No," he said.

She glanced at the statements in front of her. "They say you were 'drunk and argumentative' when they put you in a taxi at around midnight."

"They can say what they like — it doesn't make it true."

"You said you don't remember how the night ended — how can you say what's true and what isn't?"

He didn't reply.

"You see, to make your story true, the pub landlord would have to be lying; Sol and Frank Henry would have to be lying. I can't see why they would do that, can you?"

His solicitor looked across at him. "George?"

"No comment."

"I can't see why *they* would lie, but I could see why *you* would, Mr Howard."

His grey eyes met hers, wary, trapped.

"You had an appointment to see a new 'masseuse' on Thursday night. Is that correct?"

"I'm not sure."

"You're a methodical person, Mr Howard," Simms said. "As we speak, people are scouring your BlackBerry and your diary."

He dropped his gaze and she heard the compulsive *tic-tic-tic* of him picking at the scabs on his hands.

She waited, watching his eyes dart left and right under his lowered lids. Finally, he said, "It was a girl called Marta."

Simms held her breath.

"But she didn't show up."

Simms looked at Howard, and then his solicitor. Howard was sweating, but his face was grey. His solicitor, though, was bug-eyed — furious that he'd lied to her, or that he'd been found out in a lie — Simms really didn't care which.

"The murder victim's name was Marta," she said. "She worked for the Henry brothers. That is, until the night *you* were supposed to meet with her."

He dragged his fingers through his hair, and the grey of his eyes seemed to waver and drift; this was a man who knew he was screwed and couldn't understand how he'd got into this mess.

"I told you," he said, way too late to have any credibility, "she didn't show up."

"You withhold key evidence about the murder victim. You swear you don't remember what happened after you were drinking in the pub. Then, when you can't deny that any longer, you tell me that you *did* have an appointment with Marta but she didn't show up."

George Howard lifted his hands onto the table. He had picked every scab from the scratches, leaving pale pink notches and lines of shiny skin.

"Let me tell you how this looks, Mr Howard," she said. "It looks like you kept quiet about the Henrys because you *knew* they couldn't provide you with an alibi. You did meet with the Henrys. What they said made you angry, but you'd already invited Marta for a try-out, so you went ahead with it."

He groaned and rubbed the heel of one hand into his eye socket.

"The Henrys are hard men — maybe you felt hurt and humiliated."

Behind his hands he was shaking his head.

"So you decided to take it out on one of their girls."

"Please, stop!" He dragged his hands from his face. "Just stop it."

For aching seconds nobody moved, nobody spoke.

"I know what you think of me, Chief Inspector. But there are things you don't understand." He heaved a sigh.

The atmosphere in the room was one of expectation. He really was going to confess. Simms wasn't sure how she felt about that. She'd been so sure that Howard was set up, and now he was about to admit he had murdered Marta.

"I suppose," he said, tentatively, "that if a person was so drunk or traumatized by . . . something that he couldn't remember, he might plead . . .?"

"Diminished responsibility," his solicitor said automatically.

"So if he had certain . . . memories." He pressed his thumb into his breastbone as if to quell a pain. "Certain . . . images, things he couldn't understand, but which were truly awful. What might he —"

He flinched at a knock at the door.

Shit. Simms turned angrily. It was Renwick. "Not now," she said.

He stood his ground. "Sorry, Boss," he said. "You need to hear this."

Renwick was standing with Kilfoyle, the soft-featured constable who had led the canvassing teams.

"I showed the landlord the Henrys mugshots," Kilfoyle said. "It was definitely them that Howard was drinking with."

"I know," Simms said, "I have the pink slip to prove it." She looked from one to the other, trying hard not to tap her foot with impatience. If they had interrupted her interview for this . . .

"I was on my way back here when he rang my mobile," Kilfoyle said. "The picture jogged his memory." She saw excitement in his soft blue eyes. "Only *one* of the Henrys left with Howard on the night of the murder. The other — 'the tall, mad-eyed one' — left half an hour earlier after taking a call."

So, Frank Henry had left the pub a half-hour before midnight. She stared at Kilfoyle, with Howard's near-confession swirling in her head. She knew one thing for certain: the Henrys hadn't told her the whole truth, and she didn't intend to charge Howard until she had that.

She stepped back into the interview room, announcing her return for the tape.

"I'm requesting a consultation with my client before we proceed," his solicitor said. It seemed she'd shaken off her outrage that Howard had lied to her and had clicked back into professional mode again.

"I'd like Mr Howard to finish what he was saying before we were interrupted," Simms said.

Howard turned his flat, grey stare on her. It seemed he too had made use of the break to recalibrate his feelings. "I don't know what to say to you," he said. "Except I'm not a killer."

CHAPTER
THIRTY-ONE

"There are a lot of lies going around . . .
and some of them are true."

SIR WINSTON CHURCHILL

Fennimore stood in the arched entrance of his hotel, watching for Kate Simms's arrival. The temperature had dropped, the air was sharp, the pavements cold and iron hard. He enjoyed the bite in the air, needing it to clear his head; in the hours since he walked back to the city he had chased lab results, lost a couple of hundred on the races, and done something that was possibly very stupid, and which he would almost certainly regret.

Betting on the races was a distraction from the calculations he would otherwise do obsessively, compulsively, over and over in his head. But gambling was like a sugar high — peaks led to troughs — you needed to limit your intake. His two other palliatives were work and rock climbing. Work, because it required a mental immersion that excluded the helpless, despairing thoughts that otherwise crowded in; rock climbing because it required total physical commitment; the downside being there was only so much rock climbing you could do before it became a thinly masked suicide bid. So, mostly he relied on work to keep him sane.

He caught sight of her, approaching unexpectedly from the right. Her normally long, loose stride was tightened slightly by the cold, and in the hundred-yard stretch to the hotel, she checked over her shoulder twice.

As she reached the building, a few small flakes of snow drifted to the pavement, glittering and pink-tinged in the street lights.

It was too late for a bar meal, so Simms settled for tonic water and peanuts and Fennimore ordered a double measure of Jura single malt.

He listened to details of her exchange with Detective Superintendent Spry, her interviews at the Henry brothers' salon, and George Howard's near-confession.

"Amy — the girl working on reception — rang me on my mobile at six this evening. Marta's clingy punter turned up."

"By the look on your face, I'm guessing Trevor was a disappointment."

She shrugged. "Arrested, interviewed, released without charge. Trevor Hillesley was celebrating his silver wedding anniversary on Thursday night. The party finished at 12.30 and his wife reports that between 1.30 and 2 a.m., Trevor was hurling up his Indian buffet and swearing off booze for the rest of his days."

"It's still Howard in the frame then," he said. "Although you do have that anomaly in the Henrys' story."

"Big fat porky pie, you mean."

"Even if they are lying, half an hour isn't enough time to do all that was done to Marta."

"Well, I'm not going to break their alibis," Simms said. "The girls who were supposedly partying with them are word perfect."

"I can imagine," Fennimore said. "D'you really think Howard was about to confess?"

She nodded. "I'm just not sure to what. I think he's remembering things. I'm damn sure he knows more than he's telling us."

Fennimore worked back through what she'd told him. "He said that there were images in his head he couldn't understand?"

"*Awful* images, he said. And he used the word 'traumatized'. I know, you're thinking Rohypnol, but it's no use to us — we could never prove it."

"Of course we can."

She pinched the top of her nose and closed her eyes. "Am I missing something here, Nick? Because I thought Rohypnol was short-lived. It only stays in the blood and body tissues for a few hours, doesn't it?"

"That's certainly true of the soft tissues — the squishy bits that process the nasties and help us to eliminate them from our bodies — but hair is a different story. Toxins persist in the shaft of hair until it falls out." He stopped short. "Please don't tell me Mr Howard is bald."

The gleam in her eye told him that George Howard had a good head of hair.

"On the other hand, the concept of the Henrys framing their commercial rival for murder is a bit extreme if they just wanted him out of the way."

"So why would they drug him?"

"I didn't say they did."

He could see her thinking back over the last few minutes of discussion. "Didn't you?"

"Some people take the stuff voluntarily," he said. "They use it as a disinhibitor, to heighten the sexual experience."

"Seems a bit pointless," she said, "if you can't remember what you did."

"A very practical objection, Chief Inspector. Voluntary use is normally at lower dosages — reduces the amnesia risk. But the potency of illegal drugs varies enormously; it could be he simply overdid it."

She shook her head. "No, that won't wash. Doctor Cooper thought there might be two assailants."

"*Might* be," he emphasized. "He's not certain — though I would be fascinated to know where Frank Henry went after receiving that call on his mobile."

"Yeah," she said. "Me too. But I can't see him taking us into his confidence, can you?"

He didn't need to answer that question, so they sat in silence for a few minutes, Kate staring at the bubbles rising in her drink. Her eyes flickered occasionally to the entrance, and she watched the few remaining customers with more than idle interest.

"Worried about your stalker?" he asked.

"No." She'd answered too quickly, and added more casually, "Why do you ask?"

"Because you came here from the west this evening."

"Very cryptic." She took a sip of her drink and set it lightly down on the table, as if she didn't have a care in the world.

"If you had used the GMex car park, I would have expected you to appear from the east, at the corner of Lower Mosley Street."

"Did it occur to you that street parking's free this time of night?"

"And you looked over your shoulder twice, and I've lost count of the number of times you've checked the entrance in the last ten minutes."

"Leave it alone, Nick, okay?" Her voice was steely, but he saw a lingering shadow of anxiety in her eyes. "There's no sign of Candice," she said, firmly. "She's a key witness, and I haven't got the staff to find her. So now it's your turn — what have you been up to in these halls of decadence?"

Subject changed, and not subtly, either. *Do what the woman says — leave it alone.*

He thought about the two hours before her arrival, working on the aged-up picture of his daughter and what he'd done with it, and he quailed. "You want the useful or the stupid?"

She gazed at him thoughtfully, her brown eyes soft and full of warmth in the dimmed lighting of the bar. "Better tell me the useful first, in case I get so pissed off about the other thing I forget you're a brilliant scientist so all I can see is the idiot in you."

"That's probably the most backhanded compliment I've ever had."

328

She toasted him with her tonic water.

"Okay. The cross-hatch whip marks give you physical evidence linking Marta and Rika. The toxicology reinforces the link between those two *and* establishes a link to the penicillin deaths."

She took a breath — they both knew that biochemistry would be far more persuasive to a jury than a visual comparison of injuries. Chemical tests were quantifiable, hard to argue with.

"Remember right at the start of this, when life was simple and you were just investigating a few drugs deaths over the odds? You sent me samples of drugs found with the bodies. Well, the university lab has been working steadily through those in my absence, and Josh emailed with the results today. One of the tests I asked for was HPLC — High Performance Liquid Chromatography. Think of the tests you did at school with a wee blob of ink on a filter paper —"

"Skip to the results, Nick."

He flashed an apologetic grin. "The heroin that killed Rika had the same chemical profile as the deals found in the penicillin deaths, and *they* were the same as the heroin found with Marta's body."

She stared at him, round-eyed. "The same heroin batch links to *all* of the deaths?"

"Not quite," he said. "Rika's deal wasn't cut with penicillin, and the proportion of penicillin used in the later deals actually increases, so they're definitely different batches. I'm talking about the *underlying composition* of the different batches."

She frowned and he explained, "You're decorating a room — you would always buy rolls from the same batch off the production line to guarantee a perfect match, wouldn't you?"

She nodded. "Okay . . ."

"This is the same. Over the months, several batches have been made; there are subtle differences, but they all contain methaqualone — a narcotic used to bulk heroin. The key thing is, it's not *commonly* used, and that makes it distinctive, and it's present in *exactly* the same ratio in the overdose samples, the penicillin deaths, right through to the bindle found with Marta."

"So it must have come from the same place," she said.

He nodded. "The bulk supplies of heroin would probably be mixed abroad, and that's where the methaqualone would be added. But it makes sense to do most of the cutting near to the point of final distribution — smaller volumes coming through customs have a better chance of getting the stuff through unnoticed. When it gets to the suppliers, they add in the penicillin."

She took a thoughtful sip of her drink. "Methaqualone — that's Quaaludes, isn't it?"

"Quaaludes, quacks, quales, quas—" He smacked himself in the forehead with the flat of his hand.

"What?"

"You're right — I *am* an idiot," he said. "In the seventies, 'luding out' was a popular college pastime in the States. Methaqualone — 'ludes' — has several effects: it heightens sexual sensitivity, lowers inhibition

330

and the user has *no memory* of the dirty deeds of the night before."

She stared at him. "Just like George Howard." Her eyes glowed and he felt an answering flicker of excitement; they had found another possible link to the heroin deals. "Would methaqualone show up in the hair analysis?" she asked.

"You just have to tell the toxicologist to look for it. But toxicology takes time. And even if you get a positive, it won't tell you who administered the drug."

She thought about that. "Either way, I think we need to know."

"Agreed. But it won't do you any good in the short term, Kate, and so far as this investigation goes, the short term is all you've got."

She sighed. "Yup. We need to identify the supplier. I mean the real supplier — not some street dealer who jumps a red light in front of a patrol car and screams 'Catch me!' "

"The steady increase in penicillin as a cutting agent suggests a disruption of supply —"

She held up her hand. "I know what you're going to say — you need the lab analysis of drugs seized during Operation Snowstorm. I'm sorry — you really should have had that by now. I've asked Superintendent Tanford to email me a copy of his report. Speaking of Tanford . . ." She picked up her phone and opened her messaging program.

"What are you doing?"

"Texting Superintendent Tanford."

"Kate, it's a quarter to midnight."

She checked her watch, cancelled the text, opened her email and began again: "I'm *emailing* Tanford so he can pick it up in the morning. Field Intelligence said there's no significant drugs intel on the Henry brothers, or George Howard. But like Tanford said, his squad is better placed for that kind of ear-to-the-ground rumour."

She sent the email and looked up at him. "Everyone's lying, Nick — even the people I'm trying to help."

She looked about done in, and he realized she must have been working flat out for forty-eight hours. He handed her his Scotch and picked up her glass of tonic. "Churchill said, 'There are a lot of lies going around . . . and some of them are true.'"

"Profound," she said. "Churchillian."

He sipped her tonic water, trying not to shudder.

"The truth will reveal itself when you have more facts. Go home, get some sleep, let the computers and analysts and information gatherers do their work."

She tasted his whisky, approved his choice. "So," she said. "What was the stupid thing you did?"

That surprised a laugh from him. "And you say *I* have a mind like a steel trap."

"Like I'm going to forget you admitting to any kind of weakness," she said, smiling.

He saw that smile and wanted to hold on to it, which is why he didn't tell her that after working through the lab results he had in fact spent too long staring at the pictures of Rika. The photograph they had found in Marta's purse pictured a pretty, smiling girl with a

332

tumble of brown curls and dark, defiant eyes. Her estimated age at time of death was eighteen. In the post-mortem picture, one eye was closed, the other half open, and the cornea, desiccated in the hours after death, had a bluish cast. He had set the two images side by side — Rika full of life and hope/Rika dead. He couldn't make them match. Suzie — his Suzie — was only a few years younger than Rika.

Before he could reason with himself — before he could argue himself out of it — he had created a Facebook page and launched the image which for two years he'd tinkered with offline. Suzie aged ten; Suzie aged fifteen. Her name; a bio — five years too short — a picture of him, so that if she came looking she would know that he loved her and had never given up on her.

CHAPTER
THIRTY-TWO

"It is not a bad thing that children should occasionally, and politely, put parents in their place."

COLETTE

Suzie and Becky are zooming up the street on skateboards, whooping with glee. Suzie scoots up the Simms's driveway, and then down at speed, her face tight with concentration. She veers off to the left, heading for the kerb, tips the leading edge of her board and lands perfectly, a grin of exultation on her face.

Fennimore knows he is dreaming. He has arrived at Kate Simms's house to pick up his daughter. When she sees him, Suzie flips her board into her hand and tucks it under her arm. It doesn't belong to her — it's Becky's, and she knows she shouldn't have it, but she stands tall and eyes him defiantly. She is ten years old.

Becky tries to slide the board from under her arm, as though he'll forget what he's just seen if Suzie just hands over the incriminating evidence. But Suzie resists, glaring at her friend, and Becky, always the follower in their friendship, gives up and hugs her own board across her narrow chest.

"Suzie," Fennimore says, "you promised your mother —"

"I *didn't*." Her eyebrows draw down into a scowl. Becky stands very still to one side, her eyes wide with shock that Suzie should speak so boldly to her father.

It's true, she hadn't promised. What she'd said was, "Fine — but you won't stop me. I'll borrow one. Or steal one." Suzie's relationship with her mother has never been easy.

She has a healing scar on her left temple — a fall, practising "acid drops" from the kerb on her skateboard. The cut bled profusely and Rachel had rushed from the house hearing the girls' terrified screams. It was fear that made her confiscate the board, and stubbornness that made her refuse to relent. And true to her word, Suzie had persuaded Becky to loan her an old board.

Becky is tugging at his hand. "Uncle Fenn." He was always Uncle Fenn to Becky. "Uncle Fenn, Mummy wants you."

He groans in his sleep and tries to shake her off. This is a good dream; he wants to stay a while.

A fire alarm goes off further down the road and the girls stare at him, as though wondering what he's going to do about it. They're fading. The dream-ringing follows him into reality, and he realizes that his mobile is jangling on the bedside table.

"You do sleep sometimes, then?"

Kate Simms.

Half drugged with sleep, he wonders how Becky knew it was her mother on the line, then something clicks in his head and he's fully awake. He sits up, yawns, asks, "What time is it?"

"Four a.m. Can you be ready in fifteen minutes?"

"Sure."

"Good, I'm on my way."

"What's up?"

"Liz Dromer just rang." This was Kate's community partnership contact. "She's found the surviving victim of the abduction-torture up in Hull — the eighteen-year-old who was in the injuries database — Tanya Repton. She'll talk to me, but she won't give a formal statement, she won't go anywhere near a police station, and she insists that Liz is present."

By 4.25 they were heading east on the M62 in Simms's Mondeo towards Goole. It was a ninety-minute drive and Fennimore had insisted on taking the wheel, despite Simms's protests that she'd had a good three hours of sleep.

"And before that?" he'd asked.

She'd shrugged. "I'm good at power-napping."

"That's what worries me," he'd said, plucking the keys from her hand.

They drove full into an easterly wind that blasted tiny snow crystals into the windscreen like a cold white dust storm. For a time, he hugged close in behind a gritting lorry until the road began the steady descent towards the flatlands of the East Riding of Yorkshire. Kate slept through it, but as Fennimore slowed for the off-ramp, she stirred and woke.

"Take it slow." Her words were slurred with sleep. "It's a few hundred yards down on the left."

He saw the lights first, shining down on the car park in pods of three, like alien landing craft. Then he saw the big, plastic gold M and groaned. "McDonald's," he said. "Oh, joy."

"Tanya works here." She squinted at the dashboard clock. "And she's just about to knock off."

Stepping out of the car, the air felt cold enough to turn to ice crystals in his lungs, but at least it had stopped snowing. The buzz of traffic on the M62 a few hundred yards away was a constant in the background. The car park was almost deserted, but the door of an old Peugeot estate opened and a woman stepped out.

Liz Dromer was nearing sixty, grey-haired, with direct blue eyes. She hugged Simms.

"How did you find her so fast?" Simms asked.

Liz smiled. "I knew who you wanted as soon as you said the name," she said. "Tanya went through our rehab programme. But I had to square it with her, first."

Liz turned to shake Fennimore's hand. "Professor — I know you by reputation." She gripped his hand a second or two longer than was necessary, and stared into his eyes. Hers was a face that had lived through pain and learned to endure.

If not for the flaw in Tanya Repton's iris, Fennimore wouldn't have recognized her. The slate-grey irises had lost their sullen hopelessness and shone with good health. She had grown her hair out to her natural brown and when she took off her staff cap it fell, silky and shining, to her shoulders.

Carrying a tray of coffees, she guided them to a table in the far corner. Tanya was eighteen years old when she'd been abducted; she would be around twenty now, but her oval, pixyish face and shy manner made her seem much younger. Her skin was clear and flawless, but prone to delicate pink flushes. She avoided looking at Fennimore, even angled her chair and turned her head so that he could see only the side of her face.

"Back then, I was pretty wrecked," she said with a glance at Kate. "It was October; wet and cold." She stared at the table as she spoke, her voice no more than a whisper.

"I was on Myton Street, trying to . . ." She lifted her shoulders and let them fall. "Well, to earn enough for any kind of shit I could find really." She didn't sound bitter. It was as if she was talking about another girl, a distant friend, perhaps — one she pitied, but had little in common with. "Most of the girls had given up and gone home for the night. This guy called me over to his car. Said he'd pay me and give me some good grade H if I'd do something extra for him. A game, he called it."

She looked briefly into Kate Simms's face. "I'm not daft, I told him I wasn't into bondage, but he said it wouldn't hardly be anything. 'Just a couple of quick stripes,' he said. Then he grabbed my wrist."

She leaned back in her chair as if the memory still frightened her. "I'm reaching for my mace spray, but then he slaps a baggy of the whitest, purest-looking shit you ever saw into my hand."

She shrugged as if to say, *What're you gonna do?*

"He paid me upfront, said he hoped I didn't mind, but he thought we'd be more comfortable at this place he knew. He seemed like a real gent — looked away as

338

I hid the baggy down the lining of my handbag, chatted all the way there in the car, didn't try nothing — didn't even try to feel me up."

"This place he took you to . . ." Simms said.

"An old factory near the river — over the lift bridge. Cops were having a bit of a crackdown, and a lot of punters were taking the girls out of town to do business, so it didn't ring any alarm bells. He had a key to the gate and he knew where he was going, so I'm thinking maybe he's security. He had that look about him, you know?

"He goes to this door at the side and he says, 'Through here, where it's warmer.' It's filthy and stinks of piss, and I tell him, but he points to some steps down. 'Don't be like that,' he says. 'I got a nice room down there — fixed up all cosy.' And I'm like — *No way!* So he says, 'Fuck you, I want my H back.'"

She fell silent, and Fennimore and Simms both looked to Liz Dromer for her lead. With a small shake of the head she warned them to stay quiet.

After a minute, Tanya stirred and sat up. "I'm really dope-sick, so I tell him I'll do it right there. He says okay; he even lets me take a little hit to smooth the edges off the withdrawal." She exhales. "That scag was sweet . . ." For a moment she's lost in the memory, then she glances guiltily at Liz and shrugs. "Must've been good, 'cos I wake up in this room. There's white and black tiles on the floor. And there's, like, rings on the walls. And a chair — an old red armchair — and whip."

"Can you describe the whip, Tanya?" Kate asked.

She frowned. "You know, like they use on horses. Sort of like a cane, only more bendy. Looked like plaited brown leather."

Kate and Fennimore exchanged a glance. *Riding crop.*

Tanya's eyes seemed to shimmer like cold air on still water. Her chest rose and fell sharply, and Liz cupped her hand protectively over the girl's. After a few moments, Tanya nodded and slid her hand from under Liz's and let it drop into her lap.

"I rush him, but I'm still half-stoned and he's big. He spins me round and smacks me against the wall. Next thing I know, my hands are cuffed behind me and he's ripping off my trousers. I think, *Okay, just let it happen — get it over with.* But he doesn't want that. He pulls my top up over the back of my neck somehow, so I can't even lift my head up. He bends down and looks into my eyes and he just grins and we both know he's going to hurt me. He begins to pinch and twist and bite me to make —" She broke off, her face pink with shame. "Well, you know," she said.

To make her move, Fennimore thought.

"So I do, and I'm trying to act like I'm liking it, 'cos I think if I give him what he wants, he'll let me go. Suddenly I can't breathe." Her hand went to her throat. "He's choking me. I feel like my eyes are going to burst." She broke off with a sob and loosened her scarf, dragging the silk away from her neck.

Nobody looked at her directly, or at each other, and after a few moments, her face wet with tears, Tanya began again. "I must have passed out. 'Cos when I

340

wake up I'm tied face in to the rings in the wall, and all I've got on is my pop socks. He's walking back and forth, back and forth, behind me and he's got the whip in his hand, and I'm trying to keep him in sight. He doesn't hit me straight off." She looked at Simms. "I think he was getting off on just scaring me. When he did hit me, I swear, I never felt pain like it." Her pupils dilated. "He waits a bit, then he kneels behind me and starts off again, only this time he's hitting me straight." She motioned the vertical with the blade of her hand. "I thought he'd slashed me with a carpet knife. I thought he was carving my skin off."

The hairs on Fennimore's arms and the back of his neck stood up.

"He stops and I'm sobbing, and he's behind me, stroking my neck, gentle at first, but then he starts squeezing harder and harder until I know he's going to kill me. He's whispering into my neck, so I can feel his breath on my skin. He says, 'Shh . . . shh . . . it'll soon be over.'"

Tanya slapped at her neck with both hands as if she could still feel the warmth of his breath, the spider crawl of those terrible words on her flesh.

"Next time I came to, he was sitting in the chair and I was hung up from a hook in the ceiling." Her smooth forehead crinkled. "I thought I was dead, and I was in hell 'cos of all the bad things I done." Her face creased and for a second it looked like she would break down completely, but she took a huge breath and her face set in an expression of fierce determination.

"Then the pain came back and I knew he hadn't killed me, yet. He just sat there and watched me. When he got bored with that he hurt me again, and then he watched me. He hurt me and he watched me and hurt me and watched me till I thought I'd go mad. And the creepiest part? Except when he was choking me, he didn't say a word. I pleaded, I screamed, I begged him to let me go home to my mum. And he just stared at me, as if he was . . ." She frowned, trying to make sense of something no normal person could. "You know when you were in school and you had a test and you had to know stuff by heart?"

Simms nodded.

"It was like that. Like he was trying to learn my pain by heart."

For a long time, nobody said anything, and after a few minutes it was clear that Tanya had said all she was going to say.

"How did you get away?"

Tanya startled, as though she'd forgotten they were in the room. She took a few breaths before answering.

"He dumped me back in Hull in the early hours. Let me get dressed and took me outside to the car. He opened the boot . . ." Her mouth twitched; she whimpered, and for the first time it looked like she might lose control. But she swallowed and balled both hands into fists on the table and frowned at her paper cup as if she was trying to move it by sheer willpower.

"It was lined with plastic sheets." Her face had lost all expression; her voice was toneless, as if the only way she could tell this was by stripping it of emotion. "I'm thinking, *This is it — this time he really is going to kill me.* But he said he didn't want me messing up his car with —" her mouth twitched again "— the blood."

"The police didn't investigate?" Simms said.

"They took pictures, I made the statement, did a photofit. I never heard nothing, so I went back to the police station after a week. The DS says to me, 'He'll be long gone, love. Look on the bright side — he let you keep the money, and the shit, didn't he?'" She shrugged. "And that was it — the end of it."

Fennimore could feel Simms seething beside him.

"Would you know the name of the factory where he took you?" she asked gently. "Or the road it was on?"

"No." Tanya looked at Liz Dromer. Liz nodded encouragement and she heaved a sigh. "But I could take you there."

CHAPTER
THIRTY-THREE

*"It's always better to ask forgiveness
than permission."*

ROBERT RESSLER

Simms didn't want to let Tanya loose in case she lost
her nerve at the last minute, and there was a chance
that something else might drop out in conversation on
the journey, so she rode along with Tanya and Liz
Dromer, while Fennimore followed in Simms's car.
They passed rows of derelict houses, their windows and
doors secured with steel sheeting. Further on, they
crossed the bridge Tanya had remembered from her
ordeal, then onto an industrial estate, squashed on a
hook-shaped oxbow along the banks of the River Hull
with only one way in or out. The snow smoothed and
flattered the deficiencies of roadway and cracked
tarmac, but the factory itself refused its softening
effects. It remained defiantly ugly, its stonework the
colour of dust, its aluminium-frame windows ripped
out or smashed. The corrugated roof was whitened in
patches by the snowfall, but holes in the panels gaped
black under the tarry sky. The two cars pulled in at the
gate, squeezing past the rusted shell of a Ford Focus
left at an angle in the middle of the road. Fennimore

gazed at the crumbling building and suppressed a shiver.

Simms helped Tanya out. The girl pointed towards the side access, just visible through the chain-link fence surrounding the site. She was trembling from head to foot, and would not be persuaded to go any further.

Liz said, "Come on, love, I'll take you home." She shook hands with Fennimore and gave Simms a parting hug. "Don't be a stranger," she said. Seconds later they were gone, and Fennimore and Simms were alone on a snowy road in a blighted landscape.

The place had been abandoned for decades — so long that even the vandals didn't bother with it any more. Security lights around the perimeter had been smashed or had simply rotted in a succession of east coast winters; a destructive combination of salt-laden air and winds that screamed in from Norway and all points north. For a 200-yard stretch there wasn't a single working light of any sort, yet the snow seemed to give off its own eerie light, like a radioactive glow.

Signs informed the unwary that the site was patrolled by guard dogs, but the area code for the contact phone number had been defunct for ten years. Still, Simms made a note of the security firm's details — maybe Tanya's "friend" had been an employee.

A demolition notice, the text fading and laminate cracked, was tethered to the gate; there were more of them at intervals along the crosslink fence. A container services depot had been planned, the demolition date October 1999. That was over a decade ago, yet here it was, still standing, and with the whole of Europe now in economic meltdown there was no prospect of either demolition or regeneration.

They crunched alongside the fence, their breath steaming in the bitter cold. Fennimore hadn't thought to put on walking shoes, so the soft leather of his loafers was already soaked, snow had got in over the cuffs and melted, and his feet lost all feeling in minutes. About fifty yards down one edge Simms found a hole cut in the chain link.

Fennimore bent the wire to make it easier to squeeze through, but Simms hung back. "I don't know — this is way out of my jurisdiction."

He tamped down his impatience. For Fennimore, a scientist, straying onto a derelict site might be considered an annoyance, at worst a breach of protocol; Simms, a Detective Chief Inspector, had knowingly crossed Force boundaries, and was about to break into private property — the consequences for her could be dire.

"Humberside Police weren't interested in what happened to Tanya," he said. "If they weren't interested then, how are you going to persuade them to visit a crime scene that's more than two years old? We need to give them a reason, Kate. Find something they can't ignore."

Still she hesitated. "Even so, I should call someone."

"Ask permission? They'll just escort you over the Force boundaries. As Robert Ressler says, it's always better to ask forgiveness than permission."

For a while she stared through the fence at the rotting grey walls and Fennimore said, "It isn't even a crime scene yet."

She eyed him dolefully as she slipped through the narrow gap. He shoved his scene kit bag through the wire and she dragged it the rest of the way.

As he forced his bulkier frame through the damaged fencing, Fennimore was grinning. For him, the illegality of what they were doing was as thrilling as rock climbing, or slapping a hundred down on a horse he'd hardly considered just because he liked the odds.

The access door was jammed open at forty-five degrees, the bottom edge rusted to the concrete floor. Simms slid through with no problem, shining her torch into the corners of the room. Fennimore handed the scene kit to her and eased around the steel door. Old rags were piled in one corner and the remains of a fire blackened the floor. The walls and ceiling were sooty.

"Vagrants," Simms said.

Fennimore tested the edge of the heap of rags with the toe of his shoe. "Frozen — no one will be curling up in here for warmth anytime soon. We've got the place to ourselves."

She shone her torch beam towards the far end of the room. "Stairs."

They made their way slowly. It became noticeably warmer as they descended, and the reek of urine and the ghosts of other fires rose to greet them. The passageway ran left to right. It was eight or nine feet across and maybe ten feet high. The remains of a series of pipes and conduits ran off to the left.

347

"Left looks easier," Fennimore said.

"You think?" Simms's torchlight penetrated deep into the tunnel, picking up fallen plaster and startling flashes of light reflected from shredded foil pipe insulation — most of the copper pipework had been stripped out by scavengers looking for anything saleable. Treading carefully, they made slow progress; as Simms negotiated a section of collapsed roof her torch beam snagged on a hole in the ceiling, lighting up a fibrous insulating material.

"Don't touch anything," he warned her, sharply. "That looks like asbestos."

He heard her curse under her breath.

"The air is damp, and so long as we don't disturb the stuff, we should be fine," he reassured her.

They moved on, with even greater care, and came to a scratched and rusted green door at the end of the passage. A hasp was bolted in place, secured with a padlock.

"How come the scavengers didn't just break it?" Simms asked.

"My guess would be the padlock was put in place *after* the building had been stripped of anything useful."

"Well," she said, "I'd say we've hit a dead end — unless you have a bolt-cutter in that kit of yours."

Fennimore gave her a pained look. "Bolt-cutters are for Neanderthals."

He opened his shoulder bag, and snapped on a pair of nitrile gloves, then took out a leather tool wrap and slid two items from it.

348

She gazed at him, astonished. "You have lock picks in your scene kit — what are you, a scientist or a criminal?"

"It's a pen top clip and a hairgrip," he corrected. "You could hardly call that going equipped. However if it offends your moral sensitivities, you might want to look away now."

Clamping the Maglite between his teeth, he slid the bent pen clip into the bottom of the key slot and held it under tension; the hairgrip followed. Kate Simms's eyes widened; she looked as if she might try and stop him, then she let out an exasperated sigh and turned her back. Fennimore jiggled the hairgrip up and down, forcing the tumblers to drop; seconds later, the lock gave and he popped open the U-bolt and pushed the door wide.

"Black and white tiles," Simms said. "This is it, Nick. We've found it."

That remained to be seen, but he didn't want spoil the moment for her, so he stood in the doorway, silently appraising the room.

Beneath the grime, the walls were plaster, painted pastel green. The flooring was indeed laid to chequered tile, coved, hospital-style, six inches up from the floor.

"Furnace room," Fennimore said, spotlighting stubs of service pipes, still bearing faded colour codes — green for water and brown for oil. They continued the survey of the room; Kate Simms bouncing her torch beam from floor to ceiling and back along the walls, Fennimore tracking more slowly and methodically.

A minute later, she nudged him and he followed the cone of her light. There were two ring mounts on the wall, both rusted and tarnished. She took a breath, exhaled slowly.

Fennimore swept his torch beam over the ceiling. Towards the centre of the room, bolted to an exposed joist, a large metal hook.

"Any signs of footwear impressions on the tiles?"

She followed his line of sight. "Not that I can see."

"Nor me."

He stripped off his overcoat and stepped inside but she hesitated at the threshold, glancing uncertainly over her shoulder down the long, debris-strewn passage.

"See something?" His voice boomed back at him, bouncing off the tiles.

"No," she said quietly. "Just thinking how scared she must have been."

On the wall below the ring mounts he found tiny outward-splayed teardrops, typical of blood travelling at speed. "It's not a huge quantity, so not arterial spray, but there's enough here to suggest whipping." The plaster finish was remarkably good, and he sighted along its flat plane. "I see small indentations here." Either side of the ring mounts were a series of lines, four to six inches in length, each of which broke down into ridges and troughs, only visible when he shone the torch almost horizontally across the surface.

"It looks like the attacker struck the crop against the wall to clean it, or to terrorize his victim."

"Victims," Simms corrected, reminding him that there were others who might have been tortured here.

350

"*Victims*," he repeated, tracking up the wall to the single hook bolted to the joist near the centre of the room. Its shadow slashed across the ceiling in the movement of his flashlight. "Think of all the blood evidence that might have accumulated from three or more victims." He dropped to his knees and sight-lined the lay of the tiles, his right ear and cheekbone grazing the floor.

"What are you doing?" she asked.

"Looking for the lowest point, and there it is." Using his hands as a springboard, he bounced to his feet and crouch-walked to a spot a couple of paces from the side wall. On his knees again, he shone his torch along the line of grouting. "There's a dark stain," he said, air-sketching three sides of one of the tiles with his pinky finger. "Can you give me more light?"

She followed him inside at last and crouched beside him, bringing her own torch into play.

"Yup," he said. "Could be blood. Kit, please."

She gave him a look that said she wasn't about to become his technical assistant, but went back to the door and passed him his rucksack, and he stripped off his gloves, pocketing them before pulling on a new pair of nitriles and taking out a Kastle-Meyer kit. He set out the items he needed on a half-sheet of A4 paper, folded a small disc of filter paper in four, and scraped the point along a half-inch-long section of grout. He opened the filter paper and added a drop of alcohol to the centre. He capped the alcohol and took up the Kastle-Meyer reagent. In ideal lighting conditions it would be a very pale coral pink, but in the torchlight it merely looked dun-coloured. He unscrewed the cap with the little finger of his right hand and held it there, added a couple of drops, replaced the cap, then switched to the final reagent — hydrogen peroxide.

"Can you angle your lamp directly above the paper?" he asked. "You really need good light to see the change."

"Oh. Hang on —" Simms flicked a switch on the Smartlite and he was instantly blinded.

"What the hell is *that?*" He shied away, screwing his eyes shut, and she turned the torch towards the floor.

"That?" she said. "Oh, that's a million candles-equivalent." Was that a smirk on her face?

"So I see, or I will, when after-images fade from my retinas."

He blinked rapidly to clear his vision and added the hydrogen peroxide. Within seconds, the dot of matter he had scraped from the tile grout turned shocking pink. "That's a positive," he said. He bagged and labelled the sample before turning his attention to the floor again. The grout was degraded and the tile had lifted slightly at one corner. "Pass me the tool wrap, will you?"

He scraped away the grout with a sharpened spatula until he could insert the flat of the blade under it and prise up the tile. Beneath it was a patch of dark, brownish stain, beginning to flake at the edges.

"More blood?"

"Pooled and dried." He sat back on his haunches, Simms beside him, the Smartlite loose in her hand, its light skimming the surface of the tiles. Fennimore tilted his head to forty-five degrees. Something didn't look right.

"What?" she asked eagerly, and he was acutely aware of her shoulder pressing against his.

"The tiles are uneven." He placed his hand on hers, applying light pressure so that the light skimmed the floor. "See how it seems to mound, a couple of yards from us?" As the beam moved, the vaguest hint of a shadow appeared on the far side of the mound.

He edged forward at a crouch, immediately putting the area in shadow, but Kate quickly dodged to the side and lit up the tiles again. He guided her hand from the mound to an area of tile a short distance away, then back again. "Different grout," he said. "The grout in the mounded section is lighter."

He stared into her brown eyes and for a second they both held their breath.

"A dodgy repair," she said, her voice stretched tight with tension.

"Could be, but why the mounding?"

"They dug up the floor to repair service pipes. Someone botched re-laying the concrete."

"They certainly did some digging," he agreed. "But in this kind of facility all pipes, conduits and electrical services are in the undercroft, not buried under the floors. You only have to look into the passageway to see that. Which only leaves —"

"A body." The words exploded out of her. "Oh, Jesus, Nick, there could be a body under here." Unconsciously, she moved back, staring at the ground.

Fennimore reached for his phone.

"Woah, wait a minute — who are you calling?" she said.

"Doctor Steve Dearborne — an old colleague who is always up for some sleuthing." He stepped out into the passageway. It was just after 7a.m., and the first glimmer of light filtered through from the holes in the ceiling; here he might have a better chance of finding a signal.

Simms followed him. "No, Nick. This ends here — we call in Humberside Police, let them do the rest."

He stopped his slow rotational search and dropped his hand to his side. "As I said before, we need to be sure before we call in the police. Kastle-Meyer is only a presumptive test — it says blood is present, but that doesn't mean it's human blood. The archaeology department at Hull University happens to own state-of-the-art ground-penetrating radar equipment; they could provide the evidence we need."

Simms set the big, blocky torch down on the floor and crossed her arms in front of her, her hands hugging her shoulders. For two minutes she didn't move, but simply stared through the open door at the tiles. Fennimore wasn't the best at reading body language, but he knew Kate Simms better than most people and he could tell she was doing battle with her conscience. If she walked away from this, there would be no explanations to make — except an excuse for her late arrival in the office. If she followed this lead all the way, it was bound to end up messy no matter what.

He checked his mobile. He had a signal — only one bar, and it might vanish any second. "Come on, Kate," he said. "It's GPR — with a bit of luck we won't even have to touch the floor."

She closed her eyes for a second and made a low choking sound at the back of her throat. "All right," she said.

He spoke briefly into his mobile, then disconnected. "He'll be here in ninety minutes."

"That's fast," she said, eyeing him suspiciously. "Almost as if he had the van all packed and ready to go."

He chuckled dutifully.

But Simms wasn't joking. "He *did* have the van packed, didn't he?"

"Field trip, I expect," he said airily. "I didn't really ask."

She narrowed her eyes. "'Didn't really'? I've got to say, Fennimore, for such a devious bastard you are a crap liar. You warned him, didn't you? When was that? After we spoke to Tanya? Before?"

"I'm not clairvoyant, Kate. How could I have known what she would say before we'd even met her? I rang from your car after we separated. Tanya's account was convincing, so it was a fair bet we'd have a crime scene, and we do."

Unable to argue with his logic, she fell back on the personal. "You went behind my back."

"I made a judgement," he said. "Tanya was convinced her attacker was going to kill her, and he probably came damn close. I had to consider the possibility that this was his killing field. But was I supposed to tell you there and then? Tanya could barely stand to *look* at the place as it is — if she'd known what was in my mind —"

"Okay," she said. "Okay." She landed a surprise punch to his shoulder.

"Ow! What was that for?"

"Don't lie to me, okay?" Her eyes sparked amber light. "Everyone is lying to me, Nick. I need to know you'll always tell me the truth."

CHAPTER
THIRTY-FOUR

At 9a.m., Dearborne announced that they had found a void under the furnace room concrete. Simms should have been back at base an hour since, but like Fennimore, there was no way she could let this go until she was sure what they were looking at. So while they got on with the geophysical survey, she called Sergeant Renwick and asked for an update.

"If you need family time, I can handle things here," he said.

He was fishing — too wary of her to ask outright where she was and why she'd missed the briefing. For once, Simms was content to let him make the obvious assumption that a female officer with a young child must be at home, mopping up baby sick. She wasn't about to share this with anyone on the team — including Spry — until she had something more definite than a hole under an old factory floor.

It took another hour, but at last Dearborne was sure enough for them to call Humberside Police.

Nick Fennimore made the initial call, to a local DI — one of his operational contacts from his Crime Faculty years — the machinery was set in motion, and Simms was interviewed by the on-call DCI. Simms gave him an abridged version of the chain of events that had brought her to the discovery of a woman's body under a condemned factory on a derelict estate well out of her own jurisdiction. He seemed relaxed enough; as he pointed out, it wouldn't exactly be the only prostitute murder Hull had on the books.

Fennimore was known by reputation, and in scientific circles at least, that didn't seem to count against him. The forensics team welcomed his input; they even invited him back down to the basement to point out some of his observations. Simms herself had been banished to the outer cordon, beyond the fence, but she hung around anyway.

She leaned with her back to the Mondeo and stared through the chain-link at a CSI, suited, masked and gloved, climbing into the unmarked crime scene van parked inside the perimeter.

A second CSI came through the scarred green access door and exchanged a few words with the much shorter man, who had stepped down from the van with a piece of equipment. The taller man pulled back his hood and dragged off his mask, taking a gulp of air as if he'd been suffocating in the protective Tyvec. It was Nick Fennimore.

He saw her instantly, quickly stripped off his oversuit, gloves and booties, dumped them in a black bin liner at the side of the van, retrieved his overcoat and backpack and strode towards her, taking the common approach path marked out by two parallel lines of police tape. The path led to the section of wire that Fennimore and Simms had crept through two hours earlier. An opening wide enough to allow the crime scene van had been cut to one side, the gate being cordoned off and treated as a secondary scene. Along the common access and outside of the cordon, the snow was trampled and had compacted into ice; the sky pressed down, dull and off-white. The temperature had dropped another couple of degrees and the forecast said a fresh band of snow was heading in from Scandinavia.

Fennimore skirted past a huddle of uniformed officers on the far side of the burnt-out car wreck, walking fast, his gaze focused on her. His face was serious, but she could see a shimmer of light in Fennimore's blue-grey eyes that she'd seen many times, poring over crime scene photographs and lab results and witness statements, discussing their meaning. They could be having a conversation about what to eat for lunch and that light would be in Fennimore's eyes, as if he was still thinking — as if he never left off thinking — and thinking gave him joy.

Simms rushed to meet him at the cordon tape. "Is it a body?" she said. "It is, isn't it? What state is it in? Is it identifiable? Come on, Nick, will it *tell* us anything?"

"Hey, slow down," he said.

But she couldn't slow down; she felt locked out, ostracized, and there were things she needed to know. "Nick, I'm going to have to account for my actions." Electricity seemed to spark under her skin, and the muscles in her hands and arms jerked spastically.

He stared at her. "What do you mean, *account for your actions?* You found a body, Kate — you don't need to justify yourself to anyone."

She snuffed a laugh. "I found a body by conducting a search out of my jurisdiction, *without* informing the local police authority *or* consulting my next-in-command. I'm pretty sure Superintendent Spry will say I have a *lot* of explaining to do."

"Okay," he said. "Let's talk on the way back."

She stepped away from his guiding hand. "I'm not ready to leave yet."

He stared at her and, after a few moments, he shook his head and dropped his hands to his sides. "The victim is female. She's buried in a shallow grave — it's a crouch burial — she's curled in the foetal position under a thin layer of concrete."

She rifled mentally through course notes and review sessions with Nick Fennimore at the Crime Faculty, but couldn't recall the facts she needed. "I know concrete draws out water, but does it dissolve flesh? Is it mummified — I mean, does concrete preserve body tissues, or destroy them? We need to know if the injuries match our —"

Fennimore lifted his chin sharply, reminding her of the group of uniforms standing twenty yards away.

"Concrete gets hot as it sets," he told her. "Very hot. And the body's in plastic, so it wouldn't be desiccated, it'd be cooked — the DNA is destroyed."

"Shit!"

"Kate." He glanced again at the huddle standing near the burnt-out car wreck.

"What?" she said.

Fennimore caught hold of her arm at the elbow, steered her a few steps down the road. "You *do not* want uniform cops to be the first to hear what we've both been thinking for the past hour." His eyes flashed angrily. "Because once they have it, they'll spread it like a virus."

Neither one of them had spoken the words out loud; they didn't need to. A Manchester Met police officer in charge of a murder investigation had yomped over the Pennines to Hull at the suicide hour, in secret, and just happened to stumble across a body — it didn't take a huge leap of imagination to think there must be more. But while police like a major crime for the overtime and trips out on expenses, "serial killer" had implications. "Serial killer" said police at various levels hadn't been doing their jobs, crimes had gone unnoticed or, worse, ignored.

He let go of her arm and they turned their backs to the cops who were now blatantly earwigging the exchange.

"I need answers, Nick." She spoke quietly, keeping her frustration locked down so tight she could hardly breathe. "This might be their jurisdiction, but it's my investigation, and I can't do it blindfold."

"Okay. First off, even if the concrete has destroyed her soft tissues, we *will* get DNA from her teeth."

She felt the knot at the back of her neck loosen a notch.

"Now, one question at a time, all right?"

She nodded. "Will we get indications of whip marks?" It was the one thing they had which would link Tanya's attacker to Marta.

"As I said, the grave is shallow — no more than a shell scrape, really. The concrete is acting as a kind of cap over the body and the ground under the tiles is damp. If the dorsal surface of the body has been in contact with the ground, then the back and buttocks would remain damp. As you know, damp flesh can turn to adipocere, and *that* might show striations in the flesh caused by a riding crop."

"That's a hell of a lot of 'ifs'." Despite that, she felt a glimmer of hope. "When will we know?"

"It could take a couple of days just to lift the body out," he said quietly and calmly. "We can't just go in and dig her up. He buried her, then retiled and regrouted, yet there was more blood — where did that come from? Not from Tanya — her injuries weren't severe enough. So there could be other girls tortured here who didn't come forward. There could even be another body."

"Oh," she said, swallowing a wave of nausea.

"The forensic archaeologist will have to stratify the site. She'll work very slowly and *very* painstakingly, sampling, bagging and tagging the tiles, the grout, the new concrete, the old concrete, layer after layer. There could be vital evidence in or on the plastic sheeting, in the soil, or maybe he dropped something into the concrete without realizing. The wrapping itself could be traced back to point of origin —"

He broke off, and she looked into his eyes; he was telling her that they were doing everything they could.

"You need to know if we've got a definite connection," Fennimore said. "I understand that. But if it takes longer, it takes longer, and you'll have to accept it."

"I know." She bowed her head.

"It's probable the room has been sealed for some time, reducing the risk of contamination, and it's cold, and surprisingly dry, which means there's an excellent chance of finding the victims' DNA from the blood spatter. They might even get *his* DNA from the rings and the hook."

She was suddenly angry again. "Why the hell didn't they do that two years ago?"

"Scientists can only do what the police ask them to do. *Jesus*, Kate, you *know* that. The fact is, they weren't even asked to collect evidence from this building."

She exhaled through her nose. "I'd love to know who led *that* investigation."

He shrugged — that was something to pursue in the future. "We're supposed to be meeting Alastair Varley in Manchester this afternoon," he said. "I need to email him about the new developments, and my laptop is back at the hotel — we really should be heading back, Kate."

She'd forgotten about their meeting with the forensic psychologist, and she had yet to make peace with her superintendent. She nodded and they headed back to her car.

As she fired up the engine, her phone rang. She slid off her glove and fumbled in her pocket, cursing, answered without looking at the screen.

"Hello, Kate." It was Tanford. "I got your email. I noticed it was sent just before midnight last night — you're putting the hours in, aren't you?"

"Yeah, well, you know how it is, Tanno."

"You wanted to know about the Henrys . . . I'm not sure I can tell you any more than Field Intelligence." He sounded apologetic.

"Field Intelligence says the two of them are clean," Simms said.

"Depends on your definition, I suppose. For what it's worth, a lot of the girls are on drugs, and the lads probably dabble themselves, but it's a given in their trade. Like I said, it's not much."

"Thanks for checking, Tanno," she said. "I appreciate your taking the time."

"Always a pleasure," he said. Then, "I sent the Snowstorm report — did you get it?"

"I haven't got email access," she said. "I'll get to it as soon as I get back to the office."

"Where are you now?"

"Fishing expedition," she said.

Like a good cop he waited a few seconds longer, allowing the silence to create pressure on her to reveal more, but she resisted, filling the silence with her thanks.

He chuckled. "I get the message: all right, I'll butt out. Only, mind you don't hook any sharks on that rod and reel of yours."

They set off with the coming storm a hint of grey shadow at their backs, filling the rear-view mirror, while ahead the sky was clear, and, beneath it, the Pennine hills shone like new linen, twinkling under bright sunshine.

CHAPTER
THIRTY-FIVE

"Every couch potato and dim detective with satellite TV is an expert in forensic psychology."

ALASTAIR VARLEY

The Old Nag's Head was a Victorian pub off Deansgate, one of the oldest in the city and proud of it; a row of carriage lanterns hung above the etched glass windows, and the white paintwork and its rich gold-and-black trim had been recently freshened up. As snow began to fall, you could believe that at any moment a hansom cab drawn by a gleaming black horse would come trotting round the corner at a clip.

Kate Simms stepped through the door, dusting snowflakes from her hair. Fennimore knew how her meeting had gone with Detective Superintendent Spry before she'd even opened her mouth.

"That bad?" he said.

She sat down, shucking off her coat, and reached for the coffee and sandwiches he'd ordered from the bar.

"He accused me of abandoning my own investigation 'in pursuit of personal glory'."

"Ouch."

"Oh, it gets worse — the inquiry is inter-authority now, and ACC Gifford has the overview. I needn't tell you that if Gifford finds out that you've been advising me, he will not be pleased."

"Has he been in touch yet?"

She shook her head. "Nor Humberside police. Spry says he speaks for them all 'in expressing his appreciation', but 'the means and manner of disposal of the body' — in his opinion — indicate 'a disconnect between Marta's death and the Hull murder'."

A gust of cold air blew in and they looked towards the door, to a solemn-looking man in a Barbour jacket and cord trousers.

Fennimore stood to greet the newcomer, smiling.

Professor Varley did not smile; Fennimore sometimes speculated that he lacked the necessary facial musculature. His face was long and narrow, and his hairline seemed to recede by a few millimetres annually, lengthening his undertaker's visage as the years went by.

They shook hands, Varley's hand cold and hard in his palm, and Fennimore made the introductions. Kate wiped her hands on her napkin and stood.

"Sorry," she said. "I missed breakfast, so this is brunch — got to eat when you can."

Varley apparently didn't find the comment worthy of a reply.

She extended her hand. "Chief Inspector Kate Simms."

He took, squeezed and released it quickly without making eye contact.

Fennimore wished he'd warned her about the Professor, but when they exchanged a glance, she seemed to be saying in the quirk of her eyebrows, *And I thought you had zero social skills.*

She reached for the cafetière and turned the handle towards Varley. "Help yourself."

He seemed irritated to have to perform the task himself, but after a slight hesitation he poured himself a coffee and took a sip.

"So . . ." Fennimore said.

Varley set down his cup. "In my opinion — bearing in mind the geographical locations and time frame involved of course — Rika, Marta and your mystery victim were subjected to both expressive and functional violence of such close similarity in method and sequencing as to make it extremely unlikely that there is no causal connection."

Simms threw Fennimore a helpless look.

"So, in your opinion all three women were tortured by the same man."

Varley frowned, irritated. "I believe that's what I just said."

"My superintendent thinks that the difference in MO proves there's no connection between the Manchester victims and Hull," Simms said.

"*Difference*," Varley said sharply. "What *difference*?" Varley resented intrusions into his area of expertise.

"Marta was dumped at the back of a city-centre hotel; the Hull victim was buried." Kate shrugged. "Different MO."

"Oh, of course. How stupid of me. When it comes to the criminal mind, every couch potato and dim detective with satellite TV is an expert in forensic psychology." Varley's expression hadn't changed, but he might as well have spat on the floor.

"The modus operandi of a violent criminal is only a means to an end," he said, enunciating his words precisely as though she was hard of hearing. "It evolves, is subject to change, adaptive to environmental circumstances. Killers may be monsters, but they are not animals — they are human — and like any human with a modicum of intelligence, they adapt and evolve. They learn. The *method of disposal* of the body in this case is unlikely to be part of his fantasy — so he may vary it at will, and according to immediate circumstances." He paused. "Do you follow?"

Fennimore glanced at Simms; she didn't seem offended by his patronizing manner, and he guessed she'd goaded Varley so that she would have good, strong arguments to take to Spry on her return to base.

She brushed the crumbs from her fingers. "I'm just a dim detective, so I hope you won't mind if I translate that into English. You're saying he made use of what was available. The bonus for him is, if his behaviour is unpredictable, he has less chance of being caught."

Varley's eyebrows were thin and straight, and rarely betrayed any emotion, but the way his eyes swivelled from her to Fennimore and back denoted a certain level of surprise.

"More or less," he said, begrudgingly. "I do not like the word 'signature' of which our American cousins are so fond, but it may help a lay person like you to understand."

Her eyebrows twitched, but she didn't comment.

"The *signature*, therefore, is something the perpetrator *must* do to fulfil a psychological need; it fulfils his fantasy. These fantasies do not arrive fully formed. They are rehearsed mentally, over and over, sometimes for many years before selecting the first victim. Signature acts have emotional significance, and are therefore stable and unchanging. You need to look at the *consistencies*, rather than the *differences*, when comparing these assaults — focus on the actions that remain constant. In this case, those actions are physical and mental torture."

"The use of a riding crop," Simms said.

"The whip marks *are* unusual in themselves," he agreed. "The cross-hatching is highly unusual. This is expressive, rather than functional violence."

She opened her mouth, but he pre-empted her question, explaining, "Functional violence might be something like a blow to the head to stun the victim — something which helps him to accomplish the crime. *Expressive* violence is part of the script that runs through his head before the event — his fantasy. The key here is that Rika, Marta and your Hull victim also suffered bruising to their necks consistent with the use of a broad choke strap. He prolonged the torment — terrorizing his victims. The use of neck compression to choke the subject unconscious, allow them to recover, and then choke them again, is absolutely about control, and the ultimate control is of course the power of life or death over another human being." His brows drew down a fraction. "Put all of these things together, and this man's signature is very distinctive. His fantasy involves control, fear, pain — and power. He might refine his methods of torture or change the way in which he hunts his victims, but his need to control, terrorize and inflict pain are consistent."

"If he varies his MO to lower the chance of being caught, why was our victim dumped out in the open?" Simms asked. "Doesn't that increase the risk?"

"You don't need me to point out the enormous amount of good luck a person would need to avoid CCTV in a city like Manchester, and choose an alley that was not overlooked, and arrive at a time when the place was empty and *remained* empty long enough for him to remove the body from his vehicle and drive away unseen."

"It had occurred to us that he lives here in Manchester," Simms said.

"But your Hull witness said he seemed to know the factory where he took her — so it could be he's relocated from Hull to Manchester. The CCTV evasion suggests that he is also surveillance aware — so a security-related occupation is worth looking at."

"I've got someone checking the records of the firm who last covered security at the factory site," Simms said.

He nodded in approval.

"What about the different ages of the victims? It's quite a wide range."

He waved his hand dismissively. "He is selecting his victims from a vulnerable group, rather than victims of a specific 'type'. Prostitutes are more willing than most to engage in risky activities; addicts are less likely to complain, less likely to be missed. Also, as your surviving witness proves, less likely to be listened to if they *do* complain. He paid them, gave them drugs. And he was highly controlled in what he did."

"He smashed Marta's face to a pulp."

A businessman walking past with two pint glasses glanced at her in shock, and she smiled an apology.

Varley didn't notice. He sipped his coffee and nodded thoughtfully. "Yet the flogging was entirely systematic — designed to cause intense pain — no sign of rage there. It was controlling, sadistic, organized; he took his time. This man sees torment as art." He paused, still thinking. "There were no signs that your murder victim had previously undergone whippings?"

"None," Simms said.

"That in itself might account for the extreme violence. Rika had old scars and new, suggesting that she submitted herself to multiple sessions, and the Hull victim tried to please her attacker. Both were compliant — he could control them. It's possible that Marta would not comply, and it took extreme violence to subdue her."

Simms exhaled slowly. "So, who are we looking for — apart from someone who works in security?"

"A misogynist." Varley lifted one shoulder. "Obviously. He is persuasive, superficially charming, but he likes to be in control. There might have been a recent stressor — at work, or possibly at home."

"You think he has family?" she asked.

"It's possible, although the marital relationship might have broken down — a common stressor in these cases. If he works within a team, work colleagues might have noticed absences and failures; odd behaviour — he may have become unreliable and difficult to deal with. He sees women as objects. He doesn't *interact* with them, he acts *upon* them, and takes what he wants from them."

They all reflected on this for a minute or so, and finally Kate said, "Is it possible we're looking for two attackers?"

"The bite marks in Marta's PM photos *do* seem somewhat tentative," he said. "What was the situation with your Hull victim?"

"He did bite her," Kate said, "but I can't request her file from Humberside police, or the forensic images — I promised to keep her out of the inquiry."

He raised an eyebrow. "That's . . . unhelpful."

Fennimore saw her tense and mediated for Varley: "I think Alastair means that the bites are inconclusive as evidence."

Varley nodded. "I'm afraid I can't tell you either way if George Howard is your man." He checked his watch and stood. "I need to catch a train before this flurry of snow brings the entire rail network to a halt. I'll complete my report on the journey and email it to you this evening — tomorrow at the latest." He zipped up his coat and picked up his briefcase.

Fennimore thought he would leave it there — cool, professional, dispassionate as always, but his gaze lingered on Kate Simms. "Be careful, Chief Inspector," he said.

"Me, personally?" Kate glanced uneasily at Fennimore. "Why?"

He set his briefcase down on the chair in front of him and took her in with his cool, level gaze. "These killings could hardly be more sinister; and the man you are seeking could hardly be more dangerous." He looked first at Fennimore, then Kate. "Serial offenders don't stop unless they're made to stop, so the hiatus between 2007 and the present could be because he was in prison, or his victims may, like Rika, have been easy to hush up with cash and heroin. But there could be others like Marta who refused to comply.

"He didn't just spring into this from nowhere. The man you are looking for has operated with impunity for years, gradually gaining confidence." Varley went on, his eyes fixed on Kate Simms's face. "With the discovery of the body in Hull, we know that he has been fully fledged — if I may use that metaphor — since 2007. He had complete freedom to do what he liked to young women — until *you* exposed him. Worse than that, you have connected him to a murder. And now you seem to have found a burial site. He will be enraged by this gross intrusion into his sphere, and he will be looking for someone to blame. Sociopaths *never* blame themselves."

She watched him leave, her face impassive, but when she reached for her coffee cup, her hand was trembling.

"Are you all right?" Fennimore asked.

"Tell me he's grandstanding," she said softly. "Tell me he's a bullshit artist who loves to make an impact."

374

Fennimore would love to have told her what she wanted to hear, but he couldn't. He looked at her, trying to find a gentle way to say it, and she nodded.

"That's what I thought," she said, and he saw a quiver of fear in her eyes.

CHAPTER
THIRTY-SIX

Kate Simms went through the door ahead of Fennimore, brooding on Professor Varley's warning, thinking about the man who had followed her in the car park near the Midland Hotel, taken photographs of her as she interviewed Candice. Could she really be in danger?

Small dry flakes of snow were falling thickly now, and she turned up her collar against the chill. A group of men blocked the pavement and, frowning, she moved to sidestep them.

One of them said, "That's her," and she felt a stab of alarm. He held a Manchester Police warrant card in his hand. She recognized him vaguely as a DI she'd met before; he was saying something that didn't make any sense. Two others of the group had stopped Nick Fennimore.

"You are Kathryn Rebecca Simms," the DI repeated.

"Yes," she said. "Look, what's this about?"

"Kathryn Rebecca Simms —"

She couldn't work out why this idiot kept repeating her name. The two men with Fennimore were moving away and she called, "Nick." He didn't turn. She reached in her bag for her own warrant card, but the DI seized her arm at the elbow and stripped her bag from her shoulder.

"Hey!" She jerked her arm free. "I'm police — my ID is in the bag."

"I know who you are, Chief Inspector," he said. "I'm arresting you —"

"*What?*" She tried to listen, but the noise in her head was too loud, so she had to lip-read the rest.

". . . committing an indecent act in a public place —"

"This is bullshit." She turned to walk away, but the second officer moved in. "It's *crazy*."

The DI caught her again and leaned in close. "Look, ma'am," he said, "I don't want to have to cuff you. But I will if I have to, okay?"

She glared at him, ready to do bloody murder, but there was no malice in his face — this was just a cop doing his job. *Doing someone else's dirty work*, she thought with a hot surge of bitterness that almost blistered through her skin.

She nodded, breathing slow and deep. "All right, but you can let go of my arm."

He held her gaze for a few moments longer, then she felt the pressure of his fingertips relax a little, and he released her, finishing the words of the caution. He gestured towards a waiting car — unmarked — a small mercy.

As they pulled away from the kerb, she glimpsed Nick Fennimore, his hair and shoulders flecked with snow. His expression was unreadable. Nick was so sensitive about his privacy since what happened to

Rachel and Suzie; she couldn't help wondering if he felt he hadn't been roped in to this sorry mess against his better judgement.

Simms reported to Detective Superintendent Spry two hours later. The elevator doors opened directly onto an open-plan office and Simms drew a few stares immediately. She walked past desks and workstations and she could almost hear necks creaking as they craned to get a look at her.

Spry's door flew open at her knock with such force it rattled the blinds on the windows. He snatched up a bundle of lab analysis requests from his in-tray and shoved them into her hands. With finger and thumb, he teased out a request for hair analysis on George Howard and laid it on top of the pile.

"A new lab request," Spry said.

"We're looking for roofies," she said. "It might account for Howard's amnesia."

"After I told you there would be no more lab requests."

Like a magician doing a card trick, Spry found a second sheet and plucked it from the bundle in her hand. He was standing so close she could smell stale coffee on his breath. "Toxicology on the drugs seized during Operation Snowstorm," he said.

"That isn't a lab request," she said. "All I asked for was a printout of the existing report."

"Nevertheless, you contravened my *specific* and *unequivocal* orders to *stop*."

"No — I requested the Snowstorm toxicology a while ago." Her body was so tense her chest ached.

He stared at her as though she were a picture puzzle he couldn't quite grasp. "*Why* exactly did you need them?" he asked, in a tone that said whatever her answer was, it wouldn't be good enough.

"For comparison."

"You mean comparing *your* drugs deaths with a major drugs operation?" He feigned surprise. "But why wasn't I informed of this?"

"Because I wasn't sure if —"

He spoke over her. "*Because*, Chief Inspector, if you had told me, you knew damn well I would refer it to the Intelligence and Security Bureau. And *you* wanted all the credit for yourself."

That part at least was true. She bowed her head.

"When I received those, I called your office, but you weren't in; I spoke to Renwick and discovered that George Howard is still in custody, that he still hasn't been charged. Then I find out that you have been *arrested* — for *indecency*, of all things — and with whom?" He picked up a photograph from his desk — Manchester Airport car park; Simms in the back of her car, topless, Fennimore stealing a peek. He held it in front of her face, his hand quivering with rage. "That *train wreck* of a man who was booted out of the Crime Faculty."

She felt her cheeks flush hot with anger. "Fennimore has given me good advice —"

"*Irrelevant.* In a criminal investigation, the source of information is just as important as the outcome, and so far as the ACC is concerned, Fennimore is tainted. Which means his advice, his lab analysis — *anything* he's done for you in this investigation — is tainted."

"He's one of the best forensic scientists in the UK —"

"When his wife vanished, he as good as *stole* FSS resources in pursuit of his own private investigation, and he dragged you along for the ride. And now you invite him back into your life," he roared. "What the hell did you think you were playing at? Are you *actually* suicidal?" He stopped for a moment, breathing hard through his nose.

"Who gave you the lab requests?" she asked. "Who sent in the photographs?"

He stared at her, his forehead a deepening crimson, and she took the incriminating snapshot from his hand. "I'm guessing Crimestoppers. I mean, it's been such a boon right from the start of this investigation, hasn't it?"

He'd heard the sarcasm, but didn't pull her up on it; in fact, he seemed wary.

She took the photograph from his hand. "This is bullshit. But you know that, sir, because the DI who arrested me was full of apologies when he let me go, and you would be top of his calls list as soon as I was out the door."

He eyed her with dislike. "You're very sure of yourself."

"I've every right to be," she said, grateful that he hadn't heard the slight tremor in her voice.

380

He didn't say anything, but his jaw clamped so tight she could hear his teeth grinding.

"I'm guessing that the lab requests found their way into your inbox anonymously."

He glared at her, and she held his gaze, daring him to tell her she was wrong. When she was sure he wouldn't challenge her, she gave a curt nod of her head.

"I did order the tests, and I did request the tox from Snowstorm. But you've got to ask yourself why someone would consider that a *bad* thing." She shrugged. "But since the intel was delivered anonymously we can't exactly ask, can we, sir?"

Simms looked into his eyes, watching closely for his reaction, and thought she saw a shadow of uncertainty.

"I'm being followed."

"You're bloody paranoid." He spat the words.

"The man who took this —" she glanced at the photograph "— has been dogging my footsteps for days."

He seemed appalled, but not out of concern for her. All Spry wanted was a quiet life — a nice, tidy tie-up of a slightly perplexing case, and she had messed it all up. "What the hell have you stirred up, Simms?"

"I don't know yet," she said. "Give me a couple more days, I might have an answer."

"You are going home," he said.

"No," she said. "If you send me home it'll look like there's something in this shit."

"Kate," Spry said, "you need to go home."

It was the first time he'd used her given name in the entire interview, and she quailed inwardly, waiting for the hammer blow.

"The photograph is splashed all over the local press."

The room seemed to shift sideways. She bent forward to catch her breath, and discovered the photograph still in her hand.

"And you *still* say I'm paranoid?" She spun the image onto his desk.

"Look," he said. "You have the name of the victim. You have the perpetrator. That might be enough to bury this —"

"Bury *what?*" she said. "There is no case to answer."

"Maybe not, but you confused your priorities and you made bad choices — bringing Fennimore in, of all people."

"Without Fennimore's advice, none of this would have been exposed."

The look on his face said he fervently wished it hadn't. "I want you to go home and think on the choices you've made. You ignored protocols, disobeyed direct instructions and orders, brought in someone the Assistant Chief would slap an ASBO on, if he could — you're lucky he didn't suspend you."

Simms felt a spike of fear. Spry wouldn't talk about suspension unless it was a real possibility. "Sir," she said. "I have work to do — we don't have Marta's full name yet, there are lines of inquiry I need to follow up."

"Which your team will do in your absence. The official line is, you're exhausted, and you need a day or two at home with your family."

He really seemed to think that they would get on with their investigation, and Humberside would look into the murder, and everything would be kept nice and simple and clean.

"I believe there's a link between Marta and the Hull murder victim."

He huffed. "Well, you're on your own there."

Fear turned to anger. "Haven't I been from the start of all this?"

He flushed darkly. "You forget yourself, Chief Inspector."

"To hell with it, I'm going to say it — there's a serial abductor and rapist on the loose, who likes to torture his victims. Marta and the girl buried under the factory floor — they were probably murdered by the same man. Sir, I want it on record that I think this is the work of a serial killer."

The silence roared in her ears. He looked embarrassed for her, and she became defensive.

"It isn't just me, sir. I spoke to the forensic psychologist — if you let me access my email —"

"Stop!" He raised a trembling finger. "That is *enough*. You will go home voluntarily, or you will go home under suspension."

"What?" She stared at him, shocked.

"Orders of the ACC." He seemed calmer, having the full force of ACC Gifford's wrath to back him up. He went on, quietly and reasonably, "Meanwhile, I will ensure that George Howard is formally charged with Marta's abduction, rape and murder."

He waited until she was on her way out of the door, with every person in the main office straining to hear.

"Oh, and, Kate," he said, "stay the hell away from Nick Fennimore."

CHAPTER
THIRTY-SEVEN

Simms stepped out of the building into darkness and a cold so intense it made her head ache. In the hours since her arrest, the sun had gone down, the temperature had dropped by another five degrees, and six inches of snow covered the ground. She had taken a side exit to the car park from habit, remembering too late that her car was still parked in the city centre. She cursed — she didn't know the security codes for the doors, so the only way back in was by the front entrance, and there was bound to be media presence. But if she walked along the rear of the building and followed the road out, keeping to the far pavement, she might just slip past the gathered vultures unnoticed. She turned up the collar of her coat and began walking, her legs still weak from her confrontation with Spry. She felt dazed by the turn of events; not that she'd expected praise and a shiny new badge of acceptability, but this was a suspension in all but name.

She heard the dull thrum of a car engine and looked over her shoulder. A car rolled quietly over the compacted snow, headlights off, heading down the lane she was on. The car park's security lighting gave an Irn Bru cast to the snowfall, but even reflected off the snow it wasn't strong enough to see into the car. *No headlights.* Simms faced forward, the toes of her boots kicking up the powdery fall. She saw a gap between two parked cars and dodged into the next lane. The car accelerated, its wheels spinning in the snow.

Simms's heart began to thud hard; she was twenty yards from the building, with at least another fifty to go before she reached the road, and not another soul in the car park. She hesitated, uncertain what to do next, and the car skidded around the end of the row, heading straight for her, juddered to a halt at an angle and stalled. The driver's door opened and Simms braced herself for a fight.

A plump, pink-faced creature emerged, wearing a Fair Isle trapper hat with the earflaps down. It was DC Moran.

"*Jeez,* Ella, don't you know not to creep up on a woman in a deserted car park?"

"Sorry, Boss," she said. "I didn't want to use the lights — there's twenty-odd journos hanging around and I didn't want to attract attention. I thought you might need a lift."

Simms slid down as they passed the gaggle of reporters, trying to gain shelter from the snow in the overhang of the entrance, but Moran's hat was a good decoy and nobody gave them a second look. They turned left onto the road and set off at a crawl over the fresh snowfall.

"What did Spry tell you?" Simms asked, when they were safely on the A56, heading for the city centre.

"That you're taking a few days' leave. We're to work on, and you'll tie up any loose ends when you get back."

"I take it nobody's falling for that?"

The detective's forehead crinkled a moment. "There's not that many of us still around," she said, neatly evading the question.

"Has he charged Howard?"

"He told DS Renwick to do it."

It figured — Spry wouldn't want his name anywhere near this, not with photographs of the lead investigator in her scanties circulating in the media. She cracked the window, suddenly needing more air.

Moran glanced at her, but didn't comment. "Take a look in the glovebox," she said.

Simms flipped the compartment open; there were several precisely folded A4 sheets lying under a small LED torch and a Green Flag card. Nothing else — no sweet wrappers, tickets, receipts, pens or plastic carrier bags. She drew out the A4 sheets.

"The calls list from Marta's mobile," Moran said.

Simms stared at the printout in her hand. "How the hell did you get this?"

"Service provider," she said, and Simms knew from the vague way she'd answered that she'd deliberately misunderstood. "The phone's registered to Sally Hobbes."

Simms turned to face her.

"She's ninety-six and lives in a nursing home — Alzheimer's," Moran said.

Simms slumped in her seat. Why was she even bothering? Spry had taken charge of the investigation, Howard had been charged. It didn't matter that the images of her with Fennimore were bogus — in Gifford's eyes she was a liability, and he would not tolerate that. Humberside would deal with their body; she would establish Marta's identity. If there was a link — and she was certain there was — nobody was interested. It could take days or weeks for the forensic evidence to come out, and even if it proved her right, Gifford would make damn sure someone else was tasked with the job. She ached with tiredness and was sick with worry about Kieran's reaction to the photographs.

"Boss?" Moran said, and Simms realized that she had tuned her out. She stirred herself, breathing in the cold sharp air and making an effort for the young detective more than for herself.

"Yeah. Yes, go ahead, Ella, I'm listening."

"One of the calls on the list was made a few minutes before the surveillance camera picked Marta up leaving the restaurant on the night of the murder."

Simms snapped upright — Livebait restaurant was the last place Marta had been seen alive. "We need a reverse trace on all these numbers. Prioritize the one Marta dialled from the restaurant; let me know as soon as you have it."

"Already got it."

Simms shook her head. "How?"

"Well . . ." They pulled up at a set of lights and Moran tugged one of the earflaps of her hat. "The first bit of the number looked like a Firm's mobile. So I called the switchboard and said someone had rung me, but they hadn't left a message and I thought it might be urgent to the ongoing investigation." She swallowed. "It belongs to a DC Parrish; he's on the Drugs Squad."

Drugs Squad, Simms thought. *Operation Snowstorm*.

The lights changed; Moran drove on, Simms staring through the windscreen in stunned silence.

"Talk to Sergeant Renwick, ask him to request the reverse traces on the other numbers."

Moran threw her an anxious look and Simms said, "Ella, I know Renwick was on the Drugs Squad, but he's okay."

Moran didn't answer.

"What?" Simms asked.

Moran pulled over to the kerbside, as if she didn't trust herself to drive and tell Simms what she had to say. She left the engine running and folded her hands neatly in her lap. "I couldn't understand why we hadn't had the IMEI number for Marta's phone," she said, "so I called the lab myself, said I was you." She glanced quickly into Simms's face. "They told me they'd already sent the IMEI. I said, 'When?' They said, 'With the DNA results.'"

"That was Tuesday," Simms said stupidly. She couldn't process the information: two days ago, Renwick told her that the lab was backed up, hadn't had a chance to try to retrieve the number, said he'd call them and give them a rollocking. She felt suddenly cold. Renwick had lied to her.

Moran spoke, eyes forward, her voice wobbling with nerves. "Boss, I don't know what to do with this."

In truth, neither did Simms. "Were there any voicemail messages on the phone?"

Moran nodded. "The service provider sent an MP3 file, but some of them are in a foreign language — Russian or something."

"Okay," Simms said. "We'll need a translator — social services might be able to help."

"I've got a mate who works for a refugee charity," Moran said. "I'll give him a bell."

Simms nodded, approving. "Tell them to invoice me; mark it personal." That would keep it under the radar for a short while longer.

Moran moved off again, and ten minutes later they had arrived in a side street at the back of Deansgate. Simms directed her to the humped white shape of her Mondeo.

"Talk to no one," she said. "Not even Spry." She took a business card from her shoulder bag and scribbled her home address on the back. "As soon as you have anything, call me on my mobile — anytime — middle of the night if that's when the news comes in." As the constable's fingers closed on the card, she held on to it a moment longer, looking into the younger woman's kindly eyes. "Ella, remember what I said: you report back to me, and me only."

CHAPTER
THIRTY-EIGHT

*"From the deepest desires often come
the deadliest hate."*

SOCRATES

The local TV news was showing the loop of Suzie Fennimore ageing up from ten to fifteen years old. A commentator gave a quick rundown of the disappearance of Suzie and her mother five years earlier, and the discovery almost half a year later of Rachel Fennimore's body in a pond on the Essex Marshes.

Nick Fennimore sat on the sofa in his hotel suite, his laptop open on the coffee table in front of him. All it took was a quick Google search to find out that the "Grieving Criminalist" — yes, "criminalist" — had recently set up a Facebook page to "reach out" to his lost daughter. Suddenly Suzie's account was receiving hundreds of hits and had become a target for the curious and the disturbed and the sick, wanting to "friend" him.

He dumped his suitcase on the bed and began emptying his wardrobe of clothes.

His mobile phone rang — Josh Brown. He bounced the call. If Josh had fresh information, he didn't want to know; he was done with the investigation. Kate Simms had also tried his number, and his secretary, and Cooper, the pathologist. He switched the phone off and threw it onto the bed.

The TV newscaster spoke over his animated age-progression of Suzie. The next sequence showed footage of the crime scene where Marta's body had been found; then the photograph of Kate Simms changing her blouse in the back of her car, Fennimore ogling her.

A rap at the door. Journalists.

Fuck.

He stood still, but the TV gave him away. The knocking came again, louder, whoever it was hammering on the door as if the building was on fire.

Fennimore dropped a battered paperback into his suitcase, strode to the door and flung it wide. The man on the other side took a step back. It was Joe González in his on-duty uniform.

He held up both hands. "Woah! Take it easy, Nick."

"What d'you want?"

"I have messages, but your room phone is disconnected."

He'd yanked the landline jack out of the wall in his room after it rang for the seventh time — every one from a journalist.

Fennimore turned around, walked back inside and went on with his packing.

Joe followed him in and closed the door after him. He glanced over at the TV. "I am sorry for what happened to your *niña.*"

Fennimore gave him a sharp look. "I don't know what happened to my daughter."

Joe held him with his dark eyes. "Then I am sorry for *you*."

"Yeah," Fennimore said, anger hardening his voice. "Okay. Thanks." Wanting him get out so he could finish packing and leave. When he didn't, Fennimore looked into the Spaniard's dark eyes. "Was there something else, Joe?"

The concierge reached into his inside pocket and withdrew a bundle of notes. "Six hundred, fifty-three pounds."

Fennimore had forgotten the races, their long-odds bets on outsiders — had that really been only yesterday?

"Thanks," he said again, more sincerely. Joe didn't move and Fennimore tilted his head in question.

"There is someone asking for you in reception," Joe said. "He says his name is Josh Brown."

What the hell was Josh Brown doing in Manchester?

"He doesn't look like a journalist, but there is something funny about him."

Funny? "Describe him."

"He is . . ." Joe struggled for the word. *"Desalinado."*

"Scruffy," Fennimore translated automatically. "He's one of my students."

Joe lifted his chin in recognition. He himself was always *bien cuidado*. "Brown is a fake name, yes? Like Smith, or Jones." He pronounced it *John-ez*.

"Or González," Fennimore said, half smiling, impressed that Joe had sussed that Josh was hiding

393

something on such short acquaintance — it had taken Fennimore months to come to the same conclusion.

"So what do I tell this es-scruffy person with a fake name?"

Fennimore shrugged. "Tell him he can come up."

Joe nodded. "You should phone Doctor Cooper in the same time."

Fennimore raised his eyebrows. "Coop?"

"He es-says . . ." Joe frowned, trying to get the wording exactly right. " 'You should answer your friggin' phone, mate.' "

"Yup, sounds like Coop all right." As Joe slipped out of the door, he scrolled down his contacts list; Cooper had helped them out, taken time to run through Marta's PM with them, when he was under no obligation — it would be churlish not to return his call.

"Coop — it's Fenn."

"Well, it took you long enough." He sounded excited, rather than belligerent.

"Look, I'm about to head off for the train so I just wanted to thank you for —"

"You can't go now, mate," he interrupted.

"Talk to Kate; I'm off the case."

"Bollocks to that. Anyway I tried, couldn't get through. Nice shot of you two in the paper, by the way."

Fennimore clenched his jaw tight.

Into the silence, Cooper said, "Mate, I've got another body for you."

The first thing Fennimore thought was, *No, I can't do this.* The second was, *What makes him think it's ours?*

394

"No," he said, shaking his head. "I told Kate —" He broke off to answer another knock at the door; it was Josh Brown. He waved the student in and carried on. "My involvement was supposed to be under the radar. Now I *am* the damn story."

"Yeah, I saw the stuff about Suzie. I'm sorry about that, mate, but wait till you hear what I've got." Before Fennimore could stop him, he'd launched in. "Carol Watson, addict, prostitute, identified her from her fingerprints. Found in an alley at the back of Piccadilly Gardens. She'd been working around there."

Not my problem, Fennimore told himself, but he couldn't help wondering . . . "Did she have a street name?"

"Candy, Candice, Sugar Candy — take your pick-and-mix, mate."

Candice.

He heard himself say, "Cause of death?"

"She was strangled, probably with a wide leather strap or belt. *And* — little bonus for you — she had recent whip marks on her buttocks and back."

"Whip marks as in . . .?"

"As in riding crop, mate. Waffle effect. The injuries are so like Marta it's uncanny. Except he didn't bash her face in," he added with pragmatic objectivity. "And the whipping happened maybe a day or so ago."

"George Howard has just been charged with Marta's murder," Fennimore said.

"So, either he had an accomplice, or they charged the wrong feller. So, are you in?"

"I'm compromised, Coop," he said.

"You mean you're pissed off."

"Yeah, okay, I am."

Cooper laughed. "Get off your high horse, Fennimore. I've seen the pictures — and you were *definitely* peeking."

Cooper was right: he was peeking — and lusting — after Kate, which was another good reason why he should head for home. Coop was right about him being pissed off, too. As a result of the images of him and Kate in the press, his attempts to connect with his daughter had gone badly wrong. He hated the fact that Gifford had anything on him, and regretted the hurt to Kate and her family.

"A nasty fucker like this shouldn't be allowed to walk the streets with decent folk," Cooper said, speaking into the silence. "What d'you say, mate?"

Whoever took the photograph wanted him out of the way, Fennimore reasoned. That intrigued him. And he realized that he was more properly engaged, more *interested* in this case than he had been in any other for the past four years. He asked Cooper to email him the details.

This done, he turned to his PhD student. "Let's get to work."

CHAPTER
THIRTY-NINE

The Simms household was unnaturally quiet for the time of evening. Normally, Becky would be working on homework in the kitchen, or talking on the phone to one of her school friends. Tim would be getting ready for bed, squealing happily in the bathtub, later listening to a bedtime story. Tonight, sensing the tension between his parents, but unable to put a label on it, he responded with anxiety, turning his large blue eyes from Mummy to Daddy, uncertain who to declare allegiance to, finally clinging to Mummy and refusing to go to bed. Becky was hiding in her room, her iPod earphones jammed in her ears.

The journos who hung around at the bottom of the driveway for the first hour had slowly drifted off. This was explained by a call to Simms's mobile from Jim Allen.

"The nationals have been briefed," the press officer said, talking fast. "I contacted all the locals personally. You're a dedicated cop, determined to seek justice for the voiceless and dispossessed. You solved the penicillin deaths, a man has been charged — he's admitted cutting the deals with antibiotics. And now you've got the hotel murder nicely tied up."

It wasn't worth telling him they'd got that one wrong.

"They know the hours you're working, the fact that you keep a ready bag in the boot of your car so that you can be presentable on four hours' sleep. And the killer line — you've discovered a body that lay undiscovered for years. Humberside won't like it, but that's their press office's problem, not ours."

"Okay, I —"

"Just listen," he said.

She was too tired to argue and he went on, hardly pausing for breath: "This was a cheap attempt to use a perfectly innocent situation to discredit you, possibly by the criminal elements you are rooting out — the conspiracy theorists will love that. There'll be corrections in the morning papers, and updates later tonight on the online news sites. Trust me, Kate, this will be cleared up by morning; all you need to do is keep a dignified silence. If they ask for a comment, do not comment. Do not say, 'no comment' — do not say *anything*. At all. Clear?"

"You seem to have covered every angle," she said.

"Why else would a police force hire an ex-tabloid hack?" he said, allowing a hint of humour into his voice for the first time. "I know all the angles and I know how to square them off. Any questions?"

"Do we know who sent the photographs?"

He snorted. "You've got to be joking!" Then, "What?" He sounded fainter, as if he'd turned away from his phone and was speaking to somebody else. "Listen, Kate, gottago. Cheers."

She closed the phone and saw Kieran standing in the doorway, staring at her with distrust. She began to tell him about the phone call.

"Great," he said. "Terrific. DCI Simms exonerated — good for you. Pity those smutty pictures will still be out there, and I'll still have to face my year-eleven history classes knowing they've seen my wife stripped down to her bra in the back seat of a car."

"Well, thanks for the support, Kieran," she said.

The look on his face said it all. "Maybe you should explain to Becky, so she knows what to tell her school friends when they ask what her mum was getting up to."

"For God's sake!" She wanted to say that he was making something of nothing, but her cheeks burned, recalling the look on Nick Fennimore's face. Tim began to grizzle, and she stood, shushing him, kissing the top of his head.

The doorbell rang.

"I'll get it," she said.

"Don't be so bloody stupid — do you want pictures of our son in the morning papers?" He made as if to push past her, but she stood her ground.

"This is my mess. I'll sort it," she said. "Here, you take Tim."

He did, grudgingly, and she tidied her hair and composed herself at the hall mirror before opening the door.

Her heart lurched; it was Nick Fennimore.

He stamped his feet on the snowy path and looked up at her. "Can I come in?"

She slipped outside and pulled the door almost closed, tugging her jacket tight at her neck against the bitter cold. "Not a good time, Nick."

"Coop has been trying to reach you," he said. "Candice is dead. Murdered."

He was watching her, and she knew he was trying to gauge her reaction. She should have told him there and then that she was suspended — or as good as — but there was a light in his eyes that was more than simple curiosity — this was an invitation to place a wild bet with him, to join him in climbing the rock face of this investigation without rope or harness. With Kieran's silent anger at her back, she said, "There's a café about five minutes' drive from here."

Fennimore saw Kate Simms hurry past the café window twenty minutes later. She hesitated at the door, seeing Josh Brown at the table with him, but any uncertainty was over in a second and she strode confidently to the table. They were in a corner, away from the window and partly hidden by the counter and cash register — Josh's choice.

"You're here because . . .?" Kate said, offering her hand.

"I thought he might need some help."

Fennimore smiled. "He thought I was about to chicken out."

Josh didn't comment, and Kate said, "I wouldn't blame you if you did." She tilted her head, a sweet expression of regret on her face.

"I'm not leaving," Fennimore said.

400

"Why?"

He'd said it as a reflex, to stop her talking about his dead wife and missing child — at this moment it was too painful even to hear their names — but now he had voiced his decision to stay, he felt the need to explain his decision, not least to himself. "Because whoever took those photographs *wants* me to leave."

She looked immensely relieved and grateful; he didn't like that look of gratitude — a good detective shouldn't be made to feel an outsider.

"And anyway there are no more flights to Aberdeen until morning."

Josh organized the food order while Fennimore showed Simms the images and preliminary observations Dr Cooper had sent by email. There was no question in his mind: Candice had been tortured and throttled in the same way Marta had.

The photographs were arranged side by side for comparison on the screen and Simms stared at it, but Fennimore saw that she wasn't looking at the images at all.

"What are you thinking?" he said.

"Candice's killer knows we're investigating him," she said. "What if he's the one who's been following me?" She took a breath, let it go cautiously, as if she was afraid of waking a dangerous animal. "If he took these, he must have seen me with Candice."

"All we can do is work the evidence," he said. "We've a lot more than we had. Let's reassess, decide where to take the inquiry from here."

"Nick, this *isn't* an inquiry any more."

401

They listened while she told them what Spry had said to her. "He wasn't interested in Varley's report. He had the tox analysis for Operation Snowstorm actually in his hand, but he wouldn't let me see it. And he wasn't even *remotely* curious about who would want to discredit us with those photographs."

She threw her head back and looked up at the ceiling. The look on her face said she'd had enough.

"I spoke to a pal at the Forensic Science Service yesterday," Fennimore said. "Got fed up waiting for the tox screen of the Snowstorm drugs haul. It's been in my inbox since this morning, but with everything that's happened I only just checked it."

She leaned forward, her palms flat on the tabletop.

"The Snowstorm drugs appear to've gone back into circulation," he said.

Simms sat back and her hands slipped into her lap like they'd lost all feeling. "You're telling me someone is recycling seized drugs."

He didn't answer, but he didn't think she expected him to — she just needed to say the words aloud.

She rubbed her temple, the amber flecks in her eyes jumping like something alive. "Show me."

He called up a series of graphs on his laptop screen, slid his chair around the table to sit next to her. "The chemical constituents of the samples." He pointed to the peak for methaqualone. "This is the marker the lab used for your samples. But there are some smaller peaks — here, and ... here, which are mineral constituents; just crap that got into the mix because of the method of extraction in the country of origin, but useful for comparison."

He superimposed slide transparencies of Rika's OD with StayC's, adding the other penicillin-contaminated deals, and the sample taken from the bindle left near Marta's body. One after another, they matched. Then he called up the Operation Snowstorm graph and slid it over the rest.

Simms's eyes tracked right and left, searching the images. "There's no doubt?"

"None," he said.

She sat back in her chair and pushed her fingers through her hair. Her eyes lighted on Josh Brown. "I don't think you should hear this," she said.

He eyed her coolly. "Hey," he said, "you're the one with the leaky boat."

"Josh —"

"No, he's right," Simms said. "But you don't understand, Josh. It's not that I don't trust you — I don't think it's *safe* for you to hear it."

Fennimore spoke up. "Kate, he's been in this from the start. You can't cut him out now."

She looked undecided.

"And since you seem to be working solo on this, we can use all the help we can get," Fennimore added.

She took a breath and held it.

"Kate."

"Okay," she said.

She stared for a moment at a sprinkling of sugar crystals on the table. "Marta made a call on her mobile the night she died. Around the time she was in the

403

restaurant." She focused on those sugar crystals like she meant to count every grain. "The number was traced to a detective constable on the Drugs Squad — a Gary Parrish." She shook her head as if she couldn't believe what she was telling them.

"DC Moran just found out that Detective Sergeant Renwick deliberately held up the mobile phone check," she said. "And Renwick was on the Drugs Squad when Snowstorm went down."

For a while nobody spoke. Josh sat slightly back from the table, watching them both from under his lashes.

"You think Marta was acting as a go-between?" Fennimore asked.

"What else could she be doing with two drugs squad cops — one of whom we know for sure is bent."

He couldn't deny that.

"Will you take it to your boss?"

"Not until I have a clearer picture," Simms said. "I'm waiting on a translation of Marta's voicemail messages."

"So what do we think," Fennimore said, "blackmail?"

Josh looked doubtful. "Go against the police *and* a drugs cartel? She'd have to be crazy."

"Okay," Simms said. "What's your best guess?"

"Sticky fingers," he said, without hesitation. "A few grams here and there wouldn't be missed, but if they found out . . ."

"No," Kate said, "Marta wasn't an addict. She'd have no reason to steal drugs."

Her mobile phone buzzed, jittering sideways on the table. "DC Moran," she said.

Fennimore ordered more coffee and some food while she talked.

"She's found a translator," Kate told them, closing her phone and stealing a few fries from Fennimore's plate as it arrived. "She's on her way over."

Twenty minutes later the door opened as a gritting lorry ground past, flinging crushed sandstone and rock salt in its wake, and the café owner made an exclamation of protest. Moran stepped inside quickly and the translator stood back, allowing her to lead the way. He was large and dark, with soft, sad eyes and an apologetic demeanour.

Moran nodded to Fennimore.

"Professor Fennimore has been advising on the investigation," Simms said.

"The man with no name's got a name after all," Moran said. She turned to the translator, introducing him as Petr and, dragging off a pair of suede mittens as big as bears' paws, shook hands with Fennimore and Josh Brown.

Moran plonked herself down on a spare chair. "There are dozens from English friends arranging to meet for coffee or drinks, wondering where she was hiding out. A few of them mention lectures and group seminars she's missed. A few from family — Marta missed a kid's birthday. Petr says transcribing all of it will take half a day, and you need to hear this straight away." She dug in her coat pocket for her smart-phone, selected a track from her music player, and switched to speaker.

They heard an older woman's voice.

"What language is that?" Simms asked.

"Latvian," Petr said. "She calls her Martina. In Latvian, *Martina* is diminutive for Marta." They listened. "She says, 'Please, come home. Why must you be the one to do this? Veronika —'"

The woman's voice cracked, and she seemed to struggle for a moment, her breathing heavy and ragged. Someone said something, and she replied, "*Ne*," then the translator took up the dialogue again. "She says, 'Veronika would not want you to put yourself in danger. Please, please, *please*, Martina, telephone me.'" The woman broke down, sobbing, and Petr looked around the table.

Under Petr's sad-eyed gaze, Kate blinked away tears and cleared her throat. "What does that mean — 'Why must you be the one to do this?'"

Moran raised her shoulders and let them fall.

"Anything else we should listen to?" Kate asked.

Moran said, "It's mostly more of the same. The voicemail box was filled up by Monday, but give me a minute, there is one more thing . . ."

Fennimore remembered how, when Rachel and Suzie first disappeared, he had filled their mobile phones with increasingly frantic voicemail messages and texts. He hadn't even wanted Suzie to have a mobile phone. A ten-year-old — it seemed ridiculous — why on earth would she need a mobile phone? But Rachel had insisted, and they had bought Suzie a pay-as-you-go.

While the young detective searched the recorded snippets, Fennimore was dimly aware that Simms was putting together a plan of action, but he was reliving the moment, six days into the search, when they thought they might have found Suzie. It turned out that her phone had been dumped at the side of the A11 in Leytonstone, north-east London. A teenage boy found it, switched it on. He was sitting in his parents" house, quietly deleting the voicemail messages when a team of twelve armed police burst into the family home.

"Nick?"

They were all looking at him.

"Sorry," he said, feeling dazed and a little sick. "Just zoned out for a minute there."

She *knew* — of course she did — Simms could practically read his mind.

"Ella's about to play the last section," she said.

They heard a male with a strong Mancunian accent: "Hiya, it's Gary. Give us a bell, when you've got a minute, yeah?"

"Gary," Simms said. "Detective Constable Gary Parish."

CHAPTER
FORTY

Simms, Brown and Fennimore were heading back to Fennimore's hotel. Moran would talk to the Latvian embassy in London as soon as it opened in the morning — Marta was almost certainly one of their nationals. Rika was their second line of inquiry; Simms and Fennimore would deal with that while Moran put together a full list of names for incoming and outgoing calls from Marta's mobile phone. Renwick was not to be told about the calls log. They didn't want him to tip off DC Parrish. Simms would find a way to make discreet enquiries into Parrish, but she couldn't do that until the following day.

The A56 was largely clear of snow as they headed north into the city, and they made good progress. Simms's phone rang; she checked the screen and took a breath before answering. "Kieran," she said. "Hang on while I pull over to the kerb . . . Everything okay?"

"It was, until one of your lot fetched up on the doorstep."

Confused, she ran through the very limited possibilities — most of "her lot" had been reassigned to other operational duties.

"Who?"

"Detective Constable Parrish."

Oh, Jesus. Every nerve ending in her scalp seemed to fire at once. "Where is he now?"

"He's sitting in the kitchen, drinking coffee, looking like a refugee from some nineties indie band."

"Don't let him out of your sight. I'm on my way."

She swerved from the kerb, executing a swift U-turn, her wheels spinning on compacted snow on the midline of the road.

Fennimore said, "Trouble?"

"Parrish — he's in my house."

"I'll call the police." He already had his phone in his hand.

She gave a desperate laugh. "And say what, Nick? He *is* the police."

Two minutes from home, the traffic lights changed against them. Kate Simms jammed her foot on the accelerator. A lorry, fifty feet from the junction on her left, took advantage of the amber light in his favour and kept going.

"Lights," Fennimore said, bracing himself against the dashboard. "Lorry!"

She braked, hit a patch of black ice and the rear end of the car glided right. The truck bore down on them, horn blaring. Kate fought with the steering wheel, heart pounding. Josh cursed. She spun the wheel the other way, but the car glided on over the ice, sweeping anticlockwise with the ABS juddering loudly and the pedal pulsating under her foot. The lorry was coming head-on, its grill fifteen feet from them, ten, five — filling the windscreen —

The front end of her Mondeo slid past the oncoming lorry, completing three-quarters of the circle as the truck's huge wheel arch loomed inches from Kate's side window. Her heart seized.

A sharp *crack!* and her wing mirror was gone. A thin scream of metal on metal. They braced themselves for full impact.

It never came. The car shuddered to a stop with its nose pointing in the direction of home. The lorry drove on, horn blaring.

Josh muttered, "*Fuck.*" Fennimore said, "Kate . . ."

"I'm sorry," she said. "I'm really, really sorry. But please, don't speak."

She took the rest of the journey slowly, agonized by the extra seconds it took, finally turning off the main road onto the narrow leafy lane where she lived. She was out before Fennimore had his seat belt off. Josh was by her in a second.

"No," she said. "You stay here."

She ran up the driveway, slipped and jarred her knee, fumbled her keys from her shoulder bag, but Kieran must have heard the car; he opened the front door, his face dark with anger.

"You need to sort this, Kate," he hissed. "I am not about to let you turn our home into an adjunct of your office."

"Where's Tim?" She pushed past him, her fingers closing on the ASP baton in her bag. "Jesus, Kieran, I told you not to let him out of your sight."

She flung the bag from her and ran for the kitchen, slamming the door wide. Tim was sitting on one of the high stools at the breakfast bar, looking tousled and tired in his pyjamas. Beside him, a scruff with close-cut dark hair and a soul patch between his lower lip and chin.

"Get away from my son," she said.

"What?" The man didn't move.

She flicked open the baton.

"Woah," he said, "I'm a cop — Gary — Gary Parrish?"

"I *said* get away from him."

He stood back from the child, raising his hands. "Look, I don't know what you think —"

"Tim, come over here, sweetheart," she said, ignoring Kieran's protests as he crowded into the kitchen behind her.

Tim climbed down off the stool, and Kate held out her hand. He stared at the baton and she lowered it. "It's all right, darling," she said, keeping her eyes on Parrish. "Take Mummy's hand."

Without turning, she shepherded her son behind her. "Go to Daddy," she said.

For once, Kieran didn't question her, or argue. He picked their son up and retreated into the hall. With Tim out of sight, Simms brought the baton up behind her right ear, ready to bring it down hard; break a wrist, an ankle, his skull.

"Okay," Parrish said, "Ar-right. I get it — you don't know who to trust. Neither do I — that's why I'm here." He stood perfectly still, his hands raised, his voice calm and quiet. "I'm a detective constable with the Drugs Squad," he said. "And . . ." He hesitated.

"The girl found behind the city hotel — I think she's my informant."

"*Informant?*" Simms shook her head. It didn't make sense — Marta was moving drugs for Parrish and Renwick.

"Her code name was Kelly."

Not very Latvian, Simms thought. But then neither was McKinley. "What makes you think she's my victim?"

"Kelly phoned me, said she wanted to meet — she had some dynamite intel. Next day, she's in the wind, misses the meet, and her phone's off." Parrish's dark grey eyes flitted nervously from Simms's face to the baton poised over her right shoulder, ready to strike.

"Sit down," she said. "Don't move." Turning, she saw Nick Fennimore in the doorway. *Marta an informant.* This changed everything. Fennimore nodded as though she'd spoken her thoughts aloud.

"Watch him," she said, and went into the hall. Kieran was standing at the foot of the stairs.

Her smile, intended to reassure, felt weak and uncertain. "It's all right," she said.

"No," Kieran whispered. "It isn't. Look at your son."

She stared into Tim's anxious, sleepy eyes and felt a stab of guilt that almost hollowed her out. "I know," she said. "I'm sorry, Kieran."

"You charge in here like a lunatic, frighten your four-year-old son."

"Kieran." She reached out to squeeze his arm, but he shook her off.

"Whatever you're mixed up in, you've got to walk away from it. Please, Kate."

She shook her head slowly. "I can't."

He stared at her as though he didn't recognize her, then he turned away and started to climb the stairs.

Gary Parrish was sitting where she'd left him, his arms folded tight, his chin almost resting on his chest. He unfolded his arms when she came through the door, pulled his shoulders back and held her gaze.

"Tell me about your informant," she said.

His eyes went to Fennimore.

"Professor Fennimore can hear whatever you have to say."

Parrish hesitated.

"That's non-negotiable, Parrish."

He seemed to debate for a moment, then he shrugged. "Kelly'd been passing info to Crimestoppers for a while," Parrish said. "Usual set-up — anonymous, code number only. Like a guided bloody missile, she was — every tip-off paid out, always. Six months on, she calls, tells them she's got the 'in' with a big supplier; we're not talking street-corner sellers — she wants to bring the big guys down. Says she wants someone to tell her what to look for — evidentially, like."

"Evidentially?" Simms repeated.

"Her exact words. And she wanted protection. When Crimestoppers told her they could get her signed up as a confidential informant with the police, she jumped at it."

"And you were approached to act as liaison."

He nodded.

"When was this?"

"Two months ago. First few weeks, it was phone contact only. She was careful. She showed up late for our first face-to-face — turned out she'd been watching me from across the street for half an hour."

"Describe her."

"Knock-out," he said. "I mean drop-dead gorgeous."

"Height, Detective," Simms said, giving him a dry look. "Hair colour, that sort of description."

"Oh," he said. "Blonde, about five seven, long legs, carried herself like a dancer."

She looked at Fennimore. The description fitted Marta.

"Tell me about the dynamite intel."

"She worked in a massage parlour — Francine's. It's run by two brothers, Sol and Frank Henry."

"*They're* the suppliers?" she said. "That doesn't tally with what your superintendent told me."

He nodded. "Our intel was they dibbled and dabbled a bit — just on a recreational level. But Kelly reckoned they were importing and distributing smack on a *big* scale."

"How could they do that and stay clear of the law?" Simms asked.

"She told me people who cross the Henry boys disappear or turn up in bits. Literally."

That would explain why George Howard wouldn't name the Henrys as his alibi. A glance towards Fennimore said he was thinking along the same lines.

414

"Kelly was due for a try-out at Howard's place. The brothers put her up to it. They wanted her to find something they could use against him as leverage." Another piece of Marta's story slotted into place. "She rings me that same night," Parrish said. "There's a regular at Francine's — guy called Rob. A bit of a fixer, she gathers. She saw Rob go into the Henrys' office with a sports bag and come out with a briefcase in his hand and a bloody great grin on his face. Now, she's a bit of a favourite with Rob, and he's in a good mood, so he invites her for a meal. She's got the appointment with Howard, but that's not till later, and she's curious, so she says yes, thinks maybe she'll get something out of him during the meal."

"And did she?"

He shook his head. "Nah. She rang me from the ladies' while they were waiting for coffee. Rob had splurged on the booze, and he was very nicely irrigated, but she was none the wiser. He'd kept the briefcase with him — hadn't let it out of his sight for a second — so she'd agreed to head back to Francine's for a session, see if she could get a squint inside the bag."

"And you *let* her?" Simms said.

"I told her she was bloody crazy, tried to warn her off, but she hung up on me."

"I thought you said she was careful."

He shrugged. "Up to a point. But it was like she got off on it, smiling in their faces while she ripped the guts out of their operation. A couple of weeks back, she was delivering a package to one of their mixers — a mad bastard they call Bug. He locked her in his flat. No explanation. She'd been asking questions — thought they'd sussed her, thought she'd never get out of the place alive. Bug kept her for two hours then let her leave. Sol was waiting — told her there'd been a lot of police activity around the place, so he'd called Bug and told him to delay her.

"She asked Sol why Bug didn't just tell her, and Sol said, 'I didn't tell him *why*. That's the difference between you and him: Bug doesn't need to know *why* — he just does as he's told.'"

"Punishment," Fennimore said. "A warning they owned her."

Parrish nodded. "She still went back the next day though."

"And a week later, she was dead," Simms said. "Why haven't you taken this to your boss?"

Parrish's gaze skittered to the door, then back to her. "The night she died, maybe an hour or so after she called me from the restaurant, I got a panicked text from her." He took a breath and exhaled shakily. "She said someone on the job was involved with the Henrys — supplying them with drugs."

Simms slid a look from him to Fennimore.

Parrish looked confused. "You know about that?"

"We knew someone on the job was recycling drugs."

His eyes widened. "You thought that was me?"

"Not any more," she said. "But Marta . . . Kelly — whoever she was — she was right." She had to take a breath before she could say it: "Police *are* involved."

She wasn't ready, just yet, to tell him about Renwick, but what she had said was enough.

416

Parrish's face seemed to sag. "Oh fuck." He rubbed his hand over his cropped hair. "I've been sweating blood over this — couldn't make up my mind whether to tell you or go to the nearest pub and get bladdered."

"Regretting your decision, Detective?"

He considered the question carefully. After a long silence, he said, "Haven't made my mind up yet."

Simms smiled. "Why'd you come to me?"

"I'm the new boy on the squad, like I said. I don't know who I can trust. And everybody thinks you're a pain in the arse." She could see him listening back to what he'd just said, and although he didn't show any overt signs of alarm, he added, "I meant that in a good way, ma'am."

"It's 'Boss'," she said, allowing another fleeting smile to play across her features. "Did you record your conversations with her?"

"No," he said. "No way would she agree to that."

"So you've no proof of any of this?"

"Only my notes. Her calls to my mobile should be on the calls log, and I've kept the text."

"Does the text say she was in Francine's when she made this discovery?"

"No." He scrolled down his phone screen and showed her the text:

"He is police," it said. "He sold drugs to Frank and Sol."

"Why does it matter where she made the call?" Parrish asked.

"Because Francine's is probably our primary crime scene," Fennimore said. "And this Rob could be our killer."

Parrish nodded. "So what do I do?"

Simms thought about it. She should talk to Superintendent Spry — this was way above her pay scale. But Spry wasn't in the mood to listen, and they didn't exactly have incontrovertible proof. She was tired and frightened and sick to the pit of her stomach, and a part of her wanted to give up, send everybody home, get into bed and pull the covers over her head. Maybe it was pride, maybe it was Parrish standing there, asking for her help because she was the only person he knew who was bloody-minded enough to trust; maybe it was hearing of Marta's reckless courage in the face of violent men. Whatever the reason, when she looked at Parrish again, she knew she had to follow this through to the end.

"Feel like doing some digging?" she said.

Parrish replied with a cautious, "Okay . . ."

"I want to know who was in charge of Operation Snowstorm. And specifically who signed the log supervising the destruction of the drugs."

"Yeah," he said, and she could see him working it through in his mind. "I can do that."

CHAPTER
FORTY-ONE

Night fog gave way to a cold, dismal morning. It was 9 a.m. and Fennimore and Simms were in the Cemetery Office at Blackley in the northern outskirts of the city.

No, the ruddy-cheeked official told them, there was no "Rika" buried in a pauper's grave. She waved Simms's copy of the coroner's report.

"I know exactly who you're looking for," she said. "I didn't say she wasn't here, only that she isn't buried in a pauper's grave." She shoved her chair back and began rummaging under her desk. "I'll show you."

Kate winced. "Really, Nesta, that won't be necessary."

"No trouble," the administrator said, her voice muffled under the desktop. "I could do with a breath of air." She came out from under the table flustered and glowing, with a pair of shiny black rubber overshoes in her hand. She crammed her feet into them, then struggled into a bright red duffle coat which she'd hung on the back of her chair. She riffled through a pile of buff folders halfway down the high-rise tower of files on her desk, extracted one and glanced at an A4 sheet inside.

"Follow me," she said.

They sloshed their way along the slushy curve of the access road to the far north corner of the cemetery, and the tip of a wedge-shaped section, hedged in by winter-grey trees. A wood pigeon mourned in a treetop behind them, and the persistent *did-didn't, did-didn't, did-didn't* chirrup of sparrows in the lower brush sounded like children embroiled in a tedious argument.

Fennimore scanned the rows, picking out those with a plain wooden marker; state-funded burials did not run to the cost of a headstone.

"It's on the fifth row," Nesta said, pointing to a new granite upright, half buried in snow.

Fennimore brushed away some of the powdery drift. The granite was carved with the inscription, "Veronika Aizupiete, aged 19."

"Veronika," Simms murmured.

"Yes," the official said. "*Not* Rika. Though of course that was the name we had originally."

"Who paid for this?" Fennimore asked.

"Her sister. She put us right on the name when she requested permission to erect a headstone. Of course she had to cover burial costs and actually buy the plot before she was allowed to —"

"The sister's name?" Simms interrupted.

"Marta," she said. "Marta Aizupiete."

Simms glanced at Fennimore, her eyes glowing. They had a name — a genuine, verifiable name.

"Did Marta give a contact address?" she asked.

"Ye-es," the woman said. "And proof of identity — a passport and university student card."

Simms stared at the folder clutched tight to the administrator's chest. "Did you happen to keep copies?"

"Of course," she said with prim disdain.

Kate took a breath and exhaled through her nose. "May *we* have copies?" she asked, scrupulously polite.

Twenty minutes later they were on their way out of the office, the photocopies tucked away in Kate's shoulder bag, when a man wearing a sharp suit and a bright spotted pink tie intercepted them.

"You're police?"

"Detective Chief Superintendent Kate Simms, and this is Professor Nick Fennimore."

"Do you have proof of identity?" he asked.

Simms showed her warrant card. "Your turn," she said.

He held up his staff card, hanging from a lanyard around his neck. "Tyburn," he said. "Section manager." He turned to the plump administrator. "Did you get her to sign a receipt?"

"Um, well, no, Mr Tyburn," she said, her forehead colouring deeply. "They *are* police."

"By what authority are you here?" he asked.

Fennimore wondered for one mad, paranoid moment if he'd been tipped off that Simms was no longer in charge of the investigation or, worse than that, he'd recognized them from the media coverage of the airport photographs.

Simms gave him a flat cop stare. "I'm investigating a murder, Mr Tyburn." She held up her warrant card again. "*This* is my authority."

He flushed suddenly; apparently he wasn't used to being faced down. "Don't you people compare notes?" he demanded. "We do have to consider client confidentiality, you know."

"I'm not sure I follow," Simms said.

"I went through all of this with your chap on Wednesday."

Fennimore shot her a glance.

"What 'chap' is this?" Simms asked.

"Um . . ."

"What did you give him?"

"Everything — address, proofs of ID — the lot."

"And did you ask *him* to sign a receipt?" Kate asked tightly. "Did you even get a *name?*"

"He showed me his warrant card," he said. "A detective sergeant," he said. "Tall. Dark hair. Forty-ish?" He reddened and fumbled to a stop.

"A name would be really helpful," Kate said with icy civility.

"He never actually said his name," Tyburn admitted, his bravado thoroughly punctured.

"*He never actually said his name.*" She sucked her teeth. "Think you'd recognize him again?"

"Yes," he said, recovering a little. "Yes, I believe I would."

"Good. I might need to call on you. And Mr Tyburn?" she added, her voice like silk. "You might want to make a note of our names, for future reference."

"The mystery sergeant," Fennimore said, as they walked back to the car. "Renwick?"

She nodded. "It was Renwick who told me that Rika had been buried by the state."

"Rika and Marta, sisters," he said, trying it out to see if he believed it. "It explains a lot."

She nodded. Revenge, justice — they were strong reasons. "But Rika must have told her how dangerous the Henrys are. I can't imagine why Marta would put herself in the same danger."

"Maybe Parrish is right — she enjoyed the thrill. Or maybe it was better than sitting thinking about what happened to her sister."

Simms glanced at him from under her lashes. She often thought that Fennimore's restless activity was an escape from having to think.

Fennimore drove while Simms arranged for Scientific Support to attend Marta's flat with her to take safe custody of any evidence. The route from Blackley Cemetery took them through Cheetham Hill, past the alleys and tenement blocks and their bin stores, where some of the early drugs death victims had been found. The pavements here were unsalted and the snow had been trodden down to dirty packed ice.

As they reached the mean row of shops where only ten days earlier they had leafleted the locals to warn them about tainted heroin, Simms wondered if Marta had crossed the street in front of her, on her way to make a delivery of heroin. Which of these nondescript buildings housed a crazy man named Bug? That shuttered and empty shop? That flat above a greengrocer's? Marta hadn't given DC Parrish an address, said Bug was "small potatoes". It seemed that nothing less than the destruction of the Henrys' entire empire would avenge her sister's death. Simms kept replaying pictures in her head: Marta's face battered beyond recognition; the whip marks, proof that the horrible torture inflicted on Rika had also been visited on Marta, too.

Fennimore glanced at her. "You okay?" he asked.

"Just thinking — Marta's mother was right."

He nodded. "She could have gone home, made a life for herself — a bright, resourceful young woman like that. But then Rika's death would go unpunished." His face seemed calm, but a muscle in his jaw worked.

Suzie, she thought. In a way, every investigation, every case he worked on was about Suzie. "Let's see if we can finish what Marta came here to do," she said quietly.

She scrolled down her contacts list to Josh Brown and switched to speakerphone. "Marta Aizupiete," she said, spelling the surname. "She was a sociology student at Manchester Metropolitan University."

"Okay," he said. "Want me to look up her records?"

"No, I want you to talk to her friends." She hesitated. Strictly speaking, she should put this in the hands of a Family Liaison Officer. "Josh, what I'm asking you to do is highly irregular . . ."

"Not a problem," he said. "Just tell me what you need."

"Ask about her, find out if she told anyone about her background, but *do not* let them know what happened to her. Josh, it's possible Renwick got there before us, so suspicions could already be aroused —"

"It's fine," he said. "I'll get hold of a teaching schedule — I'm a friend from London, looking her up. Got her address?"

Kate read it to him from one of the sheets the admin officer had copied for them.

"Got it — I'll say I went there and couldn't get an answer."

"Well." She glanced at Fennimore as she disconnected. "Young Josh is a natural at this."

Fennimore gave her a wry smile. "I think Josh has had a bit of practice when it comes to reinventing himself."

She turned in her seat. "What does that mean?"

He shrugged. "Just a feeling."

Simms nodded to herself; a cop's curiosity wasn't always welcome.

She kept quiet until they approached the wide junction at the end of Cheetham Hill Road. From there, she gave him directions, guiding him anticlockwise onto a grey, high-walled section of the Mancunian Way. When she'd first moved north to Manchester, Simms had no cosy notion of narrow streets of terraced houses and neighbours chatting on doorsteps, but she hadn't expected something quite on the scale of the city's urban sprawl either. At Castlefield the road opened up onto a vista of leafless trees and scrubby grass; in the distance, they caught glimpses of Beetham Tower, the forty-seven-floor skyscraper looking like an impossibly tall slab of marble, reflecting the greys and whites of the sky, the penthouse wreathed in a lingering mist. They took the first left off the roundabout and drove past a student apartment block on the left.

Marta had rented a two-bed furnished apartment across the road in a Victorian Mill conversion — four-star accommodation at about double the rental on a student flat yet only five minutes' walk from the university. The place was secure on their arrival. Kate had contacted the flat owner, who had an apartment in the same building.

"Marta's a good tenant," he said. "No noise, no visitors that I know of. Pays her rent, cash every month. I didn't like it at first — cash seems a bit iffy, doesn't it? But she paid three months' deposit upfront and she's *never* been late — not even a day, not once in ten months. She's a *nice* girl, Chief Inspector. I don't know what you think she's done, but —"

"Sir," Simms said gently. "Marta is dead. She was murdered."

His eyes watered suddenly and he made a small noise at the back of his throat. "Marta?" he said. "Are you sure?"

She nodded and he placed the key in her gloved hand, then she asked him to take a step back. He stood to the side of the door and turned away for a second, wiping his face with the back of his hand.

Kate unlocked the door and swung it wide, remaining in the hallway. She looked at Fennimore and he said, "I think we both expected this."

"What?" the landlord demanded. "Expected what?" He crowded forward looking over her shoulder.

"Fucking hell!"

The place was a mess. Furniture overturned, cushions ripped apart, their stuffing feathering every surface. Books had been pulled out from the bookshelf, spines ripped off. There was no TV — removed at her request, the landlord said. A CD player was intact, but every disc had been taken. At the far end of the open-plan living space, every drawer, cupboard and shelf in the kitchen had been emptied. Rice, cereal, biscuits and dried pasta lay strewn across the floor and work surfaces, tipped out of their packs. Drawers were turned upside down, even the washing machine had been dragged away from the wall.

"Thorough," Fennimore said.

Simms nodded. "Now I know why Renwick missed the lunchtime briefing on Wednesday."

The landlord made a move to enter, but she turned and eased him back. "Sir," she said. "This is a crime scene. You can't go in."

There was no laptop, memory stick or external drive in the flat. Fennimore and Simms left the Crime Scene Unit to it and headed back to the Midland Hotel for an unofficial debrief of her unofficial team. The police constable on the door had been told to admit no one but the CSIs.

"He's been ahead of me every step," Simms said. "I thought I was doing him a favour, giving him a chance to prove himself. He's been messing with the evidence and laughing behind his hand with every supposed foul-up."

Unexpectedly, Fennimore smiled.

"Oh, you think this *funny*, Professor?"

"You know Locard's Principle — 'Every contact leaves a trace.'"

"Even when you break in to *steal* evidence?" she said gloomily, irritated by his good mood.

"Sometimes especially then," he said. "You would think he'd be especially careful, wouldn't you? But he trashed the place."

"He was panicked or angry, or both," Simms said.

"Which means he made mistakes."

"He's a cop, Nick — he's forensically aware."

"Police always *think* they know more than they do," he said. "If he was there, the CSIs will find him."

CHAPTER
FORTY-TWO

"Everybody lies."

DR GREG HOUSE

They got back to Fennimore's hotel just after midday. His suite was decked out like an incident room. His laptop stood open on a circular dining table, a flipchart lying open next to it was covered in notes, diagrams and doodles; on a whiteboard, mounted on a couple of easels, he had mindmapped the investigation as it currently stood. Hung on a stand next to it, a second flipchart summarized the mindmap in bullet points. A drift of scrapped flipchart sheets from previous attempts lay curled and scrolled against the far wall.

Josh sat in one of the armchairs, his laptop on his knee, a combined printer and flatbed scanner perched on a stack of printer paper on the coffee table in front of him. His smart-phone was in his hand and he appeared to be texting. He looked up, lifted his chin in greeting, his thumbs still moving over the touch screen. The blinds were closed — a precaution in case any of the journalists who had dogged them the previous day had failed to get the message and bribed their way into one of the buildings opposite.

Simms moved straight to the whiteboard; it was an explosion of colour.

Fennimore stood next to her. "Didn't sleep too well last night," he said.

Minutes after he reconnected his hotel landline, Fennimore had received an angry call from his in-laws; they had been trying to reach him all day. Rachel's father described the Facebook page as "a stunt", and called Fennimore a selfish, self-obsessed bastard. It was true: it hadn't even occurred to him to consult with Rachel's parents or even warn them of what he was about to do. He'd meant to apologize, but heard himself say, "I'm trying to find my daughter."

Rachel's mother came on the line, her voice raw with anger and tears. "It's all about you, isn't it, Nick? Well, we lost a daughter, too."

He shook himself free of the memory and looked at Simms; she was engrossed, studying the swirling complexity of lines on the mindmap. Fennimore left her to it, and turned to Josh.

"Did you make contact with any of Marta's friends?" he asked.

Josh nodded. "She was in her second year — told everyone she was Russian — on a placement from a university in Moscow. She attended lectures regularly; was a bit of a live wire in tutorials; had strong opinions and wasn't shy of expressing them."

"Contentious, or assertive?"

"Everyone I spoke to seemed to like her. Her grades were pretty stellar, but she got on with the rest. One of her mates told me she was aiming for a first. They were a bit mystified by her though —"

There was a knock at the door and Kate checked through the peephole. "It's Ella Moran," she said, cutting across what Josh was saying. "This will keep till later."

Fennimore began to question her.

"*Later*, Nick." Her tone brooked no argument.

She opened the door and Moran came in looking flushed and excited. "I'm supposed to be at the cemetery, checking up on Rika," she said. "Sergeant Renwick told me to get down there pronto."

Simms told her what they'd discovered about Rika and Marta, and about the break-in at Marta's apartment.

"So, what do I tell Sarge?"

"Everything I've told you," Simms said. "Just tell him I'd got there ahead of you."

"Okay."

Fennimore waited for her to say that Renwick had gathered the same information at least a day earlier, that they suspected him of the break-in, but Simms said, "How are you getting on with Marta's calls log?"

"Caller ID was blocked on a few," Moran said. "But I've got names for most of them, now."

"Good. Email it when you get back to base." Kate turned to Fennimore. "Can we use your email address?"

He gave Moran a business card.

"She also had multiple calls from a throwdown." Moran handed over her notebook, and Simms copied the number down.

Simms turned to Fennimore. "Is there any way to trace this?"

He glared at her, but she gazed calmly back at him and, eventually, he said, "Pay cash for a SIM free phone and you're basically off-grid. With an unlocked phone, you could swap providers every few days if you wanted — most garages and supermarkets sell pay-as-you-go SIM cards. It would be virtually untraceable."

"I *know* that, Nick," she said. "I'm asking if we can set up a trace and ring the number?"

"*If* he still has the phone, *and* he's still using the same SIM card, *and* you could get clearance to do a trace, *and* keep him on the phone long enough? Well, then, yes, I suppose you could probably triangulate his position. But by the time you get there, he would probably have dumped the phone and walked quietly away."

Moran looked from Fennimore to Simms. "Is everything okay?"

Simms gave a tight smile. "Just tired and tetchy."

Moran nodded, sympathetic as always, though she looked like she'd never lost a night's sleep in her life.

Simms jerked her chin towards the scanner on the table next to Josh Brown. "Does that thing do photocopies?"

"Sure," Josh said. "What d'you need?"

She handed over the forms they had picked up at the cemetery office; Fennimore noticed she held back the student ID.

"Go to Marta's flat," Simms said, as Moran tucked the copied sheets into her shoulder bag. "Get yourself noticed by the CSIs, quiz the uniform on duty about what happened, and make sure he tells you that I am the SIO — I don't want anyone thinking you're already working with me. Then take these back to the station as proof you went to Blackley. Tell DS Renwick we've got a definite ID, and make sure the Latvian embassy is informed. Spry will arrange for a Family Liaison Officer and interpreter to talk to the family."

"That'll take ninety minutes, tops — what'll I do with the rest of the day?"

"Just send me the phone log, but keep it out of sight of Renwick."

"Kate," Fennimore said, and she frowned, gave her head a little shake as if to say, *Not now.*

She saw Moran out.

As soon as the door closed, he said, "What the hell are you doing?"

"I'm protecting her, Nick."

"You're keeping her in the dark."

"Renwick has been playing with us all along, but this one time I'm a step ahead of him because, right now, Renwick doesn't know he's a suspect. If I tell Moran everything we know, it will put her in an impossible position. What if she lets something slip? What if she just looks at him the wrong way and he decides she's a threat?"

"She's already hiding the phone log from him."

"She's holding back a lead; every cop does that at some time or other. But the cemetery, the break-in — they say Renwick is dirty. I can't expect her to go back into the office and deal with that on her own."

"She is," he said. "She just doesn't know it."

She frowned. "I'm sorry, Nick — it's the best I can do."

"If it helps, I don't think Renwick's been near her university friends," Josh said. "They're assuming she's had a family emergency and gone home."

"*Nobody* was worried about her?" Simms asked.

"Like I said, Marta was a bit of a mystery. None of her friends even knew where she was living in Manchester, and one of them lived in a block of flats opposite hers."

Fennimore had listened to this with half an ear, but now he went off in an entirely different direction. "Why didn't he go to the university?"

"Who?" Simms said.

"Renwick. He has a copy of Marta's student card, yet he hasn't visited the campus."

Simms shrugged. "He couldn't blend in like Josh. He'd have to say he was police, and that would attract attention — questions would be asked." She groaned as another possibility came to her. "Or he's already got everything he needs."

A knock at the door turned out to be Parrish. He was wearing a beanie hat pulled low over his brow and a camouflage-print hoody, his hands jammed into the

434

pockets of his jacket. He came into the room fast and back-heeled the door shut.

"This is really, seriously fucked up." He snatched the beanie off his head and rubbed his close crop of hair, then noticed Josh for the first time. "Who are you?" He turned to Simms and pointed at Josh, hat in hand. "Who the fuck is *he?*"

"Josh Brown," Simms said. "He's been in the investigation since day one."

"Shit," he said. "*Shit.*" Parrish paced the floor, squeezing the hat in his hands.

"Gary," Simms said. *"Detective Constable Parrish."* He stopped for a second. "D'you want to tell me what's got you so wound up?"

He threw his head back and blew air towards the ceiling. "You were right," he said.

"About what?"

"Everything." He began pacing again and came up short at the whiteboard. "Oh, shit . . . It's here. All of it."

Fennimore's pulse rate kicked up a notch. He looked from Parrish's agitated face to the mindmap. In this version, there were three distinct strands: the drugs deaths in black; the murders in red; and the torture strand, coloured purple.

"It's good to know, Gary," he said. "But way too cryptic for me."

"Here." Parrish pointed to the branch dealing with the penicillin deaths.

On the flip chart next to it, Fennimore had bullet-pointed this strand of the investigation:

PENICILLIN
- Used to:
  - Bulk deals
- Due to — loss?
  - Snowstorm — confirmed $$$
  - Drug Squad successes
- Bulked by . . .
  - Supplier?
    - G Howard?
    - F and S Henry?
    - Bug?
    - A. N. Other?
- Dealer?
  - Anthony Newton x — set-up?

He pointed to Anthony Newton's name at the bottom of the chart. "He confessed to causing the penicillin deaths, yeah?"

Simms nodded. "After running a red light with *fifteen* wraps of heroin on him." She watched him closely. "Like he was *trying* to get himself arrested."

"Right," Parrish agreed. "Here's the weird thing: Dip Newton isn't a dealer — he's a driver. Five weeks ago, he drove a vanload of heroin onto Tesco's car park in Didsbury. He parked it up, walked away. We let him because the plan was to follow the drugs to the warehouse, identify the buyers. When I say 'we' I mean the squad. I was on a course at Bramshill, so I wasn't part of that operation. They had surveillance on the van for ten days. No one collected. Thirty K's worth of heroin unclaimed on a supermarket car park. Why?

Because whoever shipped the drugs knew the van was being watched."

"Insider tip-off," Fennimore said, and Parrish gave a grim nod.

"We went looking for Newton after the van was seized, but he was long gone."

"So, why'd he come back?" Fennimore asked. "Was he paid to take the fall?" It was common practice — someone lower down the food chain confessed for a fee, keeping the wheelers and dealers out of prison.

Parrish shook his head. "His bank account's been frozen since his arrest, he's maxed out on his credit cards, and his wife and son have just been kicked out of their flat. The CPS is about to charge him with the vanload as well — apparently he turned down a deal. I had a word with one of the interviewing officers; they said he was a wreck — traumatized, paranoid, absolutely bricking it. Which is no big surprise — they had to call out the FME when he was arrested."

"What was wrong with him?" Fennimore asked. A Forensic Medical Examiner — formerly "Police Surgeon" — would only be called out if a prisoner was in medical need.

Parrish tugged at the small beard patch on his chin. "I looked up the FME's report." He pulled a set of colour photocopies out of his jacket pocket.

Josh cleared a space on the coffee table and they gathered round. In the first image, Dip Newton had the terrified look of a kicked dog. Both eyes were blackened, and he had ligature marks on his wrists.

"He was tied to a chair and tortured," Parrish said.

Further pictures showed puncture wounds, bruises and burns around Newton's nipples.

Fennimore exhaled. "Looks like they attached crocodile clips to his nipples, connected him to an electrical supply."

Parrish nodded, avoiding eye contact. "The damage to his cock and balls — sorry, Boss, I mean, penis and scrotum — was even worse. He's still pissing through a tube."

Fennimore winced and Josh crossed his legs.

"They thought he was the police informer?" Kate asked.

"If they did, he must've convinced them otherwise, or he'd be in pieces at the bottom of the Manchester Ship Canal by now."

"So what *did* he do?" Fennimore asked.

"The Crime Scene Unit found an infrared video-cam hidden in a roof ventilator inside the van. It showed Dip Newton nicking a baccy-tin full of smack."

"So his bosses gave him a choice," Simms said. "Manchester Ship Canal, or a ten-year stretch for trafficking."

The next image showed the back of Anthony "Dip" Newton's head. Under a thin fuzz of hair, the scalp was a mass of livid burns, some of them weeping yellow ooze, some beginning to scab.

"Are those *letters?*" Josh asked, leaning closer.

Fennimore experienced an answering prickle in his own scalp. Josh was right. The lines formed letters, and the letters formed a word.

438

"They used a soldering iron," Parrish said. "Branded him. Used it on his dick as well — stuck it in there and turned it on."

Josh stood suddenly and walked away.

"Jesus," Kate breathed. "If they did that to a thief, what would they do to an informer?"

"Was it Marta tipped you off about Dip's vanload of heroin?" Fennimore asked.

"It came in through Crimestoppers," Parrish said. "So I can't say for definite. But, yeah, I think it was her."

"What about Snowstorm?" Simms asked.

"No — she made her first call to the hotline a couple of months after that all went down." He looked at Simms, and for a moment he looked like a man gingerly testing the edge of a very high diving board. "You wanted to know who was in charge of Snowstorm."

Simms lifted her chin, encouraging him.

"Oh, shit." He took a breath, let it go slowly. "Superintendent Tanford."

The colour drained from Simms's face. "No," she said.

Parrish bowed his head.

"It doesn't mean he's involved in recycling the drugs," she said, looking to Fennimore for support. "Does it?"

"As senior officer, he would have to sign off on the destruction of the drugs," Fennimore said.

"Doesn't mean he was there. Parrish?"

Parrish shook his head regretfully. "I can't get access to the log without ringing all kinds of alarm bells, Boss."

Kate shook her head in a slow, wide sweep. "No," she said again. "Tanford has supported me every step of the way."

Parrish shrugged — he looked as dazed and sick as she felt.

"You have to admit, it is neat," Fennimore said.

" 'Neat'," Simms said. "Is that how you see this?"

"It's how *they* see it," Fennimore said. "Tanford gets commended on a major drugs seizure, and he's in the perfect position to put those same drugs back into circulation."

"Well, thank you for your *insight*, Professor," she said, and he saw the crackle of amber in her eyes. "Perhaps you can advise me on how exactly I can use this information, because I haven't a fucking clue."

She was in pain. She had believed in Tanford, even looked up to him. Fennimore sympathized, but his mind remained clear.

"You can't use any of it, Kate. The recycling might *point* to Tanford, but you'd have to prove he knowingly switched a sizeable drugs haul for baby laxative, or whatever, then signed off on the burning and put the heroin back onto the streets. Dip Newton isn't about to tell us; Marta might have had proof, but Renwick took that when he broke into her flat."

"Maybe he didn't get everything."

They turned to look at Josh. He was standing with his back to the window, trying not to look at the photographs on the coffee table.

"One of Marta's friends said she'd better come back soon, 'cos she'd left a stack of textbooks in one of her lockers and it'd cost her a fortune in fines."

"I'm sorry," Simms said. "I don't see how that helps."

"Why would she have more than one locker?" the student said. "It's not like she had to hike across campus — all her lectures, tutorials and seminars were in the same building. So I'm thinking, what if she was using one of them as a safety deposit box?"

Simms nodded. "We found two Chubb keys in Marta's purse at George Howard's flat. They'll be in the evidence store by now. But I can't go there, and even if DC Moran could get clearance to pick them up, it could take an hour or two to gain access."

"Key?" Fennimore smiled. "Who needs a key?

CHAPTER
FORTY-THREE

"You can lock your door against a thief, but you can't lock your door against a liar."

ANONYMOUS

It was mid-afternoon and the sun, just beginning to lower in the sky, filtered through the trees on the small square of Queen's Park, reflecting brilliantly off the snow as Simms turned the car right at the Royal Northern College of Music.

"I shouldn't have lashed out at you like that," she said, with an apologetic glance to Fennimore.

"Forget it," he said. "I can't resist a smart-arsed remark, and you were right, it was insensitive."

"I suppose I'd hoped that this mess was down to one or two greedy cops who'd dipped their fingers in the sherbet and liked the taste," she said. "But four and a half million pounds' worth of drugs was seized in Operation Snowstorm." She exhaled slowly. "The idea of that quantity of drugs filtering back onto the streets terrifies me. And I just . . . I can't believe that Tanford is part of it."

"Don't take it personally, Kate."

"I don't —" She stopped herself, laughed. "I'm such a liar. Yeah, I do — I take it very personally."

It was good to hear her laugh, even if it was a little shaky, and caught a little at the back of her throat.

"I believed his flannel about me scaring the crap out of the dealers." She sucked air through her teeth. "And all the time the bastard was on the make."

Fennimore turned to her. "It's not just you, Kate — Tanford has fooled a lot of people — senior officers who've known him for a lot longer than you have." He quirked his eyebrows and offered a small smile. "And he wasn't lying when he said you had the dealers jumping; they were just closer to home than you realized."

The first locker was empty except for a stack of library books and a flyer advertising a guest lecture on the cultural politics of human rights. The second contained a backpack and a Next shopping bag. Fennimore stood next to Kate Simms as she emptied it into a plastic Ziploc bag. Students and staff moved up and down the busy corridor, some eyeing them curiously, while security looked on, noting each item on a receipt pad. The Next bag contained a change of clothes: a low-cut silk dress, sheer stockings and four-inch heels.

The backpack was a jumble of the usual student essentials: pens, ruler, reporters' notebook, A4 notepaper, timetable. Also a black A5 hardbound notebook and an 8-Gig pen drive.

The receipt signed, and textbooks locked in the boot of the car, Simms drove around the corner, out of sight of the security manager who had followed them out of the building and watched them leave, a thoughtful look on his face.

"I can't file these in evidence — not yet — not until I have some idea of the true scale of this."

Fennimore snapped on a pair of nitriles.

"What d'you think you're doing?" she demanded.

"C'mon, Kate," Fennimore said. "It can't hurt to take a peek."

The notebook detailed names, dates, drop points, methods and routes for drugs deliveries. He flipped through the pages and found transcripts of conversations between the Henry brothers and a man named Rob; "Rob the fixer" Marta called him.

"Listen to this," Fennimore said, reading from the journal. "Rob said, 'I can guarantee continuity of supply.'"

"By recycling seized drugs." Simms checked her wing mirror and moved off into the traffic.

"See something?" Fennimore asked.

"No, doesn't mean they're not watching though." She squinted across at the journal. "Why d'you think she wrote it in English? Why not Latvian?"

"Good question." He thought about it for a minute. "Insurance maybe? If anything happened to her, she knew that eventually her lockers would be emptied, and this would come to light — she wanted whoever found it to know exactly what they had."

He continued turning the pages, trying to absorb the sheer volume of names, dates, delivery points. "She's listed car and van registration numbers, addresses." He flipped to the next page and recoiled. "Jeez —"

Simms glanced across. "Yeesh," she said, flinching as he had. "Who's *that*?"

"Our man 'Bug', apparently," he said, reading the inscription. Marta had conveyed suppressed rage in the muscles and tendons snaking up the thug's arms and twisting around his neck like vines. His eyes bulged as if he was half-mad.

"Bug is a 'Mixer'," Marta wrote, "which means he mixes heroin with powders so it goes further. Three women do the labour. He makes sure they follow the recipe."

Fennimore glanced at Simms. "We have his address." He grinned. "She's even described the security at his flat."

"Don't suppose there's a sketch of Rob in there?" Simms said.

She was joking, but Fennimore riffled through the pages anyway. He found a photograph slipped into the back cover, held in place by the notebook's elasticated strap.

It looked like a home print, on semi-glossy paper; a dark-haired man of about forty. Taken side on, standing in a dingy-looking corridor, he was extending a hand to someone standing the other side of a doorway. The image was slightly grainy, as if it had been taken without a flash. He flipped the photograph over; it was labelled "Rob". Under that, a combination of numbers and letters: 1211<4–19. The puzzle-solver in him automatically began trying to work out what it meant.

"Fennimore, are you still with me?"

"Hm?" he said, reluctant to drag his mind away from the puzzle. "Yes, still here," he said. "And there's no sketch, I'm afraid. But will a photograph do?"

"*What?* Well, show it to me!"

He held up the image for her to see.

"Nick," she said, gripping the steering wheel as though her world had slipped sideways and she needed something to hold on to. "That's Superintendent Tanford."

Three cars back in the line of traffic, two men watched DCI Simms and Professor Fennimore. Their boss was not pleased when they told him about the removal of items from Manchester Metropolitan University. He ordered the driver to continue tailing the Mondeo, and sent the other back to demand a list of the items, a copy of the receipt — any damn thing that would tell them exactly what Kate Simms had found.

"Marta's injuries, the torture — it was Rob," Simms said. "And Rob is Tanford, which means that Rika and Candice and . . . oh, shit —"

"What?" Fennimore asked.

She fished her mobile out of her handbag and passed it to him. "Call Parrish," she said. "Switch it to speaker."

As he scrolled down her contacts list, she talked:

"The women in Hull — Tanya Repton and the other women — the murder victim we found under the factory." She swallowed. "It's all him, Nick. It's Tanford."

DC Parrish answered, and she said, "Listen, I need to know where Tanford was before he came to Manchester."

"Somewhere in the north-east, I think," Parrish said.

Simms looked at Fennimore. The north-east — Hull, Newcastle — the other victims.

"I can find out the details," Parrish said. "I'm at HQ now."

"No, Parrish," she said, "tell me you didn't go back to the Drugs Squad."

"Don't worry, I've been careful."

"Jesus." Simms took a breath and held it. "I want you back to the hotel," she said. "Immediately."

She cut the connection and rubbed her palm over her forehead.

The traffic inched forward. She stared through the windscreen for a full minute before she said, "Tanford a murderer. Tell me I'm not going crazy."

Fennimore scratched his cheek. "The evidence is starting to look strong." She began to protest, but he held up his hand. "I know you don't want to hear this, Kate — it's strong, but still deniable."

She pinched her lower lip between her finger and thumb and he could see her wondering if she should call her friend in Hull, see if she could persuade Tanya Repton to look at Tanford in a line-up.

"We still have the DNA results from the nipple stud to come," he went on. "But even if Tanford's DNA is found on it — well, it's not unknown for police officers to use the services of prostitutes — he could admit to that, which would make the evidence of no value against the more serious charges."

"What about the drugs recycling," she said. "Surely, with what's in Marta's notes, we can get him on that?"

He nodded slowly, working it through in his mind. "He'd have a harder job explaining that away. He was running the show — he's supposed to supervise its destruction. And Marta's pen drive might give us something more concrete. If we can link him to the throwdown on Marta's calls log, it would be evidence of a stronger liaison. There might even be texts and voicemail messages, but, honestly, Kate, he'd have to be stupid or monumentally arrogant to have kept the phone."

"The text," she said. "The one Marta sent to Parrish."

"She named the brothers but not Rob."

"Are you telling me this is hopeless, Nick?"

"No," he said. "Marta was a registered informant, and from what DC Parrish has said, her intel was good, so anything incriminating in the diary and on the pen drive might be enough. Tanford is bound to have at least one legit cell phone, and cell site analysis placing him with the Henrys would add weight to the other evidence. It might even put him with the body at the dump site. And we still might get fibres, hairs — even fingerprints — from the wrappings on the body in Hull."

"But I can't afford to wait for cell site, or for Hull to finish their work on the trace."

"No," he agreed.

As they sneaked through the lights on amber, Simms came to a decision. "Okay," she said. "I'm going to present the case to Detective Superintendent Spry and the ACC."

"You're taking this to Gifford?"

"Gifford and Spry are singing in two-part harmony — to convince one, I need to convince them both," she said.

He gazed at her in frank admiration.

"What?" He could see her nerves were running very close to the surface, right now.

"Nothing," he said. "Drop me at the hotel, I'll get everything in order — you're going to need it."

CHAPTER
FORTY-FOUR

Detective Superintendent Tanford closed his office door and made a call. He used the throwdown and made a mental note to change the SIM card before the day was out.

"You need to step outside your office — outside the frigging *building*," he growled.

"What the fuck you on about?" It was Sol.

"Just do like I say, then call me back — not from your car — you need to be out in the open."

Two minutes later, he got the call.

"We missed something," Tanford said. "Something big."

The silence at the other end of the line told him he'd better explain.

"Marta backed up her data. She hid a notebook and pen drive in a locker at the university."

Sol chuckled. "She told me the student get-up was a disguise."

"I'm glad you can see the funny side. You know what the big belly laugh is? Simms has got both."

"What's on the flash drive, Rob?" The easy affability was gone.

Tanford didn't answer.

"You don't know? So, maybe it's nothing incriminating — it could be essays and that."

"Did you ever run counter-surveillance in your office?" Tanford asked.

"What for? We never talked about important stuff in front of her, or anyone else. Only you, Rob." The softness of his tone sounded like a threat.

"She had audio and visual of you and Frank. On the phone, arranging deliveries."

"No chance."

"Audio *and* visual."

"No fucking chance," he repeated, his voice hard.

"Wake up, Sol. You used it yourself, on Dip — did you think it only worked one way?"

"No — *fuck*, no!" Sol's breathing stuttered down the line.

"Sol," he said. "Hey! You need to focus. We need that evidence off Simms."

Sol snorted. "Simms is your problem, mate. You've got men tailing her — send them in."

"And do what?"

"What d'you think? Arrest her."

"They can't, not without cause."

Sol barked a laugh. "You're joking me?"

"Look, this isn't some street hooker we're talking about. She's a Detective Chief Inspector. The media are already screaming conspiracy over the surveillance pictures we leaked yesterday."

"All right, you can't arrest her — just fucking take it. Tell them to stop the car and take the evidence."

"You think I can just tell them to hijack a senior officer and steal evidence in a major investigation?"

"Why not? They work for you, don't they?"

"The two lads I've got on her think they're surveilling a bent cop," Tanford said, keeping it pleasant, because he needed these morons and, worse still, he owed them.

"Tell them Simms is about to destroy evidence."

"If they take the evidence away from her, it's got to be logged."

Sol spluttered an oath. "Do I have to give you a step-by-step idiot's guide? Tell them to bring the evidence to you."

"That's not how it works, Sol."

"I don't fucking *care* how it works — we need that evidence."

He'd hardly raised his voice, but Tanford knew Sol was close to ignition point. "All right," he said. "Everyone's under pressure, let's not lose our heads over it."

Someone knocked at Tanford's door. He ignored it. The door opened a crack and a female clerk peeked around the edge.

He screamed, "OUT! GET THE FUCK OUT!"

The door swung closed hastily, leaving the blinds shivering from the shock. He snorted air like an enraged bull.

Sol carried on as if nothing had happened. "Send your goons in. Arrest her, do whatever's necessary."

"They won't do it," Tanford said through clenched teeth. "Not without good cause."

"So give them cause — pay 'em."

"These men can't be bought," Tanford said.

"Fuck off."

Sol said it in the same slightly pained way a polite person might say, "Oh, come now."

"Rob, mate," he went on, "everybody can be bought. You just got to find the right currency."

Traffic was snarled all the way to the hotel, so Fennimore took over driving while Kate Simms phoned Spry and arranged to meet with him and Assistant Chief Constable Gifford in an hour. Gifford warned her that Chief Constable Enderby would also be present.

"It seems Gifford intends to bury me once and for all," she said.

"I know Enderby," Fennimore said. "Worked with him on a cold case in 2002, when he was still just a working stiff. He's a good man."

She didn't comment — in her years as a police officer, the male perspective on what constituted a "good man" never quite squared up with the female perspective.

"You want me to speak to him?" Fennimore ventured.

"No," Simms said. "Thanks, but no." They were crawling along at walking pace, the roads clogged with football supporters on the way to a derby match between Man U and Man City; the homeward surge of commuters added to the congestion. A journey that should have taken ten minutes had already run to thirty.

Her phone vibrated in her sweaty hand, the chime alerting her that she had received an email to her personal account. She frowned; the subject line read, "Warning: hard Candy can choke." There was an attachment, marked urgent.

Puzzled, she opened it. She recognized Candice Watson immediately. She had a leather strap around her neck, and she was being choked to death.

Kate gave a muted cry and Fennimore glanced at her. "You okay?"

Her phone jingled again. Another email, no subject line this time. She opened the image.

It was her daughter, Becky, drinking coffee with school friends in a café. For five full seconds her heart stopped. A clawing sensation tore through her chest and a sound that didn't belong to her came out of her throat.

Fennimore looked at the image on the screen and across to her, a look of incomprehension on his face. She fumbled the window open and sucked in biting cold air.

Her phone rang. She almost dropped it, trying to answer.

"Becky?" she said.

"No." The voice was a man's, disguised by some kind of distorter. "But the man who took the photograph is within arm's reach of her."

"Don't hurt her," she said, hearing the panic in her voice.

454

Fennimore responded to it; his head snapped left, his eyes bright with alarm. "Speakerphone," he mouthed.

She switched to speakerphone. *Don't beg*, she thought. *Don't — it will only make it worse.*

"You have nothing to gain by hurting her." The tremor in her voice was still there, but she thought she had control of it.

"You're right," the voice said. "But I will hurt her if you don't do exactly what I say. Do you believe me?"

"Yes."

"Take the next right. Drop Fennimore on Whitworth Street first chance you get."

She glanced wildly behind them.

"Yes," the voice said, "you are being watched — so I will know if you try to make a copy or retain any of the evidence, or use your phone to alert anyone."

Fennimore changed lanes and turned right at the Palace Theatre. Whitworth Street was narrow and, either side of them, the six-storey Victorian red-brick buildings crowded to the edge of the kerb, creating a false twilight.

"What do you want?" Simms said.

"You know what I want."

She stared silently at the phone in her hand, her whole body shaking.

"You have thirty seconds to decide, then my man will make his move. If she resists, he will shoot. If she doesn't, well, Becky's a nice-looking girl, so I might find a good use for her . . ."

She saw Fennimore's hands tighten on the wheel. Simms knew those words would feel like an ice pick in his brain, but she didn't care about Fennimore — or, God forgive her, Suzie — because this was Becky, this was her daughter, *they had her daughter.*

The man's reasonable, implacable tone spoke over the screaming in her head: "Do what I say, or you will never see your daughter alive again."

"All right," she said. "All *right*, I'm doing it, okay?" Then, to Fennimore: "Pull over — you have to get out."

Fennimore braked sharply, squeezing the car into a narrow gap between a van and a Renault Espace.

He snatched the phone from her hand and switched it to mute.

"What the hell are you doing?" she said.

In the background, the man continued giving instructions, telling her to take the right fork onto Fairfield and keep driving until he gave her further instructions.

"Where is she?" Fennimore demanded.

She reached for the phone, but he grabbed her hand and held it tight. "It looks like a café," he said. "Kate, tell me where Becky meets her friends after school."

Something seemed to tear loose under her heart. "I *can't* Nick. Please, give me the phone."

"Listen to me. They'll take her anyway." She looked in his eyes and saw a wild fervour in them.

The voice on the phone demanded to know if she understood the instructions.

Kate struggled to be free of him, but he held her fast. "This isn't Suzie," she screamed. "You can't save her — now give me the fucking phone!"

He recoiled like she'd slapped him, but he did not relax his hold on her one millimetre.

"They'll take her," he said again, a strange blue light in his eyes. "And they'll keep her until they're sure you don't pose a threat to them any more. And then they'll kill her. Because by then she will know too much."

Something lodged at the base of her throat and, for a second, she couldn't breathe. He was telling the truth, she knew it, and Becky was lost to her.

"Kate."

"Starbucks," she said. "Near St Ann's Church. Go left at the next turning."

"Delay them," he said, "as much as you dare."

He was out of the car and running as she switched the phone mic back on.

CHAPTER
FORTY-FIVE

"Tattoos on criminals are as good as a bar code."

CHIEF INSPECTOR DAVE GRIFFIN

Fennimore ran past Manchester College, heading towards the city centre. These quieter side streets had not been gritted and he slithered and slipped every few steps, until he gave up on the pavement and took to the roadway. There was nothing but offices and a few seedy pubs on this stretch — no sign of a taxi. He reached a main road and looked right and left. No signs, no directions. He stopped a woman.

"St Ann's," he gasped. "Which way?"

She shook her head, avoiding his gaze, hurrying on. He turned to a group of people waiting to cross to the north. "St Ann's," he said. "The church?"

A man pointed to a side road diagonally opposite.

He dodged into the roar of rush-hour traffic. Someone exclaimed, a car blared its horn, a woman screamed. A bus bore down on him, its air brakes hissing and juddering. He leapt out of its path, and ran on.

Fifteen yards down the road he saw a motorcycle courier's bike parked outside a restaurant, keys in the ignition. He swung his leg over the seat and turned the key.

He heard a yell, then lights seemed to explode in his head and he was on the ground, staring at an empty bottle of Yanjing beer, spinning on the tarmac. The biker's engine roared and was gone.

Fennimore groaned and rolled onto his back; freezing ice-melt flooded down his neck, and the shock brought him fully conscious.

He struggled to his feet. His knee and ankle hurt and, looking down, he saw that his trousers were torn and he was bleeding. He hobbled to the next junction; the road ahead seemed impossibly long — he'd never make it in time. Then, miraculously, a taxi appeared from his left. He flagged it down, but it swerved around him and carried on going. He dragged himself fifty yards, seventy-five yards further, heading towards the rumble of traffic, onto another busy thoroughfare. He had no clue where he was, no clue which way to go. Two more black cabs swept past, refusing to stop. Then he remembered the wad of notes Joe had handed him the day before — his share of their winnings. He pulled the lot out, fanned it and waved it at the next taxi. It passed him.

He looked for the next, heard a squeal of brakes behind him, a grind of gears and the whine of an engine, then the taxicab was next to him at the kerb.

"Where to, chief?" the driver said.

Kate Simms followed directions through parts of the city she'd never seen — Lowry territory: vacant houses and disused warehouses and, as the light faded towards dusk, the occasional figures in the landscape took on a flat monochrome, like Lowry's matchstick men. She took a couple of wrong turnings pretending confusion, and kept her speed below thirty all the way, trying to give Fennimore a few more minutes to reach Becky.

She ended up at the edge of a large vacant lot once occupied by an old mill, judging by the scale of it. She drove around two sides of it, over uneven tarmac, then onto a narrower cobbled lane at a right angle to the tarmac road. It might once have been an alley, running between back-to-back housing for mill workers, but now it was a blank space, hemmed in on either side by tall spiked railings. The snow had melted in patches, creating oily black puddles, and in places the stone sets showed through. The lane doglegged left and ended abruptly at a brick wall. Tangled bone-white stems of wild buddleia and elder at the fence line boxed her in on either side.

"What now?" she said.

"Turn off your lights, get out of the car. And keep the line open."

She waited five minutes; it was almost dark. She saw the car headlights first, rising and dipping on the uneven surface of the mill road. Then she heard its tyres swishing through the slush. As it negotiated the dogleg in the lane, she was caught in the full glare of its headlights.

She recognized the LED halos as BMW headlamps, a darker centre and bright outer rim, like the eyes of an animal, a predator. A spasm of alarm shot through her: he wasn't slowing down. She cast right and left, hoping to find a gap in the railings, knowing there were none.

She dodged to the side of her car and the BMW stopped a foot short of her own bumper.

Standing to one side, out of the glare, she could read the registration clearly, and she knew before he stepped out of the car that Tanford was in the driving seat.

"Dynamic brake control on this model," he said, patting the roof of the car like it was a pet. "Fantastic."

The unreasoning terror Kate had felt since she'd received the image of Becky was replaced by a cold rage. The shaking stopped and calm settled on her.

"No questions, Kate?" he said, a look of rueful amusement on his face.

She took him in from his polished black loafers to his glossy black hair. "I've got all the answers I need," she said. "This is the car that picked up Marta outside Livebait restaurant on the night she was murdered. You took Marta to her place of execution, you tortured and raped and murdered her and you framed George Howard."

He smiled. "You were always good on the details, Kate, just not very good at working out which were relevant. None of this matters any more — you're here, and you're about to hand your entire case over to me all neatly wrapped in plastic."

"I know you have attacked other women," she went on, willing him to confess, just so she could hear it that one time. "I think you murdered Candice Watson."

He shook his head and sighed. "Open the boot," he said.

She did as she was told and he took a folded sheet from the inside pocket of his overcoat. She recognized it as a copy of the receipt she'd signed at the university.

"Just how many of you are in on this?" she asked.

He smiled. "There are *some* things you don't know, then?"

She shrugged. "I'll admit I don't know how much help you had from the Henry brothers."

He ignored her, holding each of the bags under the boot light in turn, checking the contents against the list before placing them one by one on the ground next to him.

"But I know you're recycling drugs to them," she said.

In answer, he held out his hand and she gave him the last of the improvised evidence bags: Marta's diary and memory stick. "Do you have even a shred of proof, Katie?" He smiled.

"You broke into Marta's flat, *Tanno* — you can't destroy that evidence."

"You won't find any DNA or trace evidence from me in Marta's flat, because I was never there."

"No, because like the coward you are, you sent Mark Renwick to do your dirty work. But men like you don't stop," she said. "That's what'll get you in the end."

He caught her arm, spun her around and slammed her head against the Mondeo. Dazed, she flailed with her hands, but couldn't find purchase. He had her by the scruff of the neck. A second later, he adjusted his grip and, two-handed, he dragged her coat back over her shoulders. She heard the seams tear; her arms were pinned. He slammed her forward against the car.

As she fought for breath, she felt his right arm snake around her neck, felt the scratch of his overcoat sleeve against her face. He had her in a chokehold. She kicked backward, connected with bone, heard him grunt in pain. He squeezed, flexing his forearm against his biceps and her legs lost feeling, she felt herself falling. He eased off and he slipped his free hand over her breasts and stomach, squeezing, probing, hurting — his breath hot on her skin. She grunted in disgust, tried to fight him, but she couldn't move. His hand travelled lower, groping her crotch.

She must have blacked out for a second — suddenly she was on her knees in the oily snowmelt, choking, coughing, sucking air into her lungs. He grabbed a handful of hair and forced her head up. Her phone was in his hand. He grinned and there was such violence and madness in that smile that she was paralyzed with terror.

"That you, mate?" he said into the phone. He listened to the answer. "You'll have to excuse us for a bit," he said, ruffling Kate's hair. "I'll call you back — me and the lady need some private time."

Fennimore handed the cab driver two twenties and said, "The same again if you wait for me, take me where I need to go next."

The cabbie grinned. "Fetch us a latte, I'll let you off the tip."

Fennimore walked into a pleasant fug of hot coffee grounds and warm food. He knew Becky immediately; she had her mother's dark hair and eyes. She was drinking a smoothie at a window table with two friends.

The goon was unmistakable — a man with a huge head and no neck. He wore a ski hat and a leather jacket; a Bluetooth receiver was jammed in one ear. He was sitting a couple of tables away from the three girls, incongruous and ill at ease, like a wrestler in a ballet chorus.

Fennimore limped over and Becky looked up, her face blank for a second, then she stared at him in horror. "Uncle Fenn. What happened to you?"

He made a weak attempt at a grin. "Slipped on the ice, had an encounter with a lamppost."

Her friends giggled nervously.

The man's chair scraped back and he stood, his leather jacket creaked as he folded his arms, and Fennimore had a slightly queasy notion that he'd chosen leather for its durability and convenient wipe-clean properties.

"Your mum asked me to pick you up," he said.

The man took another step, barging a chair out of the way. It squealed against the vinyl floor tiles. His skin was the colour of raw meat and now he was closer, Fennimore could see that he had a bar code tattooed just under his left ear.

"You've got blood on your face," Becky said, glancing uneasily towards the big man.

"Yeah, Uncle Fenn," the thug said, crowding closer. "You got blood."

464

Becky's anxious look told him she knew they were in danger. Fennimore dabbed at his lip and his finger came away bloody. "That was one angry lamppost." He eyed the goon surreptitiously. *What the hell am I doing? I can't take on this human meat mountain.*

But he could get in the way. He put his back to the man and took Becky's hand. "My lady, your carriage awaits."

Becky's eyes widened, and she blushed, but then he saw recognition in her face and she played along. "Lead on, sir."

But when he turned, the thug was blocking their way.

Fennimore sidestepped right, and the man moved with them. He moved left, and once more, the thug stepped in their path. Then he opened his jacket just enough to show Fennimore the Glock stuck in the waistband of his trousers.

Fennimore broke out in a cold sweat; there were twenty or more people in the place, and a goon with a gun was threatening to start shooting. Becky's hand tightened in his.

"Now sit the fuck down," the man said.

Becky's friends exchanged a frightened glance; a mother at the next table quietly picked up her coat and shopping bags and led her child out of the coffee bar.

As if by some kind of ESP, the manager turned around from the grill at the service counter and peered across the café. "Everything all right over there?" he asked.

"Fine," Fennimore said, his heart racing. He put Becky on the far side of the table, but he remained standing. "Can we get a couple of coffees over here?" He pointed to the torn leg of his trousers and smiled apologetically. "Ice-related injury."

The man scowled. "Stop pissing about."

"A tall mocha for me," Fennimore said. He leaned back a bit to get a good look at the thug. "I'm guessing you're a no-nonsense Americano man? An Americano for the man with the interesting bar-code tatt under his left ear," he said, not waiting for an answer.

The thug's eyes bulged.

"Better make that a decaf."

The man stepped up and squeezed his arm till it lost all feeling. "Go ahead," he hissed. "Keep taking the piss — I'll fucking burst you like a pimple."

"You *do* know the police keep a database of criminals with distinctive tattoos? Good as a bar code." Fennimore tapped the side of his own neck, under his left ear. "In your case, literally."

The thug shifted his weight from one foot to the other.

"How many people do you see?" Fennimore whispered. He saw confusion on the man's face. "Let me put that another way — how many *witnesses* do you see?"

Bar Code's leather creaked as he surveyed the room; he seemed to be counting in his head.

"What were your instructions? Follow her, separate her from her friends?" He looked around, lowered his voice even further. "I'm fairly certain your boss would not want you to get into a hostage situation."

466

The man sucked his teeth and stared into Fennimore's eyes, and it was only thinking about Simms on her own with the dark gathering around her that gave him the strength to hold that cold, dead stare.

At last, the goon let go of Fennimore's arm and fiddled with his headset with fat, nicotine-stained fingers. "Bit of a situation, Boss," he said, keeping his eyes on Fennimore the whole time. A pause, then: "Fennimore . . . At the café."

He listened, nodded, smiling, which Fennimore did not take as a good sign.

"So," Tanford said, "tell me, Kate — why haven't you mentioned the body you dug up in Hull?" He gave Kate Simms's hair a tug and bent to look into her face. "Oh, yeah, I know about that." He put his mouth to her ear and she shuddered involuntarily. "Are you *holding out* on me, Kate?" he whispered.

He drew back and she stared dully at him.

"Oh." He tilted his head and made a little moue of sympathy. "Are you hoping that even if you don't make it, your pet nerd will find some way to *find me out?* How noble." He shook his head. "How pathetic."

He lifted her up one-handed by the collar of her coat. The seams gave with a sharp *rip*, freeing her arms. He straightened her collar in a gentlemanly gesture, smiling into her face, and all she saw was rage.

Bar-Code Man leaned in close, his breath reeking of coffee and cigarettes. "You're right, Professor — too many witnesses. You and her — outside."

467

Oh, shit. This wasn't supposed to happen. Bar-Code was supposed to speak to his boss and then clear out. On his own. Fennimore looked at the faces of Becky's friends, he took in the other people: teens and mothers and shoppers relaxing, unaware of the danger they were in, and he looked at Becky, her eyes wide with fear.

He nodded and she stood. He put himself between the thug and Becky again, and in a second he felt the man's paralyzing grip on his upper arm.

The goon hissed in Fennimore's ear: "Just so you know — I don't mind shooting through you to get to her."

The cab driver was waiting. He did a double take when Fennimore crossed in front of him, heading towards the alley opposite. He opened his door and began to get out, but when he saw the ton of meat that was steering his cab fare, he got quietly back behind the wheel.

Fennimore looked desperately for a way out. There was a shopping arcade at the end of the alley — if he timed it right, maybe he could shove Bar-Code Man off balance, tell Becky to run. He must have tensed, or the thug read his mind, because he said, "Try it, if you want. But a skinny geek like you? I wouldn't fancy your chances. And you can't outrun a bullet."

He tried a door, then the next, and the next; these were back entrances, shop delivery doors. On his fourth try, a door swung open. Fennimore balked. He felt a sickening pain in his shoulder. He sagged and a second later he and Becky were through the door and in a scuffed and dimly lit service corridor.

468

The thug shoved Fennimore back hard. His head crunched against the wall and a thousand drums boomed in his ears. He pressed his hands to his skull and another spike of pain shafted through his shoulder.

The man snatched hold of Becky's wrist and she yelped. "Shut up," he snarled.

Tears stood in Becky's eyes, but she blinked them away and held still, sucking her cheeks in and frowning at the concrete floor.

"What now?" Fennimore asked.

"We wait."

Wait for what? Fennimore wondered. *The all-clear? Jesus, what's to stop him shooting us anyway, leave us for the shop staff to find?* He said, "Okay, but don't forget — you were seen by a lot of people. Those people in the coffee shop — they *will* remember you."

Bar-Code pulled a pack of cigarettes from his pocket, lit up one-handed, smoked it down to the filter. A minute or two later they heard a *plink plink* of footsteps, like stones falling into water, echoing off the walls. The thug crushed his cigarette under his heel and gave Fennimore a warning look. A woman rounded the corner. She froze, half turned as if she was deciding whether to run back the way she came.

Bar-Code jerked his head for her to come on and she edged past, the man still holding Becky's wrist in his massive paw.

A blast of cold air from the outer door, a quiet *thunk* as it swung closed. They waited. The thug rocked on his heels, whistling through his teeth. He stopped abruptly, tapped a button on his headset. "Yeah," he said, looking at Fennimore. "Yep."

He disconnected, dropped Becky's wrist and reached for the pistol tucked into his waistband. Becky gasped and Fennimore braced himself. The man gestured for them to back up, and once more Fennimore eased Becky behind him.

The man bent, keeping his eyes on them, and picked up the cigarette butt and slipped it into his jacket pocket. "Always clean up after yourself, eh, Professor?" He backed away to the door and seconds later he was gone.

CHAPTER
FORTY-SIX

"Maturity is sensitivity to human suffering."

RABBI JULIUS GORDON

Fennimore hustled Becky further down the corridor, moving fast away from the street exit. The man with the bar-code tattoo had most likely melted into the evening crowds, but Fennimore wasn't about to take the risk of running straight into him in the unlit alley.

Heads turned as they entered the shop through the wrong door, but staff were slow off the mark and they were out onto the main street before anyone thought to challenge them.

He tried Simms's mobile; it switched directly to voicemail. He hung up and tried again. Across the square, he saw the taxi, still waiting. He guided Becky to it, expecting Bar-Code to reappear any second.

"Uncle Fenn, what did that man want?" Becky demanded. "Why are you all messed up?"

"Becky, it's nothing to worry about," he said. "You're safe now."

"Don't patronize me!" Now the threat was gone she was angry. Fennimore, however, felt like his body had turned to jelly below the waist. And now he couldn't reach Kate.

"I'm not patronizing you, Becky, it's just — it's best if your mother explains." He'd said it without thinking, but she jumped on it.

"Mum? What would Mum know about it? What's it got to do with Mum? Where is she? Is something wrong with her?" Her eyes filled with tears and he cursed himself. "Uncle Fenn, where's Mum?" She was shaking, afraid all over again.

"I don't know," he said, helplessly, "but I'm sure she's okay."

She shoved his guiding hand away. "It's about that *bloody* case, isn't it? Why couldn't you just leave us *alone?*"

He opened the cab door, but she stood glaring at him. "I'm sick of being pushed about. Tell me what's going on," she shouted.

"All right," he said, "I'll explain, but we need to get away from here — please?"

She scowled at him for a few more seconds, but finally she stomped past him and clambered into the far side of the cab.

He gave the driver Kate's address, desperately trying to think how much he dared to tell her. The jangle of his mobile rescued him.

"Is Becky all right?"

Kate. Relief flooded through his veins.

"She's fine. Are you —?"

"Let me speak to her."

He handed over the phone.

"Mum?" she said. "There was a man — he had a gun."

472

The cab driver looked in his rear-view mirror.

"Mum are you okay? Uncle Fenn's bleeding. Mum? Mummy, I was so scared."

Fennimore heard the echo of his own daughter's voice in her words. He looked out of the window, trying not to listen, trying not to think about anything at all.

After a few minutes, Becky fell silent, listening to her mother. "Mm," she said. "Yes . . . yes . . ." She handed the phone back to Fennimore without looking at him. "She wants to speak to you."

"It's all gone, Nick," Simms said. "He handed me a lighter and made me burn everything, even the textbooks."

Fennimore wiped his eyes. "You're okay. Becky's okay. That's all that matters, Kate."

They arrived at the Simms's home just as she was pulling into the driveway.

Becky flew into her mother's arms and clung to her.

Fennimore paid the cabbie and turned to face her. She looked at him, over Becky's shoulder, her eyes desolate.

"Come on, darling," she said, kissing her daughter's forehead and face. "Let's get you out of the cold."

Becky helped Fennimore make tea, while Simms called the Drugs Squad DC to let him know where they were. She frowned and Fennimore raised his eyebrows and she said, "It's going to voicemail." She spoke into the phone. "Gary? DCI Simms. Call me as soon as you get this."

Becky handed him a pint of milk. "It was me, wasn't it?" she said.

Fennimore frowned, not understanding. "That man was using me to get at Mum."

He broke eye contact, using the bottle top as an excuse, giving himself time to think. "The man's boss, anyway," he said, picking at the edges of the foil cap, getting nowhere. "They want your mother to stop investigating a case."

She snorted. "Fat chance."

Fennimore smiled, and she took the bottle back from him and opened it with a practised movement. Simms was talking to Ella Moran.

"Where are you?" she asked. A pause, then, "Are you all right?" She listened to the answer. "Well, clear any computer searches and your desk, and get out of the office. Do you have any friends you can stay with?"

Fennimore watched Becky place a clean mug carefully on the worktop, as if it might explode, her eyes wide with fear.

"Good," Simms said. "Go there — stay put — call in sick. I'll get a message to you when I know it's safe." She became aware of Becky's scrutiny and turned her back.

Fennimore tried to distract Becky with a question, but she shrugged impatiently, her gaze fixed on her mother.

Kate lowered her voice, but they both heard her say, "Talk to *nobody* about the case. I'll be in touch."

She bowed her head for a second, and Fennimore got the sense she was bracing herself. She turned to Becky. "Just one more call."

She fast-dialled a number, left another message for Parrish.

Moments later, her mobile rang and her face flooded with relief. "Parrish?" she said. "I've been trying to reach you —"

She broke off, a frown creasing her brow. She had a lump on her forehead that was beginning to bruise and her fingers strayed to it. Suddenly, her eyes widened and a tremor seemed to run through her, then she went very still. "Thanks," she said. "I'll . . . Thanks."

She hung up. "Becky, I need to speak to Uncle Fenn in private." Becky began to object but Kate shook her head. "It's police business." She sounded implacable, but her face was lined with pain. "I'm sorry, darling. Just give us a few minutes, okay?"

Becky chewed her lip, making up her mind whether she wanted a fight. "All right," she said, sounding like a parent trusting their wayward teen against their better judgement. "But you owe me an explanation."

Simms watched her daughter leave; she listened to the thud-thud-thud of Becky's footsteps on the stairs; she waited a little longer until she heard the bedroom door close, and Fennimore thought it must be something truly horrible to make her want to put all that distance between her daughter and this fresh crop of bad news.

When she turned her eyes on him, she looked numb with shock.

"That was a DCI from Traffic Division." Her voice lacked emotion, yet he knew that whatever she was about to say, it was tearing her up.

"Gary Parrish has been killed. Hit and run. The DCI called Parrish's line manager first, and was put onto me."

"Line manager? Does that mean —"

"Tanford." She nodded, her eyes red-rimmed. "He told Traffic I needed to know."

"The bastard," Fennimore breathed. It was a threat — he could get to her family, and he could destroy anyone who tried to help her.

"It's over, Nick," she said. "We're finished. I burned *everything*. The ash is probably scattered across three counties by now. Without DC Parrish's testimony, I've got nothing."

He took her hands in his. "We *will* get him," he insisted. "The evidence is there. We'll keep after him until we have him. It might just take a bit longer."

"I'm out of time, Nick." She slid her hands from his grasp. "Even if we find his DNA on Marta, I have no sample to match to him and without Marta's notebook I've no legal justification to *demand* a sample from him. Shit — you said it yourself — even if we did get a match, it wouldn't really prove anything."

"We still have the Hull victim."

"They'd need to dig her up with Tanford's business card clutched in her mummified hand to convince Spry."

"What about the drugs recycling? Tanford was SIO during Operation Snowstorm. There has to be a paper trail; it'll lead back to him."

"Oh, yes, the drugs." She blew air through her nose as if she had a bad smell in it. "He was very cocky about that. I think he's covered his tracks pretty damn well." She smoothed her fingers across her brows. "Gifford will fillet me for this. I'm going to lose my job, Nick. So who do you imagine will go after Tanford then? Not me — I'll be working security at . . . I dunno . . . Aldi. We can't do this without Marta's evidence, and that's gone for good."

"Come on, Kate, you can't give up — not now."

"Why?" she demanded, suddenly angry. "Because you need to satisfy your curiosity, solve your scientific puzzle? He got to my *family*, Nick."

There was nothing he could say to that.

She saw him to the front door and he stepped over the threshold.

"Thanks," she said. "If you hadn't been there . . ."

He shook his head; he didn't want to hear this.

"Okay," she said. "Then, at least let me thank you for bringing her home safe." She took him by the overcoat lapels and kissed him on the cheek. Nothing in it, just a chaste kiss, a thank you kiss. Yet it set off a chain reaction in his blood and his muscles and brain. The effects of that kiss travelled through him, fizzing and popping under his skin, tingling in his fingertips and the roots of his hair. He wanted to reach out and pull her to him and kiss her lips. But she was already gone;

retreated back inside the house, closing the front door softly after her.

The euphoria of that kiss lasted to the end of the driveway, where he realized that his injured leg was giving him hell and he'd sent the cab driver away. With a sigh, he turned up the collar of his overcoat, and began hobbling slowly towards the main road.

CHAPTER
FORTY-SEVEN

"Context is the key — from that comes the understanding of everything."

KENNETH NOLAND

Josh Brown took the news of DC Parrish's death without much emotion.

"It wasn't Tanford who killed him then," he said, looking thoughtful, rather than troubled.

"Tanford was too busy forcing Kate to burn the evidence at the time." Fennimore was sitting on the sofa in his hotel suite, his leg ached and his head boomed and he felt nauseous.

"The Henry brothers must've organized it."

Fennimore thought about the big no-necked thug, and nodded. "It's a safe bet. What're you thinking?"

"Only that Marta must've got some bloody good stuff on those guys."

"And it's literally gone up in smoke."

"Yeah, but you got a squint at the notebook."

"A couple of minutes, that's all."

"Your powers of recall are a bit of a legend, aren't they?" Josh said, with a sly sideways glance.

"Well . . ." Fennimore said modestly.

Josh opened his laptop and propped it on the coffee table where they could both see what he was typing. Fennimore humoured him, reciting snippets of information — a few dates and delivery times; a van registration number; the address of the mixer named "Bug" — while Josh typed them into a Word file.

"None of this is any good without Marta or DC Parrish around to corroborate it, of course," Fennimore said.

"What about the photograph?" Josh countered. "Two of you saw that — Kate said it was Tanford, and Marta knew him as the fixer called 'Rob'."

"A photograph of a cop in a knocking shop isn't what you'd call damning evidence, Josh."

"All right, so we sit on this Bug's place. Gather evidence of deliveries and that."

"Josh," Fennimore said. "We're not police, and anyway, we haven't the resources for twenty-four-hour surveillance — it could take months."

"Okay," Josh said, his brows drawing down in frustration. "Give me something I *can* investigate."

"I've given you everything I can recall."

Josh's head came up. He looked at Fennimore, his head on one side, as though straining to hear something. He had grey-blue eyes, which habitually wore a guarded expression, but right now, Fennimore saw a flash of elation.

"You're in Kate's car," he said. "You've just picked up the stuff out of Marta's locker. How d'you feel?"

"How do I *feel?*" Fennimore looked askance at him. "Is this a cognitive interview, Josh?"

480

He shrugged. "I did a bit on my undergrad course — it works."

"I know it does." Cognitive interviewing improved recall by up to 35 per cent on standard interviews, and many police forces now used the technique. Context and state of mind were both important in unlocking memories — hence Josh's attempt to place him back in the car, and the question about how he felt.

Always up to try something new, Fennimore closed his eyes and tried to imagine himself back in Kate Simms's car.

"Kate's driving. My hands are tingling — adrenaline — I'm excited. I'm flipping through the notebook, thinking, *We've got the bastard.* Oh —" He opened his eyes.

"Yes?"

"There was a sketch — of Bug — looked mad as a badger . . . I can't believe I forgot that. It startled me, and Kate leaned across to get a look." *Jasmine*, he thought. *She smelled of jasmine.*

Josh was looking at him. "And?"

"Nothing . . . just, she . . . Nothing, it's not important."

"Come on, Nick. You know everything's important in a cognitive interview."

"It does not relate to the case," Fennimore said firmly.

"Oo-kaay," Josh said. "Tell me about the notebook."

"Plain — black, A5." He made a circular motion with his finger. "With a red elasticated strap." He felt a sudden surge of excitement — he'd just remembered something else. "It held Tanford's photo in place.

Under it she'd written . . ." He stared ahead and saw it as clearly as if it was in his hands: "Black ink, the numbers 1211, a 'less than' symbol, number 4, dash, 19."

Josh typed it in and swivelled the laptop for him to see. "Like this?"

1211<4-19

"That's it," Fennimore said.

"What does it mean?"

Fennimore shook his head. "Haven't a clue."

"Well, obviously 1211 *isn't* less than 4," Josh said. "And it *definitely* isn't less than 4 minus 19."

They stared at it for a few more minutes.

"Anything?" Josh said.

Fennimore frowned. "I feel like the number nineteen should mean something, but I can't quite recall . . ." He strained to remember. "No," he said, defeated. "Nothing."

Josh shrugged. "When in doubt, Google."

There was a fire extinguisher numbered 1211–4; several military campaigns happened across medieval Europe in 1211, a US Senate Bill on telecoms fees was numbered 1211. None of these seemed relevant.

Josh clicked on the next search result: AD-1211, an opioid analgesic. "Did they cut the drugs with opioids?" he asked.

"No — methaqualone at source, penicillin here in the UK." Fennimore stared at the digits, trying to make sense of them. "If they were letters, you might think they meant something in Cyrillic, but numbers?"

"If the numbers corresponded to letters of the alphabet," Josh said, thinking aloud, but they got ADAA<D, going from A to Z, and ZYZZ<D from Z to A. They tried the Cyrillic alphabet, but that was no help, either.

"What about a car registration?" Josh said.

Fennimore pondered. "Numbers *are* used to substitute for letters . . . But I don't see how the 'less than' symbol fits."

"Here." Josh maximized the document file he'd been working on, highlighted the figures, clicked on the font dialogue box and scrolled back and forth through the fonts.

Fennimore caught a tantalizing flash of something in the preview box. "Wait a minute. Scroll back."

Josh obliged, peering at the screen, trying to see what Fennimore had seen.

"Whoa," Fennimore said. "Go back one font type."

The preview stopped at Edwardian Script ITC. The numbers read: *1211<4-19.*

He squinted at it. "Does that mean anything to you?" Josh shook his head slowly.

"I think you're right," he said, newly energized. "Run the number one and the two together, you get 'R'."

"Oh," Josh said. "And the one and the 'less than' symbol make a 'k'." He opened the font dialogue box again and fiddled with the character spacing. "Here." He turned the laptop to show Fennimore. He had shuffled the first two digits closer, and the angle of the 'less than' symbol now almost touched the digit before: *1211<4-19.*

"Rika-19," Josh said and laughed. "A password, maybe? But why 19?"

The inscription on Rika's headstone flashed into Fennimore's head — now the 19 made sense. "Rika was nineteen years old when she died," he said.

Josh grinned. "It *is* a password." He stared avidly at the screen. "But what for?"

Fennimore thought he already knew, but he enjoyed watching his student make the connection. "Well," he said, "Marta *did* hide her notebook and flash drive at the university . . ."

A slow smile spread across the younger man's face. "F: drive."

Fennimore rang Kate Simms from his mobile.

"Nick, I can't talk," she said.

A bolt of alarm shot through him. "Has something happened?"

Her laugh sounded a bit ragged. "Only that I missed my meeting by about two hours. I've just been summoned to the Chief Constable's office. Spry told me to prepare for the worst."

He exhaled in a rush, grateful at least that she wasn't in physical danger. "Look, Kate," he said. "I think we've found something."

"No, Nick, don't start this all over again."

"Students at universities are given their own small partition on the computer's main server," he pushed on. "It's called the F: Drive. Students have their own username and password — so it's a secure, private little corner of the university computer system, just for them."

"Nick, I haven't got time for this," she said. "I'm about to get in the car."

"Wait," he insisted, desperate to make her listen. "Marta was careful — she made back-ups — the flash drive she kept in her locker, the notebook. Kate, I think she might have backed up the evidence on her partition of the F: Drive at the university."

"Jesus, Fennimore, will you *stop?*" She was shouting and, after a pause, she apologized. "Look, I know you're trying to help, but you have to stop now. It's over."

The falling notes from his earphone told him she'd disconnected.

He stared at the screen of his mobile. "She's not listening."

Josh shrugged. "So we go around her."

Fennimore shook his head. "I don't see how. We'd need Marta's username as well as the password to get onto her university account and, without a warrant, the university won't give that away. But it's only a matter of time before Tanford thinks of her university account and, when he does, it's gone. We need to get to the evidence before he does. And even if we got her username from one of her friends and broke into her account, accessing the drive would compromise the evidence."

"Catch 22." Josh sounded distant, but the frown on his face said he was thinking hard.

Fennimore pushed his fingers through his hair and leaned back in his chair with his fingers interlaced at the crown. "If Kate is suspended, that's it, she's soiled goods. I don't think her career will ever recover. She needs proof of Tanford's guilt now, or at least something to present to the Chief Constable which proves she hasn't totally lost the plot."

"Give me ten minutes." Josh eyed him critically. "You could, I dunno, shower?"

Fennimore became aware that he reeked. His shirt was still damp with sweat from the chase across town and the slow painful walk from Kate's house, and his trousers were caked in mud and rock salt from the road. He hauled himself out of the chair and limped towards the bathroom.

When he came through to the sitting room ten minutes later, Josh was texting on his phone. Fennimore had dressed in a freshly laundered shirt and trousers, but he still felt dirty, as if Tanford's corruption had drawn him in, made him part of the lies he'd woven about him.

"So," Josh said, without looking up, "I texted one of the girls I was chatting up earlier." He was leaning forward in his chair and, when he did glance up, Fennimore saw another kingfisher flash of excitement in his eyes. "I told her Marta still isn't answering her phone, and when I called to her flat, it'd been broken into. I say I think Marta should know — has she got an email address for her? She texts that she's already tried that — everyone has.

486

"*I* say, well, I don't know about her, but I keep a few personal email accounts."

Fennimore nodded; a lot of students preferred to use private email accounts — they were often faster, and less prone to outages than university networks. This had possibilities.

"She's just texted — she remembered there was this one time Marta sent her an email registered to a Gmail account." He grinned. "She's found the address."

Fennimore used his professional credentials shamelessly to gain access to Enderby's secretary. The Chief Constable was in a meeting, she told him. Fennimore told her that he had information that was highly relevant to his meeting and persuaded her to tell Enderby that he was on the line. Enderby took the call in his secretary's office. He listened sympathetically and gave instructions that Fennimore and Brown should be escorted to his office as soon as they arrived.

ACC Gifford rose from his chair as Fennimore came in. "Who let you in?" he demanded.

"I did, Stuart." The Chief Constable stepped around his desk and shook Fennimore's hand.

Josh hung back a little; he seemed uneasy around so many uniforms — the Chief, Assistant Chief and Detective Superintendent were all in full regalia.

Kate turned to face them. The bruise on her forehead looked red and angry, a white lump at the centre of it seemed almost to throb visibly.

"Nick," she said. "This isn't helping."

"I'm prepared to hear him out," Mr Enderby said. "Chief Inspector?"

Simms gazed at Fennimore, despair and exhaustion on her face, but after a moment she gave a tired nod.

Spry, who hadn't spoken, hunched lower in his chair, anticipating Gifford's response, but Gifford was a man to respect the hierarchy, and he deferred to Enderby with a grudging "Very well."

Simms closed her eyes briefly and turned to face Gifford again.

Fennimore should have felt guilty, using the Chief Constable to pull rank on her, but he didn't. He told them what Kate couldn't: that her daughter had been threatened with a gun and had narrowly escaped abduction, that she herself had been stalked and attacked and threatened. Throughout this, she bowed her head and stared at a spot on Gifford's desk.

When Gifford began to splutter at the destruction of evidence, Enderby raised a single finger, and he subsided. Fennimore told them about Marta's double life — as a sex worker and a brilliant student. He described her notebook, filled with details of drugs drops and contacts, registration numbers, sketches, the tip-offs to Crimestoppers, the man named "Rob", who seemed to have such powerful connections, the photograph he and Kate Simms had found in the notebook which identified "Rob" as Detective Superintendent Tanford. He finished with Marta's call to Gary Parrish on the night she died.

Spry murmured a few muddled words.

Gifford seemed unmoved. "As I have explained to Chief Inspector Simms," he said, addressing the Chief Constable, "sadly, without firm evidence, I've really no reason to believe this isn't all the product of a disturbed mind."

"Is that Chief Inspector Simms's disturbed mind, or mine?" Fennimore said.

Gifford raised his eyebrows and looked from Fennimore to Simms as if they were one and the same.

"And DC Parrish — is he deluded and disturbed, too?"

Gifford spread his hands. "DC Parrish isn't here to speak for himself," he said.

Fennimore held his gaze. "Only because he was killed in a hit and run a few hours ago."

Gifford blinked. He must have been told of the young detective's death, so perhaps he was offended by Fennimore's bluntness. "Are you suggesting that his death was not an accident?" he said.

"Marta had documented evidence that a senior police officer has been associating with two major drugs suppliers, protecting them, taking bribes," Fennimore said. "She was a registered informant. And both she and her handler are now dead. What do *you* think, Stuart?"

"Well," Spry said, nodding and shaking his head as if he didn't know what to think. "That's . . ."

But Gifford folded his arms and sat back in his chair. "I *believe* you've just told us that Chief Inspector Simms destroyed the evidence," he said.

489

Fennimore nodded towards Enderby's desktop computer arranged neatly to one side of his desk.

"May I?"

Gifford looked like he might leap up and shield the equipment from Fennimore's impertinent attention, but Enderby said, "Of course," and, with a frustrated sigh, Gifford subsided.

Fennimore explained the combination of numbers and letters Marta had written on the back of the photograph in her journal. He typed it in to the word processor. "A coded password," he said. "Presented in the right font, it spells a name."

"Rika-19," Enderby read.

"Marta's sister — aged nineteen when she died." He explained the purpose of the students' F: Drive — emphasizing its privacy and security. "We think the password will allow access to Marta's university F: Drive," he said as he typed in commands. "I won't risk compromising the evidence at that location, but a lot of students have multiple email addresses, and one of Marta's student friends gave us a webmail address for her."

Simms sat up, her expression changing from defeat to wonder, and then impatient anticipation.

He turned the monitor so they could all see.

There were dozens of files on Marta's Gmail account. All sent from a Hotmail account. Every email had multiple attachments.

The file names were self-explanatory: Notebk1, 2 and so on through to Notebk33. "I think she scanned pages from her notebook and emailed the images to herself," Fennimore told them. "Rob1, Rob2 and Rob3 are, I believe, photographs of Detective Superintendent Tanford, or evidence implicating him."

Simms was staring at him.

"Now, anyone with the account details can upload or access material from Gmail and Hotmail, but both service providers keep a full audit trail because of their susceptibility to attack by email viruses and bots, so I didn't see any harm in taking a peek at 'Rob 1'."

He clicked on the email attachment and angled the monitor so they could all see.

They were looking at a photograph of Tanford, caught unawares. "Clearly that's DCS Tanford," Fennimore said. "It would be a simple matter to match this image to the interior of Francine's massage parlour."

Gifford sat frozen, gripping the arms of his leather office chair.

Fennimore grinned. "Bet you can't wait to get a look at the rest of those files, can you, Stuart?"

CHAPTER
FORTY-EIGHT

"Give a man enough rope and he'll hang himself."

ORIGIN UNKNOWN

Chief Constable Enderby granted Kate Simms the privilege of arresting Detective Superintendent Tanford; she was supported by a nervous Detective Superintendent Spry. Tanford was carrying the throwdown Marta had called on the night she was murdered. Mobile phone records also linked it to the Henrys.

Four years before, Tanford was a DI in Newcastle, working Vice. He moved to Humberside Police, got promoted to DCI; he had even headed up one of the teams investigating the abduction rapes in Hull. Humberside police would want to talk to him about that, but for now he was arrested on suspicion of conspiracy to commit misconduct in a public office and conspiracy to supply Class A drugs.

The drugs seized in Operation Snowstorm were supposed to have been destroyed three weeks before Kate was assigned to the "overdose" case review. The Customs and Excise Incineration Log, which DS Renwick claimed he and Tanford both countersigned, showed only one signature — Renwick's. They had only

Renwick's word that he acted under Tanford's instruction. As Tanford predicted, there was no trace of him at Marta's flat; in fact the only trace evidence was a hair and a footwear impression, both matched to Renwick. He was wearing the incriminating shoes when he was arrested.

DCI Simms and DC Moran were to conduct the initial interview, with Fennimore watching via video link and advising Simms via audio. They discussed interview strategy, sitting in her office.

"I think we should lead with the drugs charges."

Fennimore agreed. "The strongest evidence is in the association with the Henrys and the recycling of seized drugs."

"If I can get him on the back foot with that, maybe he'll slip up on the murder."

She looked pale as she guided him to the room where the video link had been set up for him. He turned on the monitor. Tanford was already installed in the interview room with his solicitor. Moran sat opposite. Tanford looked relaxed, and even seemed to be sharing a joke with the solicitor.

Fennimore slipped on a set of headphones with integral mic and Kate said, "I'm just next door."

"Nervous?" Fennimore asked.

"No," she said, and a shiver of emotion rippled across her face. "Terrified," she admitted with a wan smile.

"He'll be confident. He's police — he knows how to clean up a scene, and let's face it, he's managed to remain undetected for a long time. But he isn't infallible, Kate; he kept the throwdown, which was incredibly stupid — Professor Varley might call it arrogant, from a psychological viewpoint — and he will have made other mistakes."

Kate nodded. They had already discussed some of those potential errors, and she would confront Tanford with them during the interview.

"He despises forensic psychologists," Simms said. "I'll see if I can needle him with Varley's profile of him."

Tanford's legal representative was Sam Carr. Known as "Slippery Sam", he mostly represented celebrities who could afford to pay his exorbitant fees.

After running through the formalities, Simms said, "You claim you weren't present at the faked disposal of heroin which had been seized during Operation Snowstorm?"

"I'm not 'claiming' anything," Tanford said. "I'm stating a fact: I wasn't there, as you will have seen from the Incinerator Log."

"You're expecting me to believe that you let a sergeant dispose of a large quantity of Class A drugs on his own?"

"My client exercises his right to silence," Carr said firmly.

"Your client is insulted by the suggestion," Tanford said.

"Detective Superintendent . . ." Carr began, but Tanford waved him away.

"Obviously I did not allow DS Renwick to dispose of the drugs unsupervised. I buddied him up with a senior officer."

"Who?"

"I can't recall."

"Isn't that odd? It was only three weeks ago."

"It's been a tough three weeks."

His solicitor sighed loudly.

"Care to elaborate?" Kate asked.

Tanford smiled, for once taking his solicitor's advice.

"We've made extensive inquiries," Simms said, "but we haven't been able to identify your elusive 'senior officer'."

"Are you surprised?" he said. "If they admitted that, they'd be admitting liability."

Carr tried again, resting his hand on Tanford's arm, but the superintendent shook him off.

"Look, I led Operation Snowstorm, why would I compromise it?"

"Self-aggrandizement," Simms said.

"What?"

"The forensic psych said to look out for that as a character trait," she said.

Fennimore saw a flicker of reaction — Tanford would not like to be reduced to a set of character traits.

"Operation Snowstorm was a joint operation set up last minute following intel from HM Customs and London Met," Simms said. "You didn't *lead* it, you just handled the Manchester end. And, as for compromising it, the Customs people were very disappointed that the big boys — the suppliers and moneymen — somehow got clean away."

"And you're suggesting I facilitated this bit of escapology?" He raised his eyebrows. "Well, clever me. But you've searched my office, my house, my police *and* home computers. Have you turned up one shred of evidence against me?"

Carr was red in the face, but Tanford ignored him — fascinated, it seemed, by Simms, watching her every gesture, devouring her with his gaze.

"Your laptop hard drive has been electronically fragmented," she said. "We haven't found anything to prove or disprove your innocence."

He smiled. "That's very Jesuitical of you, Katie."

"Please address me as Chief Inspector," she said. "Perhaps though, you could explain why you chose to electronically 'shred' the files and data on your laptop, Chief Superintendent?"

His smile broadened.

"For the record — DCS Tanford made no response."

He scratched the side of his nose, and Carr relaxed in his seat, satisfied.

"Renwick says that *you* went with him to oversee the incineration of the heroin. That it was *your* idea to switch the drugs for an inert powder that would pass for the real thing."

"Well, he would, wouldn't he? But the fact is, *Chief Inspector*, my signature isn't on the Incinerator Log, *because* . . . I. Wasn't. There." He pressed the tip of his index finger on the table three times, punctuating each word, speaking in an emphatic but entirely reasonable tone.

"Okay," Fennimore said and Simms jumped at the sharpness of his voice in her ear. "Renwick swears he saw Tanford sign the log, so Tanford only faked signing it. But his DNA could still be on the relevant page."

Tanford was watching her, one arm hooked casually over the back of his chair.

Simms said, "Low Template DNA is a miracle of science, don't you think? Say, for example, you rested your hand on the page when you faked signing the log, you might have rubbed off a few skin cells. D'you think I should ask for DNA trace on the log?"

He didn't move.

"I think I will — yes, it's definitely worth a shot," Simms said. "I've already requested cell site analysis of your mobile phones. It's always helpful to have the victim and the suspect locked together when a crime is committed, isn't it, Detective Superintendent?"

Fennimore watched as Tanford realized that the same could apply to the night of the murder — that his phones would place him with Marta when she died.

Simms waited a second, then said, "No response."

"As for your dealings with the Henry brothers — we have Marta's written testimony." She flipped through printouts from the JPEG files and Word documents they had already recovered from Marta's webmail and university accounts. "I'm looking at dates and times you went to the Henrys' massage parlour. Dates, times and duration of meetings you had with Sol and Frank Henry . . ." She glanced up at him and smiled.

He hadn't been expecting this.

"Yes," she said. "Marta made back-ups."

"Sadly, Marta is dead," Tanford said, without a trace of regret.

His solicitor raised a finger, but Tanford carried on: "It's debatable whether the CPS will allow her files into evidence."

"Well, it's good of you to show concern," Simms said. "But I can corroborate that I saw the original notebook, and I'm sure her family and friends will confirm that the electronic copies are in Marta's handwriting. So — thanks again — but I'm hopeful."

He spread his hands as if to say, *Your time you're wasting, not mine.*

"Marta *wanted* us to know everything. She filled her notebook with information written in English because she wanted us to know. She listed her code and alias for Crimestoppers on her university account because she wanted us to know."

That shook him — he'd been relying on the anonymity of Crimestoppers.

"She really messed up your supply train, didn't she? You thought Operation Snowstorm was a temporary setback. You'd get by, cutting the deals a bit thin for a few months. You'd put the drugs back into circulation when things calmed down. But things just *kept* going wrong, didn't they? Intel kept coming in via Crimestoppers — tip-offs *you had to act on* even though you were killing your own business. She must have driven you half mad."

Fennimore saw something flare in the inky black of Tanford's eyes.

"Yes," she said. "That was *all* Marta. Shall I tell you why she did it? Oh, but you know all about that. Renwick got to the cemetery before I did, so you already know that she and Rika were sisters. Marta came to England to punish the men who made her sister an addict. One brave young woman, acting alone, and she got you on the run — you and the Henrys and Renwick and whoever else you've corrupted along the way."

Tanford scratched his nose again. "I'm sorry," he said, feigning confusion. "Was there a question in all that garbled nonsense?"

Fennimore couldn't see Simms's face, but she bowed her head to look at the pile of documents under her hands and then raised slowly up again to Tanford, her back straight and stiff.

"I put it to you that you have engaged in supplying Class A substances, that you have stolen drugs seized in police operations and you have corruptly accepted payment for those banned substances from Solomon and Francis Henry. Furthermore, you have involved other police officers in your illegal actions."

Tanford watched her through half-closed eyes. "I put it to you that you're full of shit," he said.

"Don't let him get to you, Kate," Fennimore said. "He knows we've got enough to charge him with the drugs offences — you've got him scared."

"Your mobile phone log shows that you spoke to the Henry brothers around the time of Marta Aizupiete's death," she said. "Would you care to comment on that?"

The solicitor spoke up. "This is an improper line of questioning — my client has not been charged with matters relating to any death."

"No?" She found a sheet in the file and slid it across the desk. "Tell that to the parents of the addicts who died from the penicillin-contaminated deals your client and his business partners put into circulation." She left the solicitor to read the list of the dead and turned her attention to Tanford.

"I believe that cell site analysis of your mobile will put you with Marta in the restaurant where she had her last meal, and later at the Henrys' sauna. I believe it will put you with her when she was attacked. CSIs are taking apart the Henrys' sauna as we speak. A lot of blood was shed and cleaned up at their salon — we've already identified it as Marta's."

"Looking bad for the Henry boys, isn't it?" he said in a confidential tone. "Look, I'll save you a bit of time — I was with her."

"Mr Tanford," his solicitor warned, but Tanford shrugged him off.

"Marta and I were friends; we had sex."

"She was bound, beaten, and whipped with a riding crop. She was raped and choked," Simms said. "Her face was unrecognizable. She drowned in her own blood."

The solicitor looked up from the sheet and glanced uneasily at his client — this was leagues away from the marital indiscretions he was used to dealing with — but

Tanford held Simms's gaze without blinking. None of what she'd said had any effect on him.

"I left Marta safe and well at the Henrys' sauna," he said. "Your own witness statements say that one of the brothers left the pub early."

She nodded. "It's true, the pub landlord saw Frank Henry leave at 11.30 — a half-hour before George Howard and Sol."

Tanford smiled and folded his arms.

She flicked back through the pages, to a point she had highlighted in bright fluorescent yellow. "That would be a minute or two *after* you made a call to Frank Henry."

"Marta told me she was going on to a party with the Henrys," Tanford said smoothly. "She asked me to ring Frank to let him know she was ready. I can't vouch for what happened to her after that."

"Oh, you are a slippery bastard," Fennimore murmured. Tanford knew they couldn't pinpoint the moment of Marta's death. It was his word against the Henrys', and Tanford was relying on his word weighing heavier than that of two lowlifes who peddled drugs and sex. And he was probably right.

"DC Parrish told me that Marta called him on the night she was murdered," Simms said. "She was in a restaurant with 'Rob'. That's you, Detective Superintendent Tanford. She believed she'd seen an exchange between you and the Henrys — drugs for money. An hour or so later, she sent DC Parrish a text. She knew you were police. Is that what set you off? Did you find her sending the text?"

Tanford gave his solicitor a bewildered look. "I honestly have no idea what she's talking about."

"All those months of pain — the humiliating loss of standing with your criminal business associates — it was all her fault. For men like you, women who sell themselves for sex are disposable, but all the time you were screwing her, she was screwing you. That must have been devastating. You went berserk."

Tanford watched her as though she fascinated him. "Is the lack of physical evidence making Spry nervous?" he asked. "I expect it is. How long d'you think you'll be allowed to continue with this outrageous line of questioning before he calls a stop?"

Fennimore spoke again. "Talk to him about the whip."

She told Tanford they'd found a riding crop in the search of his house.

"Souvenir of my hunting days." He smiled. "I always did enjoy a good hard ride."

Simms nodded slowly. "We thought it was important — nice antique like that — your type does like to keep souvenirs."

"Type?" Tanford said.

"Sadistic, narcissistic, controlling."

Tanford bristled. Simms sneaked a look over her shoulder and Fennimore caught the glint of triumph in her eyes. "I think you kept the same riding crop *all these years*, as a souvenir. Who knows what stories it might tell?"

Rage boiled behind the flat surface of the superintendent's eyes, but it took him only a second or two to get it under control.

"Any dom/sub games I play are consensual." The pink tip of his tongue appeared between his teeth. "Marta was shy at first, but she really got into the whipping. Must be a sibling thing — Rika couldn't get enough of it."

"Her sister was addicted to heroin — she'd do anything to feed her habit."

"Hm," Tanford said. "Shared needles and shooting up in filthy dosshouses — HIV and hepatitis are a very real risk. Which is why I bleach my riding crop after I've used it. Well," he said with an expression of insincere concern. "You have to protect the submissives."

Fennimore smiled to himself. "I told you, Kate — cops never know as much as they think they know." Simms drummed her fingers on the table; she was telling him to get on with it. "Most modern riding crops have a fibreglass core, but this one, being antique, is whalebone. Ask him if he knows how long the plaited leather is on a riding crop. It's almost twenty yards — imagine that, tightly wound round and round a whalebone core."

As Simms relayed the information, Tanford's head swivelled to look up into the camera in the left-hand corner of the ceiling.

"Whalebone — or baleen, to give it the correct name — is fibrous and striated," Simms went on.

"I can see your lips moving, but those aren't your words coming out of your mouth," Tanford said. "*Striated* — d'you even know what that means, Katie?"

"If you look at baleen through a microscope, you see microscopic tubules," she went on. "Less than half a millimetre in diameter —"

"Oh." Tanford clapped his hands together, a delighted grin on his face. "Now I *know* you're there."

"— but wide enough to trap hundreds of thousands of blood cells. Baleen is really *very* absorbent."

Tanford grinned manically. "Come out, come out, wherever you are . . ." he taunted, but Fennimore saw fear behind the hilarity.

"So even a good wipe down with bleach wouldn't destroy all of the evidence," Simms finished, untroubled by his baiting.

Tanford kept his gaze on the camera. "Why don't you just come in and join us, Professor? We'll talk of many things — shoes and ships and all that. Did you know that Lewis Carroll drew Alice with dark hair? Those original drawings looked a lot like your Suzie — d'you think she followed the White Rabbit down the hole?"

"Detective Superintendent," Simms said.

He looked past her, addressing Fennimore directly. "I worked Vice before I took the step up to Drugs. I saw hundreds of girls like your Suzie."

Fennimore didn't doubt it. He knew the numbers heart and soul, and he knew the chances of finding her alive. That was the problem with understanding the odds — they said that Suzie was never coming home.

That she was dead. That if she hadn't died in the first three days after her mother was murdered, she would wish she had. The odds said that before Suzie died she was used in horrible ways by men who acted without compunction, who functioned with no understanding of compassion or morals, and who had no conscience about what they did. Men with no pity in their hearts — only the most warped and deviant species of desire.

Tanford watched him avidly. "Suzie was ten, wasn't she? The paedos love the ten-year-olds — they dress them up like princesses and fuck them like Lilli Dolls."

Fennimore's heart slowed.

Tanford winked. "Very realistic sex toys those Lilli Dolls, but silicone is no substitute for real warm human flesh."

Fennimore couldn't breathe. *He's taunting you because you've got to him. Don't rise to it.*

"Of course the shine goes off them fast; they end up being passed from hand to hand, or bed to bed, losing value with every sale."

"Mr Tanford," Simms said. "I'm warning you . . ."

"Chief Superintendent," the solicitor said simultaneously.

"What's the problem?" Tanford said. "He sent her image out into the homes of a billion strangers because he *wants* to know what happened to her." His gaze was still locked on the camera. "You won't find her that way, Fennimore. You need contacts — an 'in' on the networks. Someone to unlock a few doors for you. That man might be me."

"DCS Tanford appears to be referring to sexual offences relating to a missing child of which he has personal knowledge," Simms said.

Tanford paused, wrinkled his nose. "But thing is, I don't like you very much."

"Tanford, I really must insist that you *stop*,'" his solicitor said.

"I'm suspending this interview," Simms said. She gave the time and date and reached to press a button on the wall console.

Tanford's hand snaked out and gripped her wrist solidly. "Don't do that, Katie — I'm trying to help."

"Let go of me," Simms warned.

Tanford pulled her forward, standing now.

DC Moran moved around Tanford and grabbed his free hand, forcing his right arm behind his back, pushing him down onto the table. With her free hand, Simms hit the alarm strip which ran at waist height around the wall. The siren whooped. His solicitor tried to reason with him.

Fennimore couldn't move. He had always told himself that he'd never given up, but over the years the idea had become an abstract thought — Suzie in some kind of hinterland. But what Tanford proposed was real and horrible, and he felt a paralyzing sickness.

"Tell you what, Fennimore," Tanford yelled over the wail of the alarm and the shouting. "I'll help you if you stand as forensic advisor in my defence." He waited, his eyes flicking quickly to the door and then away again. "No? Don't care enough? Can't say I blame you — it's probably too late, anyhow. I looked in some of those kids' eyes and I swear, there was nothing left — they'd forgotten they *had* any other use —"

Fennimore tore off his headset. He covered the distance to the interview room in a few strides. Simms grabbed the back of Tanford's head and dragged him forward, across the table. He released her wrist and Moran quick-cuffed him, his arms behind his back, Simms barring Fennimore's path as he opened the door. He lunged at Tanford, but Simms shoved him hard.

"Nick," she said. "Don't."

Moran set Tanford down in his seat. He stared at Fennimore, panting and grinning like a wolf.

"He's bluffing," Simms said, her hand on his arm. "The man's a sadist, Nick — this is what he does."

"Are you sure of that?" Tanford said. "Like I say, I was in Vice. I've had close dealings across three police forces with traffickers."

Simms and Moran together forced Fennimore backwards out of the room as four officers piled in from the corridor.

"Give me a bell if you change your mind, Fennimore," Tanford shouted.

Simms sent Moran back into the room with one of the uniformed officers and sent the rest away. She led Fennimore a few steps down the corridor and pinned him to the wall.

"I'm sorry," he said, before she could really get started. "It won't happen again."

"You're dead right it won't, because you're not going anywhere near him again."

"Kate, come on," he said.

"What would be the point — he'd just use it as a chance to psychologically torture you."

He wanted to argue, but he knew she was right.

"We'll just have to go with what we've got," Simms said. "Without Marta as a witness to speak for herself most of the evidence for her murder is stacked against the Henry brothers anyway."

As well as Marta's blood and a small fragment of her nasal cartilage the CSIs had turned up in the luxury suite at their massage parlour, there was forensic evidence of the Henrys at Marta's dump site — a paint spill in the alley had been matched to a splash inside the wheel arch of Sol Henry's Lexus. Video clips on Marta's F: Drive at the university showed Sol and Frank Henry making arrangements for drug drops and restocks from their office at Francine's.

"When the cell site comes through I can have another go at Tanford. It might even place him at the dump site. But until then, the brothers are in the frame for the murder."

"And Tanford is more than willing for them to take the fall," he said.

Her eyes gleamed. "Maybe I'll tell them that — see how they take it."

CHAPTER
FORTY-NINE

The Henry brothers would take whatever the law threw at them for the drugs offences, but they were not about to sit quiet on a murder charge for a scummy cop who'd wrecked their business with his twisted sexual preferences and then tried to shift the blame onto them. Simms went through the long list of evidence against them, first with Sol, then with Frank, and Tanford's claim that he left Marta safe and well at their massage parlour. As if by some kind of telepathy, they both started talking.

Frank, surprisingly, was the most forthcoming.

Tanford was supposed to drop Marta off at George Howard's place after the meal so she could start work at Georgina's. But Tanford rang, panicked. Said he'd killed Marta. Frank left Sol and George Howard at the pub and went to find out what had happened.

"You and your brother were both at the murder scene," she said. "And we've tied you in to the dump site as well."

Frank showed no emotion. "We just helped him to clear up."

"And where did George Howard fit in?"

He shrugged. "Putting George Howard in the frame was a bit of a windfall — what you might call an added bonus."

"How did you get him to cooperate?"

"Quaaludes," he said. "Why he couldn't remember nothing."

"What about Candice?"

He frowned, confused. "What about her? She doesn't work for us no more. Pity really — she were a good worker before Tanford got to her."

"Candice is dead, Mr Henry," Simms said.

"Is that right?" He ran a finger down the groove running from his nose to his mouth. "Well, I wouldn't want to tell you how to do your job, but you might want to take another look at Tanford for that."

In a meeting room at Collyhurst Station, Ella Moran, Kate Simms and Nick Fennimore watched Marta Aizupiete and Detective Superintendent Tanford having sex. The location had already been identified by Frank Henry as the "luxury suite" at Francine's massage parlour. He had given clear directions to a self-store locker in Salford, where he had stashed a hard drive containing what he termed "security footage".

Simms caught the tech's eye and jerked her chin. He fast-forwarded to the moment when Tanford swung off the bed, naked, and disappeared around a corner. He moved carefully, with the slight overcompensation of a drunk. A second or two later, they heard the cascade of water; Tanford had turned on the shower.

510

A faint clunk — the shower door closing — then Marta slid from the bed and slipped into a white silk kimono. She was lithe and beautiful and she carried herself with grace.

"People thought she was a ballet dancer," Simms said out of nowhere.

Marta picked up a clean towel from a rack of shelves and, looking directly into the camera, she dabbed her neck and throat.

"The camera was hidden in the dresser mirror," the tech explained. "Every room was rigged up for video and audio — we found racks of monitors in the back office — but this is the only drive we've found."

Marta checked her lipstick, then, in an apparently careless action, she tossed the towel over the dresser mirror. The screen went dark.

"Wait a second," the tech said. The picture returned, but from a different angle this time.

"There was another camera," the tech explained. "We found it in the clock over the door. The film has been edited together from the two bits of footage."

Marta had placed a briefcase on the bed and was peeking inside. She lifted out a police evidence bag, and then another, and a third. The tamper-proof seals had been broken and they were empty, but it was just possible to see signatures and numbers inked on the white labelling bands.

"With a bit of tweaking, we might be able to give you the evidence reference numbers off the bags," the tech said.

Marta dived back into the briefcase and took out a couple of hefty wads of ten and twenty pound notes. She stared towards the angle of the room, where Tanford had disappeared. For a second it looked like she might run. But instead, she laid the money and the labels out carefully inside the briefcase, took her phone from her bag and clicked off a few photographs. Her thumbs flickered over the keypad.

Moran said, "The text she sent to Gary Parrish?"

"Probably, but let's hope she sent the photos to one of her email accounts as well," Fennimore said.

The tech nodded. "We'll look for anything she sent on the night of the murder."

Marta began to rearrange the bags and money back in the briefcase.

A dull *thunk*, then the rush of water sounded louder. Marta flinched wildly.

"Thought you might want to join me." Tanford's voice came from somewhere off-camera.

Marta smiled, and let the kimono slip, exposing her shoulder. She quirked one eyebrow ironically.

"Such treasures, darling," she said, putting a Russian roll into her words.

A blur of motion, then Tanford was in shot. He threw Marta face down on the bed and straddled her, seizing both her wrists in one hand, reached into the open briefcase. A second later he stood back. She was cuffed.

"I knew it," he said. "I fucking *knew* we had a rat in the kitchen."

The camera caught everything. The whipping, the rapes; he choked her with a leather weightlifting belt.

512

She told him nothing. In fact, he revealed more in his interrogation of her than they would ever have got from him in an interview. His questions were an admission to everything — the drugs recycling, the women he'd tortured before. The third time he choked her, she remained limp and still for a long time.

He muttered, "Fuck," and turned her over.

Marta lunged at him, butting him in the stomach. She sank her teeth into the flesh of his abdomen and he howled. She fought and bit and kicked but she was still handcuffed and he was twice her weight; he got free of her, stumbling back from the bed, and fell hard on his backside. He grabbed the nearest thing to hand — his shoe — and hit her hard in the face as she came at him again. Bone crunched; she fell to her knees and he hit her again, screaming, out of control. And once he'd started he didn't seem able to stop.

The camera recorded his panicked phone call to the Henrys; Tanford, trembling and still naked, on the edge of the bed, Marta choking and convulsing behind him.

CHAPTER
FIFTY

"To take revenge half-heartedly is to court disaster; either condemn or crown your hatred."

PIERRE CORNEILLE

They always keep the shoes.

And Tanford had kept his. They were steeped in Marta's blood, although you wouldn't have known it from the healthy gleam of polish on the leather. But the seams and the small creases, the lace eyelets, all held their imprint, all told their story.

Kate Simms asked him if he would like to explain how the blood got onto his shoes.

"You know what you remind me of?" he said.

"Could you answer the question, please?"

"You'll see these little birds on the beaches up in the northeast; they turn over stones looking for food. Run and turn, run and turn, run and turn, like little clockwork toys, looking under every stone."

"Marta Aizupiete's blood on your shoes," she said evenly. "The left shoe, in particular, is heavily stained."

She might not have spoken. "They don't know why they do it — half the time they don't even find anything — it's just their nature. Run and turn." He stared at her, a thoughtful look on his face. "That's you, Kate —

a wind-up toy, not even understanding why you do —"
he spread his hands "— what you do."

Simms showed him a short section of the recording.
He bunched his right hand into a fist and cupped it in
his left and the muscles of his face too were bunched
like a closed fist. He called the Henrys vicious
untrustworthy slime, his breath stuttering and growling.
His eyes glittered and a blood vessel pulsed in his
temple as he told Kate she should just have done her
sums and written up her report and left him the hell
alone.

But after half a minute, something strange happened.
It was eerie to watch: the angry pulse in his temple
stilled and the muscles of his face relaxed. He rested his
chin on his closed fists, his breathing slowed and his
gaze fixed with avid attention on the screen. With a
wave of nausea, Simms realized he was totally absorbed
in watching himself beat Marta Aizupiete to death.

He admitted that there was money in the briefcase, and
police evidence bags, which he had insisted the
brothers hand back to him — he didn't want the
possibility of them using it to blackmail him in the
future. He claimed that Marta was still breathing when
he left her, that the brothers must have finished the job.

He changed his story when a new section of video
came to light. In this fragment, a short time had passed,
and Tanford was showered and dressed.

Frank Henry entered the room. Tanford stood
nervously at the end of the bed, watching Frank's
reaction.

Frank looked at Marta's ruined body and said quietly, "What the fuck?"

Tanford began to explain, but Frank cut him short. "Is she dead?"

Tanford's face relaxed and all signs of nervousness left him. "Oh, I made sure of it," he said.

Epilogue

Four victims were eventually identified from blood spatter in the factory undercroft — Tanya, the surviving kidnap/assault victim, and three others. One was the victim they found buried — she had been whipped, but they'd found no trace of Tanford on the body, or the wrappings he'd used on her — the other two were not on the DNA database. Tanya had vanished as soon as news of the Hull murder broke. They had a close physical match to Tanford's riding crop from the walls of the basement in Hull, but close was not enough, and Candice's body was cleaner in death than it had ever been in the last months of her life. No semen, no fibres, no microscopic traces.

In late autumn, Detective Superintendent Tanford was tried and convicted of Marta's murder and the conspiracy and drugs offences. In truth, Greater Manchester, Humberside and Northumbria Police had been jointly horrified at the prospect of prosecuting a senior, decorated police officer with serial murder, but when the press release went out, they did allow Kate Simms to say that they were not looking for anyone else in connection with the murder of Candice Watson.

Tanford was recommended to serve a minimum of twenty-five years.

Sol and Frank Henry were given life sentences and sent to Manchester Strangeways and HMP Preston, respectively, for drugs trafficking. Fourteen months had been added to their tariffs for conspiracy to pervert the course of justice.

Detective Sergeant Renwick was convicted on charges of being concerned in the distribution of controlled drugs and theft in respect of the recycled drugs, breaking and entering and theft from Marta's flat, and conspiracy to pervert the course of justice.

George Howard was released, cleared of all charges. His Easter Chocolate Indulgence Weekend was an unqualified triumph.

Fennimore paced his office. Spring and summer had passed, the new undergraduate intake had arrived and was bedded in, and he was already groaning in irritation at the poor standard of literacy of their mid-term assignments. He hadn't seen Kate Simms since Tanford's trial. They had kept in phone and email contact, but today she asked for a Skype call — said she needed to see him face to face. It was 3.15 in the afternoon; it had rained heavily all day and the streets at the crossroads below his office window were wet, but the clouds parted suddenly, and the winter sun broke through like a smile, turning each micro-puddle on the tarmac roadway into a tiny prism, refracting light in shimmering rainbows of colour. The traffic threw up

518

spumes that caught the light and turned the grey streets below him into a carnival.

Or perhaps it was only his mood that made him see the Granite City with such a romantic eye.

It was nearly ten months since Kate Simms had first contacted him, and since then he had anticipated every phone call — every text and email — with keen pleasure.

His Skype alert sounded and he clicked the "answer" key without delay. Simms was peering into the webcam as if she felt that she would be able to see clear from Manchester to the shivering Aberdonian streets if only she looked hard enough. Fennimore smiled and waved to her and she moved closer to the camera, her face blurring in and out of focus, but she didn't return his smile.

"You look tense," he said. "This can't be good."

"Sol and Frank Henry," she said. "They've been murdered in prison; both shanked. Timed to happen within minutes of each other. Their sauna was torched a couple of hours later."

He nodded. "It wasn't likely that a couple of scallies from North Manchester would be the top-feeders in this particular food chain," he said. "They've been made an example for the rest to heed."

Simms agreed and they were silent for a few moments, each thinking back over the turbulent weeks of the investigation, and the dangers they had encountered.

"And . . ." She blushed. "I'm being given a commendation."

He grinned. "About bloody time."

"It should be yours," she said.

"Nonsense. I only took the job on in the first place because I owed you a huge favour."

She looked into the camera and smiled softly. "Well, the debt is repaid, tenfold," she said.

"Nuh-uh. I don't accept that," he said, not thinking to cover the alarm he felt. "I consider the debt only partially discharged and I reserve the right to do you the huge favour of meddling in your investigations whenever the mood takes me."

He saw a slight wince. "About that," she said. "I wanted you to know — I'll be heading off to the US after Christmas."

He experienced a sick thud. "For good?"

"A few months maybe. The Chief Constable thought it might help — let the dust settle. Tanford had a lot of friends on the force, and some of them are finding it hard to accept his guilt."

"What part of the US?" *Fool*, he thought, *blurting it out like that.* But he did need to know. Foolishly or not, he felt that in some way being able to picture a location would make the distance seem less excruciating.

"St Louis," she said. "It's a method exchange — you know, swapping skills and ideas."

"Sounds good," he said, trying to sound like he meant it. "Is the family going with you?"

"No," she said. "Kieran started a new job in September. It's a good school — he likes it — he's happy there." He heard the overassertiveness in her tone, and perhaps she did, too, because she stopped.

520

"Anyway, my mother has agreed to come up from London to help with Tim and Becky, just while I'm away."

There were things he wanted to say, but he knew she didn't want to hear them. He had complicated her life too much already. So Fennimore wished her well, and repeated his offer of help, and she thanked him, though both of them knew she wouldn't ever ask for it.

And as the early darkness of an Aberdonian winter closed around him, he opened a laptop that he had bought recently. Every file on the hard drive had been electronically fragmented and was unreadable. It was an exact copy of Tanford's hard drive, wangled from a computer tech who told him any data was irretrievable. It could take years to find anything usable, never mind useful. But Tanford had said he had contacts, and although Tanford was a liar, Fennimore knew that this one thing, said to wound, was true.

Suzie was still out there — he knew it. And with Tanford's contacts, he might inch slowly closer to her, even if it did take years. Because the one thing Fennimore had plenty of was time.

Sympathy for the Devil

Howard Marks

Detective Catrin Price has returned to Cardiff after 12 years of self-imposed exile to finally lay to rest the ghosts of her unhappy past. Then her ex-boyfriend Rhys, once a promising young policeman but now a washed-up junkie, is found dead.

The official verdict is an accidental overdose but Cat is convinced that there is something more to his death, something that will explain why the man who once saved her life was so unwilling to save his own.

But Cat's troubles have only just begun. Discovering that Rhys was investigating the disappearance of a troubled rock star last seen at a notorious suicide spot, she finds herself drawn into the terrifying world of a cult.

ISBN 978-0-7531-9200-9 (hb)
ISBN 978-0-7531-9201-6 (pb)

Agent of the State

Roger Pearce

A suspected terrorist is frisked for explosives on the Embankment. Operators do this so skilfully he remains completely unaware . . .

In New Scotland Yard a new brand of manager fails to deal with escalating threats — "aggressive indecision" is what Detective Chief Inspector John Kerr calls it . . .

He discovers that cocaine-fuelled sex parties in Knightsbridge are pulling in businessmen, Russian diplomats and senior members of the British government. So when Kerr's investigations are blocked by his bosses in Scotland Yard, he decides to go it alone and begins to expose a cover-up that extends to all levels of the British Establishment.

ISBN 978-0-7531-9182-8 (hb)
ISBN 978-0-7531-9183-5 (pb)